The Greatest Love

The Greatest Love Story of All Time is Lucy Robinson's debut novel. Prior to writing Lucy earned her crust in West End theatre production and then factual television, working on documentaries for the BBC, ITV, Channel 4 and Channel Five. Her writing career began when she started a dating blog for marieclaire.co.uk where she entertained readers with frank tales from her laughably unsuccessful foray into the world of Internet dating.

Lucy was brought up in Gloucestershire surrounded by various stupid animals. She recently conducted an early mid-life crisis in South America where she met The Man who, while nice, did rather ruin the 'dating' part of her dating blog. Lucy now lives with him in South London. She is writing her next novel while working on various television projects and plotting a return to academia.

For Vince, who would have been secretly delighted.

The Greatest Love Story
of All Time

*And How it was Nearly Ruined by
an Evil Cat, Gin and Unsuitable Men*

LUCY ROBINSON

PENGUIN BOOKS

PENGUIN BOOKS

Published by the Penguin Group
Penguin Books Ltd, 80 Strand, London WC2R 0RL, England
Penguin Group (USA) Inc., 375 Hudson Street, New York, New York 10014, USA
Penguin Group (Canada), 90 Eglinton Avenue East, Suite 700, Toronto, Ontario, Canada M4P 2Y3
(a division of Pearson Penguin Canada Inc.)
Penguin Ireland, 25 St Stephen's Green, Dublin 2, Ireland (a division of Penguin Books Ltd)
Penguin Group (Australia), 250 Camberwell Road, Camberwell, Victoria 3124, Australia
(a division of Pearson Australia Group Pty Ltd)
Penguin Books India Pvt Ltd, 11 Community Centre, Panchsheel Park, New Delhi – 110 017, India
Penguin Group (NZ), 67 Apollo Drive, Rosedale, Auckland 0632, New Zealand
(a division of Pearson New Zealand Ltd)
Penguin Books (South Africa) (Pty) Ltd, Block D, Rosebank Office Park,
181 Jan Smuts Avenue, Parktown North, Gauteng 2193, South Africa

Penguin Books Ltd, Registered Offices: 80 Strand, London WC2R 0RL, England

www.penguin.com

First published 2012
001

Set in Garamond MT Std 13/15.25 pt
Typeset by Palimpsest Book Production Limited, Falkirk, Stirlingshire
Printed in Great Britain by Clays Ltd, St Ives plc

ISBN: 978-0-241-95298-6

www.greenpenguin.co.uk

ALWAYS LEARNING   PEARSON

Prologue

My friends broke into my flat.

They stood scrutinizing me for a few seconds: Stefania, a vision in purple dungarees; Leonie in a massive fur coat with an inexplicable gin and tonic in one hand. Dave, wearing a patchy deerstalker, rolled a cigarette while my cat Duke Ellington sat next to them on the floor, watching me with open contempt.

Stefania spoke first. 'Ve have decided to hold Gin Thursday here at your house.'

'I love you, Franny,' said Leonie, taking a sip of her gin. 'But this has got to stop, darling. You stink.'

Dave merely laughed, shook his head and murmured, 'Fuckin' hell, Fran. We left Gin Thursday for *this*?'

Duke Ellington looked up at them as if to say, 'See? See what I've been up against?' He stood up and stalked delicately out of the room with his tail twitching. 'Whatever, Duke Ellington,' I muttered in his wake. He ignored me.

I looked up at my friends again and tried to organize my features into a calm, spiritual sort of expression. Something that said, 'Dudes! Sorry I couldn't answer the door! I was just too blissed out to hear you knocking!' *Please make them go away,* I prayed. *I just want to live like a feral animal. Please.*

'Get out of bed,' Stefania commanded, striding over to the window and opening my curtains. 'You look like someseeng zat Duke Ellington has seecked up in ze flowerbed.'

Not having seen daylight in some time I shot back under the covers, swearing. Dave muttered something about me being a nasty little ferret.

I wriggled further down my bed and fumed. What the hell did Dave know about heartbreak anyway? He lived with the most beautiful woman in London. How dare he judge me? The injustice of it! I balled myself up into a foetal position and waited for them to leave, vowing to stay in the warm fug of my bed for ever.

But it was not to be. The duvet was swept from above me, the interior of my bed was exposed and all hell broke loose. Stefania shrieked, 'YOU DISGUS-TEENG ANIMAL!' Leonie downed the gin and tonic and Dave, who was well known in war zones for dodging enemy fire without so much as a raised eyebrow, dropped his half-assembled roll-up and covered his face with his hands.

The sight that had greeted them wasn't nice. Even I could see that. A half-eaten tub of ice-cream had welded itself to the sheet and was growing fur. My pillowcases were rigid and peaked where I had let snot dry on them, and photos of Michael lay under an abandoned piece of rock-hard Cheddar. A small bottle of Morrison's brandy was resting against my feet. Scattered everywhere were crumbs, crisps and knickers.

Stefania stormed out to the kitchen, shrieking over her shoulder, 'Zis place needs to be decontaminated! Get OUT OF BED!'

I didn't move.

Dave sat down at my dressing-table and stared at me, while Leonie climbed over to my bedside table and took my phone. 'Give it back,' I mumbled feebly. She ignored me and started pressing buttons.

'Give it *back*,' I said again.

'Oh, bloody hell, Fran, what have you been doing?' she asked, taking off her fur coat. She passed the phone to Dave, who looked at it and shook his head with a mixture of pity and amusement.

'Fran, you can't send him messages like this,' he said, trying not to smile. 'That's just . . . it's just fucking madness, love.' He started chuckling. Leonie retrieved the phone and recommenced fiddling.

'I'd like to know what you're finding so funny, Dave,' I said, pulling my hood up to keep the draught out.

'Fran, where would I even start? Oh, love, you're a fuckin' basket case sometimes. Have you been sending him messages like this every day?'

'I never *sent* them,' I mumbled, tears of shame welling. Why was Dave laughing at me when my life

3

was falling apart? Did he really believe I needed to feel any more stupid than I already did? 'Stop it,' I whispered. Tears fell off the side of my nose and into my crusty sheets. Leonie was still fiddling with my phone and Dave sat back and roared with laughter, oblivious to my breakdown.

But when I started to sob he stopped laughing and jumped up from the dressing-table, arms out-stretched. 'Oh, no, Fannybaws, I was just joking . . .' My sobs upgraded to roars in anticipation of one of his big hairy-bear hugs.

But just as he reached down to scoop me up, Stefania re-entered the room and yelled, 'STAND BACK, DAVE! DO NOT TOUCH HER! SHE IS RADIOACTIVE!'

Through my tears I saw her standing in my doorway wearing long rubber gloves and one of my anti-dust face masks. She had even found the plastic goggles the plumber had left under the sink a couple of years ago. In one hand she held a bottle of anti-bacterial spray, in the other, a bin bag.

Leonie came and sat on my bed, ignoring Stefania. She took one of my grubby hands in hers. 'Now listen here, Franny darling. We've come because we care about you. We want you to be happy, and that's not going to happen if you're drafting crazed messages to Michael and rotting in bed.'

I gulped and sniffed but the crying wouldn't stop. *Happy?* Were they mad? My life was over. In thirty years I had never felt more lonely and hopeless. How in the name of God was I going to achieve happiness without Michael? Dave sat down and stroked my greasy hair with one of his great big paws.

'I just want my boy back,' I cried.

Leonie squeezed my hand. 'I know, darling. I know. And that might just happen!'

I howled.

'Franny! Come on. It's not like he's said he never wants to see you again, he's just asked for three months apart. It's ninety days, Franny! You can get through ninety days, can't you?'

I shook my head hard. I most certainly could not. Every part of me was in pain.

'Well, from the sounds of it you don't have any choice. But I can tell you right now, Franny, he's not going to take you back if you die of malnutrition in your bed.'

More sobs, with snot this time.

Leonie sighed, then ploughed on: 'So we've come up with a plan for you, Franny. A plan to help you get better. It's a sort of dating rehab. And if at the end of it you still want to fight for Michael, you'll be ready. We'll even help you. OK?'

I made a snotty noise. Dave smiled and continued to stroke my hair. Stefania stood in the doorway, looking like a pest exterminator. Leonie gazed down at me in an uncharacteristically kindly fashion and squeezed my hand again.

I nodded. I'd do anything it took to stop feeling like this.

'Great. Good girl! We'll have you better in no time! Here's the plan . . .' Leonie began.

Chapter One

February 2008: two years earlier

I'd always wanted to be a journalist. In reception class at primary school, while all of the other children told Mrs Grattan that they wanted to be a fireman, a princess or a singer, I had announced coolly that I wanted to travel to war zones and do brave things on the telly. In retrospect I can see why Mrs Grattan told Mum and Dad at parents' evening that she found me a precocious arse.

It had been a little disappointing when the only job I'd been able to get after my broadcast journalism master's was a position as general gimp to the rugby union team at Sky News. For three years I spent every Saturday hunched in the corner of a broadcast truck parked up outside the nation's rugby stadiums, transmitting live scores while the boys talked about anal.

After a particularly sordid Saturday in 2005, during which I was asked to judge a Largest Bollock competition during the Wales v. Ireland decider, I resigned and managed, against all odds, to get a job as a general gimp on the six thirty p.m. news at ITN. (I strongly suspect that I got it because Stella Sanderson, the senior specialist producer who was responsible for hiring me, had also begun her career judging testicles for the Sky rugby team. 'Is there still quite a strong crotch theme in those broadcast trucks?' she asked in my interview. I went red and talked about my overwhelming passion for current affairs. She nodded sympathetically and scribbled in the margin of my CV.)

I was twenty-five when I finally got my break; the age when my friends were beginning to settle down and do grown-up things like having relationships and getting pregnant. I started a wild and passionate affair with my career and moved into a strange little converted car mechanic's garage in a backstreet off Camden Road. It was affordable only because the conversion – involving ceilings that sloped down to the floor – had been designed solely with dwarfs in mind. But it had an *actual* wet room and a big yard where Duke Ellington could terrorize the local mice and birds, so I took it on the spot and convinced myself that Big Things were coming my way.

My job was on the entertainment and culture desk, trailing around London in the wake of our correspondent; carrying his discarded Starbucks cups and broken tripods. Occasionally I'd look after studio guests, and Pierce Brosnan once complained that my hospitality had had a lot in common with sexual harassment.

It was pretty unglamorous stuff in spite of what Leonie and my mother believed: as often as not, I'd spend shoots on bag-watch duty down a smelly alley-way with a coterie of crack addicts. But I loved my job and I gave it everything. It made me feel alive, challenged and useful. I entertained fantastical notions of one day being a foreign correspondent wearing linen trousers in a dusty land far away and in the meantime I plugged away merrily on cuts in arts budgets and the odd celebrity scandal.

Soon after starting I struck up a friendship with a cameraman called Dave Brennan. He was a big scruffy bear of a man who had been born with a camera in one hand and a roll-up in the other. He was renowned for his strange tastes: once I found him sitting in his van eating jellied eels and singing along loudly to soft rock; another time he turned up to a shoot at Buck-ingham Palace wearing a jumper that was covered with mating gnomes.

Dave was Glaswegian, tough as fuck, and had just transferred to domestic news after a long stint in Iraq. In spite of losing one of his fingers to a piece of fly-ing shrapnel and being holed up in a besieged town for ten days without food, he hadn't wanted to come home; he'd only done so because his girlfriend had threatened to further dismember him if he didn't. I'd never quite worked out how old Dave was because of his sun-abused face and poor control of facial hair, but I suspected he was in the late-thirties bracket. Regardless, at ITN he was a legend, the best and bravest cameraman we had and generally believed to be the wisest man in the world. Given the rather different nature of our news desks, I got to work with him only rarely but when I did I always sensed I was in the presence of a genius – a slightly hairy, unpredictable genius, but a genius all the same.

Dave and I bonded when he found me necking sausage and mash in a pub near work because I was too embarrassed to do so in front of my slim, tough, salad-eating colleagues. He had retreated to the same pub to down a pint of Stella after a particularly harrowing day at a murder scene. 'Well, well, well. Another outcast. Welcome to my team of one,' he said.

I blushed, mortified, while Dave got to work on his pint, drinking it like Ribena and finishing with a long, mellow belch. 'Sorry. That came out wrong. It's just nice to see someone round here who's a little . . . a little less *corporate*,' he said, and belched again. I smiled bashfully, feeling slightly less stupid.

Most weeks, unless he was in trouble with his girlfriend, Dave would join Leonie and me on Gin Thursdays, an institution the two of us had founded at the tender age of fifteen. The general rule for a Gin Thursday was to get drunk on gin on Thursday. We weren't a complex organization. Ten years on, Gin Thursdays took place at the Three Kings in Clerkenwell, not too far from work. As per our remit, we would drink a lot of gin (Dave added it to his Guinness) and as a general rule Leonie would cop off with a hot lawyer while Dave tried to encourage me to do the same. I always refused. 'I'm after something a little more special than a one-night stand with a man in a pin-stripe suit,' I had announced airily, a few months after we'd met.

'Rubbish,' Dave had replied. 'You're just shite at pulling, aren't you?'

'Yes,' I said meekly.

He smiled and ruffled my hair. 'Aye, I thought as much. Never mind. I'm sure some little scamp will whisk you off your feet soon,' he said kindly.

'Unbloody likely. Last time I tried to pull someone in here I pelvic-thrusted a Greek Cypriot and then asked him to take me home and feed me halloumi.' Dave roared with laughter. 'Oh, Fannybaws,' he said. 'You wee disaster!'

The only time I didn't really enjoy Dave's company was when his partner Freya turned up for a cheeky glass. This was not because she was anything other than nice; it was solely because she was so attractive that in her vicinity I felt like an animated rubbish dump. It was preposterous, a woman like her being let loose on an unsuspecting pub: all conversation shut down and everyone just *stared*. Freya was slim and horribly healthy; she possessed beautiful peaches-and-cream skin and gently waving hair. She wore things made of linen and always smelt amazing.

I had expected Freya and me to become excellent chums, but after a few months of stilted conversation I'd had to admit defeat. I wanted to blame this on her but, deep down, I knew it was my fault: she was calm, spiritual and smooth; I was noisy, clumsy and foolish. I just wasn't her cup of tea. Nonetheless, she tolerated Leonie and me – and our bawdy, studenty drinking – with remarkable patience. Once when he thought no one was looking I saw Dave plant a gentle kiss on her summery shoulder. I was envious. I wanted to kiss it too.

After three years in my rather junior job, I was fantasizing daily about becoming a fearless correspondent with a bullet-proof vest and a string of exotic admirers. 'What do you think the chances are of me being able to apply for a job on the foreign affairs desk?' I asked Hugh, the assistant programme editor, one day.

He looked up briefly from his computer. 'Zero.'

I carried on plugging away with my ideas and late nights, and eventually Hugh came good. In February 2008 he summoned me to his glass fortress at the top end of the newsroom floor. He told me that I was 'a lucky little fucker' and that I was being given a chance to audition for Foreign Affairs by going out to help them cover the aftermath of Kosovo's Declaration of Independence. I'd 'better be fucking outstanding' or 'you'll be working in the fucking canteen for the rest of your fucking life'.

Hugh Gormley was an enormously intelligent man with a swearing habit even worse than mine and a reputation for being a monster. Normally I was terrified of him, but the day he sent me to Kosovo I loved him madly. It was all I could do to stop myself jumping into his lap and kissing him passionately.

As I left, gasping promises of outstanding journalistic vigour, Hugh softened a little bit and smiled. 'You're fucking good news, Fran,' he said. 'You're doing really well. Now fuck off to the Balkans. And be careful. Spend the next two days in hostile-environment training, please.'

I punched the air discreetly and ran off to buy a celebratory can of Vimto, as I often did when life felt good. At last! Fran the Balkans correspondent had been born! I knew nothing about the Balkans, but who cared?

'Don't get any big ideas,' said Stella Sanderson, as she strode past me at the vending machine with a huge folder marked 'Kosovo' under her arm. 'You're at the bottom of the pile. We're going only because the main team out there need a break. It goes them, then me, then our correspondent, then Dave, then the entirety of Kosovo, then you. OK?'

'OK,' I said, nodding enthusiastically. I'd wipe Stella's bottom if I needed to.

After two days' training in hostile-environment filming I began to read about Kosovo. A few moments later, I gave up and called Dave. 'Who'd have thought it, eh? ITN's promising new talent learning her stuff from the cameraman.' He chortled.

I could hear Freya's pots and pans in the background.

'You're not a cameraman, you're a legend,' I said, feeling a bit silly. 'Of course I'm trying to learn from you.'

After a pause, Dave started talking. I listened intently. By the end I was feeling pretty scared.

'You'll be fine, kid, I'll keep an eye on you,' he said at the end, stopping to puff on his fag.

I sighed. 'Dave, I *wish* you wouldn't smoke.'

'Cut the wee princess act, Fran.' He snorted. 'I'm off for my tea now anyway. Pork chops. What are you having?'

I looked in my empty fridge. 'Um, probably some dry Weetabix.'

'You're the fuckin' pits, Fannybaws.' He laughed, hanging up.

I made my nightly call to Mum, who was drunk and complaining about something to do with the gardeners, then packed my bag, wondering how she would cope over the weekend without me coming over to do her shopping and clean her house. Well, she'd have to. If this foreign-affairs thing took off, I'd be going away a lot more. I filed my prickly sense of guilt into a remote drawer in my head and wrote a Post-it note for when I got back: *sort out Mum.*

In spite of having spent his life either attacking me or pretending to hate me, Duke Ellington always got into a panic when I went away. Tonight was no exception. Every time I turned round to put something in my bag he was sitting in it, refusing to meet my eye. 'Duke Ellington, if I ever love a man the way I love you, he will be very lucky,' I told him. He ignored me and moved over to sit down on my clean pants, purring loudly to indicate that he knew this was a bad thing to do. Cursing him, I braved a hand underneath him to fish them out but was unable to escape without toothmarks. 'Why are you such a little bastard?' I yelled, as I washed my hand. I kept a box of plasters by the sink for Duke Ellington attacks.

'You'd better behave yourself when Stefania comes round to feed you,' I told him, just as she arrived at my back door. His purring got louder. For the purpose of driving me mad, he *always* behaved himself with Stefania. I watched in frustration as he trotted flirtily over to her and sat, purring, while she stroked his head and crooned to him in an unidentifiable language.

After talking to him for a good thirty seconds, she glanced up. 'Oh, Frances. Greetings. Have you been drinking ze barley grass like I said?'

'No. It tasted of shit,' I replied.

My neighbour Stefania was simultaneously the best and most ridiculous human being I'd ever met. Since she had barged into my kitchen the day I moved in, bearing a 'dish for health' in an earthenware pot – 'It vill grow ze hairs on your chest' she hissed – she had become my friend, cat-feeder and source of inspiration.

The converted garage in which I rented my flat had retained the inspection shed that was used to assess cars on their arrival, and this shed, just inside the lop-sided wooden gates, was where Stefania lived. By anyone's standards it looked from the outside like a shack in a Comic Relief appeal, but inside it was delightful – a childhood fantasy den full of exotic silks and mad plants and just about enough floor space for her to contort herself into strange yogic shapes.

Stefania's country of origin was nebulous: when I'd first met her she'd told me she was a Yugoslavian princess; another time she'd claimed to be related to the Polish prime minister, and recently I'd heard her introducing herself to another neighbour as a descendant of the oldest family in St Petersburg. Whatever the grandeur of her past, however, the reality of her present was not so impressive. Apart from making enormous pots of stew for the local homeless shelter, she appeared to have no job and even less desire to discuss the matter. I knew that I was probably paying her gas and electricity bills but I couldn't give an arse. I loved her and her barmy ways: I wasn't prepared to lose her over a detail as minor as money. I *wanted* her there. Apart from anything else, Duke Ellington worshipped her.

'How are you anyway, Stefania?' I asked, as she removed my house key from the bunch of spares.

'I am blessed,' she replied, putting the keys down and placing her hands flat on the work surface. Just to emphasise the fact, she closed her eyes.

I smiled. This was textbook Stefania. 'Oh, good. Are you in love?'

'Do not be silly.' She kept her eyes closed.

'Well, then, what is going on?'

'Today I make the perfect seaveed lasagne. It is touched by ze hand of God, I tell you, Frances.'

'That's amazing. Congratulations.'

Stefania nodded. 'Sank you. It is truly amazing. As I tell you, I am blessed.' She scooped up Duke Ellington, who put up no fight whatsoever, and left my house, shouting, 'Take peace viz you to Kosovo, Frances!'

On the train to Gatwick, Dave was unlike his usual self. He was quiet and serious, even rougher round the edges than usual. 'You OK, Dave?' I asked, fishing a fag out of his mouth before he got us thrown off the train.

'Yep,' he said briefly. 'Yep, all good. Just up late with the missus. Tired.'

This was obviously Serious Dave, the Dave who'd lost one of his fingers in a war zone. I resolved to be Serious Fran during the trip, although I was less keen on losing part of my hand. As if he'd read my mind, Dave picked up my bandaged thumb and raised an eyebrow. 'Duke Ellington?' I nodded. 'He's a little fuckwit, that one.' Dave grinned, and returned to his paper.

I'd been sitting at the MAC counter in Duty Free for about fifteen minutes when Dave strode in looking agitated. 'What's up?' I asked him as a pearlescent black eye shadow was brushed into my eye sockets.

'Stella,' he replied, staring at my glam-rock aesthetic with confusion. 'Get out of here, Franny, we're in trouble.'

I shrugged guiltily at the makeup girl as Dave strode off. She gazed at me stonily. Not only was I leaving in the middle of her story about having it off with a minor league football player but I was scarpering without buying any makeup. 'Sorry,' I tried. 'We're journalists. There's an emergency in progress.'

'You – you are *journalist*?' she asked, with a raised eyebrow.

Damn her! 'Yes,' I said, drawing myself up to my full height of five foot four. 'Actually, I'm a foreign correspondent.'

The girl looked me up and down and smiled. 'No. I think you lie,' she said, handing me a face wipe.

When I met up with Stella in the Ladies, I saw why we were in trouble. She was crouched around the toilet bowl with a grey face and shaking hands. 'Crayfish,' she muttered in anguish.

'Oh dear, I, erm . . .' I said, dabbing ineffectually at her brow. It was cold and clammy. I withdrew my hand swiftly and ran as she heaved.

I left the loos to find Dave outside, his phone in his hand. 'She's not flying, is she?' he said. I shook my head. 'No. Let's get on to the office urgently. If someone leaves now they'll get here in time.' He peered at the departures board. Our flight was to leave in under two hours. 'No, they won't. I think we should go alone, Fran,' he said.

'*What?*' I froze. 'Dave, I'm a gimp. I'm just a junior producer! I'm the lowest of the low – I wouldn't have the first idea how to do Stella's job! I . . . can't. It'd be like asking Stephen Fry to stand in for one of Girls Aloud just because he's an entertainer. No way.'

Dave smiled briefly. 'You *can* do this and you will,' he said. 'There's only one direct flight each day. By the time anyone else gets out there we'll be going home again. Come on, Franny. Stop being a fanny.'

I gulped. Dave grinned more encouragingly. 'Are we good to go, Producer Fran?'

Chapter Two

Pristina, the capital of the brand new country of Kosovo, was still alive with people celebrating two weeks after the Declaration of Independence. Flags hung from balconies, fireworks continued to explode over the city at night and a gigantic series of concrete letters spelling 'NEWBORN' was being visited by Kosovars from all over the country. It would have felt like a carnival had there not been armed police and UN tanks everywhere. I was very glad to have Dave with me, his bulk never far from my side, insisting that I wore a bullet-proof vest and shoving me sideways into shops as soon as he thought he saw trouble. In the safety gear he'd kitted me out with, I looked awful beyond my wildest nightmares but I had never felt so alive. 'Isn't this AMAZING?' I breathed, as we hid under a truck while the police broke up a violent protest in a small Serbian enclave on the outskirts of the city.

'Shut up, you tit,' he said, but I could tell he was smiling.

After spending a day or two helping our main Balkans team cover events in the capital, Dave and I were sent up to a more dangerous town in the north called Mitrovica to make our own report. Tensions there were high and suddenly it was my job to tell the story of this angry town to, oh, just a few million people back home. Hugh's praise suddenly felt a long way away, and I was gripped with fear. Silently I thanked God for the correspondent up there, some bloke called Michael whom I'd not heard of at ITN before. He seemed to Know Stuff.

As Dave and I sped up the main road north out of Pristina, I prayed that Michael Slater would be able to run the show. ('I should never have fucking well sent you out there,' a very worried-sounding Hugh had said on the phone last night. 'Just let Michael take control. And don't take risks. A Japanese journalist was beaten up there the week before last. There've been riots too. Stay with the UN. And don't leave Dave's side.')

As we passed fields of bombed-out houses, I asked our driver, Haxhi, if we could get out and film some of them. 'No,' he replied curtly. 'You will get shot.'

'Definitely? Even if we only stop for five minutes?' I asked.

'Definitely. You may risk your life but I shall not be risking mine.'

I sat back.

Dave whispered, 'See? You're a proper producer already. They're always the ones who want to endanger everyone else's lives for a good shot.'

I gave him a distracted V-sign and watched the

unexpectedly verdant countryside sliding past. It felt good to have Dave on side.

The heavily guarded UN offices, where Michael had taken refuge for a while, were sad and grotty. An ancient tractor sat inexplicably in their front car park and the walls were covered with angry graffiti. A man on the roof of the neighbouring building stared at me as if I was an alien and picked his nose pointedly. *Don't eat it, please don't eat it,* I thought. He ate it and then fiddled with what I realized was an enormous old Kalashnikov on a belt slung over his shoulder. I scampered inside behind Dave.

We were guided along a damp, pitch-black corridor. 'No money for light,' Haxhi told us, as I crashed into a cupboard. Suddenly a door opened at the end of the corridor and there . . . There, with a sleepy, smiling face and a faded army jumper, was essentially the most attractive man I'd ever seen.

'You must be Stella,' he said, reaching forward to shake my hand. His was smooth and warm. 'You're a lot younger than I expected. I'm Michael.'

'You're a lot younger than I expected, too!' I yelled shrilly, completely thrown. This man was *gorgeous*! 'Oh, actually, hang on, I'm not Stella. I'm Fran.'

Michael raised an eyebrow. 'Are you sure?' he asked. 'You did just nod quite enthusiastically when I asked if you were Stella.'

'Yes. I'm definitely Fran. Stella was on the toilet. Well, she was under the toilet, really.'

Michael grinned. 'Interesting.'

'She ate some bad seafood. She was curled up on the floor at Gatwick last time I saw her. Her face was sort of see-through, she was so ill. I reckon it was probably coming out both ends . . .' I trailed off.

By now he was laughing. 'I think she'd be very touched by your description of her,' he said.

I blushed. 'Yes, sorry. I'm sure she didn't really get the shits, I'm sure she –'

'Fran, shut it,' Dave said, laughing too. 'Enough. Poor Stella.'

Michael, chuckling, disappeared behind something that resembled an upright coffin to make tea. It was a big, dirty, dusty room with a collection of decrepit tables and chairs at one end and various weird objects filling the rest of the space. Dave sat down on a sofa and I grabbed a wooden chair. It collapsed as soon as I sat on it. As I tried to save myself I brought a coat-stand on top of me and sprawled backwards with my jumper rucked up round my breasts. Mortified beyond all comprehension, I prayed for death. Nothing happened, other than Dave bursting into fits of laughter which subsided into chesty coughs, and Michael running over to extract me. I tried frantically to pull my jumper down over my white winter belly, but it was no use: I was pinned to the floor by a coat-stand.

'That was impressive.' Michael took a machine-gun belt from round my neck and picked up the coat-stand.

'I'm delighted you're here instead of Stella. Are you really mental or just a bit clumsy?'

I went red. 'Bit of both!' I said, climbing out. 'I like to shake things up a bit!' I tried to smooth my hair down. It bounced straight back up into the I've-clearly-slept-on-this-hair-and-then-not-washed-it style that I was going with today. (My hotel-room shower featured flashing blue lights and Balkan music, which I hadn't been game for at five forty-five a.m.)

Extreme fitness discovered in the UK building. Am acting like a twat. Will report back by 18.00 hours. I texted Leonie.

The next two hours in Michael's office were ridiculous. Forgetting entirely that this was not only my first international assignment but my big chance to prove myself as a Proper Producer, I tried everything at my disposal to work out whether or not he was single, and didn't ask one question about what was really quite a serious situation in Mitrovica. Politics, my arse! Today was about romance and passion! I concocted a new tinkly laugh, which I thought made me sound carefree and relaxed but also knowing and wise, and threw in references to cultural things I knew nothing about. When other correspondents from other channels came in, I did my best to flirt with them so that Michael could see what an amazing catch I was. My heart raced throughout. The whole thing was lamentably embarrassing.

Michael was remarkably calm in the face of my pathological lying and madness, smiling across the table with two slate-grey eyes as I babbled on about my *wonderful* life in London. 'I go to the theatre a *lot*,' I trumpeted at one point.

'Really?' Dave asked. 'What did you see last?'

I shot him a foul look. The last time I had been to the theatre, as he well knew, was to see *Dirty Dancing* with Leonie. 'Er . . . well, I like a bit of everything . . . Eclectic taste, y'know,' I muttered.

Michael sighed. 'God, I miss London. Did you see *Attempts On Her Life* at the National? Astonishingly powerful,' he said.

I stared at him and wondered at what age we would send our children to stage school.

Dave cleared his throat. 'Personally I love nothing more than a power ballad delivered by a woman wearing a good sturdy shoulder pad. "I Know Him So Well" is one of the greatest songs ever written.'

I ignored him.

As the afternoon wore on, the sun shifted round behind Michael and sliced in over his shoulder while a million particles of Eastern European dust danced round his head in a crazed halo. I was entranced. The way his eyes held mine — languidly, but with absolute intensity and purpose — was electrifying.

Dave watched the scene unfold with a face of amused despair, and when I came out with 'So, Michael, when do you think you'll be moving back to England? Just, y'know, important insight for this report . . . er . . . your life as a correspondent and whatnot . . .' He put his head in his hands and murmured, 'Fran, I think it's time we went and filmed something.'

I smiled gratefully at him. I was making an unforgivable cock of myself. We concocted a plan of attack for the report and left. Walking out of the building and into the cold, hard afternoon sun, I caught sight of Michael's bottom. I'd not realized I was a bottom sort of girl until that moment but Michael's was exquisite. Small, manly and firm, with just a hint of muscle. I wanted to cup it gently. And then firmly. And maybe give it a soft slap just to be sure. 'Ready to go?' he asked. I came out of my blissful reverie. 'Everything OK?' he asked curiously.

'What? Yes, I'm fine. Why?' I said.

'You seemed to be staring at my leg,' he said, sounding slightly confused.

'Fran was checking out your backside, Michael,' Dave said firmly.

Briefly, I prayed that Dave would be run over by a passing tank.

Michael went back to collect a couple of guards and we got into his truck. Dave thumped me. 'Will you fuckin' well pull yourself together?' he hissed. 'You're meant to be doing a job out here. This is a fuckin' dangerous city, Fran, not a fuckin' pick-up joint.'

I thumped him back. 'Why did you say I was looking at his arse?' I whispered. 'You made me sound like a total BELL END.'

His eyes creased in amusement. 'You're *acting* like a bell end. It's pure car crash, Fran! This is your big break and we're in a dangerous place. Don't cock it up over some man, OK?'

'What am I meant to do?' I whispered, as Michael and the guards came outside. 'You have no idea what it's like to be single! Particularly when you look like Barry Manilow!'

Having spent the last few days in steel-toecapped boots and bullet-proof vests, I'd stopped caring about my appearance and today's outfit was testament to my slipping standards. In addition to a pair of nineties jeans that made my legs look like flared hams, I was wearing a stab vest (on Dave's insistence) and a large pastel ski jacket of Mum's from a bygone era. On top of it all was a UN vest. I resembled a massive UN Easter egg. With a Barry Manilow hairstyle. Rarely had I felt less fanciable.

So why did I keep catching Michael's eye in the rearview mirror? And why, when we parked in the unsettled north of the city, did he fall into stride beside me and stay there for most of the next few hours? There was surely no way he was interested in me when I looked like an egg on legs and was behaving like a clumsy thirteen-year-old at a school disco.

But something *was* happening. Something exciting. It left me breathless.

In Michael's office we had come up with a plan of action that consisted largely of him conceiving a report about the Angry Men of Mitrovica and me staring at him and nodding. He was extremely clever. He Knew Stuff. He knew where we could go and not get beaten up. I was awed. I texted Leonie: I am being completely shit at my job. Help.

Her reply was swift: Do you have an initial estimate re the size of his package? That is the important matter, Fran. Don't let me down.

Serbian men talked quietly and angrily in cafés. They stared at me and my Barry barnet with confusion when we entered but soon went back to ignoring me. I didn't blame them. I'd been here long enough now to understand why they were so furious. The whole situation was completely unacceptable to them, and our presence was just another reminder of what was going on. We were on the very outer limits of welcome and no one, not even Michael's friends, was prepared to talk on camera to him. The two guards with us were on high alert all the time, hands resting on their guns and eyes always watching.

In the fifth café, I watched Michael and Dave try to cajole a group of them into talking and eventually backed outside the door to pull out a wedgie.

Before the guard had a chance to follow me I heard a chorus of giggles. Behind me a group of kids, aged maybe ten, was watching me from yet another tractor that was just parked in the middle of the city. I smiled. 'Hello,' I said, forgetting they were Serbian.

'HELLO!' they yelled back, in thick accents, cackling

with laughter and miming the act of wedgie-pulling-out.

'Hello,' I said again, pleased by the encouraging response.

'HELLO!' they roared, abandoning their tractor and coming to stand round me. I shook their hands at least once and tried to repeat their names amid much hilarity. 'FRAN! FRAN! FRAN!' they yelled.

'Do you speak English?' I asked the eldest.

'Yes. Hello. I like go to ceenema. I eat toasts for brakfast. Where is post offices please? Goodbye. Thank you,' he replied proudly.

I giggled. 'That is BRILLIANT!' Delighted, he high-fived his companions and chattered away in Serbian, repeating 'brilliant' several times.

Amid the high-fives I noticed a girl of about my age standing near the tractor, watching the scene with a shy smile. She walked up to me. She was short and pretty, in a rather haunted way. My guard clocked her and stood up straight, handling his gun in a more macho fashion. He smiled briefly at her. 'They are only learning English lately,' she said. 'They have seen many English speakers these last weeks and they like it.'

'Do they understand what's going on?' I asked.

'Yes, of course,' she said, surprised. 'Their mothers and fathers will talk about the problems in the home. Every day they will talk about the problems. Everyone knows about the problems.'

'Can you ask them what they think about it?' I asked, interested.

She raised an eyebrow but gathered them round her and listened as the answers came spilling out thick and fast. She smiled. 'They are saying that their mothers and fathers are angry about it. But they do not want the fighting. They want to go to school. They want to flirt with the girls, but the girls are all being kept inside in case of trouble.'

I heard a quiet chuckle right behind me and spun round, only to head-butt Michael square in the nose. 'Fuck!' he yelled, jumping backwards, clutching his face.

'Fuck!' I cried, mortified.

The kids roared with laughter. 'FUCK! FUCK! FUCK!' they yelled, high-fiving again. The girl laughed and covered her mouth, blushing and looking shyly at Michael.

It wasn't just me, then.

'Is it broken?' I said awkwardly.

'No ... mmffpppff,' he said, from behind his hands, eyes still screwed up in pain.

'I'm so sorry ...' I said, unsure what the best move would be. What I *wanted* to do was to grab his face, kiss his nose, then jump into his jeep and drive off into the grey hills behind the city where we would make passionate love and wake up in each other's arms the next day, ready to get engaged, but instead I just stood there, anguished, shifting my weight from one leg to the other and hoping the Serbian girl didn't know first aid.

He took his hand away. 'My fault,' he said, from behind a big red honker of a nose.

'No –'

'Fran, I think you should interview these kids,' he said, as Dave came out and joined us. 'It'd be a lovely piece to put into the report.'

I started laughing. 'That's nuts! You're the correspondent! I'm not even a real producer. I'm just –'

But Dave interrupted: 'I agree, Franny,' he said. 'Let's do this. The kids like you. You've made more progress in two minutes than we've made in an hour.' He hitched his camera up on his shoulder and sat on the ground with the kids staring uncertainly at his sprouty facial hair.

'Do you mind translating?' I asked the girl.

'Of course not. I will do anything you want.' She blushed again, smiling at Michael. 'My name is Milinka.' Dammit, I both hated and loved her.

We all knelt down to talk to the kids. At first they were silent, ignoring my questions and staring at Dave as if there was an orang-utan in their midst. After a few minutes I offered the youngest a high-five and a whispered, 'Fuck,' and they were off, gabbling away excitely to Milinka and pausing only to yell, 'FRAN,' and 'FUCK!' while I fed Milinka questions amid the general disorder.

Chapter Three

Three hours later, when we eventually finished in a striking worker's house, with a patchy but adequate report, I began to panic. I couldn't possibly leave this man: hearing Michael talking on camera about all of the Clever Shit he knew had made me quite weak with admiration and horn. And there was definite flirtation going on. Only three minutes earlier he had whispered right into my ear that I was doing a great job, and I'd known full well he was smelling my hair.

As I packed up Dave's kit, Michael saved the day. 'Um, do you two fancy coming round to my digs for dinner? It's in the south of the city. Safer. My landlady is a legendary human being and she does a famous omelette and chips for me on Thursday nights. I can't lie, it'll be a slightly unorthodox omelette . . .'

'YES!' I interrupted, at the top of my voice, terrified that Dave might say no. Then I felt guilty: he seemed so old and tired and pissed off today. But there was no way I was leaving Michael. I was intoxicated.

'She even manages to find morel mushrooms!' Michael enthused.

I widened my eyes with excitement and shouted, 'WOW! I LOVE morel mushrooms,' never having eaten one in my life. I texted Leonie as we drove to Michael's house: I broke fit man's nose and am about to eat morel mushrooms with him. He is giving me fanny gallop. Am slightly out of control.

It was true. I didn't just like this man, I *really* liked him. My stomach turned somersaults as we drove through the city in the gathering dusk. Please let me not make a fool of myself.

The landlady, Ejona, welcomed us as if we were old friends who'd just dropped by for a cup of tea. She hugged me shyly, then looked me up and down, delivering a stream of rapid Albanian to Michael. It seemed that, in spite of my shabby appearance, I was good news.

She invited some neighbours round in our honour, and soon there were eight of us sitting in a large, warm room full of worn Albanian rugs, drinking Pejes beer and not having the first clue what each other was saying. Michael and I were jammed together by the two people next to us and I felt as if someone had set fire to my right leg. 'For God's sake, make sure you say that this is the most delicious beer you've ever tasted,' he whispered, brushing my ear with his nose and setting off an eruption of activity in my stomach. He smelt of washing powder and fire smoke. I wanted to cook his dinner and wash his socks for him. I wanted to rub his back when he was tired and rub his privates when he wasn't.

'Are you married?' Ejona asked me, using Michael as an interpreter. I said no, very loudly and firmly, and felt Michael relax. Ejona smirked, her dark eyes creasing as she drew hard on a cigarette. She made a comment in Albanian and everyone fell about laughing.

'What?' I asked Michael.

'I think it's best I don't translate,' he said, smiling. 'They are, erm, speculating.'

I looked at Dave, who was smoking and watching the whole embarrassing spectacle with a raised eyebrow. I narrowed my eyes briefly – *stop it!* – but he just shook his head. I was going to have to pull my finger out when we got back to London. Dave was a friend but he was also a pillar of the news team and I could ill-afford to let him down.

Outside it was getting darker and soft lights were beginning to illuminate windows in houses across the river. Ejona served up the omelette extravaganza and Michael handed me my fifth Pejes beer. 'You're an impressive drinker, Fran. I like what I see.' My face, already red from having been out in the cold all afternoon, turned an even deeper shade.

Munching my omelette – which was more of a cake with eggs and mushrooms but delicious none the less – I wondered if I had perhaps gone mad. I had known this man for less than twenty-four hours and already I wanted to raise his children. I couldn't put my finger on what it was, even. He wasn't like anyone I'd fancied before. He was bewilderingly laid-back, completely at ease with himself and just . . . just really *nice*. And funny. *And he seemed to like me.*

Leonie texted: Has he got a decent package? Surely you must know by now.

I replied: Bear with me.

She wasn't having any of it: Fran, you're not leaving Kosovo till this Michael has popped his truncheon up your luncheon. I shoved my phone back into my jeans pocket. When I looked up again, Michael was watching me. 'Boyfriend?' he asked awkwardly, flushing as soon as the word was out of his mouth.

Before I had a chance to answer, Dave butted in with 'Och, don't be stupid, Franny's always single, aren't you, Fannybaws?'

That was it. Dave and I were over, *for ever*. The betrayal! Seemingly oblivious, he leaned over the table and ruffled my hair, chuckling quietly.

I hated him silently for a few minutes but had to give up. You just couldn't hate Dave. He was like your lovely bumbling dad and your infuriating little brother all in one big hairy Glaswegian bundle.

An hour later, by which time I was comprehensively drunk but pretending otherwise to impress Michael, Dave started making moves to leave. *Shit*. I needed to do something, fast. Haxhi was now dropping extensive hints about returning to Pristina, and although I had seen Dave hand him a substantial tip, he was clearly going without us if we didn't come soon. I panicked, letting out a little beer belch, which fortunately only Dave heard.

Shit. We were shaking hands with a beaming Ejona, who was full of knowing winks and raised eyebrows, and now we were out in the street. I was walking in slow motion, feeling Michael slipping through my fingers, while Dave thanked Ejona. *Shit.* How could I leave this man behind? A voice in my head yelled that I'd regret it for the rest of my life. *COME ON, FRAN,* it screeched. *DO SOMETHING, YOU USELESS COCK!*

Stiffly, I turned to Michael and offered him my hand, which he shook. I looked beseechingly at him and muttered how nice it had been to meet him.

And then, as he opened his mouth to reply, the quiet night was rent with the sound of yelling, banging, crashing and, to my horror, a gunshot.

Michael pulled me fast back into Ejona's house, Dave following, and double-locked the door. 'The bridge,' he said briefly. 'There's been trouble down there every night for a while.' Dave started pulling his camera out of the bag.

'Good. Let's go,' he said as Michael put a winter hat on.

'Er, guys, are you *joking?*' I asked, bewildered.

'Fran, it's fine,' Dave replied. 'This is small fry – a scuffle. I'm not about to go and stand in the middle of the street with an Albanian flag.'

'Yep. This happens every night. It's more a venting

of frustration than anything else,' Michael said. 'They shoot into the air with Kalashnikovs – they're not shooting each other. Most of the guys involved are friends. I'll talk to them and make sure we're safe. But you should definitely stay here.'

They looked at me, presumably waiting for me to insist on coming with them. No bloody chance! I was a pastel Easter egg with a Manilow haircut. If I was an angry, restless local I'd definitely take me out. More to the point, I was afraid. 'I think you're mad. Please don't go out there,' I said.

Michael smiled. 'Don't worry, Fran. I live here. This is no worse to me than rush hour on the tube,' he said, pulling on a stab vest.

I struggled hard with my impulse to jump on him. He went off into the noisy street with Dave and the two men who'd come round for dinner, all of them seeming bizarrely relaxed.

Men.

The three women who were left turned off the lights and watched the street through a gap in Ejona's curtains. They talked softly and sadly to each other in Albanian, and I reflected on how much better this scene in the sitting room would be in a report than a load of dark, confused shots from behind a wall by the danger zone.

So, when Michael and Dave returned less than five minutes later, telling me it had been impossible to get close enough to the action, I was rather pleased.

'Look,' I said, gesturing at Ejona and her two friends. 'That's the real story, isn't it? The people whose lives are being torn apart by all of this, not the angry men throwing grenades at the bridge.'

'Right again, Fran,' Michael said, smiling at me. 'You're bang on. I'll ask them.' I nearly passed out with pride.

Ejona and her friends agreed to let us film them and twenty minutes later we had a piece that brought out the emotional tumult of the situation beautifully. I grinned broadly. Perhaps I could do this, after all. 'Way to go, Franny,' said Dave later, as the disturbance died down.

'I agree. You've got a lovely human touch. You're the bollocks!' Michael grinned.

If you're not careful I'll touch your *bollocks*, I thought. This extraordinarily brainy foreign-affairs man was actually complimenting my work. I resolved to buy a library's worth of books on clever stuff when I got home. I wanted to be like him.

But back to the matter in hand. We were walking outside once more, stopping in almost the same position that we'd been in an hour ago, when things kicked off. Michael was shaking my hand again. It was warm and I wanted his children. But when I looked up at him, I saw in his face something completely unmistakable. He was panicking! 'It's been great to meet you too,' he said woodenly. 'Do keep in touch and . . . Oh, fuck it,' he whispered urgently. 'Please don't get in the car. Please don't go. Please.'

I nodded rapidly, my heart hammering in my chest. I watched Michael walk over to Dave. 'Um, Dave, I thought I'd . . . Well, I'd like to show Fran a few more sights, if that's OK, and then I'll drive her home.'

It was lame as arse. Who shows their guest the 'sights' of Kosovo's most dangerous city in the pitch black in February? If I hadn't been so nervous I'd have laughed. I walked over to the car where Dave was looking rather stony-faced. 'Sure thing, matey.' He smiled thinly at me. 'Are you OK with that, Fran?' I nodded my assent. Then the car pulled away and I was standing in the road with Michael, our breath forming small clouds of vapour above our heads.

Chapter Four

'That didn't go so well,' Michael said, with a broad grin.

'Well, we have to sign a risk assessment saying we won't leave each other under any circumstances,' I said. 'Dave made me promise not to go off on my own. I'll have to do a lot of grovelling tomorrow.'

Michael moved closer and stood right in front of me. My stomach jumped wildly round my abdomen. 'Well, tell him you're not in any danger here. I asked you to stay because I like you, not because I want to kill you. Come on. Let's go for a drive,' he said. I made a strange noise that was somewhere between 'oh' and 'yes' and followed him to his jeep.

He turned it round and started driving, revving up a hill out of the city.

I wondered how much he had had to drink, and decided I didn't care. Probably due to my sudden inability to talk, he'd put on a Kosovan radio station, which, rather surprisingly, was blasting out Duke Ellington in tinny surround sound. We were heading up what seemed like an interminable hill and the road had become narrow and rather treacherous. Had I been with anyone else I would have been terrified, but with Michael, in his stinky old jeep, Duke Ellington parping away, I felt completely safe. And thrillingly alive.

'I have a cat called Duke Ellington,' I said. The thought of my fierce grey tiger made me smile. I imagined Michael and him together and knew they'd get on.

'That's a good name for a cat,' he said. 'My mum has a dog called Alan. I think that anyone who calls their dog Buster should be punched. It's human names all the way. Although we did have a dog called Trumpet when I was a kid and he was pretty cool.'

'Eyes on the bloody road!' I yelled, as we approached a hairpin bend, Mitrovica glittering malevolently below us. 'Jesus!' We cleared the bend – just – and then the road petered out and ended with a Kosovo trademark: a half-built house.

Michael pulled over. 'Get out of my car! You're distracting me. Go on, out.' He was laughing.

'Fine. Whatever. It's a shit car anyway,' I said, flouncing out theatrically. *He had a dog called Trumpet! And another called Alan! He was actually perfect!* I slammed the door behind me and walked away from the car towards the precipice, my heart pounding now like a nineties warehouse rave. *Keep it together,* I begged myself. I stood looking down at the city, shaking violently although, in spite of the sub-zero temperatures, I wasn't cold.

Eventually I turned round. Michael was walking towards me. He didn't say a thing. When he reached me, a small smile crossed his lips. I had never wanted to kiss anyone as badly as I wanted to kiss Michael Slater right at that moment. I was gone. Powerless.

Had it been a beautiful sunset over the Tuscan hills, me in a flimsy sundress and him in a linen suit, it might have felt like a film. But we were standing by an abandoned building site overlooking a dangerous city in Kosovo on a ball-crunchingly freezing night and it felt more like a scene from a very low-budget Eastern European soap.

I didn't know Michael's age or how he liked his tea, I was wearing a terrible coat and I was drunk as a stoat – but this moment felt like *it*. The one I'd been waiting patiently for since I was a girl. I'd worked so hard, for so long, at being OK with being single, but all of the things I'd told myself about independence were disappearing rapidly into the cold night. Right now, Michael felt like the only person who mattered in the whole world.

'Now, look here, Fran. I think we have a bit of a situation on our hands. Am I right?' he said.

'Ah. Erm, well, maybe. In fact probably. Yes. A situation,' I said, through chattering teeth. I shivered hard. Michael took off his hat and put it on me. He left his hands round the side of my head, over my ears, and looked at me, smiling. 'You're a bit mad, Fran. But you're so . . . You make me feel alive again,' he said, looking suddenly helpless. 'I've been so confused out here, so out of sorts and you just – made me remember who I was. I have to see you again. Please tell me you feel the same.'

I should have lunged in and snogged him. Or at least *said* something. But for once I found myself out of words. I didn't really believe this was happening: men like Michael simply did not say such things to me. I gazed up at him and wrinkled my nose, unable even to smile. Was this really happening? Was I having a romantic moment with this perfect man?

Michael laughed softly. 'Good,' he said. 'I thought so.'

Then he slid his hands under my hair and kissed me. Softly, tentatively, at first, but then he pulled me close to him and kissed me deeply. This lovely, exciting, beautiful man. As his warm breath moved down my neck and he kissed me just above the top of my terrible ski jacket I was pretty sure that this was the best moment of my life. I put my arms round his waist and swayed slightly with lust and excitement and Pejes beer.

A few minutes later, we stopped kissing and pulled apart, giggling shyly. 'Damn you!' I said, through an uncontrollable smile. 'How could you make me wait all day?'

'Damn you too,' he said. 'How dare you just explode into my life and break my chair and ruin my job here? You with your alternative hairstyles and questionable coats.'

I punched his arm, like a stupid teenager, and he grabbed me again, hugging me so tightly that I couldn't breathe. We stood there for ages, Michael stroking my Barry Manilow hair and me smiling manically into the armpit of his coat. I don't think I'd ever felt so excited and happy and . . . well, relieved. Here he was! Here *he* was! Cue violins! Cue chubby cherubs with bows and arrows! This was it!

We got back into the car. Michael turned the jeep's ancient heater to full blast and Radio Blue Sky back on, telling me how he'd been strip-searched for drugs when he'd driven over the border from Albania. 'Did they even look in your bum?' I asked, wide-eyed.

Michael got a blanket out of the back and pulled me on to his lap. 'Yes. Right up it. Lights and everything. No, you weird woman, they did not look in my bum.' He kissed me again.

We talked all night. Strangely, having spent much of the day imagining him naked and texting Leonie predictions about the size of his truncheon, I didn't think once about sex. There was too much to say; too much to think about; too much to laugh about.

We must have dozed off at some point because I woke up to the sound of a blasting horn. Michael, too, was awake, his hair sticking up in tufts, his arms round me and his eyes smiling. 'Fran, your arse is pressing the horn.' He yawned, pulling me close to him. We kissed again, falling asleep soon after.

When it became light we woke up properly and neither of us moved. I was freezing cold, aching all over, starving – and definitely the happiest I'd ever felt in my life. 'Michael,' I began, 'I'm flying home this afternoon. I have to get back. I . . .' I trailed off, having no idea what to do.

'I kind of feel it would be futile for me to suggest that you come and live in Mitrovica with me and Ejona,' he asked, watching my face nervously. His nose was slightly bent after my assault on it yesterday. I was quite sure I was in love with him.

'Oh. I . . . probably not . . . Duke Ellington isn't very keen on flying,' I said.

He kissed me again. 'Damn that cat. I hate him already. Look, Fran, I'm contracted to stay out here until June. Will you wait for me? Please? I have to know what will happen between us. I feel like you're . . . I dunno . . . like you're the answer to everything. I know it's a lot to ask for you to wait, but to hell with it, I'm asking.'

'Yes, of course,' I heard myself reply. And then I laughed, because I'd have waited ten years if I had to. I liked the sound of being the answer to everything. I liked it very much.

As the plane banked down into Gatwick, I felt as if I'd just returned from five years on the moon, not five days in Kosovo. Dave had given me a fierce bollocking about health and safety, then followed it up with a big hairy bear hug because it was quite clear that I was in a state of total barminess. 'I'm sorry, Dave, but I had to do it,' I said lamely.

He smiled, his brilliant blue eyes creasing up. 'Aye, Franny, I know. It's no bother. Just don't ever tell anyone I let you go, OK?'

I kissed his cheek and gave him my British Airways cheese and onion sandwich. He passed it back. 'The missus'll be waiting. I can't eat that stinky shite,' he said. 'And you'll have to learn not to do things like that if you're going to get together with Mr Fancy Pants.'

I felt quite insane with excitement at this thought and was relieved when the fasten-seatbelt sign lit up. I was so high that I was liable to jump out of the emergency exit at any moment.

Freya was waiting for Dave at the arrivals barrier, even more disgustingly beautiful than normal. She was breathtaking and exotic in a fiery orange smock top with a long silk scarf, red tights and beautiful leather boots. As always, when I saw Freya, I looked down at myself and made an instant appraisal: munter. But this time, I didn't feel inferior and jealous. Michael wanted me! Freya could be as beautiful as she liked!

Dave had been carrying my bag but as soon as he saw Freya he dropped it and forgot about me, running over to her with surprise and pleasure written all over his face. It was clear that he hadn't been expecting her. I watched Freya's face as Dave approached her: it was full of love and worry and almost . . . well, almost *fear*. Why the fear? I picked up my bags as Dave fell on her like a ravenous child. I supposed that after his time in Iraq she must have grown to hate him going away. They hugged tightly. Soon after, they left with barely a glance in my direction.

Slumped in a taxi, slightly deflated, I considered calling ITN to talk about the week ahead. Instead I called Leonie. 'Fran. You total bastard. WHAT HAPPENED TO MY UPDATE? You are a terrible friend,' she yelled.

I could hear a harp in the background. 'Where the hell *are* you?' I asked, as Westminster slid past the windows of my cab.

'Oh, I'm at Claridges with a charity client.' Her voice sounded fruity, which meant that a new rich man was trying to have sex with her. 'It's lovely. Anyway, what the hell is going on? Did you have sex with him? Are you bullet-ridden? Are you about to become ITN's Kosovo correspondent?'

'Actually, I think I'm in love,' I said, hugging myself. As we swung into the Mall, I held the phone away from my face as her screams poured out of it.

Chapter Five

January 2010

I lay staring at the ceiling, trying to remember how it had felt to be that happy. Not a great deal came to me. I tried to recall the wild excitement I'd felt whenever Michael's name appeared in my inbox when he was still in Kosovo; how ecstatic I'd been when he had terminated his contract to come back three months earlier than planned.

A tear ran down my cheek. My life back then – nearly two years ago now – felt worlds apart from the rotten, painful pit it was now. I couldn't bear the grief. The loss. The sense of being so completely alone in the world. I wiped off the tear with a crusty pyjama sleeve.

You never deserved him, Fran, you knob-end! Of course this was going to happen!

The aching expanse of sadness strapped itself a little tighter across my chest. Of course I hadn't. I'd always known, deep down, that I was punching above my weight with Michael. Why would someone like him want some scruffy girl who talked to cats and got the answer to 'Who painted the *Mona Lisa*?' wrong in the pub quiz?

It had been ten days now. Ten days since Michael had picked me up from work on my thirtieth birthday, all smiles and kisses and with a ring-box-shaped bulge in his pocket. Ten days since he'd helped me out of a taxi in front of the Ritz, only to veer off into Green Park, take my face in his hands, look me deep in the eyes and tell me he wanted to break off all contact with me for three months.

Ten days since I'd stopped caring about anything, other than making sure I was still breathing.

I rolled over on to my side and bunched myself up. 'I don't know how to do this,' I whispered to Duke Ellington, who was asleep next to one of Stefania's tofu wraps. I really *didn't* know how to do this. How to tolerate another minute of the pain. All I wanted was for someone to take me to the vet and have me put to sleep. I was quite sure that the rest of my life would be miserable.

I looked at the space on the wall where a childhood picture of Michael with Trumpet the dog should have hung and started to howl again.

When I came to a few hours later, Leonie was sitting by my bed rolling a joint. Since I'd commenced my badger-like existence, she'd visited regularly to check I was alive and not eating cat food. My reading lamp had been switched on and some sort of green gunky stew was steaming frighteningly in a rustic pot on the bedside table. 'Hello,' she said briskly. 'Happy new year!'

I looked at her, then at the stew and closed my eyes again. Why was everyone so intent on keeping me alive?

Hang on. 'Happy new year?' I asked croakily, dragging myself up into a semi-sitting position.

Leonie tapped the joint against her knee and started the next one. 'Yes. I suggest you begin the year by taking a shower, Franny. You're a bit ferret-like now.'

I gazed blankly at her. I was beginning to see the world divided into two groups of people, Those Who'd Had Their Hearts Broken, and Those Who Hadn't. Leonie was definitely of the latter category.

'Didn't your mum call you to wish you happy new year?' she asked, sprinkling green skunk liberally into the Rizla.

I reached over, took the joint she'd just made and lit it, coughing. 'She did, actually,' I replied after a long toke. 'She just said I was going to become a mad old woman who smelt of urine.' After a brief silence, we laughed.

'Excellent.' Leonie was still laughing. 'Oh, God, poor Eve. What a mess. When you're feeling better, Franny, I really think you need to try to sort her out.'

I didn't say anything. Opening the Mum box in my head was beyond my capacity at present. It was just too painful. I'd failed with my own life and the idea of failing her, too, was frankly intolerable.

'She should be here, looking after you,' Leonie

added pointedly. Leonie had kept me in Lucozade and joints for ten days now; a practice she could ill-afford with her job as a charity street mugger. But if it were a choice between Leonie and Mum, there was no contest. I couldn't cope with Mum's gin breath and a lecture on how this break-up was my fault.

Leonie handed me some Lucozade ('No, Fran, you need to *drink* it, please') and reached for my hand. 'You can do this, Franny,' she said kindly. 'You really will get through it, I promise, my love. It's only three months. Ninety days!'

'But – but how do I *know* he'll take me back after three months? Why would he suggest a separation unless the relationship was dead?' I sank back into bed again. 'I just don't understand. I thought he was going to ask me to marry him.'

Leonie squeezed my hand. 'We all did, Franny. Per-haps he just had a freak-out about the commitment. Don't forget, men are complete knobs when it comes to stuff like that.' I tried to stem the flow of tears with my grubby duvet cover and she handed me a tissue. 'But stay strong. Don't contact him for three months and then, hopefully, you guys can start again once he's sorted his head out. OK?'

I cried even harder.

Chapter Six

March 2008

Sent: Mon, 01 March 2008 14:02:56 +0200
From: Slater, Michael [michael.slater@itnnews.com]
To: O'Callaghan, Frances [frances.ocallaghan@itnnews.com]
Subject: CONFIRMED!

Franny! It's all sorted! I'm coming home! I wind up things for ITN over the next two weeks and then I'm back on the 28th! I start at the *Independent* on the 30th. They wanted me sooner but no can do.

Better run. Some wannabe journalist wants to take me out for lunch so he can beg me to help his career. Yawn. Can't wait to see you.

Michael X

'Not sure about that one, Franny,' Dave said doubtfully. He was sprawled across my sofa with Duke Ellington purring innocently on his lap, while Leonie removed the next outfit from its hanger. She glanced over, resplendent in an old vintage tea-dress, fiery red hair cascading down her back, and smiled her agreement, throwing me the next ensemble.

I felt a little snag of jealousy. Leonie would never have to call an emergency Gin Thursday: Outfit Special if *her* lover was returning from Kosovo. She'd just throw together some brilliant concoction (that on me would look like a jumble-sale find) and the lover would fall at her feet in an agony of desire. As much as I loved Leonie, I did rather wish that she wasn't five foot nine, glorious, Highly Sexual and Extremely Cool.

But Michael was coming back for me, not Leonie. I felt a swell of pride and excitement. 'Don't look, Dave,' I shouted, as I hopped into the kitchen to change. I'd done a lot of shouting this evening – mostly at times when talking would have sufficed – but I couldn't help myself. It was only two days until Michael came back to London and I was jangling with nerves, anticipation and high-functioning madness.

'Don't worry about it, Frannyface. We'll find the perfect outfit by the time the night's out!' Leonie called reassuringly.

I peeped round the corner of the kitchen cupboard just in time to see her and Dave exchange despairing glances.

'Stop that!' I shouted, wriggling into a pair of ribbed tights. 'You pair of ballsacks have no idea how hard it is to be in first-time love aged twenty-eight! I need your support, not your condemnation!'

Dave patted Duke Ellington and took a sip from his can of Guinness. 'Right you are, Fran,' he said calmly.

'You sure about being in love?' Leonie asked, as

she rescued her gin from the clothes I was throwing back into the sitting room.

'YES!' I shouted. 'This is my big love story! This is IT! Michael's invaded my *soul*!' I added dramatically.

'Oh, Christ, Franny! Be careful. Just let him invade your lady garden for now and then we'll see about letting him into your soul, OK? You don't actually know him that well yet.'

I ignored her and showed them the next outfit. 'Well? Good? Bad? Fat? Too young? Too . . . ? Arrgh!'

Dave got up. 'Right, Fran, enough. You look great. Take this gin and tonic, sit down and shut up You're being a wee psycho,' he said, pushing me on to the only dining chair that wasn't covered with clothes.

'I completely agree,' Stefania said, arriving through my kitchen door without knocking, as was her custom. 'I found Francees vatching Michael's broadcasts on ze Interweb yesterday,' she added evilly.

Leonie started laughing. 'Oh, Franny,' she said, sitting down next to Dave. 'You're going to have to get this under control. Michael's only a man! He might turn out to be a complete knob!'

Stefania picked up Duke Ellington and left without any further comment.

I felt a bit embarrassed. 'Come on, Leonie, he's moving back to London for me,' I said. 'It's a big deal.'

'I know, I know. I'm just saying be careful. Has he found a job yet?'

'Yes! With the *Independent*! Isn't he clever?'

Dave got up to get some more Guinness out of the fridge. 'He doesn't mind working in print rather than broadcast? That's quite a change.'

I'd been wondering about that myself. What if he came back, realized he didn't like me and then was stuck with a job he didn't want? The idea scared me. A lot. 'He *seems* really pleased about it,' I said carefully. 'And I think I believe him. I mean, he wouldn't do it if he didn't want to, right? He told me he was up for anything as long as he could be with me.'

Leonie shook her head. 'God, you two are going to be disgusting, aren't you? Attached at the mouth.'

I threw a pair of discarded tights at her. 'Stop it. Be happy for me! You haven't been in love before!'

'No, I deal mostly in lust. And I'm very happy about that. *Look* at you! For fuck's sake!'

'Weren't you like this when you met Freya?' I asked Dave.

He thought about it. 'Aye, I was pretty pleased,' he said reflectively. 'But I'm not as insane as you, Fran.'

'Well, I bet *she* was in this state, even if you weren't.'

'I don't think so. She's pretty cool, Freya. Doesn't get worked up that easily.'

I tried not to glower. Of course Freya had been as cool as a bloody cucumber when she met Dave. She was everything I wanted to be but wasn't. Calm. Balanced. Long and wispy and Fairtrade.

Dave opened his can. 'Who's the latest shag?' he asked Leonie.

She grinned in a slightly filthy manner. 'Knut. He's Swedish. He pledged fifty thousand pounds on the street last week.'

I gaped. 'What the hell did you do to him?'

'I just chatted to him, Fran,' she replied fruitily.

I felt a little stab of envy. 'How do I learn to be as sexy as you?' I asked.

She twirled a strand of hair casually between her finger and thumb, evidently pleased. '*Having* sex is a good place to start,' she said. 'How long is it since you got some?'

I thought. 'Um, a while.' I felt a bit shy discussing my sex life in front of Dave but Leonie was having none of it.

'When? Who?'

I felt more embarrassed still and started to blush. 'Er, it was Johnny,' I mumbled.

Leonie was clearly appalled. 'Christ, Fran, he was *ages* ago!'

'I'm not sure I know how to have sex any more,' I said.

Dave put his hands over his ears.

'Would you like some instructions?' Leonie was beaming with excitement.

'Yes,' I said.

'No,' Dave shouted, looking wild and afraid.

Leonie took off her cardigan and leaned in, glowing.

'Oh, Fran, I have long awaited this day.' She pulled a notepad out of her bag. 'I think we should start off by getting you a sex toy.'

'Are you mad?' Dave said. 'She's Fran! You can't leave her in charge of machinery – she'll have his eye out!'

Leonie ignored him and started drawing a diagram of a penis. Dave got up and ran to the toilet.

'Leonie, is there any chance of you writing some sort of manual for me?' I asked, as she sketched in the testicles.

When Dave came back he ordered us to stop. We'd only got as far as 'how to get his pants and socks off simultaneously' and I was by no means done. But before she had a chance to reply, my phone started ringing and I jumped a million miles into the air
Michael?

My heart sank when I saw it was Mum. I looked at the phone for a few seconds with a screwed-up face, then answered it, feeling guilty that I hadn't been to see her for nearly two weeks.

'Mum,' I said, as enthusiastically as I could.

'Good evening, Frances,' she said grandly. She was speaking slowly, which meant she was drunk. 'I take it you're in the pub.'

'No. Just having a couple at home with Leonie and Dave.'

'I see. Well, Fran, watch your drinking, please. I don't want you to end up with a problem.'

The cheek of it! 'Sure thing, Mum. How are you? What's going on?'

'Well, Frances, in your absence, I've been having a rather trying time. The trouble with the gardening staff has continued apace and I'm afraid I had to let them go today.' She paused dramatically, obviously delighted with her role as Lady of the Manor.

'Eh? What do you mean "them"? How many do you have?'

'I *had* four.'

'But, Mum, it's only March . . . I don't understand. Why did you *have* gardeners in at this time of year?' I got up and walked outside to sit on the steps.

'Because, Frances, Cheam in Bloom starts in June and my garden needs to be in absolutely exquisite shape by then. I have held the winner's cup in my front room for the last three years and I simply will *not* tolerate losing it to Laura. I've heard she has had the gardeners in since Christmas in her attempt to punish me.'

'Right. So you sacked your gardeners why?'

When I returned to the sitting room twenty minutes later, trying hard not to give in to the gnawing sadness I felt every time I spoke to Mum, Leonie was on the phone to Knut in my bedroom, emitting filthy shrieks and shouting quite openly about her plans for his knuts. I slumped down next to Dave. He patted my shoulder. 'You're very good, taking care of your mum the way you do,' he said. 'You should be proud of yourself. She can be a right selfish shite at times.'

'Don't, Dave. I know you're on my side but she's not a bad mother. She's just miserable and wrapped up in her own world. Can you imagine being someone's mistress for seventeen years? Knowing he'll never leave his wife? Knowing his wife detests you? I just wish she'd get rid of him.'

'Did she ask you how you're feeling about Michael's return?' he asked tentatively.

'Nope.' I tensed, afraid he'd say something horrid. In spite of everything, I couldn't bear the thought of someone criticizing Mum. But Dave said nothing. He just nodded. 'And how's her drinking?' he asked eventually.

'Out of control,' I said quietly. 'I've said I'll go down there tomorrow to see her. I'm going to try to talk to her about it.'

Dave winced. 'That won't be easy. Give me a bell if you need to, OK? And well done. You're being a really good daughter.'

Leonie exploded from my bedroom with red cheeks and an unsettling dirty look in her eye. 'You'd better not have been having phone sex in there,' I told her.

She smoothed her hair, kissed me and Dave, then picked up her bag. 'People, I have to go.' She giggled. 'There is a lot of rudeness to be had over at Knut's hotel. Apologies.' She hugged me as I let her out. 'Good luck, darling. Stay calm at the airport and try not to be mental, OK?' I watched fondly as she strode off across the yard, saluting Stefania's shed.

Leonie and I had met in hospital shortly after she was born, when her mother had attended a class on how to bathe newborns led by Mum with me as her demonstration model. While the mums chatted afterwards in Kingston General, Leonie and I – me with a sort of wispy black Mohican and Leonie with a squashed little red face – were left in cots next to each other. According to Mum, Leonie had peered very seriously at me for a while, then stuck a tiny fist in my face. I had taken it on the chin.

We had been inseparable from that moment, living less than half a mile apart and going through playgroup, primary and secondary school together. We'd tried, half-heartedly, to stage a temporary separation by applying to different universities but in the end had admitted defeat and gone to Leeds together, where Leonie had set up what was effectively a knocking shop in her flat in Boddington Hall and I did slightly less well on the floor below.

We had emerged as two very different girls. While I became a career fiend, Leonie spent her days on the streets as a charity mugger, barely earning the minimum wage and living in a Stoke Newington bedsit smaller than my sitting room. A never-ending stream of men had flowed easily through her life; even under harsh interrogation I had failed to get her to admit that she wanted a real relationship.

But something was not quite right. The girl I had grown up with used to dream of being a poet with long beads, a twenties haircut and a parrot, not to mention having a husband who was a member of the aristocracy. Her current lifestyle utterly baffled me.

As she disappeared through the tall wooden gates of my yard I resolved to help her find love. Love was good. I knew she'd like it.

Chapter Seven

January 2010

Sent: Thur, 07 Jan 2010 09.08:46 GMT
From: Customer Services [no-reply@orangehelp.com]
To: Frances O'Callaghan [franocal@fmail.com]
Subject: DO NOT REPLY: Missing texts CALL REF
O22965M4

Dear Miss O'Callaghan

Thank you for contacting Orange regarding missing text
messages. I understand that you believe that you have
been unable to receive incoming text messages, specifi-
cally from phone number 07009 704462. As discussed we
have carried out a status check on the connection
between this number and yours and have been unable to
detect any faults. There is no record of this number having
sent you an SMS since 23 December.

Best wishes,
Orange

On day sixteen of my post-dump incarceration, Leonie
told me it was time to go back to work.

'No chance,' I said, appalled. 'Are you mad? Although, while we're on the subject, I've been wondering what you told ITN.' I gnawed listlessly at a horrible polenta cake Stefania had put through my cat flap last night.

Leonie started giggling. 'I told them you had gynaecological issues. It worked a treat.' She added quickly, 'They didn't ask a thing! You could probably take six months off before they dared to probe any further.'

'Well, thanks, Leonie. It's always good to have your colleagues chatting in the staff kitchen about the state of your vagina.'

'That's the spirit, Franny! Knock 'em dead, my girl!'

I glowered at her. She held my gaze. 'Fine, you can have the rest of the week off. But if you don't go in on Monday I'm telling them you have a perfectly healthy minge. Perhaps you could start things off by coming to Gin Thursday tomorrow night? We could do it in a pub near here, maybe.'

A few hours later, my phone rang. I shot out of my coma like a (smelly) firework. *Let it be Michael let it be Michael, oh, PLEASE GOD, YOU TOTAL BAS-TARD, CAN YOU PLEASE DO SOMETHING DECENT AND MAKE THIS BE MICHAEL?*

'Oh, hello Dave,' I said, disappointed, sounding deeply masculine. Sixteen days of joints and mute-ness had left me with a voice like Frank Butcher's.

'Er . . . Fran? Is that you?'

63

'Yup. Sorry about the voice,' I said croakily. 'Just had a joint.'

'Where the fuck are you, you wee skiver? What the fuck's going on?' Dave sounded quite concerned.

I wondered if he'd heard the vagina story. 'Er, I'm just not too well,' I said vaguely. I heard Dave drag at his cigarette.

'Just tell me what the fuck's going on,' he said eventually.

'Michael left me. Well, he asked for a three-month separation but, yeah, essentially he's left me.'

There. The first time I'd said it.

Dave whistled. 'Fuck. Seriously? Oh, Fran, that's terrible. Are you OK? Christ, you poor thing. Is someone looking after you?'

My throat was smarting but I hadn't the energy to cry again. 'Dave, I can't talk about it. I'll come back soon. Goodbye.' I ended the call. Talking to Dave was like talking to Dad – if I started crying I'd never stop. I hugged a sock of Michael's that I'd found under the bed and rolled over on my front, longing for a painless death.

Chapter Eight

March 2008

Sent: Tue, 18 Mar 2008 18:30:28 GMT
From: INTERNAL TAPE LIBRARY [tape.library@itnnews.com]
To: O'Callaghan, Frances [frances.ocallaghan@itnnews.com];
Subject: Change of department

Dear Frances

We notice that you have been performing the below searches on a regular basis:

- **SEARCH TERMS**: ITN REPORTS: Michael Slater + Kosovo
- **SEARCH TERMS** ITN REPORTS: Michael Slater + Mitrovica
- **SEARCH TERMS** ITN REPORTS: Balkans + Michael Slater

According to the internal phone list you currently work on the Entertainment and Culture news desk. Should we change your user profile to Foreign Affairs and increase your access to the Balkans collection?

Please advise us accordingly and state which line

manager we should contact for authorization.

All best,

Steve

TAPE LIBRARY

Sent: Tue, 18 Mar 2008 18:32:47 GMT

From: O'Callaghan; Frances [frances.ocallaghan@itnnews. com]

To: INTERNAL TAPE LIBRARY [tape.library@itnnews.com]

Subject: RE: Change of department

Importance: HIGH

Hi Steve

No need to contact anyone. I won't need to look at the Kosovo archives again. My line manager is very busy so please do NOT contact her about this.

Many thanks!

Fran

Michael came home at the beginning of spring. The day when London emerges from its winter hibernation and everyone capers around excitedly in parks full of daffodils and sunshine.

I was at Gatwick and I was a mess: breathlessly excited, horribly nervous and hoping, *praying*, that this might be it. That the man who was belted up preparing for touchdown would be the man I would spend the next sixty years picking up from airports, missing him, loving him, feeding him and, all things going well, having a fair bit of sex with him. Leonie texted me: You OK? Outfit working out?

NO. Shitting self in a serious way. Hate outfit. In Monsoon buying new one I replied from the changing room.

Five minutes later I was scanning the crowds streaming out of Arrivals in my new rather middle-class ensemble. And then there he was. Tired-looking, taller than I'd remembered and displaying freckles I'd not seen in the cold hard light of February. His hair was shorter and he was wearing a long-sleeved grey T-shirt that gave a definite impression of things I'd not been expecting to see. Biceps. Pectorals. In fact, muscles in general. Jesus Christ, did Michael go to the *gym?* I felt my stomach tighten with fear. Perhaps I should hold off sex for a few weeks while I did some sit-ups and stuff.

Finally he saw me. His face opened into that beautiful lazy smile and I hurled myself across the terminal at him, like a big, mad dog. His arms closed around me and I smelt the clean-laundry scent of his T-shirt and felt him laugh, a deep, rumbly noise that made his chest shake. I was so happy I could have exploded. He pulled me away after a few seconds and kissed me tentatively.

We stood back and gazed at each other. I couldn't really say anything: I was overwhelmed by how beautiful he was and how happy he seemed to see me.

'Franny . . . God, you're lovely. I've dreamed so much about this day.' He ran a finger under the neckline of my top and stared at me shyly. 'You are pleased I came back, aren't you?'

'*What?* Oh, my God, I haven't thought about anything else!' I coloured slightly, realizing that that wasn't particularly smooth.

'No, don't apologize. I needed to hear it. I just had a panic on the plane that I'd been too hasty . . . I like your outfit, by the way. Did you shoplift it?' he asked, with interest.

'Um . . . no. Why?'

'Just that your cardigan is on inside out and the label is still on. We may need to talk about this.'

'Right. I . . . kind of . . . Oh, fuck it. I just had a panic about how I looked so I sort of ran into Monsoon and bought this. And now you probably think I'm the biggest knob in the world,' I added, shamefaced.

Michael laughed and kissed me again. His arms locked round me and he muttered into my hair, 'I think I love you, you batty woman. In fact, I'm sure. I'm so happy I came home.'

Jesus Christ! I had an actual boyfriend! Who loved me before he'd even seen me with my kit off! A boyfriend who would love me and laugh at me and cook manly joints of beef! A further explosion of happiness erupted in my stomach, far greater and more beautiful than anything I'd ever seen in Battersea Park on Fireworks Night.

We snogged all the way to London, so much so

that a large American woman asked us to stop. We went and sat on a luggage rack and continued until the ticket collector threatened to fine us for indecent exposure. 'You've got to be kidding,' I said, laughing. 'We're just kissing!'

He squinted at us for a second. 'So you are, so you are. As you were, kids! I'll tell that lady to put a sock in it. Can't she see you're in love?'

In my excitement, I shoved my hand up the back of Michael's T-shirt and encountered a lower back rug. 'Oh, my GOD! You've got a hairy back!' I giggled, rubbing appreciatively.

'Do you ever think before you speak?' he asked.

'Not so much. But you're not insulted, are you? I LOVE your back rug!'

Michael hugged me harder. 'You're nuts,' he said into my neck. I glowed.

Arriving at Victoria, Michael stood staring at the swarming mass of people on the concourse and looked bewildered. 'Bloody hell ... Did you *have* to live in London? I'd forgotten how ridiculous it is.' He fished a bottle of something disgusting out of his bag. 'I think we should get drunk immediately. Otherwise I'm kidnapping you and taking you back to Kosovo.'

So that was what we did. We each had a hearty swig from the bottle and walked hand in hand into Green Park where the pale sun hung in a hard spring sky.

Bold beams of modest warmth crept through the still-bare lime trees and lovers held hands in striped deckchairs, trying to pretend that it was a summer's day as they shivered in short sleeves.

We drank Michael's horrible liqueur on a bench and exchanged stories of teenage love affairs. When I told him about my doomed liaison with Patrick Moorestead, whom I'd found in the stationery cupboard with his face lost between the tits of our massive-titted DT teacher, Miss Redpath, Michael was convulsed with laughter. 'Oh, God, Fran, you're scarred, aren't you? You're going to be one of those girlfriends who wants a pair of fake breasts for Christmas!'

'Shut up! I was devastated!' I cried. He continued to laugh. 'Shut *up*, Michael!' I shouted, punching him.

'Oh Fran . . . I'm sorry. For what it's worth I'm sure yours are perfect as they are. I look forward to meeting them,' he said, nibbling my ear. 'In fact, I think we should go back to your house at the earliest possible juncture so I can have a chat with them. We have a lot to discuss.'

It was all I could do to prevent myself booking us into the Ritz next door and yelling, 'TAKE ME NOW!' Instead I looked him in the eye and said steadily, 'That's fine. We'll go now. But you should know that I have a third nipple.' I cleared up our mess and smiled to myself while he stood behind me, wondering if I was serious.

On the tube to Camden Michael tried to put the bottle of meths – or whatever it was – back into his bag but I grabbed it, grimly aware that I might be required to take my clothes off soon. 'I've not done with that,' I muttered, in response to his raised eyebrow. 'I'm up for getting trolleyed.'

'Nice.' He chuckled. 'You get better by the minute.'

By the time we got back to my flat, I was rollicking. Michael ran off to the loo and I sat on the floor and talked to Duke Ellington, who was obviously angry at my late return. 'WEEOOOW,' he said crossly. While he ate his Tesco Supreme pouch with great irritation I stroked him carefully and whispered to him about Michael. He ignored me.

'So this is him. The fiend. The tiger.' Michael was standing in the kitchen doorway, so handsome I didn't know where to look. WHY WAS THIS MAN SO INTO ME?

'Yes. Duke Ellington, meet Michael Slater. Michael, meet Duke Ellington.' I tried to grab Duke Ellington's paw to offer to Michael but he withdrew it and waved his tail threateningly.

'Right. Enough,' Michael said, striding across the room and bundling me up off the floor. 'It's my turn now. Duke Ellington has had enough of your time.'

He threw me over his shoulder and marched out of the kitchen amid screams of 'I AM TOO HEAVY FOR YOU TO PICK UP! PUT ME DOWN!'

'A man has needs, Fran,' he replied curtly, throwing me on to my bed and kicking the door shut. I felt a little bit guilty about Duke Ellington but, of course, a woman has needs too.

'Where's the third nipple?' Michael said, pulling off my tights and then my dress without a great deal of regard for the buttons. I was shaking, partly with nerves, partly with the rampant horn.

'Um, not sure,' I muttered, as he took off his T-shirt and started to move a hand along my leg from my knees.

'Is it here?' he whispered, moving down and kissing my thighs softly.

'Nope. Higher,' I said, gasping as he travelled up my legs. 'Here?'

'Nearly . . .'

'Here?'

'Oh, God, yes. Yes. There . . . Oh, God . . . please don't stop . . .'

The next morning I woke up to the sight of Michael's dark grey eyes smiling at me. He was curled up, like a prawn, next to me, his hand playing with my hair and his feet resting on my leg. I decided it was time I started practising a religion.

Chapter Nine

January 2010

I sat on the floor of the wet room while water thundered on to my head, bouncing off my nose and knees. I looked blankly at my feet. The pedicure I'd had, ready for my thirtieth and possible engagement, was still almost completely intact. I'd let slip to the lady who'd done it that I might possibly be proposed to in a few days. 'Oh, love, that's great. Should we book you in for a Brazilian?' she'd said. 'Everyone wants a nice fresh foo-foo for their engagement night!'

I circled my feet with my hands, numb. It felt strange, remembering happiness. The girl giggling about fresh foo-foos felt like another person, a Fran who belonged in a parallel universe, not the Fran I was stuck with now, the Fran who felt crushingly sad and lost. The Fran who spent hours and hours fantasizing about what she would say if Michael called her and begged her to reconsider, then dissolved into tears when she remembered that contact was out of the question. The Fran who felt so empty she had no idea how to get out of bed and start the day.

What had Michael been doing while I was having my birthday pedicure and talking foo-foos? Was he out buying a ring or was he planning his dumping speech? Was he thinking about how happy we were together or how much he wanted to get rid of me?

I heard an angry miaow and reached above me to turn the shower off. If Duke Ellington hadn't been so consistent with his meal demands I probably wouldn't have got out of bed at all. In spite of all the food Stefania was leaving through the cat flap, I was still barely able to eat. He yowled again. 'All RIGHT! I'm coming, dammit.'

Unconvinced, he miaowed once more, this time with renewed force.

'Oh, my God! Shut *up*, Duke Ellington? Can't you see I'm dealing with a broken heart here?'

He responded with the feline equivalent of a bellow. My broken heart was clearly a matter of supreme unimportance to him.

I dragged myself up and into a cold towel.

Chapter Ten

April 2008

The first drop of rain splashed heavily on Michael's nose as he got started on his second pint of Kronenberg. 'Bollocks. Let's go back inside.'

'But we can't! Gin Thursday has moved outside for the spring!'

Leonie nodded in agreement. 'She's right, Michael, we're going to have to brave it. And Stefania's coming tonight – she's a stickler for the rules.'

Stefania only came to Gin Thursdays about once a month, but this was a gala celebration: it was Gin Thursday Welcomes Michael Slater. Even Mum had threatened to turn up after her busy day at Harvey Nichols and the Royal Opera House. (Guiltily, I hoped she wouldn't come. Her response when I'd first told her about Michael had not been 'Oh, how exciting!' or 'He sounds wonderful!' but 'Does he have clean ears, Frances?' In Mum's world, anyone who didn't scrub the inside of their ears with disinfectant and a pressure hose on a daily basis was probably a drug addict.)

Dave was bringing Freya. While I didn't necessarily

want to be confronted with her unnervingly serene beauty, I was desperate for Michael to see me as someone who had a large, colourful group of friends. The kind of friends who enjoyed challenging debates about social anthropology and threw organic dinner parties. I didn't want him to know that Gin Thursday was really only about Dave and me getting drunk in a corner while Leonie got off with whoever was handy.

Michael had invited his super-brainy friend Alex with whom he'd studied at Oxford ('He'll probably try to make you feel like you're really thick,' he'd warned me reassuringly), while his sister Jenny and her husband Dmitri were scheduled to make an appearance too. All in all, there were going to be a lot of brainy people around. (I had bought a Bohemian scarf for the occasion and was primed with as many pub quiz facts as I could remember.)

So far, so good. Leonie and Michael had been laughing in an easy, non-sexual way when I'd arrived late after a bit of a work emergency. He glanced up as I sprinted in and there it was: the smile that was just for me. The smile that made me want to swing from the trees screeching and thumping my chest.

'So sorry to be late,' I said as I kissed him. I felt so proud! This was my actual boyfriend! Who ran me a bath every morning, who cooked complicated meals and who slept like a curled-up prawn!

'No worries. Leonie was telling me about Knut.

Apparently he only likes back-door sex,' Michael reported, with one eyebrow slightly raised.

Leonie nodded sadly. 'It's chronic, Fran. My arse is beginning to suffer. What should I do?'

I burst out laughing. 'Wow. I'm sorry, do you two already know each other?'

Leonie batted me off. 'Fran, if Michael's living with you he might as well know the truth about me. I'd hate him to have a nasty shock later on.'

I blanched. Michael had been staying with me since he'd come back to London but nothing had been said yet about him moving in. Naturally, I wanted him to stay for ever: I wanted us to have a checked tablecloth and pots of lavender and the same bath towels, but I hadn't dared bring it up in case he got frightened and went off to rent a black 'n' chrome bachelor pad in London Bridge.

Somehow sensing my panic, he put his arm round me and whispered, 'If you've got room for a lodger I'd love to stay,' into my hair.

Man. My life was perfect.

At that moment Dave and Freya arrived, Dave marching up to Michael with one of his paws out-stretched and a roll-up hanging out of his mouth. 'All right, fella?' he said, in an unusually masculine manner.

Michael stood up and grasped his hand. 'Dave. Hi, mate. Drink?' Off they went, chatting gruffly about Derby's relegation.

I looked at Freya. 'Why are men so weird? What's with this mate and fella and football?'

She smiled politely.

Leonie rolled her eyes. 'It's to do with erections and testosterone. But anyway, hi, Freya!' she said brightly.

Leonie, I knew, felt as awkward around Freya as I did. Freya smiled calmly and offered Leonie a smooth peachy cheek, then did the same to me.

'Mmm, you smell nice!' I told her. 'I have a bubble bath that smells just like your perfume!'

'I'll take that as a compliment,' she said levelly.

Dammit. 'Yes! Deffo! It was a very expensive bubble bath . . .'

Freya merely smiled. 'I'll go and help David with the drinks,' she murmured, 'and meet Michael. I've heard quite a lot about him.' And with that she slid off elegantly, all healthy freckles and paraben-free shampoo.

Leonie and I watched her in silence. After a few seconds, Leonie turned back to me and we sat down. 'Feel like a buffoon?'

'Yep. Always.' I smiled.

'Anyway, Michael! I like what I see, Fran. Do you think he's right for you?'

I was a little taken aback. 'Does that mean you think he's not?'

'Don't be a dick. How would I know? I'm asking *you*.'

'Sorry. I'm just paranoid. Well, yes, I do think he's right for me. And the amazing thing is, Leonie, that I think I'm right for him. I just can't believe it – he wants to see me all the time! It's a frigging miracle!'

Leonie smiled indulgently. 'Well, I thought as much. You've missed two Gin Thursdays in a row and I've hardly heard from you.'

'I know. I'm sorry. It's just so new and exciting, and I . . . I just love him, Leonie. It's hopeless. I'm like this great moronic smile on legs. Hugh thinks I'm on magic mushrooms . . .' I trailed off, blushing.

Leonie got up from the other side of the table and came round to hug me. 'I bloody love you, Franny. I'm so happy for you! Of course you're allowed to miss Gin Thursday – he's only just got here.'

'I love you too,' I said fiercely, into her fur coat. It smelt of Chanel No. 19 and digestive biscuits. We picked up the glasses and moved Gin Thursday back inside the pub until further notice.

Two hours later, Dave and I were arm-wrestling for the last crisp in the packet while Leonie whupped Michael's arse on the fruit machine. Stefania was on her fifth tomato juice, talking animatedly to Freya, Michael's sister Jenny and his friend Alex. Jenny's husband Dmitri was outside yelling into his Black-Berry, as he had been doing most of the night.

Stefania was on excellent form. Since arriving she had called the barman an 'ignorant rectum', she had forced Alex to spend a week being vegan, and she had told Michael that even though I'd moved into my flat three years ago I still hadn't remembered to buy a washing line so I hung my knickers from the tree in our yard every summer. 'She's amazing,' Jenny breathed as Stefania barked at Alex about the mortal dangers of meat. I liked Jenny already. She was so easy and straightforward and, better still, she looked just like Michael in a girly sort of way. She was six months pregnant and radiated happiness. I imagined us meeting for lunch once we were sisters-in-law: she'd tell me how ugly and stupid Michael's previous girlfriends had been and how I was the best thing that had ever happened to him.

I was less sure about Alex. He was of the fashionable Oxbridge brigade, the type who lived in large flats in East London decorated with dark mahogany furniture and portraits of Victorian industrialists. He had a sharp, pointy head and a rather unsettling way of looking at you for a few seconds before answering your question. Worse still, it turned out that he also worked for ITN. Only he worked in the Special Building for Clever People in Millbank and he had my dream job: politics producer. It was exactly as Michael had warned me: I felt extremely stupid in his vicinity.

Much to my amusement, Alex seemed to be rather smitten with Leonie who, perhaps sensing my discomfort around him, was ignoring him. ('Michael's friend is a bit of a cockhead,' she'd muttered when we'd been at the bar earlier. 'He quoted T. S. Eliot at me just now and told me he only smoked cigars.')

Dave smashed my forearm down on the table, laughing at my furious face. 'Fine, have the bloody crisp, you monstrous human being,' I said darkly, watching Leonie and Michael out of the corner of my eye. I'd never seen Leonie not flirt with a man before and felt weak with relief at the complete lack of chemistry between them.

'Do you not trust them?' said Dave, catching my eye.

'Sorry?'

'C'mon, Fran, I can see what you're thinking. Do you not trust them?' he repeated.

'No, I do, I just . . . Well, you know how men go mad for Leonie. You can't blame me for being a bit scared. Doesn't Freya ever get suspicious about you and her?'

Dave laughed briefly. 'Nope. I can honestly say Leonie doesn't trouble her at all.'

That was what I wanted. A relationship free of fear, just like Dave and Freya's. I looked at Michael and Leonie again and started to grin, knowing deep down that that was exactly what I had. Michael had wanted to be with me all the time: in the two and a half weeks since he'd returned he had put me before his friends, his family and even his new colleagues. I felt like a princess for the first time in my life. *No fear!*

But Fear gave me a little kick in the gonads when, a

few seconds later, a perfectly manicured hand was placed limply over mine and I heard Mum's voice say, 'Good evening, Frances,' with suspicious precision. Precision in Mum's voice normally meant she was drunk.

I looked up: she was drunk. Even though her hands were reasonably still her eyes betrayed her: they had the bleary film I'd come to recognise as trouble at an early age. She was wearing one of her power suits in starchy peach and was shrouded in some sort of gigantic fur coat that made Leonie's vintage number look like a dirty old stoat. Harrods and Harvey Nicks bags hung from her arms and her hair was a rock-hard halo of Thatcheresque perfection. My heart sank. 'Hello, Mum!' I said brightly, as Dave got up to take her coat.

A loud cackle came to us from the fruit machine. Leonie yelled 'Take that, you fucker!' and Michael groaned loudly.

Mum stiffened. 'Leonie's language really is disgusting,' she said, with a shudder. Her eyes narrowed as Michael shook hands with Leonie to end the game. 'Is that Michael? Why is he not here with you?'

Dave went to get Mum a drink. 'Mrs O'Callaghan!' Michael arrived at the table, looking so incredibly handsome and lovely and eager that I nearly wept. I had the most perfect boyfriend in the world.

Even Mum, after God knew how many glasses of champagne at the opera, couldn't fail to be impressed. 'Well, now. You must be Michael. Fran has spoken about little else,' she said grandly, offering him her hand as if she were Queen Victoria.

'Mum . . .' I said, my cheeks staining red.

'Shush, Frances,' she said. 'You have every right to be proud of this young man. I hear you're a political journalist,' she said to Michael, with a beady stare.

'Yes. I'm still finding my feet at the *Independent* but it's mostly what I'm used to – hanging round Westminster badgering politicians, same old same old,' he said easily, as if he was working in a launderette. I swelled with pride.

'Well, I have to say I'm a bit disappointed not to have seen your name in the paper since you started,' she said, a little sniffily.

Mum disapproved of any paper other than the *Telegraph*; I was touched that she'd been buying the *Independent*. Although she was probably doing so to show off about Michael to her neighbours.

Michael smiled. 'A lot of what I do is editing other people's work so my name often doesn't make it into the finished article.'

'And you *never* get to see what I'm up to,' I said loudly, in Michael's defence. 'I'm a total gofer by comparison!'

Michael and Alex laughed – Alex perhaps a touch too much – but Dave interrupted: 'Not true, Fran. And I've heard a little rumour that your job description's about to change anyway.'

I swung towards him, surprised. 'How?'

Dave grinned. 'I shouldn't tell you,' he said.

'But you will,' Leonie commanded.

Dave batted her away. 'Well. Hugh pulled me in earlier, wanting to know what I thought of your performance in Kosovo. And I told him you'd been a fucking legend, Fran, and how much you'd impressed me.'

I felt my face flush with gratitude and pride. Freya smiled prettily, watching me with interest. 'And he said – if it doesn't work out you can't hold me responsible – that he was going to make you a proper specialist producer for ents and culture. Frances O'Callaghan, specialist producer!'

I stared at him open-mouthed. I tried to talk but nothing came out. And then, eventually: 'OH, JESUS! SHITTING BOLLOCKING – OH, MY GOD!' I launched myself at him and sent the remainder of his pint flying. 'Thank you thank you thank you,' I cried, into his sideburn.

Dave pushed me away. 'Oi, off. And go and buy me another drink, you mad beast.' He looked delighted. Dave was so kind; Freya was a lucky woman.

As she glided calmly to the toilet I saw her smirk. It was almost imperceptible but I knew it was there. Disgust at me and my swearing and my poxy little career. *Well, sod her*, I thought, smarting. And Alex, who had watched with a raised eyebrow. They could be as superior and grown-up as they wanted. I had Michael Slater and a very exciting promotion.

'This calls for champagne,' Mum said loudly. She looked pointedly at Michael, a section of hairsprayed quiff falling into her eye. I felt simultaneously embarrassed and appalled. Mum was not this person.

Michael sprang up. 'Quite right, Mrs O'Callaghan,' he said brightly. 'You've got a very special daughter!' Everyone, except Alex, smiled. 'Don't worry about him,' Michael said, when I joined him at the bar. 'He can be a right wanker. Ignore!'

I felt safe and warm and loved. 'OK,' I said, beaming up at him.

Another hour later, Mum was absolutely steaming and I was in hell. I sat rigidly next to Michael with a sickening tension headache pounding at my temples. Mum had already told Michael about my 'shabby' father leaving her when I was thirteen and was now slurring on about the affair she'd been having ever since, with all of its attendant petty dramas. Leonie and Dave had seen this often enough, but for this to be Michael's introduction to my family was crucifyingly awful.

'His wife, Laura, is one of the most poisonous women you could ever hope to meet,' she whispered conspiratorially. 'And the way she keeps their house is disgusting. I've only been there once but I saw all I needed to see. There was a *multipack of crisps* in their downstairs cloakroom,' she told him, with a shudder.

Michael's lips twitched as he shook his head politely. 'Disgusting,' he said, with just the right level of affected horror. I squeezed his hand under the table.

'It's time to get you into a taxi, Mum,' I said eventually. Seeing her like this was too sad. I wanted to enjoy the last hour of Gin Thursday with Michael's and my friends, who were giggling about something at the other end of the table – probably Knut's fixation with anal sex. Stefania had finally given in and had a glass of wine. Now she was red-cheeked and shrieking with laughter at whatever Leonie was saying. She was really quite pretty, I thought, as she fell sideways on to Dave mid-laughter. On the rare occasions that Stefania actually drank, she always flirted with Dave. Freya looked on calmly; she had seen it all before. Alex was staring at Leonie with guarded eyes but she was ignoring him. Jenny and Dmitri had gone home.

Mum stood up, then sat down again. 'Dear me, Fran,' she said, 'that wine hasn't done me any good at all. And, you saw me, I only had two glasses.' As Michael got up to fetch her coat her eyes beseeched me not to take her to task on the bottle of champagne she'd probably downed at the opera. Or the gin and tonics she'd probably had at Harvey Nicks. Guilt and shame hovered wetly in her eyes.

''Bye, Eve,' Leonie said, coming over to kiss Mum's cheek.

'Ah, Leonie, goodbye,' Mum said, trying to sound grand again. 'You've heard about Fran's promotion?'

'Yep. She was always destined for big things,' she said enthusiastically.

'So, too, were you, dear,' Mum said shrewishly to her. I froze.

Leonie's eyes stopped smiling but her mouth stayed fixed. 'Fran's flying the flag for both of us,' she said carefully. She went to sit down with Stefania and downed the rest of her gin.

'I'll get in the cab with you to Victoria, OK, Mum?' I said, unable to abandon her. Michael looked sharply at me. *Sorry*, I mouthed at him, shrugging. He shook his head briefly to reassure me that it didn't matter and kissed me quickly as I walked past, Mum swaying on the end of my arm. ''Bye, guys,' I muttered, as we teetered away.

Dave sat back. 'Take care, Fran,' he said. He didn't look impressed. I ignored him. My *boyfriend* got it, even if Dave didn't.

Stefania looked away: she had always disapproved of Mum's drinking.

As soon as I'd put Mum on a train to Cheam, I sat on a bench in a deserted Victoria station and stared at the picture of Mum and Dad I kept in my wallet. They were sitting on a beach in Devon, Mum with long hair, a hippie headband and poncho, Dad with a mop-head haircut and tight swimming trunks. They were hugging each other and Mum was doing some sort of ballet thing with her left leg. Both of them had beautiful grins stretched across their faces. I was in the background, chubby and determined with a mound of patted-down sand in front of me and a cloth hat on my head.

I still had no idea how or why it had started. Mum and Dad were in love, they had a child upon whom they doted and 'enough money to afford a cleaner once a week', as Mum used to say to her own mother on the phone. Mum always seemed so happy – I remember her singing softly in the kitchen and sweeping me up into her skirt, hugging and tickling me until I begged for mercy. Yes, there had always been bottles of wine at dinner but none of the hidden whisky bottles and the Drink Voice that I'd come to dread by the time I was a teenager.

'This illness affects everyone. It doesn't care how much money they earn,' said the man at AA, whom I'd phoned for advice when I was twenty-five. 'Get her to come and say hi. You can come with her, if you want,' he added, when I found myself too choked to respond.

Three years on, I was still no closer to getting her anywhere near an AA meeting. The first time I'd brought it up she'd laughed in my face, the second she'd burst into tears and told me that she was shocked and appalled by my disloyalty, and the third she had thrown me out of her house ten minutes after the last train back to London had left. After that I'd stopped trying. She simply wouldn't have it. I knew further intervention was needed – but what sort?

'She'll get here when she's ready,' the AA man had

said, when I called again two years later. 'Not before. Just make sure she knows we're here.'

I put the picture back in my bag, watched a lone tramp combing a platform dustbin and fought the tears that were gathering in my eyes.

After several years of scraping Mum off the floor and being shouted at and generally abused, Dad had run off with Gloria, the once-a-week cleaner of whom Mum had been so proud. They lived on the Costa del Sol now and he had turned into a rotund but very jovial man with leathery brown skin and a string of upper-crust fry-up cafés in the wealthier resorts. Leonie and I periodically went out to stay with him, and before he had even greeted me, he'd always ask if Mum was still drinking. His disappointment when I nodded was evident.

In the meantime, Mum had begun her affair and in the process had become a person I barely recognized. It was only when she passed out in bed and I came in to check that she was still breathing that she was the mum of my childhood. Wavy-haired, pretty, vulnerable. Watching her sleep, I'd entertain lonely fantasies of torching her power-suit collection and carrying her off to some remote hippie commune where she could overcome her drinking and become Mum again. I wanted her back.

Michael was asleep when I got in, warm and prawn-like in a corner of my bed. I crept in as quietly as I could but he rolled straight over and hugged me, nuzzling the back of my neck. 'Don't worry,' he said sleepily.

I squeezed his hand gratefully. 'Thanks.'

'Does she do that a lot?'

'Yes. Sorry. I need to sort her out.' I closed my eyes. 'Michael?'

'Mmm?'

'I was wondering why your name isn't in the paper too. Does that mean you're, like, the political editor or something?'

'No. Actually . . .' He paused and I turned over to face him. The shadows falling lengthwise across his face made him seem suddenly sad. 'To be honest, I'm a bit gutted. I've not been allowed to write anything yet. I just said that about editing because I didn't want your mum to be disappointed. But it's early days. I can't expect to take over during my first month.'

'No. Well, I think you're the cleverest man on earth.'

He pulled me closer. 'Do you really?'

'Yes. In the universe.'

He kissed me. 'Thank you. That's good to know.' He closed his eyes, smiling.

'Michael.'

'Mmm.'

'I'm a specialist producer! Howzaboutit, eh? High five!'

He raised a hand, smiling sleepily.

'Alex looked a bit scornful,' I said, after a careful pause.

'Not surprising. He's a snob, Fran, he doesn't approve of ents and culture.'

'But that's ridiculous! I've just spent the last week at the British Museum – it's not like I'm working on *Heat*! For fuck's sake, I'm a specialist producer aged twenty-eight. He knows what that means! I can crack politics another time.'

'He has no idea what you do. Just thinks it's a soft option. You're a princess, he's a prick. No contest.'

I smiled myself to sleep.

Chapter Eleven

January 2010

Thursday night came, and Gin Thursday relocated itself to my local, but I didn't go. And when I heard their voices outside and, later, heard them knocking at my door, I didn't answer. Dave had been texting, Leonie had been calling and Stefania had been shouting through my cat flap but I couldn't face human company. I just didn't see the point in socializing: I wanted to die quietly in my bed and have a moving obituary in the *Observer* stating that I had died of natural causes, leaving an evil homeless cat. Hopefully Leonie would give them a picture of me when I was sixteen and a size eight.

The knocking continued. 'Fran, let us know you're OK or we're kicking the door down,' Dave shouted.

Duke Ellington stared at the window with an expression of such black fury that I couldn't help smiling.

Then I heard a very loud noise and realized my friends were breaking into my flat.

Once they'd confiscated my phone and stared, shouted and laughed at me, they settled down to tell me about this 'amazing' plan they'd drawn up. The plan that would allegedly prevent me dying of malnutrition in my bed and maybe even help me get Michael back after our three months apart.

Leonie cleared her throat. 'It's . . . er . . . it's called the Eight Date Deal.'

I sniffed. 'The what?'

'The Eight Date Deal. It's simple, Fran, you go on eight dates with eight different men before you meet up with Michael in ninety days' time. You'll see what else is out there and then, *only then*, can you think about getting back together with him.' I raised an eyebrow. 'And we've just taken his number out of your phone to be on the safe side,' she added.

I gazed at them with complete incomprehension. They gazed back at me. 'I can email him. You can't stop me doing that.'

Stefania butted in. 'STOP being stupid,' she barked. 'Do you vant to get better?'

'Yes.'

'Zen you need to go and meet ozzer men. As soon as possible.' She came over to my bed and pulled my sheet to dislodge me.

'No, Stefania. I'm staying here.'

Dave snorted.

'You are filthy animal,' she replied, shooting a warning glance at Dave. 'It is time you vere alive again. Come now. Up.'

'No.'

'DRAT, Fran, do you vant Michael back?'

'Yes.'

'Zen you get out of ze bed and start ze dating. NOW.'

'Stefania,' I asked, incredulous, 'are you on drugs? You expect me to start dating *now?* When I'm in the middle of the worst heartbreak of my life and I can barely even eat?'

She looked a bit uncomfortable. 'Frances. Ve have done many things for you for nearly three weeks. Many things. Ve are asking one thing of you in return. Please vill you do it for us. It is all ve ask. Please.'

I glanced at Leonie, waiting for her to get Stefania off my back. But she was smiling and nodding.

Dave? Oh, my God, even Dave was grinning. 'It's a good plan, Fran. You need to meet some other men. Get your mind off Michael. Pay these girls back for looking after you.'

My eyes fell on the packet of weed that Leonie had brought round yesterday and I knew I couldn't say no. These people had gone out of their way for me. They had even kicked my door down. I had no option but to nod numbly.

Chapter Twelve

The day after my friends had set me their stupid task, I decided to disobey them and email Michael. Enough was enough. I *had* to know.

'Thought you'd been clever, confiscating my phone,' I muttered, as I fired up my laptop. Cretins! Emailing was just as good. In fact, emailing was better. Why hadn't I thought of it before? An email was a blank canvas, an unlimited space in which I could lay out my plans for being a model girlfriend when Michael took me back!

My heart pounded as I scanned the 168 messages in my inbox. 'Dear Friend, Your Penis is definitely too small,' I read. Then: 'Colonic irrigation for only £19.99!' and 'Don't let incontinence spoil your fun.' A lot of gynaecology and bum stuff; less on the Michael front.

And then, among the penis extensions, I found a name that made my heart leap: Jenny Slater. My stomach turned itself inside out.

Dearest Fran,

I don't know what to say. I'm so very sorry to hear about you and Michael – I just can't believe it. We are all devastated. I have absolutely no idea what went wrong but I really hope that you two manage to work it out after this trial separation. If it helps at all, he is in pieces. I just hope to God he sorts himself out over the next three months because you two were made for each other.

If you want to meet up for a cup of tea and a hug, I'm totally here for you. I'm huge at the moment but still mobile!

Lots of love and big hugs
Jen XXXXX

Jenny. So perfect, so lovely, so . . . so *mini*. I'd always felt like a big fat hairy gorilla next to her. But she'd become a good friend over the last two years. She must be due any day now; the no-doubt-perfect second baby she had made with her perfect husband Dmitri. I read the email again and again, as if it were from Michael himself, hoping desperately that him being 'in pieces' meant that he'd changed his mind already.

I wondered if my friends would allow me to see her.

Fat chance! Well, bugger them. I wanted to see Jenny more than anything else in the world. Through her I could get close to Michael. It was a simple equation.

Guiltily, I picked up my phone.

'Fran! I'm so pleased to hear from you!' she cried, in her safe, kind, comfortable little voice. I wanted to be her. (Actually, thinking about it, I wanted to be anyone other than me. Even Peter Stringfellow's girl-friend.)

We arranged to meet for lunch on the South Bank at two o'clock.

Getting ready, I jangled with nerves, the Michael-shaped hole in my chest suddenly replaced by pumping adrenalin. This was much better than emailing Michael! The allure of an hour with Jenny and the information she could give me about her brother was overwhelm-ing. *I'm the crack whore, she's the crack*, I thought, as I stabbed myself in the eye with my mascara wand.

Jenny, waiting for me on a sofa in the BFI restaurant, looked nothing like a lump of crack. Her clean, mousy hair was clipped to one side and her face was glowing, even though she was wearing only a dab of lip gloss. She wore a beautiful grey silk maternity dress that covered her well-proportioned bump very stylishly, with a grey cashmere cardigan over the top that must have cost the sum total of everything in my wardrobe. There wasn't so much as a centimetre of fat on her.

I wondered briefly how I'd be in pregnancy – vomit-ing, bulky, pallid – then cut myself short, remembering that pregnancy was not likely any time soon. 'Wow, Jenny, you look lovely!' I said, hugging her awkwardly. 'Where's that dress from?'

'Dean LaRonda, actually. I've been so lucky, Dmitri's great friends with their PR who's given me all sorts from their new maternity collection. Lots of nice soft cardigans and stuff, just the sort of thing you want when you're pregnant!' she said happily. It was impossible to hate her.

Jenny and Michael really were so similar, I thought, as I sat down opposite her.

Michael.

'How is he?' I blurted out, unable to bear it any longer. She looked at me with such sadness and kindness that the familiar stinging in my eyes started before I had time to leg it. Warm, salty tears fell out of my eyes as I said, 'Oh, sorry, it's fine, just, you know . . .' She let me cry it out, ordering a tonic water plus a large glass of red for me. As my sobs subsided into snuffling piglet sounds, she rubbed her tummy, wincing slightly. It couldn't be comfortable hauling yourself across London when you were that pregnant.

'Franny, my brother is an idiot. I know he'll come round. If he had an actual reason for it then that'd be different but he's not talking to anyone. I think we should just assume that he's gone mad,' she added firmly. I gulped, trying desperately to control myself. 'It's just that, I just really . . . I miss him so much and I don't understand what I did but it must be my fault and I feel so wretched and miserable and I . . . ugh . . .' I sobbed.

'I know,' she said, rubbing her tummy and shifting in her seat.

' . . . and I can't imagine ever not loving him and not caring about how he is and what he's doing and . . .'

'Fran . . .'

'. . . and I don't understand why he hasn't contacted me. I mean, I know that's what we agreed but doesn't he *care*?'

'Of course he does. In fact, I wasn't going to tell you this, but . . . Oh, shit, Fran . . .'

' . . . and worst of all, worst of all, is imagining what will happen if the three months comes to an end and he decides he doesn't want me back,' I wailed dramatically. Then I looked up at her. 'Hang on, *what* weren't you going to tell me?'

But Jenny was clutching her stomach, the other arm braced against the side of the sofa. 'Fran, I need to go to hospital,' she said quietly. 'I just had a mini contraction. They're expecting complications and they told me to go in as soon as this happened. Can you take me to the Portland? Do you mind?' So polite, Jenny, even with a baby in her birth canal.

With the help of a terrified waiter, I helped her downstairs to the road where we hailed a taxi. 'The Portland,' I said, 'as fast as possible.' I felt like a bad extra in a bad film.

Just as we pulled away, Jenny grabbed my arm and literally roared into my ear, 'FUUUUCK!' Then 'CUUUUUUUNT!'

I tried not to laugh. This was most unlike her.

The roar subsided and she panted in my ear, 'Oh, my God, that was another.'

I stopped feeling amused and started feeling

panicked. 'Don't worry, Jenny,' I said unconvincingly. 'Contractions start hours before the baby's born, don't they?'

Jenny's eyes were shut and she muttered, 'I think it may happen quickly, Fran. It didn't take long with Molly so they told me to come as soon as . . . CUU-UUUUUNT!' She slammed her back against the seat, face contorted with agony.

In the rear-view mirror, the driver's eyes were filled with pure fear. 'St Thomas', I said to him. 'It's three minutes away and you don't have time to crawl across town.' She began to protest. 'I'm not a midwife, Jenny, and I'm not delivering this baby. Come on, now, try to keep calm.' I squeaked as she pulled a clump of my hair out and screamed again. This was awful! What on earth had happened to nice calm labours in birthing pools where women sang songs and did yoga and arts and crafts between contractions?

The driver floored it.

As I watched Jenny being wheeled out of sight, taking her information about Michael with her, I cursed myself for feeling so angry. *What the hell was she about to tell me?* I swayed grottily in the corridor outside, still rough as arse from two and a half weeks of being stoned.

Jenny had given me her mobile and asked me to call Dmitri. I did so; he said he'd be there within half an hour. And then, as I went to hand her phone back to a nurse, I paused. *No. Don't do it.*

Calmly, quietly, as if it were perfectly normal to stalk your ex using his sister's phone, I breezed into her inbox. The first message was from Dmitri; the second from me; the third was from Michael. My finger hovered over the 'read' button. Over the years I'd bollocked endless girlfriends for hijacking their boyfriends' phones but now, standing by the lifts on the sixth floor at St Thomas', I got it. Nothing would stop me reading whatever it was he had to say, however much it was going to hurt me. I was, after all, the crack whore now.

Feeling blood pumping loudly up round my ears I pressed 'read': Am with Nellie. We've got some lovely new jumpers for you. Hope you're OK. Speak later X

I sank slowly on to a bench and watched a woman being wheeled past by a porter. Outside, it had begun to rain. I stood up and walked over to the window. The London Eye cruised slowly around, unhurried, unbothered by the weather, uninterested in what was happening to me.

Michael's name was still highlighted on Jenny's phone. 'Call?' asked a prompt at the bottom of the screen. I shrugged. Why the hell not? Things couldn't get any worse.

He answered almost straight away. 'Jenben! I thought you were in labour already! Look, I'm going to walk Nellie home and then come straight over . . . How's it going? . . . Jen . . . ? Jenny? Hello . . . ?'

*

Gulls wheeled overhead as I walked along the Thames Path, past the bookstalls under Waterloo Bridge where tourists sheltered from the rain and talked brightly over takeaway coffee. Rain had streamed down my face and neck and was now inside my clothes; small sharp darts of cold on my back and chest that stung my skin. I was freezing and my teeth were chattering but I couldn't stop walking, on past the Oxo tower and then the Globe theatre, where a smiling Korean couple asked me to take their picture.

Nellie. Nellie. Nellie. The rain got harder, hammering directly into my face. The Thames was brown and uncharacteristically angry; it looked swollen and deadly as it flowed fast and silent under London Bridge. Where the hell do suicidal people get the courage to chuck themselves into that? I wondered. (And why aren't I one of them?)

Who in the name of God was Nellie? Had Michael left me for another woman? Was this separation a sabbatical so he could go and knob someone else before popping the question? Or, worse still, had he just left me for her and wimped out of telling me? Surely there was no way. We had lived together; he'd always told me where he was going. I'd have *known* if there was someone else on the scene. It was just impossible.

No, it isn't, said a voice inside me. *It happens all the time.*

FUCK OFF, I yelled in my mind, but the internal

voice was insidiously soft and cruel as I pushed the wet slicks of my hair off my face and walked up the ramp to London Bridge station. The possibility of feeling even more rejected and unlovable than I already did was making me feel dizzy.

A few minutes later I was on the Northern Line, imagining a smiling stranger sitting in the waiting room at St Thomas', her small gloved hand in Michael's.

Chapter Thirteen

'Who in the hellfire is called Nellie anyway? This name is for an elephant, no? Not a girl. No mozzer has called her daughter Nellie since 1900, Francees. She will be nasty like a badger's bottom. And nothing you are telling me suggests that Michael is banging viz her.'

Silence. I sat in bed staring at Stefania, who had taken it upon herself to storm into my house again, although this time she'd decided against kicking my door down. Her wild hair was piled on top of her head and her tiny boyish figure perfectly enclosed in an eye-watering leather miniskirt and Take That T-shirt combination. It was Saturday and I had been in bed since I'd got in from the hospital yesterday, back in my tracksuit and working towards becoming human compost. I was drinking brandy and had been imagining Mario Testino taking big, bleak photos of me alone in my bed.

Stefania started opening windows. 'Right, Francees. You have two options. You ask Jenny who zis Nellie elephant is, or you forget about it. Zose are ze only two options, you understand, yes? You do not have ze facts so you cannot sit here in a goulash.'

I sniggered and had another nip of brandy. 'Stew?'

'Whatever ze dish,' Stefania snapped, 'you cannot do zat to yourself. Or to me,' she added, as she got up and started to clean out Duke Ellington's bowl, which had become a little crusty of late. 'And stop drinking zat disgusting spirit,' she added. 'Do you vant to turn into a steenking drunk?' *Like your mother* hung in the air.

Duke Ellington shot through the door at high speed and galloped over to Stefania as if she was the last human being left on earth after the apocalypse. He could spot a reliable feeder a mile off, Duke Ellington.

She turned back to me. 'Which are you going to take then, Fran? Option one or two?' She gave Duke Ellington a late breakfast and he wove round her legs, purring, pretending to be a normal, well-mannered cat. The little scrote.

'I've decided to take option three,' I said. 'I'm going to stalk her.' I opened up my laptop and logged on to Facebook, taking a little tot of brandy as I did so. It was beginning to do the trick.

'You vill *not*,' Stefania barked. 'Are you out of your mind? Option sree vill lead to earthquake and disaster, Francees.' She removed the brandy from my bedside table but failed to grab my glass in time.

'Stop it, Stefania,' I said irritably.

I began scouring Michael's list of friends. There were far too many girls, all posh and sexy and clever. 'Bunch of hoes,' I said, under my breath.

I continued scrolling down, knowing there definitely

hadn't been a Nellie among his friends a few weeks ago. But there was a Nellie now. Oh, fuck. There she was. Nellie Daniels. Long, shiny brown hair, a black dress and a glass of champagne, laughing at something off camera. A man's arm lay on her shoulders. Michael's? I felt sick. 'Shit. SHIT. Stefania, I've found her already. She's a friend of his on Facebook!'

Stefania strode over. 'Step away from zis computer,' she yelled, grabbing it from me. 'You're being a foolish penis. She could be anyone! Being friends on myface does not mean that he has seen her naked. You are jumping into conclusions!' She marched off with my laptop and put it into the oven, for no discernible reason.

I stormed off to the toilet, tears of panic rising. I needed her onside. I needed her to understand how frightened I was. I'd thought I'd hit rock bottom already: the possibility of there being an even deeper chasm for me to fall into was making me feel faint. I simply couldn't cope with Michael having a girlfriend called Nellie Daniels. I thought about his hands roving over her back and her mane of shiny brown hair and nearly puked.

In the mirror my face was like a boiled dumpling, all puffy and bloated from crying with the dregs of yesterday's makeup under my eyes. A cold sore was forming by my mouth. Faced with a choice between Nellie-the-fucking-champagne-girl and myself, I thought I'd probably choose her too.

'I sink ve should do some yoga,' Stefania said, when I came back into the sitting room. 'You are like ze advert for ze Camden Sexual Health Clinic.'

I sat on the sofa and downed a good inch of cognac. 'Piss off. I don't want to do yoga. I want to talk about Nellie Daniels.' Stefania shook her head and turned on the TV. Even though she always behaved as if TV was the enemy of mankind, she often forgot herself and sat absorbed for hours in front of my screen. 'OK. Ve vatch television. You need to know vhat is happening in the world.'

She'd chosen a bad moment. For there, smiling at his front door with his arm round his Teutonic wife, was Nick. A strap line underneath read, 'Nick Bennett joins Tory election campaign team.'

A little jolt of fear shot through me and I sat down. This was not good. Not good at all. I glanced uneasily at my phone.

'I hate zis man! He looks like he has sex viz his hand many times each day.'

I smiled weakly, wishing I could tell her the truth about Nick. But of course I couldn't.

Soon after, Stefania got up and went to her shed to make lunch, issuing a barrage of threats to end my life if I didn't get into the shower and do something productive with my day.

I slouched back to bed and brooded. Seeing Nick's face again was making me wonder.

The day before Michael had dumped me, I'd told

him I was going to ask Hugh if he'd consider me for the election-coverage team.

Michael had raised an eyebrow. 'Really? Is that a good idea? You'll be working fifteen hours a day, Fran,' he said. Duke Ellington stared at him from atop the work surface, licking his paws.

'I know. But I want to do it, Michael. I'm thirty years old tomorrow, and it's time I tried my arm with politics. I've wanted to do it for ages. I reckon the time's come – it's nearly two years since I was made a specialist producer in ents.' I shifted to the other foot. 'Fran does Westminster, innit.'

He scratched his head and blinked, reminding me of how he'd looked when I'd first met him. 'Are you sure it's right for you?'

'You don't think I'm clever enough, do you?' I'd blurted out, after a brief pause. For no reason other than a vague need for moral support, I picked up a carrot from the work surface.

'What on earth makes you say that?'

'You're just trying to stop me making a fool of myself by asking Hugh. You don't think I can do politics!' I pointed the carrot at him.

Michael looked slightly irritated. 'Don't be silly. I'm just anticipating what Hugh's going to say. His first question will be "Have you got any contacts?"'

'And I *have!*' I cried. 'I've got a bloody direct line into the Conservative Party!'

Michael smiled exasperatingly.

'You think I'm some fluffy little bumstain from entertainment who can't hold down a job in clever politics! Well, I can! I can, Michael, I know I can.' I thumped the carrot against the side of my leg, feeling suddenly close to tears.

Michael shut his laptop and walked over to stand in front of me. He took the carrot out of my hand and put it on the work surface behind me. 'Listen, you mad carrot-waving woman, I don't think you're fluffy and I definitely don't think you're a bumstain. But what I *do* think is that you've been working long hours for months now and you need a break. You need more time for you. And us. I miss you!'

What had I done to deserve this man? I put my arms round his waist. 'OK. I'll have a proper think. Maybe you're right. I can't remember the last time we just sat around and watched TV.'

He smiled and kissed my forehead. 'I think we should down tools – laptop and carrot respectively – and go and make use of the last few hours of your twenties,' he said, leading me out of the kitchen.

'Stop it,' I hissed at Duke Ellington, who looked at me with stony disapproval as we passed him.

I had emailed Hugh the next morning. I couldn't not go for it.

And just as I'd been about to leave work for my birthday dinner/potential engagement with Michael, Hugh had hauled me into his office. 'I got your email about the election team,' he barked, as I closed the door behind me. 'Fran, if you wanted to join the Mill-bank lot, why the fuck haven't you said anything to me? Why the fuck did you wait till the fucking election came along? It's a big fucking deal – how do I know you won't fuck up?'

I'd tried not to smile at Hugh's interview technique. 'You don't,' I replied. 'But you do know that I haven't fucked up anything else for you and that I'd work so hard my arse would probably fall off.'

Hugh said nothing.

I took a deep breath. 'What you don't know is that it's my thirtieth birthday today and that there could be no greater present than a place on the politics team. It's why I got into journalism, Hugh. It's what I want to do. I read about politics, I think about politics, I blog about politics.' (That last one was a surprise. Did I?)

Hugh raised an eyebrow. 'I couldn't give a fuck about your birthday, Fran. That said, happy birthday. But I could give a fuck about your interest in politics. Who's going to win this election?'

'Cameron.'

'I see. And if he does, who are the rising stars of his party?'

Fuck. 'Well, Nick Bennett is one to watch. He's been playing an increasingly important role in policy over the last few months.'

Hugh wrote something in his notebook. 'You think so?'

Shit. Did I?

'Yes.'

'And contacts. You can't just blaze into Westminster with the duty number for the press office, Fran.'

'I know. I've got contacts.'

Hugh had glanced vaguely at his BlackBerry, which was making loud popping noises. 'OK, so suppose I said we have a feature on tomorrow's bulletin about the rising stars of politics.'

I waited.

'Fuck that. How about I'm *telling* you, right here, right now, that we have a feature on tomorrow's bulletin about the rising stars of politics? I want some of them in the studio. And you say Nick Bennett. Get him in for us. Go.'

What a bastard. 'OK,' I said, turning on my heel. 'Give me a few minutes.'

Hugh had roared with laughter. 'Good fucking bluff, Fran,' he called. 'That's half the fucking job.'

I'd looked at my watch. Michael had been due to collect me from reception half an hour ago. I paused briefly to picture him sitting there on the sofa with his chin deep in one of his scratchy Scottish wool scarves. I wondered what he'd bought me for my birthday and imagined his eyes creasing into a smile as I opened it. A ring? *Everyone* was convinced he'd propose tonight. Even Mum.

I'd buzzed through to Reception and asked them to tell him I'd be out in five minutes. Then I'd picked up my mobile and scrolled down to Nick's number. I glanced back at Hugh's office, where for no good reason he was sticking pins into a Plasticine dog. That would be me if I fucked this up.

Nick had answered almost immediately. 'Fran, I really can't talk. I'm at home. Laura is here.'

'Yes. I know, but it's business. Nick, I need your help. We'd like a rising star from the Tories to be in the studio tomorrow night. I proposed you as one of them. Can you do it?'

I'd heard the cogs of his ego machine beginning to turn. 'It'd be great exposure,' I added, wincing. Damn him.

'OK. I'll need to involve our press people but I don't see why not. As you say, I've been very prominent of late.'

'Oh, my God. Thank you, Nick – thank you so much. I – I really – Look, thank you. I'll organize a car to come to Portcullis House at about five o'clock. Is that OK?'

'Yes. Please confirm the car details via the press office. Don't ring me again.'

In typical Nick style, he ended the call without recourse to traditional pleasantries such as 'Goodbye.'

'Nick Bennett will be here at five thirty p.m. tomorrow,' I said, walking back into Hugh's office.

He'd sat up. 'Are you serious?'

'Yes.'

Hugh had chuckled. 'Fran, you could do with smartening up a bit — those bloody floral jumpsuit things you wear are fucking horrible — but I won't lie, I like you. And you're quite right about not letting me down. So I'm going to give you a chance. You can have a month's trial in the election team, starting on the fifth of January. But if you fuck up, you're out. That fucking simple. What do you say? Don't you fucking *dare*,' he added, as I forgot myself briefly and ran towards him with open arms.

'Wow! Good for you,' Michael had said, when I exploded into Reception. But he'd looked uncomfortable.

He'd probably foreseen what had come next: a call from a none-too sober Mum, saying, 'Frances, I'm rather shocked that you've organized this television jaunt with Nick. You of all people should be aware that the better known he becomes, the greater the strain on our relationship.'

Was that it? Had Michael got fed up with the constant drama of going out with the daughter of a politician's mistress? *Surely* not. While I was happy to change almost anything if it meant getting him back, I couldn't do anything about Mum's relationship.

By the time Stefania returned to ensure I wasn't stalking Nellie, I had got to the bottom of the brandy bottle and was playing Starship very loudly. She stood surveying the scene while, from my cosy spot on the floor, I howled that nothing was going to stop us now.

She stood surveying the scene. 'Right,' she said, and walked out with my phone. I increased my singing volume, gearing up for the key change, just as she came back in and turned off the music. 'Oi! Stefania! What the hell are you doing?' I asked, sitting up. Whoops. Floor was better. I lay down and giggled a bit.

'Your mozzer is on her way,' Stefania said stiffly. 'You are out of ze control.' She sat on the sofa and put on the TV, petting Duke Ellington. Glad of sane and sober company, he climbed into her lap and sat staring down at me haughtily. I passed out.

When I woke up, Mum was tapping me on the head gingerly. 'Frances? Are you alive, dear?'

'Mum!' I tried to sit up but my head hurt. The clock said 8.16 p.m. What kind of drunken tramp had a hangover at a quarter past eight on a Saturday night?

'Mum. I saw Nick and Laura sodding Bennett on the news earlier, joining the election team. Did you?' She nodded. 'Are you OK?'

'Well, darling, I've had better times,' she said. 'But let's not worry about me, let's worry about you. Stefania called me and told me that she found you singing power ballads in your knickers. Is this true?'

'Pretty much,' I admitted. 'I think Michael's seeing someone called Nellie Daniels. You and I are as fucked as each other now, right?'

She patted down her hair as she sat on the sofa above me. 'It's not meant to be like that, though, Frances,' she said. 'I'm meant to look after you, not the other way round.'

There was a silence. I knew Mum had never *wanted* to stop being my mum. But we both knew she was right. Our roles had been reversed a very long time ago.

'Mum, I think we should open a bottle of wine,' I said, getting up.

She looked guilty. 'That's a great idea,' she whispered, just in case Stefania could hear.

Stefania couldn't hear, but she heard later on when Starship went back on and Mum and I started duetting. Her furious face, as she showed Mum out of my flat and into a waiting taxi, was something I wouldn't forget in a hurry.

'Oops . . . Stefania's cross,' I said to Duke Ellington. His enormous haughty yellow eyes stared, unblinking, into my face, and then he stalked delicately off to my bedroom.

Dave texted just as I passed out drunk for the second time in one day: If you're not back at work on Monday I'm calling the police. Come back, kid, we'll look after you.

Chapter Fourteen

'But how . . . how do you *know*?' Leonie asked, when I told her about Nellie Daniels.

I told her the tale.

'Oh, Fran, you're being ridiculous. How the hell do you know he's seeing her?'

'Come off it, Leonie. Why else would he be dropping her home before visiting his sister? That's what men do in new relationships. They stick like bloody glue to your side. You never get a moment's peace because they're always walking you home, walking you to the bus stop, walking you to the fucking toilet. That's what he was like with me. And now he's doing it with her!' I yelled into the phone.

'You're being insane,' she said briskly. 'You have no proof whatsoever. Until you know for sure that he's seeing her I absolutely *forbid* you to stalk her, you mad journalist. OK?'

'Fine,' I muttered. Leonie was no use: I needed to take this up with Jenny Slater.

'Franny! Wow! How lovely to hear from you!' Jenny trilled, sweet and lovely as ever.

'Hey!' I blustered. 'How's it going? Girl or boy?'

It was a girl: Lily. She was six pounds six ounces, tiny, an angel with soft blonde hair who, apparently, had only cried twice in her two-day life. But, happy as I was for Jenny, I wanted to know only one thing. And it had nothing to do with epidurals.

Unfortunately, I got my chance quite soon. As Jenny lowered her voice and started telling me how badly she needed her milk to come through, she was interrupted by the arrival of some visitors. And before I had a chance to ask who it was, I knew. I could hear Michael's soft voice as clear as day. His and that of a girl I'd never heard before. I heard her say a cheery, Sloanish 'Hi, babe' and felt my stomach drop out.

'Who's that?' I whispered.

'It's Michael and . . . a friend,' Jenny faltered.

I ended the call. It was time to stalk this bitch.

'NELLIE DANIELS', I typed into Google, in furious capitals. I ran my hand through my knotty, greasy hair, drew a breath and pressed SEARCH.

There were quite a few links all relating to a company called Spikey PR. It was a medium-sized agency off Brompton Road, dealing mostly with contemporary fashion houses and a few restaurants. Nellie Daniels was a senior account executive and her photograph was flawless. It was black-and-white but that did nothing to detract from her high cheekbones, long eyelashes and miles and miles of fucking luxurious hair. My heart sank even deeper. *Game over*, I thought.

'Arc you Michael's girlfriend?' I asked her picture. She stared back, porcelain and expressionless. A Rolex was clearly visible on her slim wrist and she wore an immaculate fitted shirt that was definitely not from Topshop. A wave of monstrous jealousy broke over me. I'd never win in a fight with anyone who looked like this. She probably had twice-weekly manicures, a sister called Tamara and a flat off the King's Road. Since when had she been Michael's type?

I thought about us both; Nellie who looked like Angelina Jolie, who probably wore silk knickers and had exquisite taste in wine, and me: after several hours' makeup application I might just scrape a comparison with Billie Piper on a bad day, with my faded BHS pants and secret love of Irn-Bru WKD. Viewed in those terms, it'd be a clear choice.

I scanned her client list. She looked after a restaurant on Westbourne Grove, a Savile Row tailor, a couple of jewellery designers, a Kensington restaurant and . . . And Dean LaRonda. For a minute I couldn't remember, but I knew it was a bad sign. My heart thumped as I sifted quickly through my mind for a connection. And there it was. Jenny had told me that a friend of Dmitri's did the PR for Dean LaRonda; she hadn't mentioned that the same friend was now boffing Michael. *This* was who he'd been choosing jumpers with; this was who he'd been walking home on Friday! *Shit.* It was her! This smooth-skinned monster was going out with Michael! *My* Michael! She was the reason I'd been dumped! I got under the duvet and hugged my knees, shaking.

I knew I had to see her. I had to meet her. *I had to know more.*

I thumped my pillow in fear and frustration. Duke Ellington got up disdainfully and squinted at me as if I were a savage. I swear I saw him shaking his head as he stepped out of the cat flap. 'Whatever, Duke Ellington,' I called.

The cat flap closed daintily behind him.

And that was how it started. That was the moment at which I decided to go in search of Nellie.

Chapter Fifteen

The day after I decided to go in search of Nellie, I walked stiffly into ITN, a cold wind roaring angrily around my head. I prepared myself for sympathetic comments about the state of my vagina.

'Hi, Fran, how are you doing?' said Stella Sanderson to my crotch.

Thanks, Leonie, I thought, as I fumbled with the coffee urn. Hugh came in shortly after and ignored me completely. He seemed convinced that I was dying of syphilis.

A tall, skinny man, wearing tight jeans and brogues, was sitting at my desk. As I approached him uneasily from behind I noted several warning signs: a Fashion hairstyle, a Fashion cravat and a Fashion cardigan. 'Er, hello there, I'm Fran,' I mumbled, waiting for him to spring up and clear away his stuff.

'Fran,' he said, turning slowly.

Oh, fuck. Oh, FUCKING FUCK. Oh, fuck up the bottom.

It was Alex, Michael's best friend. Oxford-educated Alex who'd smoked cigars when he'd come round to dinner and who had once told Michael he was 'surprised' by Michael's choosing me. I'd done my best to ignore him ever since. I'd thought he worked at the fucking Millbank office!

'Oh, my God . . . Alex!' I said, feeling the blood pumping into my cheeks.

He looked me up and down slowly. 'Hi. Welcome back. Make yourself comfortable and I'll get you up to speed when you're ready.'

'Er, well, this is my desk.'

Alex smiled languidly. 'OK, Fran. You can have the desk if you want. No problem.' He shifted his neat piles to the hotdesk next to mine. 'How have you been?' he asked. 'Are you OK? I mean, are you OK?'

There was no hope of a bogus vagina story here. This was hideous: it was almost as if Michael was sitting in front of me. 'Why are you here, Alex?' I said, as confidently as I could.

He smiled slowly. I'd always disliked his thin, aristocratic face: it was the kind of face that gazed solemnly at itself in a mirror for several hours each day.

'Election show,' he said silkily, sitting back in his new chair and logging in to the computer. 'The team's going to be based here, not Millbank. I've been doing your job,' he added, when the incomprehension on my face failed to clear. I blushed again. Michael's best friend, doing my job? Was this actually the worst joke in the history of the world?

I tried to regain my composure. 'Ah. Well, thanks for that, Alex, much appreciated. I tell you what, I'll get logged in and then you can start handing back to me.' The idea of getting my teeth into Clever Politics was all that had got me out of bed this morning.

Alex looked me straight in the eye. 'Sorry, I'm not explaining things very well. I took your place on the election team because they had no idea when you'd be back. They seem to think you're suffering from some sort of gynaecological problem so I didn't say anything about you and old Slater breaking up. Sorry about that, by the way,' he added, clearly uncomfortable.

'I'm fine about Michael,' I said stiffly. 'And we haven't broken up, it's a trial separation.'

He looked sceptical.

'And I wasn't having gynae problems either,' I added quickly.

'Well, either way, I'm sorry.'

The *weasel*. I resisted the urge to punch him in the crotch and set fire to the building, yelling, 'YOU

NEVER THOUGHT I WAS GOOD ENOUGH ANYWAY.'

What had happened to my smooth transition back into work, during which I was smothered with sympathy and affection? My eyes filled with tears and I looked away towards Hugh's office. He seemed to be watching me.

Alex snapped back into action. 'Hugh wants you to stay on entertainment but I suggest you go and talk to him. In the meantime Eddie's emailed you a handover from ents. Have a good morning.' He put on some expensive Bose headphones and logged on to the election drive. I looked at my screen: I didn't even have access to it.

'Fran. Glad you're better – sounded like a nasty illness.' Hugh was walking past with a ginormous coffee in his hand. "Fraid it's back to ents for you – we needed the election team starting three weeks ago. But I'm giving you the Brit Awards to cheer you up – OK? The launch is at Renaissance tonight. You've got jis up your sleeve,' he added, striding on.

I should be so lucky. It was butter.

As soon as Alex went to lunch I clicked on to Spikey PR and stared at Nellie Daniels's page. What grooming, what poise, what crisp Chelsea coolness. She held my gaze defiantly. The idea that Michael could have seen her naked made me want to stick my head in an oven. And then, quite without warning, my hand did something exceptionally stupid: it picked up the phone and called her direct line.

'Hello, Nellie Daniels speaking?'

Her voice was deeper than I was expecting, but unmistakably Sloanish. I was mute.

'Hello?'

I twirled the cord round my hand, my heart thumping. Lunchtime yoga said an email that had popped up in the corner of my screen. And out of nowhere I started speaking. 'Hi. My name is Yolande and I'm calling from Inner Calm. We're a new yoga and, erm, meditation centre in West London set up with the high-flying executive in mind.'

'I'm sorry, I'm not interested.'

'No problem. But let me at least send you our brochure?'

WHAT THE FUCK?

'OK, fine. You must have found me on the website. My email's there too. Thanks.'

Shit. *I had to see her, I had to see her, I had to see her.*

'One more thing, Mrs Daniels . . .'

'Miss.'

Bollocks.

'Ms Daniels. Our meditation classes for busy execs start on Wednesday next week and you've been specially selected for a free trial! It's no strings attached and I know you'll just love our set-up. The session is candlelit, with free healthy refreshments before and after. Ms Daniels, it's *Paradise*!'

A pause. Bloody hell, she was actually thinking about it! I imagined what Leonie would say if she knew I was doing this. Or, worse, Stefania. She'd cut my head off, probably. Well, sod them. I was going in search of Nellie and no one was going to stop me. I needed to know what she had that I didn't.

'Well, I can't say it doesn't sound appealing. Where do you meet?'

'We meet at . . . er . . . sorry, we're new, as I said, so I keep forgetting! We're based in a private suite at Renaissance in Notting Hill. Oh, and did I mention that you're welcome to bring a partner?'

'Thanks, but no – it's early days with my boyfriend. Well, Yolande, I'll say yes. Please email me the details. I have to go now. If you could copy in my assistant Tara Jenkins I'd appreciate it. Thanks.'

'Great! See you a week on Wednesday, Ms Daniels.'

'Nellie. Goodbye.'

It's early days with my boyfriend. How could she be going out with Michael? This abrupt, businesslike woman with a husky Prada-sunglasses-type voice and a personal assistant? Did Michael have to schedule blow jobs via Tara Jenkins? What the hell *was* this?

Then, sitting bolt upright, I realized what I'd just done. A meditation class for high-flying media execs? At the fucking Renaissance? The most expensive members' club in town? This was the work of a complete mental case! *Cancel, Frances, cancel!* I picked up the phone and called Renaissance.

Hoping that perhaps they'd be booked up for months ahead, I was alarmed to find out that yes, they did indeed have just such a room available. It was late January and still freezing after all. After twenty minutes' hard negotiation I managed to get them to reduce the hire fee to a mere two hundred pounds because I'd be bringing in a raft of desirables to whom they could tout membership. Within minutes, a hire contract had arrived in my inbox and I was entering my credit-card details.

And that, suddenly, was that. I had a room, and an exec seeking inner peace. I only needed to find an understanding Buddhist and nine other high-flyers. Piece of cake.

Oh, God.

I went to the toilet and rested my forehead on the cold white tiles, wondering if I had actually lost my mind.

I texted Leonie: Fancy a meditation class next Wednesday?

Of course I don't. How's work going? You OK? she replied.

No. Bloody Alex got transferred over here. Has taken my job on election team. Sitting next to me. Too fucked up for words. I texted back.

Oh dear! she replied. It seemed a little jolly, given the circumstances, but I had bigger fish to fry.

Over the next week I nearly died with the effort of not calling Michael. On several occasions I started

126

emails but I just couldn't shake his words from my head: 'If we have ninety days of total blackout, Franny, I'm sure we can sort things out.' What 'things?' *What* had gone so badly wrong and, more importantly, how had I failed to notice it? Pondering this painful conundrum, I felt more frustrated and stupid than ever. How had I failed to notice whatever was wrong? I must have seemed to Michael like a child so intent on eating her apple that she couldn't see it was rotten.

'I honestly don't know,' Leonie said tiredly, when I called her from a meeting room one lunchtime, crying uncontrollably and asking why the hell I'd been dumped. 'He's just . . . urgh, Fran, I don't know what his fucking problem is.'

Sitting next to Alex was pure torture. It was like staring at a delicious cake I couldn't eat, its still-warm sugary scent floating softly into my nostrils invitingly. The temptation to wrestle him to the ground armed with a staple gun and demand information about Michael and Nellie was unbearable. How long had it been going on? Was it serious? Was she great at oral? *WHAT THE FUCK?*

But, of course, I remained silent. My pride could not take any further blows.

Scraping together the enthusiasm to do the job I'd loved for the last five years bordered on the impossible and the entertainment team seemed to be doing quite well without me. Most of my time, therefore, was divided between stalking Nellie and finding media fools to join my meditation class.

By the end of my first week Alex had drawn up a ten-page dossier on David Cameron and I had put together a ten-page fully illustrated dossier on Nellie Daniels. (It was an outstanding piece of work by anyone's standards. I had ten different pictures of her, featuring seven stonkingly crisp, tailored outfits, and a list of fifteen of her Facebook friends who had open profiles through which I could stalk her in the coming days. I had worked out that she lived on the Fulham Road and had discovered via her friend's Facebook that she was going to a party at Boujis on Saturday. I knew her birthday, I knew how she'd met Michael's brother-in-law Dmitri (a power lunch at Kensington Roof Gardens in 2002) and I knew that she was a member of the Richmond Park Running Club.

Most of all, I knew that I hated her. And that her life couldn't have been more different from mine. My dossier on her read like a manual on how to be young and successful and glamorous in London: where to shop, where to eat, who to go drinking with, where to live. I imagined what a dossier on me would look like. It would probably have been dropped down the bog at some point and would be curly and dog-eared. It would note things like 'eats kebabs' and 'wears dirty tracksuits' and 'has alcoholic mother'. Next to Nellie's power-lunching existence, my life felt like a lumpy old cowpat. Of *course* Michael wanted ninety days off from me if he'd got lucky with Nellie stinking Daniels.

It was unbearable.

On Thursday morning Alex received a call that I knew straight away was from Michael. 'Hi,' he said quietly. 'Yes, hang on.' He got up and sidled off into an empty edit suite. Naturally, I followed. 'Sorry, she was sitting right next to me . . . No, I don't think she knows. How could she?'

I felt sick.

'Yeah, she just seems to be spending most of the day on the Internet.' After a pause he started to laugh.

I fled.

Later that day I was roused from Nellie-stalking by a voice behind me saying, 'Someone told me there's a washed-up old bint who goes by the name of O'Callaghan sitting round here . . . You don't know where I could find her, do you?'

I yelped and jumped up into a Dave Brennan hug. He'd been in Copenhagen doing climate change since I'd been back and I'd missed him. He pushed me away and held me at arm's length, looking me up and down. 'Fran, are you eating?'

'Sort of.'

'You have to eat, you scrote. Otherwise you'll die. Get some pie, love. What happened to the girl who crams bangers and mash down her gob on her own in the Union Tavern?'

Alex looked round and smiled. 'Really?' he said. 'You do that, do you?'

I went red. Dave turned to him. 'All right, Alex. Great outfit, mate,' he said casually, peering at Alex's Hackney waistcoat. God, I loved Dave. Alex reddened and turned back to his Cameron dossier. Dave raised an eyebrow. 'Seriously, kid,' he said more quietly, 'you've got to eat. Got to keep up your strength!' I nodded and, without warning, began to cry.

Dave pulled me away, shielding me from Alex's view. 'Oh, Franny, don't cry,' he said, as he thumbed away the tears that were pouring down my face. 'Please, don't cry.' His kind, weather-beaten face showed his concern.

'Sorry, Dave. I just – I just miss him so much. I think he's seeing some posho called Nellie and I might just want to die with the horror of it all,' I mumbled.

After a while he pulled me back into a hug. He smelt of fags and an old-fashioned spicy cologne. 'I know how it feels,' he said quietly.

'Shut up. You're going out with the most beautiful woman on the planet. You don't know the first thing about heartbreak,' I cried into his armpit.

He pulled away. 'Fannybaws, *you* don't know the first thing about my love life,' he said, after a pause. 'Of course I've been where you are now. But it gets better. OK? Easier. Come on. Go to the loo and wash your face – you look like road kill.' He handed me a tissue from his pocket.

'OK. But while we're on the topic of your beautiful girlfriend, could you spare her for a meditation class on Wednesday at Renaissance? I've organized one and I need to fill it up.'

Dave suppressed a snigger. 'Seriously? Since when were you into meditation?'

'Stop it, Dave. I need inner calm. Just make sure she's there.' He ruffled my hair and loped off into an edit suite where Hugh was watching his footage.

'How're the election plans going, Alex?' I asked, in as companionable a fashion as I could muster. I'd enjoyed Dave's put-down very much but I couldn't really afford to fall out with Alex. 'Stressful?' I added hopefully.

Alex laughed. 'Not really,' he said, swinging his chair round to face me. 'No. Politics is my heartland, just like entertainment is yours. It's second nature. I'm just beginning a dossier on Nick Bennett, actually.'

I didn't like his raised eyebrow. Was he giving me a Significant Look? No. I was being paranoid. 'Oh, right! Lots of material there,' I said brightly. But he was still looking at me like he Knew Stuff. 'You picked him at the right time,' I continued. 'Bound to be in the cabinet if the Tories win!'

Alex smiled. I decided I definitely hated him.

'I'm not so sure. I think he's got some issues in his private life that might get in the way of that,' he said.

My palms pricked. He surely couldn't know about Nick and Mum. No one knew! Not even Mum's bloody sister! He continued to watch me with a rather awkward expression on his face. 'Oh? How do you mean? Has he been fiddling expenses, too, then?' I asked. My voice was a little shrill.

'No. I was referring to his . . . to his family life. I've been spending a lot of time with his aides during my research. I discovered some surprising stuff,' Alex said. 'But it won't go anywhere.' He winked at me.

What the fuck?

He knew.

I felt suddenly like I might like to be sick and knew I needed to change the subject immediately. 'How's Michael?' I blurted out.

The name hung in the air like a fart on the Victoria Line.

Alex seemed a little surprised. 'He's good. But I don't think we should be talking about him. You're upset enough as it is.'

'I'm not,' I said tersely. I started to hammer out a report on Tiger Woods's latest indiscretion. This was not good at all. Mum needed security and peace, not a starring role in a national sex scandal. And I needed a soft re-entry to my workplace: I did not need Michael's fucking best friend sitting next to me and taking my job.

I should have stayed in bed.

Chapter Sixteen

It was Saturday night. I'd been back at work for a week and I was sitting in Stefania's rocking chair while she cooked what appeared to be a pan of stewed testicles. She was burning sandalwood oil by her bed and the shed smelt heavenly.

'You look very nice,' Stefania said, as she stirred in a rotten old tree root.

I was touched. 'Thanks, Stefania. I don't feel nice but one has to do one's best.'

Armed with my Nellie dossier as a guide I had hit the Westfield shopping centre that afternoon, loading up on sexy tailored outfits and expensive shoes and stopping off in Toni and Guy to get my hair highlighted and properly conditioned. It now sat in an uncharacteristically neat, shiny bob and incorporated a media-style fringe. (I'd even toyed with buying clear-lensed glasses but had slapped my face sharply at that point.)

Financially I was ruined but I was enjoying a temporary reprieve from the pain of heartbreak. Project Glam Fran was go! By the time I'd finished with myself I'd be a match for Nellie sodding Daniels any day. I would engineer a 'coincidental' meeting with Michael and he would draw in his breath at my glamour. His glance would linger on my well-turned ankle and exquisite high-heeled shoes and he would throw himself at my feet, begging my forgiveness.

Stefania started to ladle the testicles on to two plates but I declined. 'Vhy not?' she asked irritably. 'You look like a toothpick. Eat zees. Is very, very good for you.'

I gazed at the testicles in dismay.

'Zey are not bollocks, Fran. I am a vegetarian,' she said, with a slight smirk.

'I didn't think they were,' I said brightly, picking up the fork.

'Bollocks,' she said, through a mouthful of bollocks.

'Sorry, Stefania. And sorry, generally, that you've been having to look after me. I know you have a life of your own and I don't want you to ever feel duty-bound,' I said. 'Heartbroken people are awful. I'm sorry.'

'Ees OK. I care about you,' she mumbled.

'Why?' I really meant it. Why was I worth caring about at the moment? I divided my time between crying and stalking; even Duke Ellington had stopped pretending to hate me and now actually *did* hate me.

'Because you are like my stupid child,' she said simply. 'I vant to punch you many times but I also vant you to be happy. You are good to me.'

This surprised me. I knew I was probably paying for her gas and electricity and maybe even her water – but was that being good to her?

I must get her drunk, I thought, *and try to find out what her real story is.* But there was a time and a place and it would need to be a careful attack: I'd been trying for five years to work out where she had come from and how she had ended up in the shed. I wasn't going to stumble on the answer halfway down a bottle of Malbec.

'Well, I actually came round to ask you another favour,' I said shiftily. 'But I think you might like it. I, er, wondered how you'd feel about running a meditation class for me?'

She put down her fork, excitement patently visible. 'Vhat? But vhere? I cannot afford to hire room,' she said.

'That's taken care of. All you have to do is turn up, guide ten uptight bitches from the media through an hour's basic meditation and then you're done.'

'Zat is it?'

'Well . . . I suppose I'd also like you to make some treats for them too . . . maybe some vegan canapés and some raw-chocolate fudge?'

Her cheeks coloured faintly.

'Don't worry. I'll pay you. And I'll buy the ingredients. It won't cost you a cent.'

She reddened further, horribly embarrassed. This was the first conversation we'd ever had about money.

We discussed the details, Stefania becoming increasingly enthusiastic and me increasingly panicked. Of the many stupid things I'd done in my life, this was definitely the crowning glory.

'But once sing, Franny, vhy are you doing this? I do not understand. What is ze reason, please?'

Ah. 'Well, the stress of the last few weeks has all but killed me, Stefania, and I've decided that perhaps I might benefit from a more alternative lifestyle. I couldn't find a meditation class that felt right and I . . . I thought I'd set one up. For people like me. Media twats.' I was becoming an exceptional liar.

Stefania held up a cup of oolong tea and toasted me. 'You have a deal. Zis is *dubious*! Cheers!'

'Fabulous.' I chinked her cup. 'Hey, Stefania, you don't fancy going to a party at Boujis tonight, do you?'

Her eyes narrowed. 'I vould rather eat my own solid vaste,' she replied. 'Vhat are you up to?'

'Oh, nothing. Just a friend invited me. It sounded cool.'

She wasn't convinced. 'How are you feeling about Michael, Frances?' she said eventually.

'As before.'

'Vell, zat is not true for a start. You have been out of bed for more zan a week and you are looking less like a peasant's goat. Perhaps it is time to start ze dating.'

'I don't want to date. Now or ever. I've said I'll do it, Stefania, but you can't expect me to begin straight away. It's just madness. I'd only end up crying through the whole date.'

She munched her testicles, nodding. 'I understand,

136

Fran. But if you vill not do it for yourself, can you do it for me?'

I tried not to lose my temper. 'But why? You still haven't given me a decent explanation why you want me to do this. It just seems like a completely mental idea.'

Stefania nodded again. 'I know, but there is logical. I promise. I vant you to find love, Frances, real love. Not ze love you had for Michael,' she continued, as I tried to butt in. 'A deeper love.'

'And you think I'm going to find that by dating? Stefania, I *have* a deep love. I love Michael and I want him back. I want to get him back from this Nellie bitch and that is that.'

Stefania pushed back her chair and took our plates over to her tiny sink. She looked distraught. 'Fine. Zen call him. Call him now and make ze arrangement to see him.'

'I can't. You deleted his number from my phone.'

'Vell, zen, get it from Jenny. Or email him. Go. Now.'

I didn't move. This didn't feel right at all. Stefania looked round at me. 'Vhy are you not doing zis?' Her eyes were flashing.

'Because it's making you upset, Stefania. Or angry. And I don't want that.'

Stefania shook her head.

'Stefania, I just don't understand why this is so important to you, but if it really is, I'll do it. I'll go on eight bloody dates. But date number eight is going to be Michael. I'm going to get him back. And don't expect me to put any effort into the others. OK?'

She smiled. 'Good. Zat is better. And I vill allow you to see Michael for the eighth date. Vhy not? So how vill you find ze ozzer men?'

'Well, if I want to get this out of the way quickly there's only one way, isn't there? I'll have to get them off the bloomin' Internet.'

Stefania giggled. 'I vas hoping zis was ze way you vould attack ze problem. I hear zat ze Internet is ze perfect place to find love. Let us start immediately!'

And so, rather bewildered, I let Stefania into my flat and fired up my laptop for her. 'FRANCES!' she shouted, as I opened a bottle of wine. 'You have been stalking ze Nellie Daniels. Vhy are you doing zis? Frances, you do not even know zat zey are togezzer!'

I ran into the sitting room, hoping against hope that there weren't any photos of Nellie up. If Stefania recognized her at Meditation on Wednesday I'd be sunk. Fortunately it was just an article I'd been reading about her and the Savile Row tailor for whom she did PR. It had left me feeling awed and depressed by her knowledge of luxury brands and heritage. Was there *anything* this bitch didn't know about?

'I vill do your dating page, Frances,' Stefania announced, when I had set her up with a browser. 'Ve vill do ze site vhere you recommend your friend, OK?'

'Fine by me,' I said. The less I had to do with this, the better.

She got to work.

'Promise me you von't call Michael until his three-month thing is over,' she said later, as she got up to leave.

I crossed my fingers behind my back. 'Promise.'

Stefania grabbed my arm and hauled it round in front of me. 'Horrible girl,' she muttered.

'OK, OK. I promise. You have my word. I won't contact Michael. I *promise*.'

As she walked out of the door, Stefania put a hand on my cheek and smiled the most kindly smile I'd ever seen. 'Good girl. You vill sank me for zis one day.'

A few minutes later I texted Leonie: Fancy going to a party at Boujis later?

I was viewing my dating profile with great unease. Apart from the fact that it looked very much as if it had been written by a woman of unknown (but not British) origin, there was a whiff of madness about it that only Stefania could have injected. She had seemed to relish the process, starting up a search as soon as my profile had gone live. 'Zis one! Look! He is divinity!' she yelled, pointing to a toothy man called Hilary. Eventually I'd had to throw her out because she'd added seventy-six men to my favourites folder, all of whom were so bad I'd sooner have slept with a woman.

Leonie replied: Er, no. It's nearly midnight. Are you drunk?

No, just heard there was a wicked party on. Don't worry, I texted.

This had better not have anything to do with Nellie Daniels, she replied.

I was going to have to go underground with my Daniels hunt. There were people who wanted to shaft me at every turn.

Chapter Seventeen

FRAN, YOU HAVE A NEW MESSAGE FROM **BOB**!
HERE'S WHAT HE HAD TO SAY!

All right Fran
If I could rearrange the alphabet, I'd put you between F and CK.
   Mail me.

FRAN, YOU HAVE A NEW MESSAGE FROM **PETER**!
HERE'S WHAT HE HAD TO SAY!

Hi Frances
I'm a selfish, fucked-up waste of space who likes a bit of rough
   sex every now and then.
If this sounds like your sort of thing then bell me on 07065 333891.
   Cheers
      Peter

FRAN, YOU HAVE A NEW MESSAGE FROM **KERRY**!
HERE'S WHAT SHE HAD TO SAY!

Hi babes, you don't ever do girl on girl do you? If not, try it . . . ; -)

FRAN, YOU HAVE A NEW MESSAGE FROM **ANDREW**!
HERE'S WHAT HE HAD TO SAY!

Hi Fran.
I am Andrew. I am man. You are woman. Interesting woman, by

the look of things. With even more interesting friends. Who did your write-up? Can I go on a date with her?! However if she's unavailable I'd definitely be interested in a date with you. Do you like beer? If so, let's meet up and have one (each).

Andrew X

FRAN, YOU HAVE A NEW MESSAGE FROM **EDDIE**!
HERE'S WHAT HE HAD TO SAY!

Hi Fran, er, surprise! Fancy seeing you here . . .(!) Look love could you keep this quiet please? I won't say anything to anyone at ITN if you do the same for me! Thanks hun, see you soon, E x

'STEFANIA!' I yelled, striding out into the yard. I blinked in the unexpected winter sun as Duke Ellington sprinted up the tree that overhung Stefania's shed. I rapped on her door. 'STEFANIA! COME OUT! Surrender yourself, woman. You are in a world of trouble.'

Silence.

I was sure she was there.

Duke Ellington glowered fiercely at me from the bare branches of the tree. 'Count yourself lucky that you'll never have to Internet date,' I told him. He crouched on the branch, preparing an assault, and I moved away. He'd never launched himself at my head yet but I wouldn't have put it past him.

Stefania's shed door was flung open. 'FRAN-CEES!' she screeched, even though I was only a few feet away.

'Don't you shout at me, Stefania. You just wait until you see what's been arriving in my dating inbox. You'll be getting down on your hands and knees begging forgiveness.'

She rubbed her hands with glee and cackled. 'Ha-*ha*! Is all part of ze plan! Show me your inbox!'

Inside, Stefania held her sides and wept with laughter while I made lunch. 'Franny, thees is vonderful!' she gasped. 'Vhich one vill you pick?'

'None of them!' I replied, flopping down next to her with two plates of cold falafel and salad. Her eyes narrowed suspiciously. 'They're organic,' I said tiredly.

'Francees. Now, listen to Stefania. I looked after you, I took your bullsheet day after day and I never complain, no? All I ask of you is zat you go on zese eight dates. Zat is all. It is not too much to ask.'

'I still don't understand it, Stefania. But I've given you my word so I'll do it, OK? I just hope you can explain to me what the hell this was all about one day.'

'I can explain now. I vant you to be happy. Is zat simple.'

I put down my falafel and smiled at her. 'Thank you. You mad, weird woman.'

She batted me away, clearly embarrassed. 'Peess off. Now, vhich one are you going on a date viz? I like ze sound of Andrew. I sink you go on a date viz Andrew. He makes funny joke about Stefania. Yes. I vill email him now.'

'Get off,' I yelled, reaching for the laptop just a little

too late. Nimble little bugger that she was, Stefania sprinted off with it and locked herself into the bathroom, laughing evilly. A few minutes later I heard her shouting, 'I set you up on date viz Andrew now! You go on Thursday, do you understand?'

'I HATE YOU,' I yelled, grinning. Andrew it was, then. God knew who else she emailed: it was a full fifteen minutes before she re-emerged from the bathroom.

While she sent poorly spelt messages on my behalf, I put the remaining falafel back in the fridge. There was a picture on the door of me and Michael sitting on Brighton beach in the rain, eating each other's ice cream and laughing like toddlers. As I stared at it, I imagined him sitting on Brighton beach in the brilliant sunshine with Nellie Perfect Daniels and felt my stomach churn. The jealousy was almost overwhelming.

When we were together I'd never really been jealous of Michael: he'd been so committed, so into me, wanting to be with me all the time - although, for reasons that eluded me he had often been jealous about me and other men. Over the last couple of years he'd thrown out some inexplicably paranoid theories, including a conviction that I was exchanging significant glances with some Essex entrepreneur Leonie had been knobbing last winter, and even some fierce cross-questioning about Dave. Dave! Dave, who couldn't have been further from what I was looking for; Dave, who had the most beautiful partner in the world and was no more interested in me than he was in handbags.

The weird Michael/Dave incident had happened in the summer of 2008: Leonie, Dave and I had been enjoying a particularly raucous Gin Thursday, which had culminated in a prolonged karaoke session at Lucky Voice. I had sung 'I'll Stand By You' in what I believed to be ethereally beautiful and tragic tones and then proceeded to knock out so many power ballads that Leonie had eventually wrestled me to the floor to get the microphone. Drunk as I was, I decided to stay there for a little kip. When Lucky Voice closed and I refused to wake up, Dave had had to sling me over his shoulder and carry me all the way up to Clerkenwell Road to hail a taxi. He'd sat with me back to Camden and had been discovered by Stefania an hour later.

Stefania had been doing some sort of mad-sounding equinox worship and had noticed us outside: Dave was sitting uncomfortably on my doorstep while I slept with my head in his lap, snoring loudly. I had apparently lost my keys and Dave had decided to stay with me until I was sober enough to knock on the door and explain myself to Michael. Needless to say, Stefania had hissed so loudly and dramatically during her conversation with Dave that Michael woke up. He came out, took me inside, tight-lipped with fury, and the next day questioned me for nearly an hour about Dave, refusing even to let me go to the kitchen for emergency hangover toast. 'Are you completely *barmy*?' I'd shouted at him, from my pit of pain in the bed. 'Dave is like my bloody *dad*! I'd set him up with Mum if he was a few years older!'

He'd stared angrily at the ceiling for a few more seconds and then had sat down suddenly on the floor, putting his head in his hands. 'I'm so sorry, Franny. I'm insane. Please, please, forgive me. I just had a really bad day at work and I wanted to talk to you last night.'

I'd been overcome with remorse and had dragged myself out of bed to comfort him. I wagged off work and made him a lunch of Tesco sandwiches and mini chocolate trifles, washed down with a back massage and some hungover sex, which made me feel even more ill.

After that he had stayed even closer to me. We always knew where each other was and I liked it that way: Michael was my shadow. My much better-looking shadow. I felt safe, secure and completely certain of his feelings for me.

So how the frig had he managed to start an affair with Nellie Daniels? How, when I knew his every moment, had I not noticed? And why had I gone from being his prized possession to Just Not Good Enough?

Three days to go until Meditation.

Chapter Eighteen

Great! Yes, I'm free on Thursday. Soho? If you work in the media you will probably feel at home there. I love watching all the frustrated media-type men with their steel-rimmed glasses and striped jumpers and futile once-a-week yoga habits. How does 8 p.m. corner of Frith Street/Old Compton Street work? Ax

'Sounds great, Frances, count me in.'

This was Mona Carrington, head of New Media at ITN, signing up for my meditation class tonight. Or Stefania Mirova's meditation class, as I put it. (I didn't know Stefania's surname but that one felt right.) I'd briefed Stefania to treat me like any other class member and she suspected nothing.

It was really quite exhilarating, all this lying. I just needed one more media type to fool and then I was done. 'I am Frances O'Callaghan and I am a massive bullshitter,' I said to my reflection in the ITN toilet mirror. I pouted, enjoying my sleek, short-skirted image, and flounced out.

Back at my desk I pretended to watch a Brit Awards news report while plotting how I could find my final media bitch. In my book there were two types of people who went to meditation: first, there were the genuine carob-munching, bean-sprouting, recycled-Fairtrade-cardigan wearers, and second, there were the wealthy middle classes who didn't really give a shit about meditation or yoga or alternative well-being but suspected that it might just give them an advantage over other people.

It was these self-absorbed types that I wanted at my class. And I knew Nellie would be one of them. I knew because she had a PA called Tara and a Rolex and hair like Cheryl Cole's.

An email from Mona Carrington arrived in my inbox. Hi Fran. A contact of mine would like to come along tonight. Is that OK?

I sat back and rubbed my hands. My bitch quota was complete: I was good to go!

The only problem was that I had lied to Stefania. That part felt less enjoyable.

But I couldn't put a stop to it. There were only nine hours to go until I could meet Nellie and the anticipation was almost unbearable. In fact, I wasn't sure I could wait that long. I went out and bought a packet of beef Monster Munch to tide me over for a few hours.

That evening, as I helped Stefania lay out her carefully prepared healthy treats, I felt paralysed with fear. I was about to meet the woman who was now sleeping with my man. I'd dreamed last night of her expressionless face staring frostily at Michael's bottom while he slept, and had woken up crying and determined to cancel the class. Determined to bloody well *call* him and find out what on earth was going on.

But when I'd picked up my phone, I'd been paralysed.

Stefania was humming; her eyes bright and her typically car-crash sartorial style radically transformed. She was wearing a simple long raw silk dress Mum had donated to her a few years back; it fitted her perfectly and made her look significantly less mad. If I wasn't mistaken she was even wearing mascara, and her hair was clean and shining. As she propped up a little statue of Buddha on the table at the front, I marched over and hugged her tightly. 'Thank you so much for doing this, Stefania,' I muttered into her hair.

She laughed, surprised and delighted, and pulled me away, studying my face. 'Ees OK! Zis is a vonderful day for me! Vhy do you sank me?'

'Just because. You're a really good friend to me, Stefania.' *A mother*, I thought, with a little twinge of sadness.

'Shush, little cabbage. You are going on a date tomorrow and zat is all I require. Anyvay! Ze vomen vill be here soon! I can feel their angster!'

'Angst.' I laughed, lighting a candle. 'And remember, Stefania, I'm not the organizer of the class. I just want to enjoy it and join in. Just another class member, OK?'

'No problem!' She saluted.

The women began to file in. They were an uptight, pushy bunch all right. 'Hello, Fran,' Mona Carrington boomed, walking in with . . . with a *man*. An extremely attractive man. But a man all the same. This was a class for media bitches! Not bloody fit *men*!

I walked over to remove him but Stefania got there first, welcoming him with her palms together in some sort of Buddhist greeting. I stopped. If she was happy to have a man there then so be it. I shrugged. Perhaps he and Nellie would fancy each other and then she'd leave Michael.

Five minutes later, as the media types removed their expensive shoes and stashed their beautiful handbags at the back of the room, there were only two women left to arrive, Freya and Nellie Daniels. So when Dave shuffled in with a roll-up behind his ear, coughing loudly into his dirty hand, I was appalled. 'Er . . . Dave?' I hissed at him. 'Where's Freya?'

Dave made no attempt to lower his voice. 'All right, Fran. This is a fuckin' triumph, girl! Yeah, I decided to come along myself, actually. Get some of this Zen shite.' I stared at him furiously. 'Dave, this is meant to be a class for women! For crying out loud!'

Dave laughed, taking off his big army coat and throwing it on the floor next to a bowl of rose petals, most of which flew across the floor in the tailwind. 'Och, Fran, I need some inner calm. It's fine! And there's another fellow over there. What are you on about?'

Stefania had come over.

'Oh, all right, Stefania, how's tricks?' Dave said conversationally, as he pulled off his workman's boots.

Stefania smiled coyly. 'Ees vonderful to see you, as always, Dave. I am glad to have man in my class. Men have vonderful experience of meditation! You are very velcome!'

Dave beamed at her and turned to me. 'See?'

I was gearing myself up to have a quiet tantrum when the door opened and in walked Nellie. With one hand she was turning off her BlackBerry, with the other she was pulling out her hairband . . . and there it was: that mane of perfect hair. I gawped, suddenly breathless. She was, if at all possible, even more flawless than the porcelain-faced Rolex woman in the picture. She was far taller than me, probably nearly five foot ten, and she had the figure of a gazelle. Long, long legs in expensive seamed tights, beautiful spikey shoes and a charcoal pencil skirt with a tight black, flawless shirt tucked into it. A small gold pendant saying 'Nellie' hung round her neck and she carried the Heritage Bayswater satchel that I longed for but would never own. I felt physically sick. This? This was my competition? Never before had I felt quite so inadequate.

The hot man smiled at her in a way that said 'Ah.

We're the two best-looking people in this room. We must therefore fuck.' Not even having spoken to him, I felt betrayed. He was MY hot man! In MY class! He should be after me, not bloody *Nellie*! I looked at Dave. He, too, even though he was with the Mrs bloody Natural Flower Meadow Woman, was staring open-mouthed.

Annoyed, I removed my socks while Stefania introduced herself. I winced, as Nellie said, 'Yah, I'm *really* pleased to be doing this. I think it'll really help me.' What the fuck did *she* need help with? She was stunning, successful, clearly rich, fashionable . . . oh, and she now had the best boyfriend in London.

Stefania asked her name and I held my breath. *Don't say your surname. Don't say your surname, don't say your surname* . . .

'Nellie.'

Phew. Stefania looked at me and smiled slightly: OK, she was saying. Nellie isn't just a name for an elephant.

Stefania sat us down and began. After a lengthy chat about the benefits of meditation, she finally closed her eyes and asked everyone else to do the same.

Of course, I did no such thing. I now had an uninterrupted forty-five minutes to stare at Michael's new girlfriend. Why had I doubted myself? It was a bloody brilliant plan! I stared at her waist, which I was reasonably confident I could get my hands round. Her ankles, too, were delicate, yet sexy and powerful.

There was a tiny mark on her chin. Was that a

stubble rash from Michael? I remembered him kissing me every morning with his chin all spiky and felt my eyes smart. I'd never get him back if he'd fallen for this woman.

'Just focus on the sensation of breathing in and out . . .' Stefania was saying. 'Ze air feels colder on the back of your nose as it goes in, zen varmer as it comes out.'

Did they have better sex than we'd had?

Nellie and I were at the back of the room and I was closest to the door where everyone had put their bags. I gazed at her Mulberry with envy: not only did she have the love of my life, she had the bag of my dreams. Her coat was folded next to it, some frighteningly expensive cream thing that made my grotty trench look like a dustman's overall. The pocket nearest to me was flashing.

It must be her BlackBerry.

Don't do this, I told myself. Seriously. If she finds you with your hand in her coat you'll be arrested. You are decent, sensible Fran, not the sort of weirdo who goes into other people's pockets!

But I was the crack whore again. In a second, I leaned over and then it was in my hand, smooth and cold, blinking quietly.

I opened up her email inbox; it all seemed pretty boring. When Dave snorted loudly for no discernible reason I jumped a mile in the air but his eyes were still closed. Furtively, I switched over to her phone messages. When had I turned into this person?

Her screen was large enough for me to be able to see eight messages, all with 'Michael xxx' in the sender line. Michael with three kisses? For crying out loud! My stomach flipped as I clicked on the most recent.

Enjoy this evening. You deserve it. I'm sorry if I've been grumpy recently, it's just a difficult time for me. But what I said last night stands: I am over her. I only have eyes for you, Nell. I love you. XXXXX

The BlackBerry went quickly back to the coat from which it had come. I felt dizzy. That was it. I was going to have sex with Andrew from the Internet tomorrow. Even if he was a boss-eyed Nazi with wooden teeth and halitosis.

'By now you should be feeling blissfully calm. All zere is in your head is your breath going in . . . and out . . .' Stefania was purring.

Panic charged through me and I dug my nails into my hand, willing myself not to cry before I got home. What a fool I was! I looked at Dave again, hoping that his blissful state might rub off on me. But instead of a mane of wild hair, I saw two crinkly blue eyes. Two blue eyes that were staring at me, one eyebrow raised.

He'd seen the whole thing.

At the end of the class, a radiant and beaming Stefania did the rounds of the media bitches with her platters of health food. Dave had left as soon as the class finished; I'd been unable to meet his eye. No doubt he was off to tell his beautiful girlfriend what a complete fuck-up I was. Not that she needed to be told.

I seized the opportunity to talk to Nellie about Spikey PR. Clearly it hadn't crossed her mind that I might just be being polite because she was holding forth with unbridled enthusiasm about her newest client: a trendy members' club for posh new mums in Chelsea. It sounded like utter hell to me: swarms of Range Rovers arriving with ghastly, messy-ponytailed women carrying babies called Claudia and Archie, guzzling designer coffee and organic cake while they helped each other through the devastating hardships of motherhood.

'It's just such a cute little venture,' she breezed. 'Rully, *rully* talented guys who've set it up, y'know. They *rully* know their shit. They know *just* how hard it can hit these women when they have a child – they've always been so successful and suddenly they're run ragged and alone all day. The club's all about support and friendship, y'know.'

I nodded enthusiastically. 'Yes, it sounds *wonderful*,' I trilled. Nellie consulted her Rolex and I panicked slightly. I needed more. More crack. 'Actually,' I gabbled, 'I work for the ITN news at six thirty and we've a strand of reports coming up in the next couple of weeks about the aftermath of the recession . . . We'll deffo look at how it affected luxuries like members' clubs, gyms and whatnot – how about we come and do a feature about these guys and how their business is booming in spite of the recession?'

Nellie paused, thinking about it. 'Well, yuh, sounds *great*!'

I hesitated as I handed over my number and promised to call her in the next few days, wondering what would happen if Michael found it. But why not? Why wouldn't I meet her at a meditation class and set up a feature?

Stefania arrived with a plate of raw-chocolate fudge and offered us each a piece. 'Er, thanks,' Nellie said doubtfully. 'How is this raw? I don't understand.' Her voice was so posh and husky. I wanted to stab her with her Patrick Cox shoe.

'Ees damaging to many foods to cook zem,' Stefania explained. 'Viz many foods ees possible to sprout zem or rehydrate zem to give zem ze same texture as cooked foods vizout damaging ze nutritional structure.'

Nellie smirked a little. 'But why would you bother? I mean, if you're going to eat chocolate then surely you're fucked anyway, aren't you?'

I bristled. Nellie was not allowed to say 'fuck' to Stefania. She didn't *know* her. The bloody arrogance of it.

Stefania laughed. 'You're not fucked if you eat zis,' she said. 'Try it. Ees delicious!'

I felt a stab of protective love for Stefania. If Nellie messed with her, I was taking her out. But I didn't need to: Stefania's years in that shed had made her a brilliant chef. Nellie's brown eyes widened as she chewed. 'It's bloody *delicious*, babe,' she said. 'A*maz*ing!'

'Yah, I agree,' said the preposterously hot man, who had somehow joined our group and was standing next to Nellie, smiling confidently into her eyes. 'Really good stuff, this. I love healthy, simple food!'

'Totally! She's an angel,' Nellie said, enjoying the attention.

I tried not to vomit over them.

But Stefania was beaming. I thought she was going to throw down the plate and hug them both: I'd never seen her so rosy-cheeked. I'd have to encourage her to continue with the class after today. She patted Nellie lightly on the arm of her perfect, uncreased black shirt and said, 'Ah, sank you ... er ... Vhat is your name again?'

Nellie flicked her mane over her shoulder. 'Nellie. Nellie Daniels. Spikey PR. I'm looking forward to the next session. Please do get that woman Yolande to sign me up for the rest of the course.'

Stefania's head dropped as she realized what I'd done. While the guests drifted out of the door she stood still, staring at a spot by my feet, white with anger.

Chapter Nineteen

Date one: Andrew

In spite of the fact that I had recently acquired a broken heart and a stalking habit, I felt my heart lift as I walked into Soho. The cold February air smelt of garlic and seafood while the chink of pint glasses and carefree laughter spilled from behind steamed-up windows, reminding me of what normal, sane, happy people sounded like. Out-of-towners screamed as their tuk-tuks hurtled the wrong way down the one-way system and gay men in designer parkas drank coffee at pavement tables. A pigeon sat fatly on the first-floor windowsill of Little Italy, deciding who to take a shit on.

It chose me.

I stood, frozen, as the white blob slid delicately off my shoulder and landed on the front of my left bosom. *What the flaming Jesus was I doing?* Why was I standing here with shit on my tit when I should be at home crying over my ex-boyfriend? Who on earth would put themselves through this horrible, gut-wrenching experience of going on a date with a *total stranger?*

I ran into Little Italy and begged the maître d' to allow me to wash my breast.

I emerged back on to Frith Street a few minutes later with a top so wet that my entire bra was visible. It was light grey and, now, completely transparent. To compound the situation, I was wearing a T-shirt bra so you could even see my nipple if you looked hard enough. The maître d' looked hard enough.

Dammit! Nellie Daniels wouldn't turn up on a date with her nipples showing. I had been playing our conversation over and over since last night. I was now more obsessed with her than a child with Father Christmas. Feeling rather conspicuous, I cowered in a doorway next to a chef who was having a fag break, shouting into his phone in an unidentifiable language. He broke off mid-conversation and stared at my breasts with great wonder.

Where was Andrew from the Internet? I briefly pondered the possibility of escaping. It wasn't too late to call him and say I had fallen down a drain and fractured my leg. Or unexpectedly given birth. But I knew I had to go through with it. I was missing Gin Thursday for this date and, in an act of solidarity, Leonie had gone on one too; while I was sweating it out in Soho she was on some trendy urban date in Spitalfields with a man who was probably wearing Victoriana.

As I scanned Frith Street once more, I wondered what the hell had happened to us. Only five minutes ago we were two little girls holding hands at the gates of Chiswick Park Primary on our first day of school. At what stage did it go so badly wrong that we'd ended up Internet dating together aged thirty?'

My phone rang and I hoped it was Andrew, calling to cancel the date. It wasn't.

'Mum,' I whispered, even though I was on a noisy street. Nothing. Just what sounded like a gale-force wind.

'Mum?' Louder this time. Still nothing.

'MUM?' Now I was shouting.

Finally, she replied. 'Ah, Frances, hello.' She sounded as if she was in the middle of a hurricane. 'I was just having a melancholy moment on Wandsworth Common and I felt I should share it with you.'

'What? Why are you on Wandsworth Common?'

'I am pondering my relationship, Frances. I am wondering how Nicholas and I will survive the new-found fame he appears to have acquired for himself. I have seen that repulsive wife of his twice on television now. She is a very unpleasant piece of work.'

'Mum, you've been having an affair with her husband for the last seventeen years,' I said gently. 'You can hardly write her off.' I kept an eye on Frith Street.

'OK, Frances. Well, I shall leave you to it. I don't know why I expected you to understand. I tell you what, you get back to your Internet date and don't worry about me.'

She hung up.

Bollocks. I kicked a step. My expensive boots scuffed

immediately. 'Fucking BOLLOCKS,' I said, louder. 'AND COCK.'

The chain-smoking chef was studying me with renewed interest.

I texted Leonie: Bird shat on my tit. Had Mum on phone telling me I wouldn't understand being unhappy. Date not even started yet.

She ignored me. Knowing Leonie, she was probably naked already.

At first, I had had little enthusiasm for this date. Stefania's message to him on Sunday had been pretty bad: Hello ANDREW thank you for DATE OFFER Yes I will date with you we will date on Thursday, thank you from Frances XXX – and out of pride, rather than interest in Andrew, I'd had to send another message explaining what the hell was going on.

He'd been reasonably understanding and, if I was honest, quite funny about it. So eventually, looking at his smiley photo, I had decided that a date with him wouldn't be all that bad. But I'd woken up this morning and nearly crapped my pants with fear. Whoever had invented Internet dating deserved to be strung up: it was a *terrible* idea.

'Fran?' said an Australian voice on my right.

Andrew wasn't Australian.

'No,' I said briefly, fiddling with my phone.

'Are you sure? You look just like her!'

Oh, my God. Seriously. Was I out of my *mind*?

Why shouldn't Andrew be Australian?! 'FUCK! Andrew!' I shouted. 'Yes! I'm Fran!'

Andrew was every bit as nice as he seemed in the photos. He kissed me on the cheek, drawled, 'Nice to meet you at last,' and smiled easily, appraising me from underneath long eyelashes. He was *really* good-looking. (A brief scenario ran through my head: we went out, fell in love, he asked me to marry him but I had to say no because I couldn't move to Oz and leave Mum here. Then I'd settle for a bald ex-con and spend the rest of my life whispering tragically that I had once allowed the love of my life to get away because blood was thicker than water.)

Andrew grinned at me, waiting for me to say something.

In an attempt to seem fun and friendly, I started gabbling about the fact that (a) I was really nervous, (b) I had had *no idea* that he was an Aussie and (c) that a bird had just taken a shit on my shoulder so I'd had to go and wash my top and it was now so wet that he could probably see my bra. 'AND EVEN MY NIPPLES!' I finished off in a yell.

Andrew began to snigger.

'Sorry,' I muttered lamely. 'Just nervous.' He was doing a heroic job of not looking at my tits. Maybe I *would* fall in love with him. Maybe he would be the one to take all the pain away. He would heal me with guitar songs and trips to the beach where he would teach me to surf and we'd eat kangaroo.

Andrew (the real-world Andrew, rather than the fantasy Andrew) gestured towards Old Compton Street. 'Well, I think all of this can be solved by a beer. Do you fancy the French House? Oh, and I'm a Kiwi. Totally different accent. But never mind.'

I smiled gratefully and we wove off along Old Compton Street. He was nice. And he was *hot*. And he didn't seem to mind that I was borderline mental and that I was wearing a wet top that showed my M&S bra. Maybe I'd only need to go on one Internet date, because Date One was actually *The* One. As I dreamed about our future together, we were buffeted by a swarm of Japanese tourists en route to Mamma Mia. Andrew smiled at me, moving into Dean Street.

And then I saw it.

Oh, please, God, no. It was gigantic. It was monstrous. It was . . . oh, help.

Jiggling softly along in front of me, Andrew's bottom was the most enormous, wobbly, womanly, wide-hipped ELEPHANT of a backside I'd ever seen. I was transfixed with horror, hypnotized by its gentle left-right sway. I looked at his upper body: normal, nice, blokish; not too wide, not too narrow. And then my gaze travelled back to his gigantic hips and huge, marshmallowy bottom.

Cursing myself for being so utterly shallow, I knew immediately that it was all over for me and Andrew. Men were meant to have muscular hinges, not billowy bottoms.

While Andrew queued at the bar, Leonie phoned me. 'How is it?' she whispered furtively, sounding like she was holed up in a toilet.

I sighed. 'It's terrible, Leonie. His backside is bigger than *me*.'

She screamed with laughter and I smiled grimly as her howls reverberated round the cubicle. Eventually, she drew breath. 'Fran, I don't know which is worse. Mine is six inches shorter than me and he's got two spiky front teeth like fucking Dracula! I'm terrified he's going to lean over and suck blood from my neck!'

'Shit,' I said, aghast. 'I thought he was taller than you?'

'He lied. But here's the best bit: he's got plucked eyebrows.'

And with that we were reduced to helpless laughter, me crammed into the corner of a steamed-up pub in Soho and Leonie crouched in a toilet in Spitalfields. As Andrew wobbled back over to me I pulled myself together, preparing myself for an evening during which I must do everything in my power to avoid talking about bottoms. I resolved to murder Stefania.

Chapter Twenty

Hello, Fran.

I was rather taken by your profile. You write yourself up well with a most enjoyable turn of phrase.

About me. I have a rather pretentious-sounding job but don't be put off; I'm really quite normal underneath it all. I do not spend my life arguing about Nietzsche. I like wine, cake and eggy toast soldiers (although not together). I like my steak rare and tend to over-cook pasta. I downloaded Shakira and Shostakovich this week.

Do I pass muster?

Yours respectfully,

James

'Are you going to tell me what the fuck you were up to with that girl's phone?' Dave said, picking at a scab on his forearm. It was the following Wednesday and we were in the Union Tavern, where I was having an impromptu Wine Wednesday.

'No,' I replied, sipping my wine as quickly as I could. Alex had had at least three 'mystery' phone calls today and I had had to spend a large part of the afternoon with Max Clifford. This glass of not-quite-cold-enough Chilean white was the undisputed highlight of my day.

'Tough tits, Fran. If you don't tell me, I'll go back to Meditation tonight and tell her I saw you reading her phone.'

'DAVE! Where's your loyalty? Can't you accept that I'm heartbroken?'

He blinked, unimpressed. 'That's true. But you're not mad, Fran. Well, you are, but you don't need to be. So come on, spill.'

'I . . . I thought she was really hot and I was trying to find out if she had a boyfriend. I think I'm having feelings for another woman.'

He raised a bushy eyebrow. 'Stop wasting my time. Tell Uncle Dave why you're being such a psychopath.'

I sighed. 'Oh, fuck it. The girl, the one with the brown hair –'

'Oh, aye, I'd give her one.'

'Shut up,' I said, hurt. 'That girl is called Nellie Daniels.'

I watched him try to work it out. His eyes widened. '*Michael's new bird?* Fuckin' HELL, Fran, what the fuck are you playing at? How did you know she'd be there? Jesus!' He downed the rest of his Guinness.

I didn't say anything, just fiddled with my non-Mulberry handbag sheepishly.

It finally dawned on him. 'Oh, fuck, you invited her, didn't you? You mad fucking pervert. Oh, my

God.' He started chuckling, then broke into a full-scale roar of laughter. 'Barman, another drink for this fucked-up wench, please' he called, slapping the bar with one of his big paws.

'No, I can't. I have to go. It's time for Meditation. Which, for the record, Stefania is organizing from now on. I don't even know if Nellie will be there,' I said primly. I wasn't in the mood for being laughed at.

Dave stood up and put his coat on. 'Well, I sure as fuck am coming. I wouldn't miss this for the world!' He threw his satchel over his shoulder and offered me his arm. 'Come on, you bell end. Let's meditate.'

Stefania had forgiven me for lying to her, partly because I'd agreed to arrange another date for this week and partly because Renaissance had asked her to stay on, offering the room to her for twenty-five pounds per night after a whole load of my media bitches had signed up for club membership last week.

But although she had forgiven me, I hadn't forgiven myself. The Nellie-stalking was bad enough, but to lie to Stefania was unforgivable. Had she not spent three weeks putting meals through my cat flap and cleaning my disgusting flat when Michael had demanded this hellish separation? What kind of a repayment was this?

'Vhat the holy hell is zis outfit, Fran?' she asked, as I walked in. 'Vhy are you dressing like a banker zese days? And vhy are you so thin?' She turned on some Zen music.

'Nellie here today?' I asked, with a face of burning shame. Stefania came over and touched my head. 'Come on, my silly child, stop thinking about her. You do not know she is banging viz Michael. She left a message to say she is at running club tonight. She is running ze marathon in April.'

Of course she was running the marathon. Of course.

Mona Carrington's friend, the hot bloke, had turned up in a suit today. I wondered if the suit was part of an effort to show Nellie he was one of her number. As Stefania started the class he glanced disappointedly at the door, as did Dave. Frigging Nellie. Frigging men.

At home I had a lonely gin and tonic with Duke Ellington, who abandoned me to go and kill birds.

Desperate to get out of my own head, I scrolled back to a message Mum had sent a few hours ago while I was in Meditation. It yelled drunkenly, I have heard nothing from Nicholas in 48 hours. Mum. It broke my heart to think that she might be about to be dumped too. But how could Nick possibly continue the affair if he was about to become a big cheese in British politics?

Mum seemed to be permanently drunk now, from what I could tell. And, I realized, if she was going to be dumped I would need to be prepared. I downed my G and T and – heart pounding a little faster – called Nick.

'Er, Frances,' he said hesitantly. It sounded like he was still at work. 'How may I help you?'

I swallowed. 'Hey, Nick. I, erm . . . well, I sort of wondered if we could talk about Mum.'

Nick said nothing but I heard the sound of his leather-soled shoes clicking out into an echoey corridor. 'Frances, are you out of your *mind?* Why are you calling me about this? It is *none* of your business.' He sounded quite terrified.

I held my ground. 'Nick, I'm not calling to make trouble. I'm asking because I'm worried about Mum. If you're about to dump her so you can go off and be a big Tory star I need to know. I need to be prepared.'

I watched Duke Ellington emerge through the cat-flap and march over to my bed, where he took a spot right in the centre.

'I don't know, Fran,' he said eventually. 'I don't know what to do. I must keep my family and the Party safe but you know I care about your mother.'

'You promised you'd always look after her,' I said dully, accepting the inevitability of what would happen next.

'Things were different then. I need you to guarantee me your discretion,' he said shortly.

I nodded sadly. 'Of that you can be very confident. The last thing Mum needs is some sort of press scandal. It would kill her, Nick.'

Someone called his name from further down the corridor.

'Like I said, it's difficult for me. But I have to go, Fran. Please don't call me about this again. I'm doing the best I can.'

'Well, this is all just great!' I said brightly, to an empty room. 'Life is wonderful!'

I turned the TV on and made a cheese sandwich with some rock-hard yellow Cheddar. Dave texted: Just checking you're not thinking of calling Michael.

No I replied, truthfully for once. I was eating a mouldy sandwich. But thanks for your concern.

Good girl.

I couldn't believe that Dave – of *all people* – was getting involved with this crazy Eight Date thing too. What the hell was going on?

Chapter Twenty-one

Sent: Sun, 7 Feb 2010 19:33:50 GMT
From: Fran O'Callaghan [franocal@fmail.com]
To: LEONIE [LeonieBlythe@fmail.com]
Subject: Fuck

See below. Is he being serious? I can't tell. HAVE ALREADY HAD IT WITH THESE CUNTING DATES, LEONIE. PLEASE CAN IT STOP? I want out.

YOU HAVE A NEW MESSAGE FROM JAMES! HERE'S WHAT HE HAD TO SAY!

> Did you use the word 'cunt' that many times just to test me?

> I propose we meet on Thursday night at the Bridge House pub in Little Venice. According to my calculations it is equidistant between our two houses and I do not want there to be any resentment if we do not get on and one party has had to travel further than the other. I should say now that I believe in buying the first drink but after that I prefer an 'even stevens' policy. Please, tell me what time is convenient. Yours, James

I shifted around in the back of the taxi, trying to find

a way of sitting that didn't involve being cut in two by the crotch of my high-waisted trousers. How did women like Nellie manage to dress like this every day? It was like having a cheese slice in your crack.

I looked over at Alex, who was slumped elegantly on the other side of the cab, fiddling with his iPhone. The effort of being near him over the last two weeks had been intense and I was developing facial paralysis from the effort of fixing a smile I didn't feel. And now here he was, gatecrashing my fake shoot at Nellie Daniels's posh Chelsea mums' club.

As I had crept furtively into a taxi on Grays Inn Road earlier on, he had appeared out of nowhere and grabbed me. 'Where are you off to?' he'd asked, his gaunt features framed by his stupid trendy hairstyle. He was wearing a black shirt with a slim grey tie and an extremely expensive military jacket. If he wasn't such a tosser I'd probably have to admit that he was quite attractive.

'I'm shooting a recession story about the Chelsea set and I'm in a hurry. I'll tell you all about it later,' I replied, leaning over to shut the window. But before I could, Alex jumped in. 'I'll come,' he said. 'Hugh gave me the afternoon off because he was so pleased with my Nick Bennett dossier. It's good to get out with a camera every now and then.'

Why had Michael's best friend – of all the people in the world – been sent to torment me? Why couldn't I stalk Nellie in peace? As usual, I felt small and stupid in Alex's presence, like Bridget Jones fannying around with her press releases.

As I stared out of the window it occurred to me that it wasn't just Alex who made me feel this way. I'd often felt like a total moron around Michael too. His Oxford PPE degree and air of *knowing* stuff had scared the living hell out of me so I'd positioned myself, from the outset, in a place of deep intellectual inferiority. It was easier to play the buffoonish simpleton than to try to have a conversation with him about Clever Stuff and end up exposing myself as a buffoonish simpleton.

'God, the *brazenness* of all these bloody countries, pretending to be working *multilaterally* in the Middle East . . . What a fucking *joke*. Doesn't it just *incense* you?' he'd raged one night about a year ago. I'd frozen, a piece of steak and ale pie halfway to my mouth.

'I, er . . . Yes. Incenses me. Does the same to Duke Ellington, doesn't it, Duke Ellington?' Duke Ellington hadn't even bothered to look my way.

Michael was clearly frustrated.

'Go on. Tell me, clever Michael Slater. Tell me what's wrong with these countries.'

And he did, for about three hours. While Michael talked, I ate a steak and ale pie, then ate Michael's steak and ale pie. I had a bath, I shaved my legs and got into bed. And when he'd finished, I got out of bed, padded over to my dressing-table, where he was sitting, and put my arms round him. 'You are intelligent beyond my wildest dreams. I love you,' I said.

His grin had stretched from ear to ear. 'No, I'm not. Don't be silly.'

'Yes, you are, Michael. That's why I fell in love with you. Your amazing brain. Well, I suppose you don't look that bad either.'

He buried his head in my stomach, smiling uncontrollably. 'I'm not clever,' he said delightedly.

I stood back and looked at him. Then I let out a little growl and whispered, 'Take me now, Michael Slater, you intellectual fiend.'

We'd had probably the best sex ever that night. He was on fire.

As I fell asleep, an uneasy thought had flashed across the back of my mind. *Michael was too clever for me. I wasn't good enough.*

Turn the taxi round and come back to work, you fucking basket case, Dave texted.

No.

You'll get yourself sacked Fannybaws, came the response.

I turned my phone off and brushed down my posh trousers. It may well be time for me to purchase a proper handbag, I thought, clutching my Primark holdall.

How was I going to keep this made-up shoot a secret now Alex was here? As we inched down Brompton Road I considered throwing myself out of the taxi by way of escape. But I wanted a bit more crack first. A bit more Nellie. I wanted to know where her soft side was; how well she looked after him; what she liked about him. I wanted to know who was in charge in bed; I wanted to know if she was in love with him yet and I wanted, more than anything else, to know if he was in love with her. It was Monday, five days since last week's Meditation when she'd failed to turn up. And I hadn't been able to take any more of the waiting.

'So, anyway, Alex, this is going to be pretty low-key. I'll shoot the interview on this camera and you can monitor the sound, if you want. Any interference or distortion, give me a nudge and I'll sort it out. OK?'

'Yeah, whatever,' he said languidly, continuing whatever he was up to on his iPhone.

'It was a bit last-minute organizing this, actually, and I've not had a chance to run it past Hugh and everyone, so until I do, could you keep it to yourself?' My face was going red.

Alex peered at me suspiciously. 'That's fine, Fran, but I don't want any trouble.'

'No, no trouble.'

He stared at me for a moment, then said, in deceptively friendly tones, 'Fran, you know you can trust me.'

I thought about all the things he'd said to Michael about my 'jazz hands' ents and culture department and buttoned my mouth. I'd sooner trust Mugabe.

Isabelle Langley-Gardiner had been banging on about the horrors of parenthood for twenty minutes before I realized that I hadn't taken in a single word of what she was saying. I was transfixed by Nellie, who was tapping away at her BlackBerry to our left. She looked outrageous. Slim, groomed and perfect in a black cashmere jumper dress with exquisite tan boots and two small diamond studs in her ears. She was wearing a strong fifties power fragrance, and I imagined Michael inhaling it on her neck. The thought made me long to garrotte her with my tights.

The only mercy was that she and Alex showed no signs of having met. At least Michael wasn't at the meet-my-friends stage with her.

When I snapped back to the present I discovered that Alex had started setting up the camera to interview Isabelle himself. 'Er, Alex, I can take it from here, thanks,' I said.

He stepped away from the tripod. 'Sorry, Fran, I was just trying to help,' he muttered, and arranged himself on to a leather armchair as if he were in a painting. I couldn't deny it, he *was* beautiful in a sort of thin, aristocratic way. 'What kind of set-up are you aiming for?' he asked interestedly.

I bristled and resisted the urge to wallop him with the tripod. 'Simple, businesslike and tight on her face,' I replied briskly. 'We're interested in what Isabelle has to say, not how the room's furnished. We can get some shots of the club later.'

'Not too close to my face!' Isabelle trilled, winking at Alex with one of her mad eyes.

I ignored her. Nellie was now on the phone and had walked off to the end of the vast day room. I couldn't hear what she was saying but I could tell, from the way she wiggled her hips, that she was talking to a man.

I excused myself to go to the toilet so that I could walk past her and eavesdrop. 'Yes, but your mum thinks I'm the best girlfriend you've ever had!' she was squealing.

Dammit! Michael's mother would *never* have said that about me. When we'd driven down to see her the first time I'd had visions of her throwing her arms round me, crying, 'You're the daughter I always wanted,' and inviting me to bake scones with her while Michael and his dad smoked pipes and tinkered with classic sports cars in the garage. Instead she'd merely asked me to take my shoes off because they were muddy and gone back to her newspaper. Why would any mother want their son to be shacked up with a girl who had muddy shoes, crap handbags and an unfortunate reliance on toilet humour? Nellie was every mother's dream daughter-in-law.

Freeing myself briefly from the womb-crushing trousers, I sat on the toilet and thought idly that a little gin and tonic would take the edge off things very nicely.

Back outside, I was in no way surprised to discover the camera running and the interview in progress. Alex, in headphones, one hand on the camera, was chatting away animatedly to Isabelle, who was delighted by his attention. The Mother Teresa of Chelsea, I thought bitterly, as Alex asked a devastatingly brilliant question about something to do with egalitarianism.

'Pushy little bugger.'

I spun round. It was Nellie, murmuring in my ear. Was this a moment of solidarity? An imperceptible nod in Alex's direction confirmed that it was. Was Nellie Daniels trying to be my *friend*? 'I have a colleague just like him. The moment I turn my back he's all over my clients,' she whispered conspiratorially.

I smiled awkwardly. 'I want to punch him in the testicles.'

Nellie folded her arms and leaned against the wall next to me. It was Youth Dew she was wearing, I realized. I bet Michael loved it. She whispered, 'When you were in the toilet he said that he had recently taken over your job. I'm presuming that's not true?'

'The fucker! I just had a long period of sickness and he grabbed my place on the election team,' I said.

'*Galling*, hon.'

I looked nervously at Alex. What was particularly annoying was that I hadn't planned to press record; I was simply going to point the camera at Isabelle and let her think it was on. That way there was no chance of any tapes being found.

Nellie's Youth Dew wafted over me like opium.

Intoxicated, I decided to start digging, 'Us girls

need to get married off quickly before these pushy little shits make us redundant,' I said in a faux-conspiratorial voice.

She smiled. 'I'm working on it, trust me!'

I felt dizzy. 'Go on.'

'Well, it's early days but I'm just *madly* in love! It's one of those awful ones when you know you should slow down but you just can't . . .' She was grinning uncontrollably.

I gave her a lame thumbs-up, feeling as if my stomach was falling out of my privates.

'What about you?' she asked.

'Er, well, actually, yes, there is a man in my life,' I heard myself saying. What the fuck? 'His name's Duke.'

Great, Fran.

'Now that is a *rully* cool name, babe! Good work! And is he as fabulous as his name suggests?'

I thought of Duke Ellington who had last night ambushed my foot as I slept. 'He's quite passionate,' I replied. I scuttled off to Alex to stop the filming.

His face was flushed and happy. 'What a great interview!' gushed Isabelle, her mad eyes even madder. 'You've got a really brilliant colleague here, Frances!' she tinkled. 'He'll be running ITN before the year's out!' I tried not to make eye contact with Alex.

'Ah, not at all. Isabelle's a star!' he said.

Nellie caught my eye and grimaced behind her folder.

I smiled reluctantly, thinking that I *rully* didn't need

an alliance with my ex's new girlfriend. But just for a moment, as I watched Isabelle fling her arms ecstatically around Alex, it felt comforting.

'Thanks so much for doing this, Fran,' Nellie said. She was so controlled, so measured, so powerful. Once more, her long slim hand was extended towards me. I took it, wondering when it had first held Michael's. And I knew I had to see her again. 'I'll call you,' I babbled. 'I'll let you know when this is going out . . . and in the meantime we should talk about your other clients, see if there's any stories there.'

'Yup, sure. Let's have lunch next week to discuss, yuh? Or see you at Meditation on Wednesday?'

'Oh, no,' I replied. 'I can't, I have a date.'

'*Really?*' said Alex, putting the camera bag down.

'*Rully?*' said Nellie, who thought I was seeing someone called Duke.

'Ha-ha! I like to call them dates still!' I trilled at Nellie, and manhandled Alex out of the building. 'Keeps the romance alive!' I yelled through the door.

'So, tell all, Fran,' Alex said, as I struggled to hoist the camera and tripod bags on to my shoulders. 'What's going on?'

'Ah, just doing a bit of casual dating,' I said airily.

Alex stared at me. 'Good for you,' he said eventually.

'Well, I'm sure Michael hasn't been wasting his time.'

Alex gave me an impassive smile and walked off to

the main road. 'I hope I was of use today,' he said, jumping into a taxi. 'Just shout if you need help.'

I crumpled on to the camera bag as he sped off.

So Michael would find out I was dating. I couldn't decide how I felt about that. On the one hand, if this three-month separation was just a sabbatical during which he could knob Nellie Daniels, then it would do no harm for him to know that I was in high demand. But if, as I feared, he had never intended us to get back together after the separation – and was as into Nellie as she said he was – the news of my dating activities would give him an easy excuse to get rid of me completely.

At least he hadn't introduced Nellie to Alex yet.

And if I didn't get these trousers off soon, I'd be rendered infertile.

When I'd taken the camera back to the office I found myself with twenty minutes to spare before my pre-Brit Awards meeting. I opened up a Word document to jot down some brilliant, show-stopping ideas. Staring at the blank page, I pondered how badly Nellie's attempt at solidarity had thrown me. In my haste to write her off as an evil posh bitch, I'd failed to consider the possibility that she might actually be a decent human being.

I miss you so much, Michael Slater, I wrote. *It's driving me completely insane not being able to talk to you. I miss the sound of your voice and the confusion in your eyes when you wake up.*

I even miss our morning-breath snogs. And then: *I just pretended to your girlfriend that I am going out with my cat. You'd have found this funny once.*

When I felt the familiar heat round my eyes I got up from my desk, left the office and jogged round the corner to the Apple Tree for a little gin to take the edge off my sadness.

Chugging it guiltily at the bar I noticed that I was by no means the only smartly dressed Londoner indulging in a stiff one. So *this* was how the high-flyers dealt with days that felt like a load of bum.

I felt pleasingly cool and relaxed as I minced back into the office on my high heels.

That was, until Dave's hand fell on my shoulder as I turned into Grays Inn Road. 'What the fuck are you doing, Fran?' he asked.

I bristled. 'Nothing. Why are you manhandling me?'

Dave sighed. 'Mid-afternoon drinking won't solve anything, you fucking doofus. I should know. Please, let's sit down and sort you out. You mustn't lose it, Franny, you've way too much going for you.' He looked me up and down. 'And why are you dressed like a prostitute?'

'Piss off, Dave.' I walked round him and tried to carry on up Grays Inn Road but he grabbed my arm. 'GET OFF!' I shouted.

'Oh, will you shut up?' he said. 'Franny, you're acting like a fanny. You've got to stop this, kid, because if you don't you'll get completely out of control. First you stalk Michael's new burd and start dressing like a tosser, and now you're making up fake shoots and sneaking off for a fucking drink mid-afternoon. I thought the point of these three months was to sort yourself out and get Michael back. Wake up, Fran. Get a grip.' Dave had a hand on each of my arms and he'd stopped shouting.

'OK,' I said briefly, and shook myself free.

'Fucking Glaswegian cunt,' I muttered under my breath. I had a hot date with a mad philosopher called James on Wednesday; I didn't need Dave.

But he had upset me, I couldn't deny it. As I swaggered back to work and into my Brit Awards meeting, I smarted.

Just as I walked into the building, my phone buzzed in my bag. I bristled, expecting it to be some patronizing admonishment from Dave.

But it wasn't.

It was from a number that my phone didn't recognize but my broken heart most certainly did. Michael. *Michael who must have just found out that I was dating.*

I miss you Franny. So much. There isn't a day when I don't wonder if I've made a massive mistake. Xxxxx

NO. ABSOLUTELY NO NO NO NO NO. DON'T EVEN THINK
ABOUT REPLYING.
Sender: Leonie Mob 07111 996945
Message centre: +447999100100
Sent: 08 Feb 2010 23:58:01

Fannybaws do not text him back. That is an order.
Sender: Dave Mob 07222 444333
Message centre: +447999100100
Sent: 09 Feb 2010 00:05:23

I FUCKING MEAN IT
Sender: Leonie Mob 07111 996945
Message centre: +447999100100
Sent: 09 Feb 2010 00:07:01

Confirm you aren't planning to reply or I'll send Stefania round
Sender: Leonie Mob 07111 996945
Message centre: +447999100100
Sent: 09 Feb 2010 00:09:16

HELLO?
Sender: Dave Mob 07222 444333
Message centre: +447999100100
Sent: 09 Feb 2010 00:20:55

Chapter Twenty-two

Date two: James

. . . OK. *That's Nietzsche covered . . . Who else was there?* I flipped through the pocket guide to philosophy that I'd bought last night. *Oh, that's right, Hegel. Hegel was the dude who thought that human existence was moving towards perfection.* I laughed to myself despairingly, thinking that Hegel couldn't have seen Internet dating looming ahead in his perfect future. I was fast reaching the conclusion that you were as likely to find perfection on the Internet as you were to find buggery classes at the Women's Institute.

I tried to straighten my now frizzy fringe with the aid of a lukewarm finger. There was a heavy rainstorm raging outside so it had decided I was lost somewhere on the equator and had stuck itself to my forehead like . . . well, like blonde pubes. I was not happy.

This was the second time in a fortnight that I'd waited in terror for a random man to arrive. Why the hell was I doing this?

Date Two, James, was a philosophy tutor at King's College London. I still couldn't decide whether or not

I found him attractive. In his picture, he had a honking nose and a very craggy brow, plus he was wearing distinctly academic glasses. I kept imagining him cramped over a 1950s typewriter in a small dark office, knocking out angry poetry and pausing only to howl like a dog at suitably dramatic moments. His appeal was definitely not of the let-me-rip-your-clothes-off-and-sit-on-your-face school but those men were more Leonie's thing and, besides, he had intelligence.

You're an impressive young lady, he'd written a few days ago after I'd spent twenty minutes searching GreatLitaryQuotes.com for something clever to say in response to one of his emails. I must say I'm getting a bit depressed with meeting girls on this site who say they 'read' when actually they're talking about chicklit.

Ha-ha, yes, fucking terrible stuff that chicklit! I'd replied, my eyes running over the shelves and shelves of it that I'd devoured since Michael had left. I could start a mobile chicklit library with that lot. I'd travel round the suburbs of London with a chicklit gypsy caravan and knock out books for 50p to miserable stay-at-home mums who'd read the sex scenes over and over in an attempt to bring back the memory of carnal embrace. I'd wear an ethnic scarf in my hair and keep the money in my knickers.

James was now ten minutes late. I got out my phone to Wikipedia a few more philosophers and heard the sound of high heels approaching me as it loaded up. I ignored it: I wasn't here to meet women.

But then the high heel noise stopped at my table and a male voice said, 'Hi. You must be Frances.'

It was craggy James. I scanned down quickly for a huge bottom – which he didn't have – but I did discover the source of the high-heel noise. James was wearing cowboy boots. Not only was he wearing cowboy boots but he was wearing them tucked into tight black jeans. With a Pink Floyd T-shirt and a leather jacket. Not a nice retro leather jacket or even a vague, sloppy academic's leather jacket: it was a jacket designed to be worn by a man who rode a Harley Davidson with a horned helmet. Oh, and somewhere between the moment when his photo had been taken and now, he'd dyed his hair platinum blond and parted it at the side. In fact, our hairstyles were very similar.

'Oh, hello,' I said brightly, standing up to kiss him on the cheek.

He held out his hand and leaned away from me. 'Er, let's start with a handshake, yeah? I don't understand why people are always kissing each other when they've just met.'

Fuck, he even had sideburns. Bleached ones.

'Oh, sorry!' I said, flustered. 'I know what you mean. It's like people who put kisses at the end of emails and text messages when they've only just met you. Why do people do that?'

James paused a minute. 'Yes, I agree. It betrays a sad need for intimacy, doesn't it.'

Aha! This was my chance to drop a fat one. 'Yah,' I

said, in a scatty academic kind of way. 'But I suppose that in our godless Kierkegaardian universe that sort of need is inevitable.'

James raised an eyebrow. 'That sounds rather like Wikipedia to me, Fran. *Why* do women do this before they go on dates with me? Do you all think I don't know what you're doing? Kierkegaardian universe indeed!' He smiled unkindly. 'What are you drinking?'

I was speechless. I wanted to tell James to shove his drink up his philosophical anus. But I stayed, asking politely for a gin and slimline, because I was weak and a retard.

The pub was full of fringe-theatre types knocking back pints of continental lager before going upstairs to watch a piece of performance art called *Pain, Sex, Birth*. I presumed it was about a day in the life of a vagina and wondered if I should ask James to buy tickets. That, surely, would be enough to end this hellish rendezvous. I checked my phone, just in case by any remote chance Michael had texted me again.

My friends had strictly forbidden me to reply to him and – to my absolute amazement – I'd actually obeyed. Thus far. *Their* reasoning was that I needed to complete their ridiculous challenge before contacting him; *mine* was that the news of my dating had clearly made him jealous, and if jealousy was a tool that I could use, I'd damn well use it. Sitting here waiting for a platinum twat in cowboy boots to return from the bar reminded me all the more astringently of how much I wanted Michael back.

'So why are you Internet dating, then?' James asked, as he arrived back at the table with drinks. He tucked his bizarre blond hair behind his ear and looked as if he didn't care much about my answer.

I thought about his question. What I *wanted* to say was 'I am dating online because the love of my life wants a three-month break from me and I'm stalking his new girlfriend and going on these dates to keep my friends happy and make him jealous because no one else will have me. Will *you* love me, James, will you – *will you*?' but instead I muttered something insipid, like 'Well, I'm single because I'm not going out with someone.'

'I exist so therefore I am,' he said, nodding sagely.

'Yes!' I tittered, despairing. Why was I sitting here with this withered scrotum of a man? I swigged my gin and tried a mini belch in case that persuaded him to abandon the date.

He winced but remained.

'I am a vegetarian, of course,' he announced, an hour or so later.

'Oh, right. I'm not. I eat meat with the blood dribbling down my chin. I love meat so much I have to eat it every few hours.'

Surely that would work.

James merely nodded slowly. 'You don't love yourself very much, do you?'

'James, are you a philosophy lecturer or a crap psychology student?' I asked irritably.

'At last, the real Frances,' he said. 'Your vulnerability is beautiful.'

Right, that's it, I thought grimly. *As soon as this is over, I'm texting Michael back. Enough is enough.*

At the end of the night, by which time I was wasted, I got up to shake his hand again. I felt weak with relief. But as I did, he grabbed my hand, yanked me over to him, hooked an arm round my neck and whispered roughly, 'I have to kiss you. Right now. You are the essence of sex and pain.'

Stunned, I looked on in the third person as I wrapped my arms round this horrid spectacle of a man and snogged his face off.

Chapter Twenty-three

Sent: Sun, 14 Feb 2020 12:12:47
From: Eve O'Callaghan
To: FRAN PRIVATE [franocal@fmail.com]
Subject: VALENTINE'S DAY

Dear Frances,

I wanted to wish you a hAppy St Valentinesd ay. I did try to buy you some chocolate but I'm afraid I got rather sidetracked with some housework., and then I ate it.

Nicholas is spending St Valenintines' day with bloody Luara & I am not happy between you and me Franny not happy. IT was nice to see you yestrerday please do come more often I have plenty of time on my hands at the moment speaking of which I need a manicure & maybe a pedcure.

I have called Nicholas three times today he hasn#t answered maybe you could give me a call and cheer me up./

Mum

Duke Ellington sat watching me beadily as I got ready for my day at the Brits. I opened my wardrobe and kept my eyes firmly to the right, avoiding the empty space where Michael's stuff had been. Clinging to the hope of rousing his jealousy, I'd somehow managed not to reply to his message and had not heard from him again. I presumed that, having got over his little moment of madness, he was now happily ensconced in Nellie's four-poster. The thought made me want to eat doughnuts until I passed away. I missed every bone in his body.

What does one wear to report on a trendy music awards ceremony? I wondered. I tried on a slouchy eighties jumper with my new spray-on jeans and spiky boots, but removed it hurriedly when it took me straight back to my date with James last week. At Warwick Avenue tube station he had snogged me manfully against a wall and then – I trembled to think about it – he had actually begun to bump and grind against me. Thank God my handbag had been stolen just then by a moped-mounted thief.

I went for a short striped dress and biker boots.

Ninety minutes later I was plunged into the madness of Earls Court on the biggest day in its calendar. Eddie-the-entertainment-correspondent's job for the day was to vox-pop bands as they came offstage from their sound checks. And my job was to snag them. Eddie was More Senior Than Me, and since my promotion he'd spent the last two years making sure I knew this.

An achingly cool blonde girl wearing skinny jeans and a man's shirt, eating a Mars bar (just because she could), handed me my pass. 'Don't hassle anyone,' she said, without meeting my eye. 'They're here to rehearse, not to chat. If I get any complaints, you guys are out. OK? Marcel, can you send Robbie Williams to the stage, please?' she barked into her walkie-talkie.

'Robbie Williams?' I asked, amazed. '*Actual* Robbie Williams?'

She raised a haughty eyebrow. 'Yes. Actual Robbie Williams. He's picking up Outstanding Contribution. Do me a favour and leave him alone, yeah?'

It quickly became apparent that I had lost all of my celeb-badgering abilities since coming back to work. I was tongue-tied, shy and completely flat, watching hopelessly as act after act sped past me without so much as acknowledging my existence. Those who weren't coked off their tits were too busy running to the toilet to get coked off their tits or flirting with the blonde bitch to pay any attention to me and my timid approaches.

'FRAN!' Eddie yelled, as Calvin Harris walked past me and disappeared into the green room, from which we were strictly banned. 'We've only got two interviews in the can and they're shit. What's *wrong* with you?' He stormed off for a fag and Sean-the-mediocre-entertainment-cameraman-who-should-have-been-working-at-MTV looked at me with pity.

'I'm shit, aren't I?' I said to him.

'Yep' he said briefly.

I sat down, my head in my hands. I felt stupid, fat and ugly. I didn't have the confidence even to *look* at anyone here, let alone chat to them with a big TV voice. Maybe I should text Michael back.

'Everything OK?' said a rather plummy voice above my head. I looked up and saw a face I had definitely not banked on seeing today. Standing above me, ten different passes hanging round his neck, was the preposterously attractive man from Meditation. 'You look suicidal.' He smiled.

You're not far off, I thought, as I got up. 'I'm meant to be getting musos to vox pop,' I said. 'It's going very badly. I've only got one of JLS and a backing minger.'

Preposterously Attractive Man laughed. He had thick dark hair, the same suntan he'd been sporting two weeks in a row at Meditation and the relaxed demeanour of someone who knows that he's extremely attractive. 'One of them even told me I looked like a lesbian,' I muttered, glaring down at my offending biker boots.

The man laughed. 'Charlie Swift,' he said, grabbing my hand. 'I missed you at Meditation last week.'

'I was on a shit date,' I said, taken aback. Why did he even care who I was? 'My name's Fran. I work for ITN. What about you?'

'I'm a DJ. I do the drive-time shift on Love FM for the pennies but really I'm a club DJ,' he breezed. 'Just got back from a stint in the Caribbean, in fact.'

'Right,' I said. I wasn't sure how to respond so blurted, 'Weather must be nice out there this time of year!'

Charlie touched my arm briefly. 'Actually, I've been wondering who you are –' He stopped as Eddie and Sean stomped back from their fag break. 'Hi, guys,' he said.

'Oh, *hi*, Charlie! How's stuff?' said Eddie, switching on his showbiz voice. Gross.

'Stuff is good. I've just bumped into Fran who I meditate with.' Eddie's eyebrows shot up. 'Right,' Charlie said, getting out his mobile phone. 'Let's fix you up some interviews.' And, within minutes, there was Lily Allen, all tumbling curls and angular fringe. I shook her hand, speechless. Next came Dizzee Rascal. I couldn't believe my eyes. How come I'd been working on the entertainment desk for years and never even got close to people like this? Charlie laughed and put his arm round me. 'Fran's my clever journalist friend,' he told Florence Welch. I nearly passed out with pride and Eddie looked sick with envy. Straight though he was, he looked, from where I was standing, like he wanted to bum Charlie.

Charlie's trump card was a short interview with actual real-life Robbie Williams as he left his sound check. I stared throughout Eddie's interview as if I was in the presence of God.

Under the megawatt beam of Charlie's brilliant

smile I forgot completely that I was a heartbroken thirty-year-old spinster with alcoholic tendencies and a dangerous stalking habit.

I hope you've been keeping busy today, said a text from Leonie. And I hope you're still on for Gin Thursday this week. I'm having withdrawal symptoms!

Fuckloads of gossip, I reported back. Met Robbie Williams. Yes we're on for GT. X

As I handed over my pass to a security man at the exit I felt a hand on my shoulder. 'I hope I'll be seeing you later on, young lady,' said Charlie.

'Me?'

He laughed. 'Yes, you!'

'But I can't . . . I'm not invited and, besides, I look like a dyke,' I said, going red.

He roared with laughter. 'But you've been making me laugh all afternoon. I can't get through tonight without my new favourite lesbian by my side,' he said, as he walked me over to a makeshift reception area. 'And there's plenty of time for you to go home and transform yourself.'

This whole thing was plain weird. Why was he even talking to me? I looked awful and, apart from the odd gaffe about my outfit, I wasn't aware of having said anything remotely interesting.

Charlie seemed to read my mind. 'Of course I want to see you again. You're a breath of fresh air! Most of the people I come across in my work have their heads up their own arses. It was just nice to hang out with someone who didn't give a shit.'

'Was it that obvious?' I said, as we walked out.

'Yes. And it was delightful. Let's get you a wristband for tonight. How many?'

'Well, two, I suppose . . . if it's OK for me to bring a friend,' I said, somewhat dazed.

Charlie was back a minute later with two complicated wristbands and Brit Award passes on shiny silver lanyards. 'See you later, lesbo,' he said casually, kissing my cheek. He lingered there a fraction longer than necessary, then smiled at me. 'Yves Saint Laurent,' he said. 'You smell lovely.'

And off he walked.

As I watched his back retreat into Earls Court my phone started ringing. 'Er, how do you fancy going to the Brit Awards tonight?' I asked Leonie.

After a rather crazed leg-shaving session and a tumultuous throwing on and off of a million outfits, I emerged into Camden Road in one of my new micro tunic dresses with massive cage heels and far too much makeup. I got into the taxi that contained a sleek, vintage-dressed, red-lipsticked Leonie. She stared at me in some surprise. 'Fran, you've turned into a transvestite. Are you all right?'

'Thanks, Leonie. Yes, I'm fine. Not much going on for me at the moment – losing my boyfriend, getting shoved out of a job by his best mate . . . Oh, and did I mention that my self-confidence is at an all-time low and you've just made it worse? Yes, all things considered, I'm great.'

'Oh, Fran, stop it. Tonight will be fine. If you can't cope, we'll go home. Or, at least, I'll put you in a taxi. I'm not missing this for the world.' She squeezed my hand.

I wanted to jump on her and hug her tightly but her belted red dress was spread carefully across the taxi seat and I didn't dare. Instead I smiled at her and squeezed back. 'How's it going with Alex, anyway?' she asked.

I rolled my eyes. 'Hideous. He keeps going off to have secret phone calls, blatantly with Michael. It's killing me.'

Leonie winced. 'So you currently hate him, correct?'

'Correct. He's always bloody sniffing round my work offering to "help",' I said, shuddering. Leonie just shook her head.

Charlie spotted me almost as soon as I arrived. 'Looking good, little lesbian.' He chuckled. 'Let's do the red carpet together, yah?' I shivered as he put his hand on the small of my back and walked me past the photographers. They shouted his name and papped crazily.

'Are you actually famous, then?' I asked, turning my back on them.

'Turn round, you fool!' He laughed. 'Yes, reasonably.'

I kept my back turned.

'Fran, have you invited me here as your wingman?' Leonie asked, staring suspiciously at Charlie when he went to sign a housewife's autograph book.

'Wingman? Leonie, I've just lost my boyfriend! I've got as much interest in pulling as I have in fucking crochet.'

'Liar,' she whispered.

I wasn't having this. 'Do you honestly think I give a shit about him or any other man in the world? Because, let me tell you, I don't. He's absolutely nothing to me.' My whisper had got a little loud.

'Charming,' said Charlie, behind me. 'Why don't you two make friends and meet me down the front?' he said, gliding off to the flash of camera bulbs.

'Well done, Fran,' Leonie said tightly.

She and I stood glowering at each other like we had done as small children. She'd always won. 'Come on,' I said grudgingly. 'I'm sorry I shouted. But I didn't invite you here as my wingman. I'm not interested in Charlie and I wanted you to come so we could have fun. OK?'

'You're a cock, Fran.' She smiled, following me into the main hall.

It was an incredible sight. Acres of candlelit tables stretched away in front of us, all containing faces that we'd spent years perving at in magazines and on the TV. Music boomed fatly over the chink of champagne glasses and the buzz of excitable conversation.

Slightly overwhelmed, I grabbed Leonie's arm and hung on to her as she wove minxily through the tables to the front, where Charlie was waiting. He'd got us into a small roped-off bit just to the side of the stage. 'How did you *do* this?' I asked, thrilled.

'My station is this year's main sponsor,' he shouted. 'And I'm the face of the station. Tonight, Frances, your wish is my command!'

The ceremony passed in an increasingly drunken blur. Leonie and I shamed ourselves quite comprehensively by screaming our heads off, dancing like apes and reaching out to try to grab Robbie Williams like the teenagers at the front of the audience. Charlie, miraculously unfazed by our regression, stood very close to me all evening. He whispered gossip into my ear about the acts and presenters and, although I tried not to, I couldn't help enjoying it.

When the cameras stopped rolling and Charlie shoved us into a taxi to the after-party in Knightsbridge, we were impressively drunk. There were six of us in a five-man taxi and Charlie put me on his knee. I beamed like a toddler until I realized that I was thinking rather rude, un-toddler-like thoughts about sitting on his lap. Of course, I regarded myself as being far too mad and tragic to be *considering* other men – but this was *fun*. Maybe some paparazzo would picture us and Michael would see it and beg me to come back . . .

Leonie watched disapprovingly and I wondered if

she was jealous. Charlie and his patent dirtiness were, after all, right up her street.

At the party I pushed the thought of Michael out of my head and concentrated on staring at the unhappy-but-pretending-not-to-be musos around me. It really was very nice and comforting to be in the company of people who were as mad as I was, I thought, as I watched a Best International Female contender honking up into a champagne bucket. But after half an hour I was bored: they were ignoring me as studiously now as they had this morning *and* Robbie Williams hadn't shown up. I gave in and turned my attention to Charlie. His hand had been resting lightly on my waist since we'd arrived. I could feel his breath on my neck as he talked and – after several large gin and tonics – I was really rather enjoying it.

Trying to look sexy, I tried a little experimental move on the periphery of the dance-floor, which involved some reasonably unsubtle breast-jiggling in Charlie's direction. After watching me for a few minutes he moved over and, really quite matter-of-factly, pressed himself tightly against me. Much encouraged, I expanded the dance move a little more. *Why not?* I thought drunkenly. *A hearty rogering would do me the power of good right now!* Clearly of the same opinion, Charlie suddenly leaned even closer and slid his tongue slowly down my ear, bringing about an almighty stirring in my knicker region. Smiling, I turned round and, before I had a chance even to look at his face, he kissed me hard, pressing his hands into the small of my back. Bolts of desire shot through me, surprising me.

'FRAN!' It was Leonie in my other ear, grabbing my shoulder.

I shot her an I'm-otherwise-engaged face and turned back to Charlie. She ignored me and dragged me off to dance with her. 'Leonie, I was busy!' I shouted, but she put her hand over my mouth and wagged her finger in my face.

'Too early! He's dirt! You'll get hurt!' She started dancing with a tiny bloke from JLS.

I minced around for a minute or two, then staggered off to the loo.

When I got back, Leonie had ditched the JLS hobbit and was now dancing with Charlie. I watched suspiciously, unsure how much I liked this. She looked pretty damn hot in that red dress.

'Can I talk to you outside?' I shouted in her ear.

'What's up, Franny?' she asked, as we emerged into the freezing air. The paparazzi jerked up but then calmed down, realizing we were Insignificant People.

'Oh, just wondering if you've been shagging anyone recently,' I improvised.

'Eh? No, I haven't. Why?'

That didn't sound too good. Was Charlie next on her list?

'Well, it's unlike you not to be shagging anyone, that's all . . . I was a bit worried.'

Leonie put her hands on her hips. 'Are you calling me a slag, Fran?'

I put my hands on *my* hips, looking somewhat less commanding. 'Are you flirting with Charlie?' I teetered slightly on my heels.

'What the fuck? You think I'm flirting with *Charlie?* Are you out of your mind?'

'No, I'm not. You were dancing with him. You haven't had a fling in at least three weeks. How do I know you're not after him?' I knew I was being a bell end but held my ground.

'Oh, my God,' she said slowly. 'You do think I'm a slag, don't you?' She was disgusted and hurt.

No, I thought. 'Yes,' I said. 'Yes, maybe I do.'

What the fuck was I saying?

Leonie inhaled slowly and stood up to her full height, which in heels was a fairly terrifying six feet. 'Do you know what, Fran?' she said, suddenly monotone and eerily still. 'I've spent weeks looking after you. Weeks. I've forked out a small fortune keeping you alive and not once have you said, "Thank you", or "Sorry", or even fucking "How are you?" Not once have you offered to pay me back, even though you earn three times more than me. Fran, I didn't try to get off with your fucking cheesy love interest tonight, but I damn well should have done, you ungrateful wanker.'

And with that she stomped off to a taxi, opened the door and shot off into the night. I watched it disappear up Knightsbridge and then fell off the pavement, much to the delight of the assembled paparazzi.

Chapter Twenty-Four

HEY!!! Thanks for replying! God you remind me soooooo much of my sister. Is that weird (legal)? Anyway totally hear you on Chelsea, it makes me want to wear a tracksuit with white socks and go and vandalize a car. I saw a kid in his teens wearing a fucking cravat there last week!!! WTF!!! Give me some cheap cava in Bar Soho anyway babe! So are we going out or what? Let's go DANCING! Toni x

For a few seconds when I woke up, I didn't remember the night before. But an angry miaow from the bottom of the bed reminded me. Duke Ellington was sitting staring at one of my shoes, which he had been forced to share the bed with. He looked comically outraged; a grey spiky cat next to a gold spiky heel.

I scanned back through the evening.

Going out looking like a prostitute: check.

Getting off with a well-known DJ in public: check.

Brawling publicly with best friend over said DJ: check.

Being photographed falling off kerb after doing all of the above: check.

On paper, I had to admit, it didn't look good.

I got out of bed when Duke Ellington started trying to ambush my shoe. 'You're a scrote,' I croaked, crashing into the door frame on my way to the kitchen. I was still a bit squiffy. 'How am I going to get to work?' I asked him. He walked over to his empty food bowl and miaowed at the top of his lungs.

Some nookie with Charlie would have helped no end, I thought sadly, as I leaned against the wall of my wet room, hot water streaming over my head and down my face. Nellie Daniels would *definitely* have sex with someone like Charlie. In fact, she probably already had.

I, on the other hand, had staggered off in search of a kebab and in so doing had somehow deserted both Charlie and my coat.

I put on some old jeans and a faded jersey top. Fuck fashion. Fuck glam Fran. She was dead to me.

As I tried to force down a slice of toast, my phone beeped. Are you alive? I have your coat and I'm only returning it if you agree to go on a date with me. Cx

I tried not to smile, but I couldn't help it. Glam Fran was back! She was going to get a rogering from Charlie Swift! I tore off my bargain-bin outfit and crammed myself into a tight pencil skirt and heels.

OK. But only for the purposes of getting my coat back, you understand . . . I did a little squeak and karate-chopped the air.

Charlie replied straight away: Good. Hakkasan, Saturday night then. Cx

What the hell? He was very, very pretty. It was 17 February, fifty-six days since Michael had dumped me, and if I played my cards right I'd be waking up next to another man – who was very easy on the eye – by day sixty. *Ha! Put that in your pipe and smoke it, Michael!*

But I didn't really believe myself. I missed him more than ever.

'I'm a cock. I'm a tyrant, a fannyface, a fool, a knobber and a dullard,' I informed Leonie. 'Please, please, *please* forgive me.' I handed her a gin and tonic.

She regarded me sceptically. 'Are you drunk?'

'No! I've only just got here!'

'You look drunk.'

Actually, I was. I'd had a horrid day missing Michael – in spite of the cheeky messages I'd been getting from Charlie since yesterday morning – so it had seemed perfectly reasonable that I should finish work early and start Gin Thursday at five o'clock.

'Nope. Sober as a judge,' I lied. 'Anyway, Leonie, the point is that I'm truly sorry. I behaved like a stinking bastard and I can't apologize enough. You've done so much for me, not just in the last few months but in life. I am really, truly sorry.'

She looked at me a few more seconds and then, eventually, her face softened into a smile. 'OK. Well, I'm sorry for bringing money into it. It was vulgar of me –'

'No, it wasn't. It was fair enough. Please, take this,' I said, trying to shove a couple of twenties into her pocket.

'Fran! Don't be a dick! No *way*,' she said decisively, pushing the money back towards me. 'I'm not your frigging stripper!'

'Leonie, please take it. You were quite right – you earn hardly anything and I took advantage. I just want to pay you back. If you feel uncomfortable taking it then you can show me your tits so there's a proper trade. OK?'

Leonie coloured. 'Can we not talk about my financial situation?' she said stiffly. 'I'm working on it. I don't need handouts.'

How had I fucked up *again*? I really was on a roll. 'Oh, God, I'm sorry. For everything. I don't care how much you earn, I'm sorry to embarrass you, I'm sorry about Tuesday night – I'm sorry I'm sorry I'm sorry.' I was close to tears.

Leonie put her hand on my arm and lowered her voice. 'Hey. It's OK. Forget about Tuesday night. We were both drunk. And Stefania's just arrived. She looks like she's about to eat you.'

She wasn't wrong. 'FRANCES!' she yelled, as if I was on the other side of the Thames rather than on the other side of a bar stool. She was looking really quite foxy, it had to be said, in a pair of slinky jeans and an uncharacteristically restrained stripy top.

'Hi, Stefania. Before you start on me, I've got

another date lined up.' Stefania's thin little face broke into a dazzling smile. 'VAY TO GO!' she shouted, high-fiving me and slapping my bottom at the same time.

I collapsed into laughter. 'What the fuck was that? In this country we slap bums or hands – not both!'

Stefania grinned. 'I am just pleased zat you are doing vhat I say. Vhere is Dave?'

Once Dave had arrived and we were all sitting round the table, Stefania called for silence by hitting the side of her glass with the fork from my basket of wedges. The glass cracked: she put it to one side and carried on talking without turning a hair. 'Silence! It is time for a formal update from Frances O'Callaghan about her Eight Date Deal!'

Leonie whooped and clapped and Dave drummed the table.

'Well, you all know about date one,' I started.

'Massive bottom like big pillow,' Stefania hissed, just in case anyone hadn't got that the first time round.

'Date two was, well, pretty bad, too. He was insane, he wouldn't let me kiss him hello but then he face-raped me all the way back to the tube.'

Dave sniggered.

'Did he fondle your lady bits?' Leonie asked interestedly.

'He was seconds away from it. But I got robbed, remember? I've never been so grateful for the presence of a thief.'

'So. Who is ze third date?' Stefania asked.

I smiled coyly. 'Well, I actually got a date in the real world.'

Leonie was surprised. 'Charlie?'

I nodded.

'Who's Charlie?' Dave asked. He hadn't shaved in weeks.

'Charlie is a DJ. I met him on Tuesday at the Brits,' I replied.

Dave was appalled. 'Charlie Swift? The fuckwit?'

'Er, I'm not sure. Charlie who goes to Meditation.'

Stefania, too, blanched. 'Vow . . .' she said uncertainly.

I looked at them all. 'What's wrong?'

They looked at each other; at the floor.

Dave spoke first. 'He's dirtier than an alky's carpet, Fran. Don't go there, you'll get fanny warts.'

Leonie smirked behind her hand. 'To be honest, Fran, I'd agree. Even *I* wouldn't touch him.'

I turned to Stefania. 'And what's your objection?'

'Vell . . . I find him to be sexual in ze classes. He is always talking to ze ladies . . . I feel zat he lives his life guided by his penis,' she said.

'Anyone else?' I asked, bitterly disappointed. Charlie was meant to be the answer to my problems!

Then, just to top things off, Alex arrived at our table. 'Hi, guys,' he said languidly. 'Good to see Gin Thursday's still alive. Mind if I join you? For old time's sake,' he added, glancing at me.

'Of course not. The more the merrier,' I said tightly, and got up to go to the bar.

I sat on a stool and worked myself up into a beastly funk, not even bothering to pretend I was queuing for a drink. 'Charlie's bad news, I promise,' Dave said, as he came to sit down with me. 'If I were you I'd stick to men from the Internet.'

'But they grind their crotches into mine at Warwick Avenue tube station!' I cried, dismayed. 'They have bottoms as large as Australia! What's the point?'

Dave ordered another pint. 'How are you feeling about Michael?'

'How do you think? Terrible. I miss him so much it hurts. And, no, I didn't reply to his message. Can I have another G and T?'

Dave didn't look happy but he ordered one anyway.

I took a long, grateful glug as Stefania came sidling up. 'Vell? Are you going on a date viz Charlie?'

I nodded and nicked one of Dave's pistachio nuts. 'Yes. But if he's as bad as you say then I'll use a condom. OK?'

Stefania grimaced. 'No, Frances, do not make ze sex viz zis man. I do not like him at all.'

Dave nodded. 'Seconded. Don't do it, Fannybaws,' he said quietly. 'Stick to the nice chaps from online, OK?'

I sighed. 'Guys. This Eight Date thing is stupid and it hasn't changed anything. I want Michael back and, quite frankly, the longer you guilt-trip me into playing this stupid game, the more he'll be getting into Nellie and the more impossible it'll be for me to get him back.'

Stefania thumped my arm. 'Zis is *not* a silly game,' she said fiercely. 'Zis is a plan for your recovery! Ve have it all vorked out!'

I stared sullenly at her and her face fell. 'Don't let me down, Frances,' she said less fiercely.

I realized, with a little pang of guilt, that I was going to have to stick at it a little longer. Stefania had never asked anything of me before. 'OK, OK,' I said. 'I'll sort out another date.'

'Vhen?'

'Christ alive! There's some bloke called Toni who's been emailing me, I'll see if I can get a date out of him this weekend. OK? He spells his name T-O-N-I.'

Dave raised a bushy eyebrow as he washed back his Guinness. 'Wow.'

When I swayed out of the toilets an hour or so later, Dave was deep in conversation with a wildly gesticulating Stefania. And Leonie was in what seemed suspiciously like a flirty conversation with Alex. I stopped and looked at them just as Leonie did her head-thrown-back laugh and touched his arm. Oh, God, no. *Why?* Of all the men in London, why would she flirt with Alex?

Slightly repulsed, I went over to Stefania and Dave,

who stopped talking abruptly. 'What?' I said. They said nothing.

Dave looked over at Leonie and Alex.

'I sink zey vant to make ze sex,' Stefania hissed in my ear.

'Oh, gross! Vombags, Stefania! Take that back!'

She shook her head. 'Mark my vords. She vill seduce him no problem.'

I felt sick. I didn't know if it was the vast quantity of gin that I'd drunk, or the sight of Leonie flirting with Alex, but I realized I needed to get home fast.

As I ushered my weary corpse into a cab, my phone started ringing. I felt a fleeting sense of dread, knowing there was only one person it could be at this time of night: Drink Voice Mum. She was calling me more and more these days, making less and less sense. In fact I couldn't remember the last time I'd spoken to her when she was sober.

Just for a moment, I let myself wallow in overwhelming resentment. Why? Why was it *my* job to deal with this?

Because you are all she has, beyond that shitbag Nick Bennett, I reminded myself. Sighing, I got my phone out of my bag.

It was Michael.

Michael was calling me.

I froze. A million different feelings exploded in my

brain – joy, fear, amazement, relief, love – but before I was able to move again, my phone went dead.

I stared at it, stomach churning. Had that just happened?

What should I do? Call back? What the flaming Jesus would I *say*? 'Hiya! How are you? Long time no speak?' Oh, shit. Leonie. I needed to speak to Leonie.

With shaking hands I fumbled through my address book to 'L' but as I did so a message arrived. I took a deep breath, braced myself, and opened it. And then I started to smile.

Still love you. Still miss you. Still waiting impatiently for our 90 days to end. 33 days and counting. Mxxxxx

Chapter Twenty-five

Hi Fran, I wrote to you last week but you didn't reply. Were you
taught any manners as a child?? I ask you to PLEASE REPLY by
the end of the week. I am going on holiday and need to know
whether or not we will be going out on my return. Many
thanks. All the best, Perry

On the morning of my date with Charlie I got up early
with the aim of cooking bacon and eggs and doing
something about my bikini line, which bore more relation to a tropical rainforest than it did a muff. Duke
Ellington sat as close to the frying pan as was possible
without actually being fried himself. 'What are you up
to today, my little prince?' I asked him. He closed his
eyes. 'Got any hot dates lined up for tonight?'

He stared meaningfully at my bacon.

'Because I have.'

He yawned.

'Oh, Duke Ellington, come *on*. Don't be horrible
to me. Look how strong I'm being, ignoring Michael
and going on a date with Charlie Swift!'

Nothing.

I flipped my bacon over, smiling. Duke Ellington was significantly wiser than most human beings and probably knew that the only reason I had resisted the overwhelming urge to reply was that (a) my friends had threatened never to talk to me again if I did and (b) I was really quite convinced that he was in a state of agonizing jealousy now he knew I was dating. If – in spite of his affair with The Daniels – he was tortured at the thought of me dating then maybe it was just sex with Nellie and love with Fran. Maybe he just needed to go out and sow some final oats before settling down. Maybe I had a lot more control over this situation than I thought.

I turned my egg over for two seconds, then slid it clumsily on to a plate, not entirely convinced. The effort of not replying had nearly killed me.

'Oi! Stand back,' I said to Duke Ellington, who was preparing to eat my breakfast. I was going to need my strength tonight.

I was a bit surprised, as I logged on a little bit later to organize a date with Toni the gay, to find my dating site at the top of my browsing history. As far as I was aware I hadn't logged on for two days. Perhaps I *was* drinking too much. Had I been having virtual sex with strange men after too many gin and tonics at home?

I scanned through my inbox. The usual pondlife lurked slimily: bragging, lies, desperation and 'off-the-cuff wit' that whiffed of having been written and rewritten over five hours. A man calling me Sarah. Another man whose picture was of him naked apart from a plastic bowler over his knob.

I sighed as I clicked on the last.

Freddy was described by his friends as 'handsome, tall and amazing'. I was quite impressed by his photo. It was a classic black-and-white shot; he looked distinguished and handsome, gazing off down a street in a casual sort of manner. His eyes seemed a little bit vulnerable but his stance suitably confident.

I opened his message.

Hi Fran

My name is Freddy and I am not a wanker. According to my friends I am a rock. How I feel about that I'm not sure.

What I am sure about though is that your profile is lovely. Not just the rather alternative write-up that your friend has given you but the funny self-deprecating write-up that you gave yourself. Is your cat really that bad or were you just trying to make your life sound a bit more interesting? Because, seriously, if he IS that evil he sounds like a legend. Purry cushion cats are shit.

I was going to write you a sharp witty email full of devastating one-liners like your own profile but I suspect you probably want something a bit nicer than that, in spite of the way you've described yourself. So for now I will just ask if you could explain what you mean when you say that your friends have taken an unhealthy interest in your

online dating exploits. Does this mean they will be there if
I manage to snag a date with you?
Have a nice Saturday.

Freddy

I sat back, smiling. What a nice email! I scanned
Freddy's profile again and couldn't find anything that
I objected violently to. It appeared that he was able
to cook and (bizarrely) sew and he didn't smoke. On
their final up-sum his friends had said that he was
'basically the best person in the universe'.

Perfect, I thought, hitting reply. Freddy the Rock. I
liked it.

'I smell cooking peeg. Is it organic?' Stefania yelled,
bursting into my kitchen in a pair of Bermuda shorts
and a floral vest I'd given her last summer.

'Morning, Stefania. I'm fine, thank you. How are
you?'

She folded her arms across her chest, unimpressed.
'Vell?'

'No,' I said firmly. 'No, it was not. I can't afford to
buy organic *everything,* Stefania. Sometimes a girl just
wants some dirty bacon and eggs, OK?'

'You are a peeg,' she muttered crossly, stroking
Duke Ellington.

I got up and took my plate to the sink. Grease was
congealing on it, mingled with ketchup and mustard.
She had a point. 'Fine. I'm a pig. But I enjoy eating
pig too. Sorry.'

She tried not to laugh but let out a little Slavic snort before she was able to control herself. 'Oh, Frances. I despair of you.'

'Thank you. Is that all you came over to tell me?' I asked, squirting washing-up liquid all over the taps by mistake.

'No. I came to tell you not to go on zis date tonight. I do not like ze penis man. Is zere no one else you can go on a date vith?'

I thought of Freddy and smiled a bit. 'Get off my back. I'm doing what I'm told. The next date will be soon.'

'OK, Frances, I make a deal viz you. You go on the date tonight but you do not make ze sex viz Penis Man.'

I started to laugh. 'And what's your side of the deal?'

'I do not steal Duke Ellington and take him to live in my shed.'

'Stefania, you're welcome to take Duke Ellington to live in your shed. He's started sitting on my pillow staring evilly at me when I'm sleeping. I keep waking up to these demonic yellow eyes – it's like being in a nightmare.' Stefania shrieked with laughter and patted Duke Ellington on the head. Then she stared accusingly at me again. 'Fine. OK. I won't sleep with him. But you can't stop me going on a date.'

'You vill not be able to stop yourself once you have started ze drinking,' Stefania pointed out.

I reddened. She was probably right. Charlie had been sending me fairly dirty messages since Tuesday. Much to my surprise, he had somehow hoicked me out of my pit of sexual stagnation and into a boiling cauldron of quite overwhelming horn.

'True,' I said slowly. 'I tell you what. I've got a muff like a rainforest right now. How's about I leave it on and then there's no *way* I'll be able to let him near me?'

Stefania was clearly unconvinced.

'No, seriously, Stefania!' I whipped up my T-shirt to reveal my knickers and the heavy forestation that spread out in all directions.

'Vow,' she said, shocked. 'OK. Zat vill be enough. Just be careful, Frances. I am convinced there are better men out zere for you. Now, I have been vondering how your mozzer is.'

An unpleasant feeling of heaviness settled over me. I sat down. 'She's the same as ever. No, that's not true. Worse. She really seems to be losing it, Stefania. I think Ni–' I broke off, remembering that not even Stefania knew about Mum and Nick. Now, more than ever, I had to keep her safe. Nick was in the press more and more every day. If Mum ended up there too, it would finish her off.

What I'd *wanted* to say to Stefania was that I was quite sure Mum knew she was about to get dumped. It killed me, the thought of her sitting in her house waiting for the phone to ring. I imagined her, inert on one of her damask sofas with her hands in her lap, gin lined up neatly on the coffee-table next to the phone. Would his next call be an invitation to dinner or an announcement that he was ending a relationship that had lasted seventeen years? I couldn't imagine how wretched she must feel.

Stefania was watching me as if she could see everything that was happening in my mind. 'Vhy does she drink, Frances?' she asked quietly.

Sadness overwhelmed me. 'I don't know. I really, truly don't know.'

Without warning, Stefania hopped over to the sofa and hugged me. 'She must get help,' she said. 'You can help her do zat. And, Frances, please do not go ze same vay yourself.'

I smiled and shook my head. 'I don't want to. Trust me, that's not what I want, Stefania.'

She kissed me on the cheek, took a clump of my hair briefly in her hand and left. I watched her crossing the yard, a mad pixie in Bermuda shorts. Then I went to the phone, picked it up and hit speed dial two.

'Sunny Side Up?' a familiar voice said.

'Hi, Gloria. It's Fran. Is Dad there?' I tried to remove some of the dust on my phone cradle with my sleeve, suddenly nervous.

'Oh, all right, darling. How you doing? TREVOR? TREVOR! IT'S FRAN, BABE.'

I heard the clatter of crockery and Dad chuckling. 'Oh, wonderful,' he said, as he approached the phone.

I imagined him drying his hands on the Fulham FC tea-towel he always kept thrown over his left shoulder.

'Franny! Hello, darling! What a lovely surprise!'

I curled up on the sofa, instantly comforted. Talking to Dad *always* made me feel better. 'Hey, Dad . . . how are you?' I got out my wallet and stared at the picture of Dad and Mum on the beach while he told me about his plans to open a branch of Sunny Side Up in Barcelona and the new contract they had with an artisan baker who'd just arrived in Marbella. He sounded quite beside himself with excitement. I felt warm and fuzzy, listening to his ramblings, and wished desperately that I had just eaten one of Dad's trendy fry-ups overlooking a lovely beach in the winter sun, rather than one of my own slimy efforts, served with a view of empty flat and a side of damp grey sky.

'Anyway, to what do we owe this unexpected pleasure?' he asked eventually.

I swallowed, a little nervous again. 'Actually, Dad, I wanted to talk to you about Mum.'

There was a silence, then I heard Dad shut the door of the office. 'Go on, love. Is everything OK?'

Tears gathered in my eyes. 'No, Dad, it's not. Nick's part of the Tory campaign team and he's in the press all the time. He pretty much told me he's going to dump her. She's drinking more than ever. It's . . .' My chest heaved with the effort of not crying. 'It's pretty much all day long now.'

Dad sucked in his breath. 'Oh, Franny love,' he said. 'Would you like me to come over?'

'No, I don't think there's anything you can do . . . I just . . . wanted to know, did you ever try to persuade her to get help? Like a clinic or something? Alcoholics Anonymous? Can the NHS help? I just can't let her go on like this.'

Dad sighed. 'Franny, I know it's hard but it's out of your hands. The only person who can get help for your mother is your mother. I tried, Fran, God knows I tried. But until she accepts she's got a problem she ain't going anywhere.'

'But that's ridiculous. There must be *something* we can do. I can't bear it, Dad!'

I heard another sigh.

'I went to Alcoholics Anonymous in Sutton one night, Fran, not long before I, er, started my relationship with Gloria. I didn't know what else to do. But they told me she'd only get help when she was ready.'

'Yeah. I called their head office and they said pretty much the same thing. But, Dad, I can't just wait and watch her kill herself,' I said. 'I think I should talk to her about it again.'

'Again?' Dad sounded surprised.

'Yes. I've tried three times to bring it up. Each time it went really badly.'

Dad's chair creaked. 'Hmm,' he said. 'When I told her about the AA group she threw a marrow at me.'

I smiled briefly, and felt Dad do the same. 'Why did she start drinking?' I asked eventually.

'TREVOR! TEN COVERS!' Gloria yelled, through the office door.

'Oh, Fran, I'm going to have to go. I'm so sorry. Tell you what, I'll drop you a line after the brunch rush finishes, OK?'

'OK. Thanks, Dad.'

'Love you, Franny.'

I signed off with a sort of grunt: I was choked with sadness. I looked at Duke Ellington. 'Fancy going back to bed?' I asked him. He left through the cat flap without a glance in my direction.

From: Trevor O'Callaghan [Trevor.Ocallaghan@sunnysideup.es]
To: Frances O'Callaghan [Franocal@Fmail.com]
Sent: 19 February 2010 15:04
Subject: Eve

Hello Franny! Was wonderful to hear from you my little girl!

Well it sounds a bit awful over there. I can get on a plane tomorrow if you want some moral support. Must be tough doing this without Michael. The little shit. I know you want to get back together with him Fran but if I saw him now I'd land him one on the nose.

Anyway love I've been racking my brains all through lunch trying to work out what to tell you. I wish I knew why Eve started drinking, darling. They told me at AA that there doesn't need to be a big event. Apparently most people just have it in them and eventually it gets out of control. I found that hard to believe but the longer it goes on the more I think they must be right.

It seemed to start when she was made redundant but I do believe now it was going to happen anyway. Her mother drank really heavily, and her grandmother. None of them ever accepted they had a problem. I just pray that Eve does, because she needed help seventeen years ago so I can only imagine how she is now. And if Nick Bennett is going to dump her for his Tory career then she must be worse than ever.

Sorry darling, I'm not sure what else to say. Are you sure you don't want me to come over?

Hugs,
Dad

Chapter Twenty-six

Date three: Charlie

I was more than halfway down my second gigantic cocktail when the waitress finally showed us over to our table. Hakkasan was throbbing; absurdly chic girls sipped cocktails at the bar with men who looked like they'd been made in a Los Angeles factory, while small, efficient waiters shimmied between the densely packed tables wielding massive trays of steaming dim sum. I'd been here before I met Michael and had liked it but tonight, dressed immaculately and sitting across the table from a man who made Michelangelo's *David* look like a dog's bottom, I really got it.

So far, so good. He'd turned up at my flat to pick me up like a proper gentleman and had sat at my kitchen table, chatting easily while I'd run around my room with hairspray and Marks & Spencer tights. Then a posh taxi had arrived, swished us silently into town, and Charlie had ordered exquisite cocktails. This was a Good Date.

When we sat down at the table, Charlie ordered wine without consulting me and then, while I tried to decide whether I found this sexy or annoying, he leaned over and kissed me full on the mouth.

Definitely not annoying. Sexy.

He held me there for a minute, staring at me at point-blank range. Then he let me go and we leaned back into our seats, me flushed, him infuriatingly casual.

'Well, then. Good evening, Mr Swift,' I murmured, in as alluring a voice as I could muster. It was no good: I fancied him desperately. Everyone did. Even the bloody waitress was ignoring me and fawning over Charlie.

'Hello to you, too, young lady,' he said, leaning in and twirling a bit of my hair between his finger and thumb. 'I've been thinking about you a lot this week. Do you have any idea how attractive you are?'

'Well, I'm better than Roseanne Barr, I suppose,' was the best I could do.

Charlie roared with laughter and I noticed two girls, dressed like high-class prostitutes, staring at him and whispering.

I leaned back and poked my breasts out in case it helped. Charlie was clearly in demand.

'I don't know,' he said. 'I've always had a thing for Roseanne. The thought of screwing a larger lady has always given me a bit of a hard-on.'

Ah. Less good. Did he favour the larger lady? (Was that why he was out with me?)

'Have you listened to my radio show at all this week?' he asked.

'No,' I lied.

'Shame. I dedicated something to you.'

'Oh, my God! What?' (It had been 'Can't Get You Out Of My Head' by Kylie. Bit weird, but nice.)

'Well, you'll never know now, Fran. Tell me, how long before I get to take your clothes off?'

I blushed. 'I'm not sure. It depends how well you behave yourself, Charlie Swift.'

'Really? OK, well, how about this for now?' He leaned in. 'How's about I put my hand inside your knickers – purple lace, I noticed, very nice – and then make you come?'

I nearly came, handsfree.

'CHARLIE!' The first set of dim sum arrived. 'JESUS!'

'No relation. Sorry.'

I was bright red as I picked up my chopsticks. And then, maybe because I'd now drunk two yards of cocktail, I said, 'Actually, they're blue lace. And if I push my chair in just a little bit further you'll be able to do just that.'

He groaned quietly, and muttered, 'Please, don't do that to me.'

'Your fault,' I said, with affected nonchalance, picking up a steaming prawn parcel expertly. Less expertly, I dropped it just as it got to my mouth and it splatted into a tiny bowl of something brown, which splashed all over my dress. I'd gone for monochrome: a thick cream dress with black tights and black heels. Now I looked like a Friesian cow.

Charlie laughed but his eyes glazed over slightly. 'I

need you to know how much I want to be inside you right now,' he said, without bothering to lean in.

'Well, tough. You'll have to wait. Besides, we haven't even talked yet,' I said firmly. Having a man this good-looking begging me for sex was the best therapy I could ask for. I couldn't remember the last time I'd felt sexy with a man. With Michael it had just become . . . well, normal, I supposed.

Charlie put his hands up. 'Fine. Fine, let's talk. What do you want to talk about? How about the general election? Who's going to win? See? I can do clever stuff, too, y'know.'

'Um, the Conservatives?' I replied doubtfully.

'I hope not but it's looking pretty likely. Mmm. How quickly do you come if you're doing a sixty-nine?'

'Charlie!' I said, reddening. He was impossible. I tried to cover up my excitement by taking a large gulp of my cocktail. Trying to guzzle every last drop, I tipped the glass and a clump of passionfruit seeds slid out on to my lap. I froze. 'Fuck.' Charlie leaned over and stared at them. 'Charlie! I look like I've just made frogspawn!' I gazed beseechingly at him. 'What shall I do?'

He got up and walked round the table. 'You just remove it, that's what,' he replied, taking a napkin and gently rubbing it off. When he deliberately rubbed the tissue in a frogspawn free zone, I gasped. He studied me with narrowed eyes.

No, no, no. *No.* I was not going to have some man trying to bring me off in the middle of a restaurant with a napkin covered in passion fruit seeds. Not without some effort, I made him remove his hand. 'Stop it. Now. Sit down.'

'Sure. Sorry.' He sat down. 'Actually, Fran, I'm *really* sorry. I'm coming on far too strong with all of this sex stuff. Let's chat and have dinner, OK? It's just unusual for me to fancy someone and *like* them at the same time. I'm a bit overwhelmed!'

I peered at his face and suddenly he seemed so earnest, so genuine, that I leaned over and kissed him. 'That's a lovely thing to say,' I said. 'Shall we start again?'

He looked eager and relieved. 'Yes! Thank you. So, I'm Charlie, I work in music and I'm thirty-seven. Tell me all about you. From the beginning!'

By the time we'd finished dinner and got through a bottle of wine, three Chinese vodkas and another cocktail back at the bar, I was nicely drunk. 'Let's go dancing!' Charlie yelled in my ear, above the shriek of the beautiful people.

'OK! I need to get changed first, though,' I said, pointing at my soy- and seed-splattered dress. 'How about we go somewhere in Camden? We can get a taxi and I'll run in to get changed quickly.' He nodded and paid the bill. I felt totally euphoric: I was with the hottest man in London who didn't just want to have it off with me, he *actually* fancied me. Michael and I had never gone dancing, really: he'd always said he found it a bit embarrassing and distasteful.

In the taxi Charlie and I snogged like the world was going to end. He was an exceptionally good kisser and had a way of handling me that left me absolutely weak with desire. Sort of firm and soft but rough and with just the right suggestion of dirtiness. *Just go dancing, go home alone, and have sex another time,* OK? said the voice of reason. Remembering the Amazon in my pants, I took note.

We stopped briefly at my flat. I left Charlie in the taxi and ran in, throwing my dress off. I caught sight of myself in my underwear and stilettos as I sprinted past the mirror. I stopped and looked. For once, I felt really sexy.

And suddenly Charlie was in the room, crashing through the door, running towards me. 'But the taxi . . .'

'Shut up,' he said, standing behind me in the mirror and running his hands roughly over my breasts and belly. I gasped, shoving myself backwards into him. He kissed my neck and shoulders roughly, undoing my bra. My nipples were rock hard and he ground himself against me as he touched them. Still behind me, he surveyed me in the mirror with his right hand still on my belly and his left on my breasts. 'Fuck, you are too hot for words,' he said, plunging his hand down inside my knickers. His fingers worked me quickly, and within seconds I was gasping, my head thrown back on his shoulder, an orgasm ripping through me as he bit hungrily into my neck.

He spun me round and threw me on the bed, flinging away my shoes and pulling off my tights. I lay completely naked while he stood above me, slowly unbuttoning his shirt. It dropped to the floor. I was twitching all over, completely frantic for him now, desperate for more. Slowly, very slowly, he started to undo his belt, all the time staring at me. I couldn't take any more. In a second I was up, pulling off his belt, ripping open his trousers, taking him into my mouth.

Just before he came he plunged into me. I shoved him even harder into me, losing control as another monstrous orgasm got closer and closer and deliciously closer.

I'd never, ever, ever come at the same time as a man before. Not even with Michael. As Charlie rolled off me, breathless, he kissed me hard. 'You are completely fucking hot, Fran,' he gasped. 'I think I'm going to have to fuck you all night.' Dazed, I went to the toilet, but within seconds, Charlie was in there too, throwing me into my wet room – quite an appropriate name, in the end – where we started round two.

I woke the next morning to a piercing miaow. 'Shut it, Duke Ellington,' I croaked, pulling a pillow over my head. I shot a mile high when someone next to me burst out laughing and said, 'You have a cat called Duke Ellington?'

And there he was. All six magnificent feet of him: Charlie Swift, DJ. Not to mention the best shag I had ever had in my life. He was stretched out with his hands propped under his head, his perfect, disconcertingly tanned body smooth and firm, his quite sizeable manhood on full display. I went red. 'There's plenty more where that came from,' he said, taking my hand and leading it down. In a second he was hard. I started to move my hand but then came another furious miaow and I stopped. I turned, acutely embarrassed, to see Duke Ellington at the door, looking appalled. I tried to shield him from the sight of Charlie's erection but he just turned and walked away.

Slightly guilty, I padded off to feed him, feeling horribly rancid but extremely perky. There was a gorgeous naked man in my flat! Charlie came after me, yawning and stretching. He helped himself to bread and slotted it into the toaster, reaching over to put the kettle on. There was something about a man's bottom, I thought, as I watched him, that makes him seem somehow defenceless and, well, a bit silly. From the front he's all face, hair, chest, meat and two veg: powerful, angular, arresting. And yet from the back he's a bit defenceless and shapeless with two small peachy buttocks. I walked over and hugged him from behind, then felt immediately embarrassed, realizing that this was what I'd do with Michael. I moved away again and sat at the kitchen table. I glanced down at myself.

OH, GOD! THE RAINFOREST!

My eyes widened with horror, which Charlie saw just as he turned round. 'That's quite a muff you've got there,' he said conversationally, putting some toast in front of me.

'I left it on so that I wouldn't sleep with you,' I replied. 'Don't forget, after all, that I'm a lesbian.'

He chortled. 'It's OK. I managed to find my way around. So, what are you up to today, Fuck-me Fran?'

'Excuse me? Fuck-me Fran?'

'That's what you were yelling last night.'

I blushed. 'Well, I thought I'd go and see my mum, actually. She's been having a bit of a hard time of late.'

'Really?' he said, through his toast. 'Sounds bad. When can we meet up next?'

So he wasn't interested in talking about Mum. Well, fair enough. We'd only just slept together. Perhaps it was a bit early to be talking about future in-laws.

'Soon,' I said, eating a piece of his toast and peeping at him from under my eyelashes. This felt amazing!

Suddenly the door opened and in walked Stefania. She took in the sight of Charlie and me, naked, munching toast and drinking tea, crossed herself and walked out again. Duke Ellington followed her, keen to get away from the spectacle.

'Ah, the meditation teacher,' Charlie observed. 'Interesting. Well, these alternative types like a bit of nudity, don't they? Speaking of which, I do, too. Get back into the bedroom this minute, please.'

An hour later, Charlie left. I asked him what he was up to as I went round my room picking up underwear. 'People to see, things to do,' he said breezily. 'I'd like nothing more than to do it again tonight, but needs must.' He pulled me tightly to him and kissed my forehead.

I staggered back into bed, bow-legged and bruised, blushing as I caught sight of myself in the mirror. As I sank down into bed, my phone beeped.

My heart leaped: it was Michael again!

Franny. You probably hate me but I just want you to know I am sorry. I miss you. Xxx

What *was* this? Did he have cameras rigged up in here or something? I struggled hard not to punch the air. My boy wanted me back! I smirked, trying to drag a 'Ha! Up yours, Daniels!' out of myself. But I felt guilty. In spite of everything, Nellie was *actually quite nice*. And she was clearly in love with Michael.

So what was happening?

I needed to get to the bottom of this. If I didn't do so soon I was at risk of texting Michael back and then it'd be game over – I'd be back at square one, staring morbidly at my phone, waiting impotently for a reply.

After the Chelsea club shoot I'd banned myself from any further Nellie-stalking – as Dave had pointed out, I could have lost my job using ITN's equipment for my covert Chelsea mission the other week – but desperate times called for desperate measures. And I knew exactly how, where and when I could carry out one final stalk. It would take place this week.

'You're a bloody genius!' I told Stefania, when I strode into her shed five minutes later. 'I love the Eight Date Deal! Charlie wants to have loads of sex with me, some bloke called Toni is counting down the days till our date next weekend, there's a brilliant bloke called Freddy wanting a date with me and Michael is begging me to talk to him *behind Nellie's back*! It's amazing!'

'GET OUT!' she screamed. 'Hose yourself down! You have been making ze sex all night! Do not touch anysing in my room!' But she was smiling.

Later that day I had a long bath and tried to work out what I wanted from Charlie. He was glamorous, seemingly wealthy, well connected, flashy and stylish, all the things that Michael was not. And that, I was now quite sure, was what I needed. Moreover, he seemed genuinely nice. He'd woken up in the middle of the night and said, 'Are you OK?'

'Mmpfff,' I'd replied, asleep. 'Why?'

He kissed me. 'I don't know. I just wanted to check. I couldn't hear you breathing.'

I smiled. 'I'm alive. Just worn out. Some man broke into my house last night and shagged me till I couldn't move.'

Charlie chuckled, and kissed me in the dark. 'You make me laugh,' he said softly.

But who was I trying to fool? It was the sexual chemistry I wanted more of. It was electric. I'd forgotten what it was like to be with someone who excited you in every sense of the word, who thrilled and frightened you in equal measure.

When I was eleven I'd started a band in the playground called Fran and the Bitches. I didn't know what bitches meant, of course, but I knew it was edgy and fierce. And I was a fierce lead singer, a massive attention-seeker, bumping and grinding long before I learned what bumping and grinding actually was, screwing my face up in affected emotion and performing to the (largely uninterested) kids in the playground from atop the green Grundon bins while my bitches jived below me.

Daniel Ashcroft, the school hunk, a boy who used actual hair products and kept a picture of Madonna in a locket round his neck, put out a rumour that he wanted to go steady with me after he'd been to one of our lunchtime recitals. For three weeks, that summer, I was his girlfriend. We'd snog each other with our hands between our mouths; we'd exchange gifts (biscuits we'd stolen from our parents' kitchens) and sometimes we'd sneak off and sit in the evergreen tree behind the kitchens and listen to the dinner ladies slagging off our headmaster while they washed up. He'd solemnly cup my non-existent breast while gazing studiously into the middle distance and I'd cup his arse awkwardly while staring at his face, hoping he might look at me. Those were heavenly times. Everyone knew about me: I was Fran-Daniel's-girlfriend-and-founder-of-Fran-and-the-Bitches. My stock was up. Then the summer holidays came and, like all good childhood relationships, we forgot about each other for six weeks.

Unfortunately for me, Daniel Ashcroft hadn't forgotten about me temporarily: he'd forgotten about me completely. When we came back to school the following September, he had moved on to Stella Cartwright, who was from a tower block in Bermondsey. She had an earring and a fake tattoo and patent leather shoes. She out-cooled me by a good 400 per cent and Daniel knew it.

My stock went down. My Bitches resigned from the band because they were fed up with my spotlight-hogging tendencies and, besides, Stella had offered to audition them for backing-singer roles in her new R&B group, which rehearsed at lunchtime in the car park.

I was toast. After two weeks' wandering around completely on my own, I had to make emergency friends with Crispin Ghanaba, a quiet, studious Ghanaian who was popular with no one in particular because he was far too good at schoolwork to be cool. But Crispin and I had a wonderful time together. We'd talk from the start of lunchtime to the end, making dens in the dust and discussing eleven-year-olds' politics. I wanted to be Kate Adie, he wanted to go home and take over as president of Ghana. When he was sent to a private school the following term, I was secretly heartbroken. Crispin may have been radically uncool but he was the best boyfriend I'd ever had. So when Daniel Ashcroft tried it on again at the leavers' disco, I punched him in the face and stalked off, spending the rest of the evening sitting on the toilet, writing a letter to Crispin.

The similarities with my current situation had not eluded me. Michael had always been like Crispin: clever, fascinating, warm, quiet, reserved. But Charlie was what the egotistical part of me had always longed for: danger, sexiness, popularity, style, unpredictability. The kind of man who'd always keep me guessing. Just one night with him and I'd already started to wonder if perhaps I'd spent the last two years in a comfortable coma.

There was only one way to find out, I thought. *Treat yourself to life in the fast lane with this man. Nellie Daniels lives in the fast lane. I bet she doesn't sit around talking to her cat on a Saturday afternoon. And she sure as buggery doesn't have a muff like a rainforest. This, Frances O'Callaghan, is what proper girls do. They dress up. They party. They have sex. They go to spas and their fridges contain organic produce. Are you serious about Glam Fran? Lemme hear you!* I punched the air and extinguished my candle with a tidal wave of bubbles.

By the time I'd got out of the bath and fed Duke

Ellington, I'd decided that things were probably going to be OK. Michael would come back, I'd get some sex with a divine and exciting man in the interim, and I'd sort my life out.

I reached for my phone to call Leonie and update her on my plans, only to discover that while I'd been in the bath I'd missed twenty-seven calls. All from Mum. And the text that had just arrived in my inbox was from her. It read: Please come to my house urgently. Emergency.

Chapter Twenty-seven

Fran, I think it is extremely rude of you not to have replied to my
text messages since our date. However, having read the
newspaper I am rather glad you haven't replied and would ask
you not to contact me again. Best, James

I ran to the tube as fast as I could, trying not to throw
up last night's cocktails and redialling Mum every few
seconds, but her phone was switched off. Something
serious had happened. Mum had trouble remembering to call me on my birthday, let alone twenty-seven
times in one day.

So when I arrived at Victoria to get on a train to
Cheam, I was strangely unsurprised to see her face
staring out at me from the corner of the *Mirror* on a
newsstand. 'Bennett's Bit,' the headline yelled. '*Tory big
hope forced to admit extra-marital affair*'. In slow motion I
picked up the newspaper and turned to page four.
There, clutching a bottle of champagne and stagger-
ing across a carpet at some posh reception with her
hair in her eyes, was Mum. And next to the picture,
above a caption that read 'Like mother, like daughter:

Bennett's bid for top cabinet post is in tatters' was me, falling off the kerb outside the Brit Awards. My knickers were plainly visible. If you looked hard enough, you could even see my tropical muff.

I handed the newspaper vendor a fiver and wandered off, clutching the newspaper to my chest as waves of nausea washed through me. I stared at a man who appeared at my elbow, trying to give me money. Ah, the newspaper vendor. I smiled distractedly at him and took it, drifting on towards ThickCrust kiosk where I ordered a salami baguette.

Perhaps this wasn't really happening. Perhaps Charlie had drugged me last night and I was just entertaining an odd hallucination. Perhaps James from the Internet had been looking at crotch shots of someone else who just had the same name and knickers as me. I nibbled a mouse-sized portion off the end of the baguette only to find myself with a mouthful of armpit-flavoured salami. Past caring what people thought of me, I spat it into a bin and threw the rest of the baguette after it, leaning heavily on a pillar as another wave of sickness pummelled me.

Then I froze. Was some dirty little paparazzo following me right now? I pulled my hair over my face and glanced around furtively. The only person looking at me seemed to be the newspaper vendor, who was probably more interested in the fact that Knickers Girl from page four had just bought a paper from him than he was in my bin-hugging.

I breathed deeply and lurched off to Platform Nine where I curled up on a lurid red and orange train seat and hoped that everything would stop.

As the train pulled out of the station, I sat up and looked again at the paper.

It appeared, rather unfortunately, that this really *was* happening. There was Mum, drunk, half obscured by her champagne bottle. And there was me, drunk, half obscured by my pants, which were hogging most of the picture. The article was grim. I read it with an increasing sense of despair and humiliation.

Power-suited Eve O'Callaghan has been helping herself to Tory hopeful Bennett for nearly twenty years, we can reveal. The sordid affair has been conducted in O'Callaghan's £400,000 semi in Cheam, right under the nose of Bennett's pretty wife Laura who is president of three local charities, mother of two, and pillar of the local community. Our source revealed that stiff-haired wine lover O'Callaghan often threatened to go to the press if Bennett ever left her. 'It was pitiful,' our insider told us. 'She'd get wasted in the Prince of Wales and then leave crazed messages on his phone until he had no option but to go round.'

Who the fuck was this 'source'? *No one* knew about the affair. It was possibly the best-kept secret in the history of politics! Nick's wife knew, of course – she had done for at least ten years, but she would be the last person to tell the press. (Laura's recent attempt to upstage Mum's Cheam in Bloom contribution was just the latest in a long line of suburban war tactics. My personal favourite had been when Laura had persuaded the director of the Cheam Players to demote Mum from the role of Hermia, in *A Midsummer Night's Dream*, to Nick Bottom. Unfortunately Mum, drunk, had put up an unintentionally outstanding comic performance and received a standing ovation and several gushing local newspaper reviews.) Laura risked losing her husband and pride if she went to the press. It *couldn't* have been her.

One of Nick's colleagues? It felt unlikely. Nick had always been so sure that they knew nothing. He was almost as proud of his secret as he was of his wine cellar.

For months Bennett has feared that his dubious dealings might taint his political future, our source revealed, and so he recently started planning his escape from the toxic affair. It's believed that his decision to leave booze hound O'Callaghan and her chip-off-the-old-block daughter were what prompted them both to go out and get slaughtered, as these pictures reveal.

If the Conservatives, widely tipped to win the General Election in May, aren't able to form a scandal-free cabinet, then Cameron stands to lose widespread public support. Mother and daughter may be in need of help but Mirror *readers have the right to know that there's more to Bennett than meets the eye.*

And there was the answer, right there in the text. *There's more to Bennett than meets the eye.* I sat up and rested my head against the cold window, suddenly clear. 'I've been spending a lot of time with his aides during my research,' Alex had said pointedly. 'I think there's more to Nick Bennett than meets the eye.' Then he'd winked.

Alex. Of course Alex. Alex who considered himself a *serious journalist.* Michael had said Alex would sell his own bloody mother if he believed she'd done something newsworthy. Instead, he'd sold mine. My vulnerable, confused, lonely mother, who would now lose the only person in her life she seemed to care about. My stomach churned furiously. How could he? How *could* he? What about *Michael?* Michael loved Mum!

Alex. The rotten, stinking *scumbag.* Hot tears gathered in my eyes as I began to scrabble around in my bag for my phone.

'Hi, this is Alex Sutcliffe. You know what to do.'

I gathered all my strength, enough to sound like I wasn't crying, and began to speak: 'Alex, you are disgusting and despicable. I cannot believe you sold my mother to the press when you knew full well how vulnerable she was. Nick might be a fucking moron, Alex, but at least he loves her. But why would I expect you to know anything about love? If anything happens to her, you'll have blood on your hands. You *scum.*'

When I put the phone down and slouched back in my seat, a large, kindly face framed by mousy curls was staring at me from between the two seats in front. 'Erm, are you OK?' the face said.

Clearly, I was not. 'Yes,' I croaked, with a weak smile. 'Never better.'

The face smiled kindly. 'You poor thing,' she said, in a broad Dorset accent. 'I've just bin reading about it all. Get your mum into Alcoholics Anonymous, OK? It's *'mazin'*. Totally sorted my husband out.'

I tried to smile again. 'I'm working on it. Thanks.' And then I wept into my salami napkin, realizing I'd just admitted to a complete stranger – probably another fucking reporter, knowing my luck – that my mum was an alcoholic.

When I got off at Cheam, the sky was overcast and the air damp. Planes moved slowly across the sky above me, banking down into Heathrow as calmly and slowly as a feather falls to the ground. I jogged along the street as fast as my hangover would allow, praying that Mum hadn't drunk herself unconscious and wondering how on earth she would cope if Nick really was leaving her.

As I rounded the corner to her house I stopped dead and caught my breath. Outside there was a small gaggle of paparazzi and – far worse – four news cameras. In the middle of them, wrapped up in a grubby army coat and a strange Bolivian hat, was Dave.

'Oi! Fran! Great photo in the *Mirror*, doofus!' It was Raza, one of our political correspondents. I turned puce as I walked slowly towards them in my hoody, with tear-stained cheeks. The journalists' code of honour was evidently not in place: every single camera, except Dave's, turned and pointed at me. Raza trotted up to me as I began to run through the crowd towards Mum's house. 'Look, get Eve to give us a quick comment and we'll leave you alone, my love.' I ignored him. 'Fran, come on, dear, you know I have to do this. It's that or some dick misquotes her in the *Daily Mail*.'

As I made a run for the front gate, Dave piped up: 'Leave her alone, Raza, you cunt,' he said. And then, as I fumbled with the latch, he called, 'Fannybaws, I'm coming with you. Without the camera,' he added, appearing next to me. I looked briefly at him and considered punching him hard on his craggy nose. 'They didn't tell me who it was,' he muttered. 'They just told me to meet Raza down here urgently. You know I'd never have come otherwise.' He grabbed my hand and followed me up the path. I let him; I wasn't in any state to start scrapping. His hand felt rough and alien in mine. Right at this moment I missed Michael more than I'd ever missed him before.

Dave took the keys out of my shaking hands and let us into Mum's house.

'He's told me we can't ever see each other again and that I'm not to contact him,' said Mum, when we sat down in the lounge a few minutes later. 'Ever.' She was drunk, of course, although not as badly as I'd feared. She was still in her dressing-gown, looking old and heartbreakingly vulnerable. Her hair was flat and her eyes were glazed.

'Oi, Fran! Come on, babe!' yelled Raza, through the door.

'I'll sort it,' said Dave, abruptly, and went outside.

'Don't come back,' I said, following him out. 'You'll get sacked. It's not worth it. I'll explain it all to you next week.'

He looked uncomfortable. 'Seriously, Dave,' I said. 'Hugh will whup your ass. But thanks for coming in.'

Dave stood his ground. 'Why didn't you tell me things were this bad with your mum, Fannybaws?' he asked softly. His normally inscrutable face was kind and concerned, enough to tip me over the edge.

'Because I . . .' I stopped, unsure.

'Because you didn't want to believe it was happening, aye?'

I nodded. Dave hugged me. 'She'll survive this, Fran. Just be there for her. Listen to her. Don't tell her what to do. She'll get help when it's the right time.' Without any further ado, he disappeared out of the front door, yelling, 'Raza, if you don't fucking piss off, I'll knock you out.'

'Surely Nick'll change his mind, Mum,' I said, knowing he would do no such thing. 'Surely Laura will kick him out and he'll come running.'

Mum just shook her head and then she started crying. 'Be a dear and go and get me a bottle of Gordon's,' she said pathetically. 'Franny, I have none left and I can't take another moment of this. Please, darling.'

I started listing every reason I could think of why this was a very poor idea indeed but was interrupted by a phone call from Leonie. Terrified she was ringing to say that further pictures of my lady garden had made their way into the press, I answered.

'God, Franny, are you OK? Are you with your mum?'

'Yes. Not good.'

'Oh, God . . . is she drunk?'

I nodded, although she couldn't see me, and shuffled into the downstairs loo.

'Franny?'

'Sorry. Yes. But she's not too bad. She's run out of gin. She wants me to go and buy booze. She looks like she's going to top herself. I think I'll have to.'

'Oh, fuck, Fran. This is awful.'

There was a lengthy silence and then I heard a sniffly noise. 'Leonie?' Nothing. 'Leonie, are you crying?'

'Yes.'

Further silence.

'Fran, I need to tell you something.'

'Go ahead,' I said dully, bracing myself for some further breach of our privacy.

'Fran, it wasn't Alex.'

'Er, it *was*,' I began, and stopped. Hang on. 'How

do you know I thought it was him?' I asked. A small tendril of something not nice had begun to wind its way around my stomach.

Leonie exhaled nervously. 'Because I'm with him right now. We listened to your message together.'

The tendril got larger. A snake, perhaps. 'Excuse me?'

'I'm with him now. Fran, I'm sorry you had to find out like this but I've been seeing Alex for a while now. Since, erm . . . since you broke up with Michael.'

I watched a money spider swing awkwardly from the bottom of the basin.

'No,' I said eventually. This could not be true. Of that I was quite sure.

'Yes,' Leonie said firmly. 'Yes, I have. I'm sorry, I know the timing's poor but I'm with Alex and I plan to continue being.'

The snake in my guts was going fairly mad now. This news was simply too preposterous to take in. 'Leonie, I hope you're lying. Because this would be a betrayal of the worst kind,' I said, as clearly as I could.

'No, I'm not lying. It's not a betrayal at all. It happened. And I'm telling you, Alex did *not* sell the story to the *Mirror*.'

'He fucking DID!' I yelled, suddenly furious. 'He fucking TOLD me he knew about Mum and Nick – and the article was in the same fucking WORDS he used. He's a cunt and a weasel and a fucking scummy, pushy journalist. He cares about politics more than anything else. You fucking KNOW THAT.'

'Fran?' Mum was in the hallway. 'What's going on?'

'Stay there,' I hissed at Leonie, and opened the toilet door. 'Mum, remember Michael's friend Alex? He spent a lot of time with Nick recently. Do you think he found out?'

Mum nodded meekly. 'Yes. Nick's been a bit worried about it, actually. But I told him we could trust Alex, what with him being Michael's friend –' She broke off, her voice faltering. 'Oh dear. I really do need that gin, Frances. Can you go now?' She shuffled off, clutching her stomach.

'Did you hear that?' I asked Leonie quietly.

She replied strong and clear: 'He wouldn't do it. He *didn't* do it. Sorry, Fran, you're just going to have to accept that.' She ended the call.

Chapter Twenty-eight

Hello Fran.

Thank you for filling me in. Your friends sound mental. I particularly like the sound of the one who lives in your shed – she sounds as fierce as your cat. Who is obviously a right little ballsack.

Why did you brush off your job like that? I've got a friend who works in News so I KNOW that you've got a really posh job. You should be showing off.

Er, in answer to your question: 'Love Over Gold'. Have you heard the intro to 'Telegraph Road'?

How's your weekend been anyway? Did you date any munters? How'd you feel about going on a date with me? I'm abroad for another two weeks; you've got plenty of time to prepare yourself. It will be the best night of your life, of course.

Freddy X

Dave took one look at my outfit – a shoulder-padded power dress from Jaeger in royal blue – and fell about laughing, stopping only for a coughing fit. 'This is the *best* outfit I've ever seen, Fannybaws,' he said reverentially.

In spite of myself, I smiled. 'You're jealous. You're secretly wishing that Freya didn't wear Fairtrade linens and instead dressed like this.' He merely stared at my ensemble, shaking his head in wonder. 'How *is* Freya by the way? I haven't seen her in . . . well, in ages.'

Dave fixed me with a Stern Look. 'Stop evading the question,' he said. 'Tell me what's going on with your mum.'

We were sitting in the staffroom at lunchtime, where I had taken to hiding when I wasn't required at my desk. It was now Wednesday and everyone at ITN had been pretending I was invisible since Monday. After all, what could one say to a news producer whose crotch had been a noteworthy feature of Sunday's news? Alex – the *scumbag* – had moved to a bank of desks round the corner from the main newsroom floor and was avoiding me like the plague. This worked well for me: I was still overwhelmed with rage and did not need a homicide on my record too.

Hugh had merely sent me an email on Monday saying that in light of my sudden infamy he would prefer me to base myself in the office for the foreseeable future and not to make or receive any telephone calls. I had less status than Jacinta, the eighteen-year-old work-experience girl, but none of the popularity or sex appeal. And because I'd had to stay at Mum's since Sunday night I'd had to spend the week wearing polyester power outfits from her wardrobe.

'Mum's pretty shit,' I replied. 'And I'm running out

of ideas. Dad agreed that I should take her to AA but she refused. I tried to talk to her about it last night and she just started crying and saying she couldn't believe I'd start shit-stirring when she was going through hell. If I don't go and buy her booze she literally goes mental, Dave. I can't take much more.'

Dave got a bag of Krispy Kremes out of his satchel and offered it to me. 'Oh, Fannybaws, that's rough,' he said.

'Thanks.' I took a Kreme-filled monster. 'It breaks my heart, Dave. She's only OK when she's got a drink in her hand.'

Dave nodded reflectively. 'Of course.'

'Do *you* know an alcoholic then? You sounded like you knew what you were on about the other day.'

'Aye. My cousin Rosa.'

'What happened?'

'She died.'

I sat back. 'Jesus. I'm so sorry.'

He shook his head. 'No, you're OK. Her sister, Betty, went to AA. She's in fuckin' great shape, these days.'

'Really?'

'Aye. I think they're the only folks who can help.'

'I know.' I sighed, feeling suddenly exhausted. 'But I can't drag her there.'

'No. But I reckon she'll be ready soon, Fannybaws,' he said reflectively.

I helped myself to another doughnut and slumped

over the table to scoff it. Dave watched me for a while with a mixture of pity and concern. 'Fran, you need some time off. Go home, get some kip and some normal clothes. You look like Thatcher. You can't help your mum when you're this shagged out.'

I finished the second doughnut in three bites. 'Yeah. I'll go home tonight maybe. I just don't want to leave her on her own.'

I reached for the bag again and Dave raised an eyebrow. 'Really? Three doughnuts?'

'Oh, piss off.' I took the third, hurt. Why did Dave have such a remarkable ability to point out my most embarrassing behaviour?

'So. Did you decide what to do about Charlie?' he asked, after a pause.

'Er, yes. I went on a date and shagged him.'

Dave sat back and whistled. 'Really? I hope you were careful, Franny . . .'

'Yes yes yes, I was. And you know what? It was great sex. I'm glad I did it.' I was pretty sure I believed myself.

Dave looked slightly ill. 'Erugh. Now, Fannybaws, listen. I was at a party on Saturday and I met someone who knows him. Told me Charlie's got a massive coke problem. Apparently he stole some jewellery from her house last year.'

I scowled at Dave over the Krispy Kremes bag, wishing that, just for once, my friends had something nice to say about my love life. 'Really? Well, he didn't steal from me. He just gave me a jolly good bang. I needed it, Dave. I'm in hell over Michael. I needed to know I'm not . . .' I felt miserable tears swelling fatly in my eyes. 'I needed to know I'm not completely disgusting to men any more.'

Dave began to roll a cigarette. 'Don't be a pillock. You've got loads of men lined up on the Internet wanting a date with you – you're in demand, girl!'

'Oh, who cares?' I cried, letting out an almighty sob. Dave put his cigarette down to pat my hand awkwardly. 'The only person I *want* is Michael. He's sent me three messages now. I miss him. I need him. I can't do this shit on my own. I'm going to text him back.'

It was true. I was done. I needed my boy.

'But, Fran . . . he's riding Nellie Daniels! You can't want him back!'

'Of course I do. I still love him,' I said quietly, tears falling off my nose and into the Krispy Kremes. Dave moved them and leaned forward to give me a proper hug. 'Listen here, Fannybaws,' he said, into my hair, 'I think you should keep your distance. You don't know what he's up to and you've got another month till the ninety days are up. Why don't you have it out with him then? When you know more about him and Nellie?'

I wiped my eyes on Dave's sleeve. 'I'm just so tired, Dave. I'm tired of coping with Mum, I'm tired of having to do this fucking stupid Internet dating, I'm tired of trying to do this job, I'm tired of restraining myself from punching Alex and, most of all, I'm tired of not being able to just crawl into bed with Michael for a cuddle.'

Dave sat back. 'You're doing OK,' he said quietly. 'You really are. Don't give up. It's only another month. Think how much saner you'll be then, eh? No offence, love, but I'm not sure I'd take you back in this state.' He smiled cheekily but I failed to see the comedy. I put my face in my sugary hands and howled.

'Frances.'

We both jumped. Nikki, Hugh's PA, was standing in the doorway with an asymmetric fringe and Bad Tidings written across her face. 'Hugh would like to see you in his office, please.'

I brushed doughnut crumbs off my polyester lap. 'About . . . ?'

'Not sure. But he wants you now.'

I got up to go but Dave jumped up, blocking my path. 'Er, Fannybaws, you, er . . .' He hovered awkwardly, staring at my face.

'I've got mascara all over my face and I look like Dracula?'

'Aye. That one.'

'COME IN!' Hugh screamed, a few moments later.

That didn't sound too promising.

'Shut the door,' he said, not looking up.

I did so and sat down. I was beginning to feel rather afraid. Hugh picked up a tape box from his desk. He showed it to me. It was marked 'New Life House (Chelsea) shoot: Isabelle Langley-Gardiner/Nellie Daniels, 8 February 2010'.

My heart sank.

'What the fuck is this, Fran?' he asked, sitting back in his chair.

Slumped in the back of a taxi thirty minutes later, I decided that the worst of it was not that Hugh had given me a formal written warning for going on a made-up shoot at a Chelsea mums' club, not that he had said my appearance in the *Mirror* was one of the greatest embarrassments of his career, but that he had told me, really quite sadly, that I had turned out to be an enormous disappointment after such a brilliant start.

That part was unbearable. Feeling myself spiralling into a silent panic, I did my best to remember some of Stefania's meditation mantras. But nothing came, only a voice telling me that I was a complete fool and deserved all of this. I had had the best job in the world but I'd chosen to spend my work time stalking Nellie Daniels using ITN's computers, cameras and time.

'Every time I walk past your fucking computer you're doing your fucking Facespace,' Hugh had yelled. 'You're never fucking working. What the fuck happened to you during your three weeks off sick? Why was Fran replaced by a fucking moron who looks like something from the Young fucking Conservatives one minute and some reject from Greenham fucking

Common the next? I don't fucking like it. I swear I even smelt booze on your breath yesterday. And, my God, if that happens again you're out of here quicker than I can say "fuck".'

I'd sat trying to control the tears forming in my eyes and nodding blankly. All of the years I'd worked for fifteen hours a day, all of the times I'd sat up until four in the morning watching the news wires, all of the times I'd blown out my social life in favour of work, and now I'd cocked it up.

'But I'm giving you one last chance. One last FUCK-ING chance,' he said. 'Nick Bennett is big news right now. And I need you to get him for us. Two-hour interview, exclusive to us, location of *our* choosing, ready for Friday night's bulletin. Do I have a deal?'

'Hugh,' I began. My voice was wobbly. 'Hugh, I'm not sure I . . .' I struggled.

Hugh made things simple for me by slamming his fist on the table. 'The deal is non-negotiable, Frances. You get us Nick in the next forty-eight hours and you keep your job. You fail, you will no longer be working at ITN. And this isn't blackmail. I've had IT compile a review of your recent Internet use. There's enough in it to have you fired fifty fucking times over. Understood?'

I nodded stupidly, appalled.

'One last thing. Alex will run this project once you've secured access to Nick. Professionally he's worth twenty of you at the moment. So don't fucking well take this out on him, OK? I'm watching you, Fran. Oh, you can be fucking well sure of that. I'm watching. Now fuck off home, sort yourself out and get me Nick Bennett. You come back tomorrow *ready to do your fucking job.* No more chances. Goodbye.'

Why did Alex hate me so much? There was no way anyone other than him could have given the tape to Hugh. I shivered. Was it not bad enough that he'd sold Mum to the press and bedded my best friend?

As I let myself into my flat, numb with shock and shame and clutching Dave's bag of Krispy Kremes, I encountered Duke Ellington, fresh from a fight with a cat far bigger than him. His left ear was torn and he was limping slightly. 'Oh, my God . . . Duke Ellington, are you OK?' I asked him. He miaowed dismissively and ambushed my ankle, tearing Mum's shiny tan tights.

Duke Ellington would not lie down and die amid a pile of Krispy Kremes, I thought grimly, as I removed him from my leg. He would fight on. And if that little grey monster could deal with anything that was sent his way, so could I.

I took a deep breath, threw the doughnuts into the bin, sat down at my kitchen table and dialled.

'Frances. Why in the name of God are you calling me?' Nick hissed furtively. 'THIS HAS GOT TO STOP. I could be being *tapped*!'

I swallowed. 'It's a work call. They want a two-hour with you for Friday's bulletin. I think you should do it.'

He said nothing for a few seconds.

'They don't want to screw you, Nick. They just want to hear the truth.'

'I'll speak to the press office. But, yes, I think I should. I deserve the chance to remind the public of my otherwise unblemished record. But for obvious reasons you cannot be anywhere near the filming location.'

'Very well.'

'Right. Well, Fran, thanks for calling and all the best for your career. And, um, I hope everything goes OK with Eve.'

'That's it? You "hope everything goes OK"? And now you just waltz off out of her life after seventeen years? Shame on you, Nick,' I cried.

But he'd ended the call.

Poor, poor Mum. It was unimaginable. Seventeen years and then – boom. Nothing. A wall of silence. I sighed, knowing I would have to go back to her house tonight. The mere prospect of an evening in her company made me feel despairing. *You need Michael. You cannot do this alone,* my head told me. I looked at my phone.

'I'll just let Hugh know about Nick,' I said to Duke Ellington. 'And maybe have a bath. And then it's back into Stefania's care for you, young man. I'm needed elsewhere.'

I reawakened my laptop, which had been hibernating since Mum's SOS message on Sunday. As the screen came to life, I wondered vaguely if I might have heard from Freddy again, but instead I found the email I'd had from Dad on Saturday afternoon. I read it again. How true it had been: my certainty that Nick was about to dump Mum, and Dad's recommendation that she go to AA.

Suddenly I felt uncomfortable. I didn't know why, but something wasn't right.

My phone beeped. Charlie! I'd been worrying that he'd seen the *fanoir de Franoir* in the *Mirror* on Sunday. Wednesday, after all, was quite late in the day to be getting in touch after a Saturday of passion.

Hey. Me want more Fran. She hot. Next weekend?

I smiled stupidly, remembering how disgracefully attractive he'd been as he'd sat in this very seat on Saturday night while I'd been running round my room getting ready.

I think I could fit you in

I stopped.

Oh, dear God.

. . . *as he'd sat here in this very seat on Saturday night.*

Right in front of my computer. With this email wide open, facing him. Charlie the alleged coke-head who thought nothing of stealing from his friends for the next few grams.

I stared at his text message again, panic balling in my chest. Panic that turned very quickly into anger. He had come here, nicked a story to sell for some fucking coke, then had *sex* with me – and had the *cheek* to ask me on a second date?

Oh, my God, Mum, I'm so sorry. My mind was racing.

I deleted the text I'd started to Charlie. Instead I typed: Fuck you. I cannot believe what you did. But then I felt even more afraid. I couldn't send this! He could use it as proof if Nick denied the story.

Don't reply, I told myself frenziedly. *Go to bed. Lie low. No, go to Mum's. No, kill yourself. No, kill Charlie. No, kill . . . ARRGH.*

My phone started ringing. It was Nick. 'Hello?' I shouted wildly, terrified that he was going to pull out of the interview, then Hugh would sack me and I'd end up being a bag lady for the rest of my life.

'Fran, er, I have a situation,' he said quietly.

'PLEASE DO THE INTERVIEW. PLEASE! MY LIFE DEPENDS ON IT!'

'Yes, yes, it's all being organized now. Fran, I need you to come and get your mother. She is sitting on my driveway in a red-and-white deckchair with a bottle of champagne in her hand.'

I stared at Duke Ellington. '*What?*'

'I said, she's sitting on my driveway drinking champagne. If you don't come and get her, Fran, I'm going to have to call the police. I cannot have a photographer see this. Or Laura. I need her gone within fifteen minutes.'

'Oh, Nick, I'm so sorry. Actually I'm not, it's your bloody fault. But – but I *can't* get there in fifteen minutes! Please! Don't do this! She's at the end of her tether . . .' My voice was getting more and more hysterical.

Nick sounded equally terrified. 'Fifteen minutes,

Fran,' he said. 'This is my life. My career. My family.'

He ended the call and I burst into tears again. 'My life is DOWN THE TOILET,' I yelled at Duke Ellington. My phone started ringing again.

'Hello?' I cried, gulping.

'Fannybaws, I've got some serious news. Charlie Swift is even more of a cunt than we thought. It turns out he stole a whole load of money from –'

'I know he's a cunt. It was him who sold Mum to the *Mirror*. I just found out.'

'So it's over, then? Och, sorry, Fannybaws, I didn't want to wreck –'

'It's not important. Dave, Mum's set up shop outside Nick's house in a fucking deckchair and she's drunk and Nick's told me I've got fifteen minutes before he calls the police and I – Oh, God, Dave, I don't know what to do.'

'I'll be there in ten minutes if I put my foot down. I'm on the A24. There was a pile-up and I got diverted.'

'What? No, you can't –'

'Shut it, Fannybaws. Get down to your mum's as soon as you can. I'll wait for you there.'

'Mum?' I whispered. The room smelt of stale champagne and sadness. A bottle of Bollinger gleamed from her bedside table. In spite of everything, I smiled. Mum wasn't wasting her time with Morrison's cava, at least. Then I spotted an empty cognac bottle next to the bin and stopped smiling.

'Frances.' She sounded very sleepy. 'I'm sorry. I . . .'

'It's OK. Go to sleep. But we need to talk tomorrow, OK?'

Mum shuffled up in her bed and turned on her bedside lamp. I tried not to start: she looked terrible. *Keep calm, Fran.* I felt frightened and completely exposed. The one person in the world who was meant to be able to look after me was like a tiny helpless baby, propped up on her pillow looking desperately at me for help.

'I . . . I had a moment of madness, Frances,' she said eventually.

I thought about Dave losing his cousin to this thing. I wasn't prepared to let Mum go the same way. 'No, Mum, it wasn't madness,' I said, sitting on her bed and taking her hand. 'Mum, you need help. You have a real problem with drink. Can you see that?'

She dropped her eyes.

'Mum. Look at me. I'm your daughter. I'm your little girl. I'm afraid. I'm afraid I'll lose you if this carries on. You're ill. Ill people need help.' My voice was shaking but I held my ground. I meant it. There was a distinct feeling of last-chance saloon in this room and this time I wasn't going to give in.

Mum's eyes had filled with tears. 'I don't want anyone's help,' she said hopelessly.

I squeezed her hand, terrified that she would shut down and throw me out. 'I know. But, Mum, this is a common problem. There's nothing to be ashamed of.

It's not like it was in Granny's time. You can get help now without being judged.'

Mum nodded. 'Dave . . . Dave told me about the AA group in Sutton,' she said hesitantly. 'But I just don't think I can face it, Franny.'

I sat up straight. 'Mum, you *have* to go to the meeting. Just try it. One meeting. For me, Mum. Please, please, *please* – just go.' I squeezed her hand again. 'Please, Mum. I can't lose you.'

She sank back down in bed. 'OK, Fran,' she said, in a small voice. 'I'll try it. There's a meeting tomorrow, Dave said. I'll go.'

'I'll take the day off work and go with you. How do I know you won't get drunk and make an excuse?' I said. Getting Mum to that meeting felt like the most important thing in my life right now.

She tried to pull herself back up to hug me but slumped down, exhausted. 'Trust me, Fran. I will go. I *will* go.'

I watched as waves of sleep washed over her and she began to drift away. My lip trembled. 'Well done, Mum. I love you.'

'I'll never be able to thank you enough,' I said to Dave, who was texting someone, presumably Freya, in the lounge. He seemed ridiculously out of place among Mum's formal three-piece suite with his army coat and scuffed trainers.

''S OK,' he said, yawning. 'I've had practice with this,

remember. Betty told us she couldn't start AA until she got to rock bottom. I reckon your mum's there now.'

'Yeah, that's pretty much what she just said,' I replied, flopping down on the sofa next to him. 'Seriously, Dave, what you did tonight was absolutely incredible. I'm more grateful than you'll ever know. And finding out about the AA group – you're amazing. I properly love you.'

'It's fine,' he said shortly. 'I was only four miles away.'

'Was Nick a cunt?'

'Och, no more than normal. He was just shitting himself. Anyway, look, Fran, I've got to go, OK? It's late.'

'Sorry, yes. Freya must be really pissed off.'

Dave grimaced. ''Bye.'

'Dave, wait! Let me show you out!'

'You're fine. See you.'

'DAVE! Come back! Let me give you some wine! Or a hug! Or something!'

'It's fine. I just need to get back,' he called, as he strode off down the path to his van.

He was clearly desperate to get away from us.

You can hardly blame him, Fran, I thought, peering at my reflection in the mirror in the hallway. I looked like a strippergram who'd spent the night sleeping in a bin. I was still wearing Mum's hideous dress; my tights were full of cat-shaped toothmarks and ladders; and my eyes were surrounded by smudges.

*

A cup of tea later, overwhelmed by my day and at a loss as to what to do, I got my phone out and reread Michael's messages. They had become a little bit like his old smelly sock that I'd hugged so voraciously when our separation had started in December. They were a nice place to go in my head. An escape from reality. A cup of mental hot chocolate.

I just want you to know I am sorry. I miss you, his most recent message had said. Sunday, 1.37 p.m. I smiled mushily. *I miss you too*, I thought. *More than you can possibly imagine.* Maybe it really had gone wrong with Nellie. Maybe it had just been a fling and she'd got too keen too quickly. I opened my diary and drew a smiley face on 23 March: day ninety. There were twenty-seven days to go. Twenty-seven days until I could see my boy. I'd forgive his indiscretion with The Daniels. I'd do anything. Learn to cook. Take up exotic massage. Take up erotic massage. Anything. I just needed some stability in my life again.

Chapter Twenty-nine

Frances Frances Frances . . . if you were a bogey I'd pick you :)
Govinda

I was in the changing room at Richmond Park Sports
Centre, limbering up for a ten-mile 'warm-up' run
with the running club. This being the first run that I
had undertaken in approximately ten years, I was a
little anxious. But I'd already spotted Nellie out of
the corner of my eye and was filled with an almost
sexual excitement at the idea of an evening in her
company. Fran the crack whore was BACK!

I thought guiltily about Mum, who had hugged me
tearfully when I'd left her house that morning. 'I'm
proud of you, Frances,' she said, her hand shaking as
she held on grimly to her dressing-gown belt. 'I really
am.'

I'd decided there and then to abort tonight's stalking mission. Mum, dumped less than a week ago, was
going to get into her car and drive to some poky
church hall to ask for help from a bunch of strangers
tonight – and I, dumped nine weeks ago, was going

to try to run ten miles on unfit legs just in the hope of perving at my ex-boyfriend's new love interest?

But here I was. Doing just that. This mission was stupid and dangerous but what could I do? I'd had three 'I still love you' messages from Michael in a week! And if I didn't find out what was going on RIGHT NOW I would lose it altogether.

I'd narrowed down three possible explanations for Michael's texts:

1. He was having a rough time with beautiful shiny confident Nellie and wanted minging, grubby, mental Fran back. (This one was my favourite.)
2. He was jealous about my dating and trying to fuck with my head.
3. He was clinically insane and needed electric-shock therapy.

It seemed abundantly clear that the only way to ascertain which of these it was, without directly consulting him, was to go underground and tap The Daniels.

'Just one last time,' I muttered to myself, as I shoved my clothes into a bag. Dave and Stefania would never know and Leonie . . . Well, I needed to talk to Leonie. And maybe Alex. But the idea of apologizing to either was a little beyond my mental capacity today.

I locked my clothes away, said a short prayer to any

God who might still be interested in me and marched out into the cold. 'Hi,' I said, to the human bouncy ball who appeared to be in charge. 'Fran O'Callaghan. I emailed.'

'Oh, Fran, hi!' He beamed. 'Welcome! Everyone, shut up a minute. Let's say hello to our newest member: THIS IS FRAN!'

I smiled awkwardly, feeling my cheeks redden, as a shiny brown column – Nellie's hair – emerged from the crowd cooing, '*Babe,* what a coincidence! Hi!' She kissed me on the cheek.

This was ridiculous. *What was I doing?* 'Oh, hi, Nellie! God, how weird. Of all the running clubs I could have joined! Bizarre!'

My voice was at least two octaves higher than normal. But Nellie seemed oblivious. She put her perfect hair into a thick elastic band, and said, 'Well, hon, great to have you here. Let's run together, yuh?'

'I'd LOVE that!' I cried enthusiastically.

Fool! She was running the marathon! I'd failed to qualify for the 800 metres at Sports Day and I ran like an animated vegetable! *But I had to know what was going on.* As we set off, I said, 'You'd better do the talking, Nellie – I have asthma so I can't talk and run at the same time.'

She looked at me doubtfully. 'Me, too, babe. It's just about fitness.'

Balls.

But it wasn't hard to get her talking. 'So,' I said,

'how's it going with the new man? What's his name again?' Without even needing to look I could see the extent of her smile as she jogged along with exaggerated slowness next to me.

'Michael. And it's amazing! God, babe, I am just out of my mind on this one! He came to my office at lunchtime today and took me out to Gordon Ramsay! I mean, can you *believe* it?'

'Wow,' I said sadly, thinking about the ham bap I'd eaten at my desk. 'Go on . . .' I wheezed. Nellie actually jumped properly off the ground and let out a little whoop. My heart sank. If this perfectly poised, sleek posh girl was at the whooping stage she must be in love.

'It's moved really fast, y'know, he's just so into me! I honestly think he might be about to *propose!*'

I tried not to be sick. 'Wow!' I gasped again.

'I *know!*' Nellie gushed. 'I feel like the luckiest girl on earth. And do you know what, babe? He even runs me a bath every morning!'

Enough. 'Need to stop and take some Ventolin,' I gasped. 'So excited for you. See you back at the club.' I peeled away from the group and started to walk back along the river to the centre of town, trying not to lose it entirely. *If you can't take the heat then stay away from the fire*, I told myself furiously. Why was I doing this to myself?

But it didn't matter. The point was that Nellie and Michael were in love. He ran her baths and I was toast. The texts must have just been an ego-massage: a little bit of bait to keep me keen. After all, why have one girl in love with you when you can have two?

He had run *me* a bath on the day he'd dumped me. Had he already met her then? 'Please, Michael, don't propose to her,' I whispered. 'I can't bear it.'

I stomped into the White Cross and pulled my purse out of my bra. 'Gin and tonic,' I said miserably to the barman. He looked at me with disgust. I was red and mad and sweaty. 'Don't worry,' I muttered. 'I'll sit outside.' I wouldn't want me in my pub either.

As I sat on an already frosty bench outside, my breath still coming out in fast, steamy clouds around my face, I wondered how I was going to get out of this crack habit. Perhaps there was a branch of Stalkers Anonymous in London. I felt an overwhelming wave of self-hatred. Mum was at Alcoholics Anonymous right now and I was *here*? *Please, God, make it work for her.*

I heard steps crunching towards me and then husky laughter. It was Nellie, holding a gin and tonic.

Of course.

'Oh. Er . . . I was so far behind after taking my inhaler . . .' I trailed off, smiling ruefully. It was very clear that I was lying and, besides, I was past caring. I'd lost the battle. She chuckled again. 'I stopped to check you were OK, babe, and saw you duck into the pub. It made me laugh. Sod running! I've been training every day – I'm allowed one drink, aren't I?'

She sat down next to me, without so much as a

drop of sweat on her, her face smooth and clean and her expensive Lycra clinging to her toned legs. I shrank into my old jogging bottoms and pulled my hood up, wishing I could just expire on the spot, as she opened, '*God*, so Michael's ex is apparently MAD – she keeps calling him and crying down the phone begging him to get back together with her and –'

The Nokia tune cut in and saved me. Never before had I been so grateful to hear it and never before had I been so happy to see Dave's name. He was calling from a very noisy-sounding pub. 'Where are you, Fannybaws?' he yelled.

'I'm in Richmond,' I whispered, moving swiftly down the pub's river terrace. The Thames looked hard and black and I was beginning to shiver.

'WHAT?' Dave roared.

'I said, I'm in Richmond.'

Dave moved outside his pub and asked what the bloody hell I was doing down there. I glanced at Nellie: she was watching me intently, no doubt presuming I was on the phone to my boyfriend (cat) Duke. 'Er, I'm running,' I said, as quietly as I could.

Dave burst out laughing. 'You? Running? Fran, you run like a scarecrow! What's going on?' As I cast around for a reply, though, he got it. 'Oh, for fuck's sake, Fran. You're not following Nellie, are you?'

'No,' I said obstinately. Then: 'Well, yes.'

Dave sighed. 'Stop it, Franny. Come up to Clerkenwell. Get in a taxi. You shouldn't be anywhere near that girl. God knows what's going on with her and Michael, but you're only torturing yourself, love. Come to the Three Kings.'

Hang on. 'Dave . . . are you at Gin Thursday?'

I could hear him puffing on a roll-up. 'Aye. Get your scraggy arse out of Richmond and come and join us.'

'You mean Leonie's having Gin Thursday *without* me?'

Dave chuckled. 'Well she couldn't very well have it with you. You've been cancelling her calls. Stop being a big gay and come and make up with her.'

'Is she there with Alex?'

'Yes,' Dave said, drawing on his cigarette. 'They're properly together, Fran love,' he added gently.

'That girl has the loyalty of a stray cat in the mating season,' I fumed. 'Michael has ruined my life and she responds by shacking up with his buttfuck of a best friend? Who has hated my guts from day one? He tried to get me *sacked* yesterday! What the fuck, Dave? Is Leonie going to start getting her muff waxed with Nellie fucking Daniels next?'

'I thought you were with Nellie "fucking" Daniels right now?'

Oops. I *was* with Nellie fucking Daniels. I looked round briefly but she was yacking away on her own phone, presumably to Michael, who was updating her on the latest fictitious outburst from his ex.

'You can't help who you fall for,' Dave said mildly.

'Fine, enjoy yourselves,' I said resignedly, ending the call. Fucking Dave with his smug little life in Wimbledon.

I began to walk back up the terrace towards the pub again. Maybe I should make friends with The Daniels. I was fast running out of other options.

Chapter Thirty

Fran,

Sounds like you've had a shit time of it. Whatever's going on, I'm
sorry. Make sure you look after yourself. Remember to eat
breakfast. Take a bath. Oh, and change your socks, you munter.
Joking. Hope you're OK. Say yes to a date. Two weeks tomorrow?
Sunday, 14 March?
I'm eating a massive pastrami sandwich. It's so beautiful I might
cry. Just so you know.

Freddy X

Date four: Toni

To my delight, the Backstreet Boys started playing as
I walked in. I suddenly felt a lot more confident about
tonight's date. It was the following Saturday and,
since I'd discovered that Michael had taken to lunch-
ing Nellie at Gordon Ramsay, I'd been doing my best
to accept that I'd lost him and divert my attention
elsewhere. It wasn't going that well but as Stefania

hissed 'encouragingly', as I left my flat earlier, I was at least trying.

Toni seemed 90 per cent homosexual but I didn't really care. My evenings were currently spent staring at my phone and fighting with Duke Ellington; anything else marked a vast improvement. And, of course, there was always Freddy in two weeks. Although I'd got to the stage where I'd gladly go on a date with a badger, I did feel a little bit excited about meeting Freddy. He made me smile.

Toni and I were meeting in the Islington Diner for a burger and milkshake and, if we got on, a bit of a rave-up in the Old Queen's Head across the road. I was ten minutes early, purposely so: I wanted sufficient time to scoff an extra milkshake before Toni arrived. I loved milkshakes with an unhealthy passion. Dirty, fatty, sweet and wrong. I *loved* them. I smiled at the waiter as he made up my chocolate and banana fix. He was beautiful and dressed in a skin-tight stripy top, like Jean Paul Gaultier; he wiggled his bottom as he sang along to Backstreet Boys. I resisted the urge to join in with my best karaoke voice.

Just as I started imbibing the satanic pleasures of the Diner's banana and Nutella shake, a very feminine northern voice behind me said, 'Frances?'

I turned round guiltily, straw in mouth, mid-slurp. Yup. Toni was gay.

He looked at my milkshake and sniggered excitedly. 'Hi, babe! I got here early so I could neck an extra milkshake in private but you've beaten me to it, you milkshake whore!' Toni was all giggles and raised eyebrows; he was as camp as tits. He kissed me on the cheek, smelling absolutely delicious. 'Mmm, you smell nice, Toni,' I told him, patting the stool next to me.

'Oh, *thanks*, babe! It's Jean Paul Gaultier!' he twinkled, crossing his legs and opening the menu. I chuckled. Perhaps he and the waiter would bond over their common Gaultier theme. The waiter evidently hoped so too: he came breezing over to our end of the bar, rolling up his sleeves to reveal two gigantic biceps. 'Hi, there,' he growled, completely ignoring me now. 'What's it to be?'

Toni pondered, without looking up. I clocked the waiter flexing his arms quickly and giggled to myself. It was going to be a funny afternoon.

'So, Toni, you're a celebrity booker then?' I asked, as we slurped hard and loud. I already wanted Toni to become my GBF. We could bond over our love of dirty milkshakes and maybe become gym buddies, staring at hot men's bottoms and making tits of ourselves in the free weights area.

'Yah,' he replied, turning towards me with an enormous smile. 'And I just LOVE it!!!' Toni, I could already tell, was someone whose speech would involve a lot of exclamation marks if it was written down.

'So what does a normal day entail?' I asked.

He giggled. 'Well, I work on *Coffee Break*, so all of the celebs you see on Matthew's sofa were booked in by me. I basically spend all day chatting to agents on the phone!'

I already loved Toni. He was my kind of gay and he was already making me smile in a way I hadn't since Michael had dumped me. He was wearing tight jeans with a torn vest and cardigan. 'Wow,' I replied. 'That sounds totally awesome! Do you know Katie Price?'

Toni smiled fondly. 'Oh, yeah, Kate and I have been working together for years. She's such a doll, never causes trouble. Whereas . . .' He rolled his eyes and whispered the name of probably the most popular woman in the UK.

'*Really?* Oh, my God, tell me more!'

Two hours, two milkshakes and two mojitos later, Toni and I left, giggling like children. Toni was in the middle of some catfight on Facebook via his iPhone and was punctuating our 'date' with outraged screams every time a bitchy update came through. I loved him.

By now it was half past nine and there was a queue outside the Old Queen's Head. Friday-night drinkers in fashionable outfits huddled over Magners at heater-warmed tables on the pavement, and a woman who looked like Meatloaf sat on a high stool divesting people of their cash and stamping their wrists. A sign outside announced that we could expect 'Broken

Beatz n breaks + vigorous nostalgia' upstairs tonight. My heart sank a little.

We got into the queue but, like me, I could sense that Toni was feeling a little reluctant. He was chattering away about his Facebook catfight but kept breaking off to stare with dismay at girls who were wearing Ray-Bans even though it was dark. Tentatively, I said, 'I hope they mash up their beatz with some Abba,' and before I knew it, Toni had bundled me into a taxi, yelling, 'Let's just go to fucking Popstarz!!!'

Thirty minutes later we were dancing to 'Billie Jean' in a sweaty gay club that smelt of poppers and fart. I felt a fleeting stab of sadness that I couldn't text Leonie, with whom I had a long and glorious history of dancing in farty gay clubs to 'Billie Jean', but pushed it away. I still hadn't decided what to do about Leonie.

Toni was the best dancer in the world, of course, and he was an immediate hit with the boys. To his left there was a child who looked like Brad Pitt aged twelve, to his right an enormous bald chap who looked like he lived in a gym, and behind him two lovely-looking boys with complicated hairstyles who couldn't decide if they wanted to kiss each other or kiss Toni. I giggled to myself. This was easily the best date of my life.

An exquisite specimen of a man wearing jeans and a waistcoat was dancing next to me, smiling. As the final rhythm section of 'Billie Jean' began to fade out and the opening bars of 'Holiday' tinkled in, he shouted, 'I can't believe Michael Jackson is DEAD! I had to take a fortnight off work when it happened! Would you like a pill, darling?'

I smiled and shook my head. Lovely Waistcoat Man laughed and grabbed me round the waist, guiding me through a dance routine that looked like something from an S Club 7 video. 'This is like an S Club video!' I screamed into his ear.

'Yeah, I did their choreography, love,' he replied.

Amazing.

I glanced about for Toni just as his back disappeared into the crowd surrounding the bar. In a normal club I'd have panicked, but here, in the farty environs of Popstarz, I felt totally content. I tried an experimental spin and crashed into a bony shoulder, which I grabbed and stroked apologetically, following the arm up to a man's face, which was staring at mine in utter amazement.

It was Alex.

No. I looked away again. This was not possible. Alex in Popstarz? And, in the crook of his arm, wearing an elasticated bandeau dress from the eighties, was Leonie. She was staring at me with abject fear, her arm dangling awkwardly at her side. It had clearly just been round Alex.

I stared at them both, at this utterly improbable spectacle in the middle of the dance floor at Popstarz, and tried to work out how to react. Alex might not have outed Mum but he'd handed my Chelsea tape to Hugh in an attempt to have me sacked. He was a weasel who had told Michael my news desk was for thick people and then gone on to steal my best friend. So, as far as I was concerned, the declaration of *jihad* that I'd left on his voicemail last week was still good.

But there, standing in his arms, looking at me beseechingly, was Leonie, my very best friend, the girl I'd been to playschool, primary, secondary and university with, the girl who had taught me how to kiss boys and forced me to eat when Michael dumped me. I missed her. Horribly.

Surely I wasn't going to have to deal with this at 1.36 a.m. in Popstarz?

Just as I decided that it would probably be best for all parties if I just turned round, resumed dancing with Lovely Waistcoat Man and pretended this wasn't happening, she detached herself from Alex and threw herself at me. 'FRANNY,' she yelled in my ear. 'I love you so much and I AM SO SORRY. PLEASE CAN WE BE FRIENDS AGAIN?'

After a few stiff, angry seconds, I relaxed. I couldn't live without Leonie. I smiled into her hair, which smelt of the same Tesco apple shampoo she'd been using since she was eight years old. 'Yes,' I shouted into her ear. 'Your love life is your business. I miss you too, you old slapper.' She screamed and hugged me even tighter.

A week without Leonie was a bad week.

'And Alex?' she shouted, looking at him with an uncharacteristically slushy face.

I shook my head. 'I'm sorry, Leonie. I can't.' Alex was watching us, clearly feeling exceedingly awkward. I wasn't bloody surprised. The devious, stinking bastard, trying to have me sacked like that. 'I know it wasn't Alex who sold Mum to the *Mirror*,' I said.

Leonie was delighted. 'NO! OF COURSE IT WASN'T!'

'And I will talk to him about it on Monday and sort it out. But he tried to have me sacked,' I shouted. 'I just can't go there. What you get up to is your business but I can't play happy families.'

'RIGHT!' she shouted, grabbing my arm and dragging me off towards the stairs. 'We need to talk.'

Alex watched us go with pure fear in his eyes.

Settled into a velvet booth in the even fartier indie room upstairs, surrounded by thin teenage boys who were dancing to EMO music and studiously ignoring each other, we talked. 'You're serious. You actually like him, don't you?' I said, starting to laugh.

Leonie reddened but laughed too.

Then Toni appeared, out of nowhere, plonked a vodka and Red Bull in front of me and minced off, winking. Now Leonie looked confused. 'That,' I sniggered, 'is my date. Toni.'

She looked even more confused. 'The guy from the Internet?'

'Yes. I'm on a date with a homosexual man, Leonie. Welcome back to my world.' And with that we lost it.

'It was Charlie Cunt-face Swift who sold Mum to the press,' I told her, when we'd recovered.

She nodded slowly. 'That makes sense. Dave said he'll nick anything for coke money. But how did he find out? I mean, presumably you didn't just tell him your life story while he went down on you?'

I explained that Charlie had had unlimited access to family emails for a good thirty minutes on Saturday.

'Poor you. Poor Eve. That's fucking awful, Fran. What a bastard.'

'At least it's got Mum going to AA. She's been to the group every day since Thursday. Maybe it needed to happen.'

'Yeah, Dave told me. I'm so glad, Franny. I've been thinking about her a lot. But, God, Charlie. What a total bastard.' Then she nicked my vodka and Red Bull, drank half of it, and yelled, 'But I bet he was amazing in the sack, right?'

I couldn't help but grin. 'Mind-blowing! He even rogered me in the wet room!' We both collapsed with laughter again.

'So, Alex. Fran, we really do have to talk about this. I know about the tape thing at ITN. Alex didn't give it to Hugh. He would never try to get you sacked. He really isn't like that, Fran. He didn't even want to do the Nick Bennett interview yesterday because he knew Hugh blackmailed you to get Nick in.'

'Of course he bloody well gave Hugh the tape. No one else even knew about it!'

Leonie shook her head. 'No. I know what happened, Fran. The tape was in the bin – presumably you threw it away – and the work-experience girl . . . what's her name?'

'Jacinta?'

'Yes, that's the one. She sounds vile. Far too keen. Anyway, she saw it in the bin and gave it to the tape library because she was told that that's what you do with lost tapes. No one there knew what the interview was for so it was passed around and eventually ended up on Hugh's desk. And he already knew you'd been stalking Nellie because he'd had IT do some report on you. He bollocked Alex, too, you know . . . C'mon, Fran, do you honestly think I'd get involved with the sort of guy who sneaks round trying to get my best friend sacked? As if!'

I looked at her guardedly. I wasn't sure about this story. Why would the tape have been in the bin? I'd hidden it in the bottom of my drawer.

But she was obviously serious about Alex. And, I realized, with a slightly heavy heart, I was going to have to Be Nice. 'You mean this, don't you,' I said slowly. 'You actually like him.'

She blushed and nodded shyly. 'Erm, well, for now, yes. Yes, I do.'

I sat back and sipped Toni's teenage drink while Leonie admitted to having fancied Alex since she'd first met him. 'I know he's a bit ratty in the face,' she giggled, 'but there's something about him . . . At first I just thought I wanted to scrub that smug smile off his face and, well, you know, ruin him a bit, but then I bumped into him in Borough Market a few days after Michael finished with you –' I winced '– sorry, but it was a complete coincidence – and we went for tea and cake and, I dunno, Franny, he just seemed genuinely concerned about you and really sad about it all . . . I just realized that he's actually this really sweet bloke. I think he's a bit lost. A bit insecure.' I stared at her in astonishment. She smiled weakly. 'You don't agree, do you?'

'Well, forgive me, Leonie, but it's not very easy to. He's always said *vile* things about me to Michael. I don't understand what his problem is.'

Leonie hung her head.

'And you've always been so vile about him!' I said, clutching at straws. Then I started to smile. 'Ah. You're never vile about men. I should have spotted it. It was cos you liked him, wasn't it?'

She smiled. 'S'pose. That first night I met him at Gin Thursday when Michael arrived in London I felt a bit crap, like I was about to lose you. I sort of think he felt the same about Michael because you two were so in love' – my stomach lurched painfully – 'and we got chatting. And then after that afternoon tea it was sort of like we were the survivors of this horrid fall-out. We chatted for hours on the phone and went on a date to Southend. He bought me fish and chips, Fran, and he kissed me and it felt incre– No, too much, sorry. I did try to stop it, Fran, I went on that date in Dalston with the man who had vampire teeth and shaved eyebrows, remember? But it didn't work. I couldn't think about anything other than Alex all night. I'm a massive disappointment to you, aren't I?'

'Shut it,' I said, patting her hand. 'Not at all. I just . . . It's so *messy*!'

Leonie looked tormented. 'I know.'

There was a brief pause while we watched the skinny teenagers shuffling around the farty dance-floor.

'Have you talked about me? And Michael?' I asked eventually.

She shook her head vigorously. 'No. I said to him almost as soon as he kissed me that we could never talk about Michael because it would do my head in knowing anything about him, wondering whether or not I should tell you. So he hasn't said a *thing*. He actually really understood and then he said, "Well, Fran's fine, anyway. She's dating, isn't she?" and I told him, yes, you were a total hit. He was impressed.'

I pondered this for a bit. 'Well, I don't think you could have chosen a worse man to fall for' – she coloured – 'but you're obviously smitten so . . . well . . . Just don't talk about Michael, OK?'

Her face cracked in two and she hugged me fiercely, shouting, 'I'm damn well going to bring you the man of your dreams with this Eight Date Deal!'

And with that we downed the remaining dregs of dirty Red Bull and went downstairs just as Britney started. Alex was still in the same spot on the dance-floor, looking like a frightened vegetable.

'I owe you an apology,' I said politely to him. 'I'm sorry. The *jihad* is off. I know you weren't responsible for what happened to Mum.'

'Absolutely not, Fran. Or the tape at ITN. Nasty business, that. Very unfortunate.'

I looked at him, long and hard, then gave him a watery smile. I didn't really believe him but I'd been backed into a corner.

'Well, see you around,' I said carefully.

He beamed like an eager child. 'I'd like us to be friends again,' he said. *Friends?* Since when had we been friends? But, because I was a useless knob, I nodded. And just as he held out his hand to shake mine, I leaned in to give him an insincere hug and thus delivered my right breast into his outstretched hand.

I fled to find Toni.

He was at the bar surrounded by adoring young men. 'Babe, something *fucked up* is going on, isn't it?' he said, handing me another vodka and Red Bull.

I smiled. 'Yep. That's my best friend, shacked up with my enemy. I'm quite sure he tried to get me sacked only four days ago. Oh, and he's also my ex-boyfriend's best mate! Ideal, no?'

Toni roared with laughter and swept me into his arms. 'Fuck 'em all! Let's DANCE, OK?' he yelled.

We danced for ages, him with style and rhythm, me with neither. Leonie and Alex twirled around us several times and, much to my amazement, I observed that Alex was in fact a remarkably good dancer. I smiled awkwardly at them, wondering how this was ever going to work. The way he was looking at Leonie was scary. His pointy, angular little face was literally aglow.

Somewhere in the region of four a.m., 'I've Had The Time Of My Life' came on and Toni dragged me on to the stage, yelling that he had Big Plans for us. Essentially we were to do the routine from *Dirty Dancing* where Patrick Swayze runs his hand down Baby's knockers, she jumps off the stage into his arms and the whole place starts dancing in unison. After a slightly unpromising start we began to make headway – like most other ten-year-olds I'd spent hours working out the dance – and before I knew it, it was time to launch myself off the stage. A gaggle of gays stood by, whooping and clapping as I broke into a run.

Heavy and uncoordinated after the milkshakes and Red Bull, I flew into the air like a polar bear. I crashed down on Toni's head as his arms gave way, and we ended up in a heap on the floor, helpless with laughter. Toni gave me a smacker on the mouth and we hauled ourselves up, coming face to face with Leonie who was laughing and shaking her head despairingly. 'You're the most embarrassing person I know,

Franny,' she yelled. 'And are you sure this man is homosexual? He's all over you!'

I twirled her round and yelled that Toni was my favourite man in the whole world. And that, yes, he was gay, was she actually blind?

Toni put his arms round me and started some sort of bump and grind routine as 'Africa' came on. I whooped loudly. Leonie, watching me over Alex's bony shoulder, continued to send me fairly obvious visuals regarding Toni's sexuality. 'Don't be ridiculous!' I shouted at her, as he got side-tracked dancing with the twelve year-old Brad Pitt-alike. 'Look at him! He's seen more cock ends than weekends!'

'Well, just keep an eye on it!' Waistcoat Man danced up and stole her from Alex.

Back from his brief romp with Brad Pitt, Toni grabbed me and screamed, 'HAVE SOME POPPERS, BABE!' shoving a bottle under my nose. I hadn't done this since I was twenty-one – the novelty of what was essentially glue-sniffing had kind of worn off at that point but, well, what the hell? I inhaled deeply, and a few seconds later my head caught fire and the helpless laughter and whooping came on. Toni kissed me on the lips and yelled, 'Oh, babe, what are you like?!' in my ear. I had another toke, then stopped because I could feel my brain frying and Toni had started snogging me. With tongues. And, dear God, he had his hand up my top. I sat down suddenly on the dance-floor, my head spinning.

In a blissful, glue-sniffed haze, I saw Alex remove Toni from my environs and Leonie bent double with laughter. Then I went back upstairs to sit on the velvet sofa and have a sleep. This was a strange night.

An hour later, wedged against the window of the 29 bus with Leonie on my knee and a deadly kebab spilling its guts over us both, I found myself helpless with laughter again. Leonie had decided to come and stay with me 'just in case you die of popper-poisoning' and we were talking blow jobs.

'I really believe it's an important skill,' Leonie said, as if she were talking about Photoshop proficiency. She fed me a mouthful of unidentifiable animal. 'Of course I enjoy it, but I think a lot of women get it badly wrong and need to learn.'

I laughed even louder through my kebab. 'Maybe you should write a book about it, or upload tutorials on to YouTube,' I suggested. 'I'm sure we could all learn a lot from you.'

She smiled enigmatically.

'NO! STOP IT! STOP THINKING ABOUT LAST TIME YOU GAVE ALEX A BLOW-JOB!' I yelled, occasioning the noisy bus to come to a standstill. Leonie smacked me lightly round the head, going red. 'Sorry,' I whispered noisily. 'You see, I'm drunk. That's the problem.'

'I'd noticed,' she hissed back. 'So please shut it! And, for your information, we haven't slept together.'

I was aghast. 'Oh, my God. It's been *weeks*! You're going to fall in love with him, aren't you?'

She took a bite of the kebab, looked me in the eye and said, 'Let us resume conversation on the topic of blowjobs.'

I'd missed this. Me and Leonie on a night bus with a kebab and a thorough analysis of the Blowjob. I could barely remember the last time we'd done it; being with Michael, wonderful though it might have been, had not provided the opportunity for many night-bus-and-kebab scenarios. Our Saturday nights had tended to be more of the sharing-a-bath-with-a-bottle-of-wine-and-the-papers variety. On the occasions when Leonie and I had got together, Michael had never joined us.

When we arrived back at my flat, ready for further bread products and an assault from Duke Ellington, I looked at the picture of Michael and me on Brighton Beach and, in spite of the usual blow-to-the-stomach moment of sadness, I felt an unexpected sense of liberation. I was thirty. Thirty years old. Night buses and kebabs were still very much part of my agenda.

Chapter Thirty-one

Frances, I am much loving. I like cats and woman maybe you will like come at Tunisia for visit and maybe wedding with me, I, live in Tunisia, my mother is waiting for you come tomorrow for visit us! We cook great food for you! Come to Tunisia! Come! We marry ourselves! Frances I want to have wedding to you!

'What did you get up to this weekend, Fran?' asked Stella Sanderson. We were in the kitchen and she was eating what appeared to be a piece of grey card with faeces spread on it. 'Want one?' she offered, following my gaze.

'Yes!' I replied immediately, grateful for any communication whatsoever after the silence of the previous week. Stella pulled a jar of homemade poo out of the fridge and started spreading it on another slab of card. My stomach heaved. After Saturday night's drinking and glue-sniffing efforts, Leonie and I had had to take ourselves down to the Grand Union for brunchtime burgers yesterday, at which point I'd got on to the Bloody Marys. Hard. Having checked in with Mum this morning – she had not had a drink in three days and sounded exhausted and utterly terrified of the task ahead of her – I felt very ashamed.

'Er, this weekend I was mostly researching stuff for work,' I said vaguely. And then, lest she cross-question me, had a bite out of her horrid-looking offering. It was surprisingly good.

'Oh, great. Sounds like we've got you back! Your *Alice in Wonderland* special on Friday was cracking,' she said briskly. I blushed and had another bite. 'So, what were you researching?'

Bugger.

'Erm, it was mostly – Blimey, Stella, this is delicious! What is it?'

I realized I was actually shouting. She smiled and spread some more. 'It's sprouted millet crackers with plum jam that I sweetened with stevia. So, what story are you cooking up?' She handed the cracker to me and brushed down her skirt, waiting for me to tell her precisely what I'd been researching all weekend. I scrambled around mentally for a few seconds. On the copy of *Metro* folded on the table behind her there was a trail for an article on the forthcoming Bloggies. 'Oh, I'm working up a story about the Bloggies 2010,' I said airily. 'They're an annual award for the world's best blogs . . .' I trailed off and had another bite, chewing with gusto. Stella was still looking at me expectantly. 'We Brits have won quite a few over the last ten years,' I improvised.

Stella raised an eyebrow. 'I see. Lots of reading this weekend, then. Is the awards ceremony over here? I thought a lot of these people were anonymous.'

'They are,' I replied. 'Actually, there isn't an awards ceremony, they just announce the winners online. The prize is tiny – it's more about the kudos.'

'Oh, right,' Stella said politely. 'So what shape is your report going to take if you don't even have an awards ceremony to film?' I took another bite, turning cold. Good bloody question.

And then, suddenly, a beautiful thing happened: a Useful Thought emerged deep from the bowels of my history A-level classes, most of which I'd skived off with Leonie in favour of all-day breakfasts at the Tesco café in Chiswick.

'Samuel Pepys began his diary four hundred and fifty years ago, in 1660,' I said matter-of-factly. 'I'm working up a piece about how the average London blog compares to Pepys's diary. These guys are just as important to the Londoners of the future as Pepys is to us now . . . And they're all writing about the same old London – all that's changed is the detail. I'll meet some of them, get into their lives and try to take out a few snotty historians who think that blogs are the devil's diarrhoea. It'll be fun. Irreverent. Contemporary. Character-based.' I took another bite, colouring.

Stella nodded slowly. 'Yes, that's interesting. I like the Pepys part of it.' She smiled.

'How come you've gone all health-food on us?' I

asked, popping the last of her hippie snack down the hatch.

'Just trying to look after myself better,' she replied. 'We have to take responsibility at some point, eh? Take control of our lives?'

She's not wrong, I thought, as I wandered back to my desk, wondering if it was OK to take paracetamol and aspirin at the same time for a hangover. I could do with looking after myself a bit more. Even if Michael *was* knobbing Nellie, I didn't need to drink myself to death. Much as it felt like a nice alternative right now.

There was an email from Dave in my inbox. He was up in Glasgow, having a long weekend with his mum, and I smiled, imagining his massive hairy frame being ordered around by the sharp, sprightly little woman in the photo he'd shown me. Mrs Brennan was a force to be reckoned with, by all accounts. Freya had once told me that the first time she'd been taken up to Glasgow and presented to Dave's mum she had been ordered into the kitchen to assist with dinner-making, handed a tumbler of Scotch and told quite firmly that Dave needed looking after and that if Freya didn't feed him broccoli at least three times a week there would be murder.

Morning Fannybaws! Heard you and Leonie patched things up. That's fuckin grand news! Next action points:

* Stop fuckin drinking

* Get dating

* And leave that fuckin Nellie girl alone, OK?

Sound advice, I thought. It was time to step away
from The Daniels once and for all. I'd lost; she'd won;
I'd never get Michael back. I promptly brought up
Nellie on Facebook and added her as a friend.

> Dave, I am insane. Just read your email and then added
> Nellie as a friend on Facebook. Please help.

I sat drumming my fingers on the desk and waited
for him to reply. While I waited, a Facebook notifica-
tion plopped malevolently into my inbox, telling me
that Nellie had accepted my request. Dammit! Why
was she on Facebook at 10.12 a.m. on a Monday
morning? Why wasn't she poncing around on Savile
Row or talking strategy around a sturdy white table in
Kensington? Helpless, I clicked through to her page.

And what I saw made my heart stop. No bloody
wonder she was on Facebook at 10.12 a.m. on a Monday morning.

Nellie Daniels is engaged!!!!!!!!!!!!!!!!!!!!!!!!!

Below it, among the mushroom cloud of comments
that had gathered overnight, was Jenny, Michael's
sister, with a gigantic, capital-lettered WOOOOOO-
OOOOOO!

The final twist of the knife.

I called Leonie and stared at my hands. My vision

had begun to tunnel and my mouth had gone dry. This could not be happening. It just *couldn't*. If they got engaged it would be the greatest rejection of all time. The largest imaginable demonstration of my inadequacy as a human being. Michael getting married to a Pantene model from Chelsea? Save for him getting married to Leonie, I couldn't think of a worse scenario.

Leonie didn't answer. My heart was pounding. I needed help. *Now*. My desk phone rang and I ignored it. Hugh had not yet lifted his embargo on me speaking on the phone and, quite frankly, there wasn't anyone work-related I wanted to speak to right now. I carried on staring at my hands, trying frantically to get a handle on my feelings. My phone started ringing again. I looked at it and registered, vaguely, that it was an 0141 number. Glasgow! I snatched it up, relief exploding through my veins like heroin. 'Dave! They've fucking got engaged . . .' I trailed off as my voice began to break.

There was a pause. Oh, treble fuck. 'Oh . . . er, news desk – hello?' I added.

A dry, papery cackle came down the line. 'Well, good morning to you, Frances. It's Glenda Brennan here.' She sounded exactly as she looked in the picture: small, efficient and sharp as a razor.

'Oh. Mrs Brennan . . . I, oh, blimey, I'm sorry. I sort of expected it to be your son –'

'David was just after telling me about your situation.

I told him it sounded like you needed some common sense drilled into you.'

'Right,' I mumbled.

'Still, it seems that the situation has progressed further since you emailed him just now,' she said briskly.

'What's going on, Mum?' Dave said in the background.

'Och, the girl has got engaged to Michael, that's all,' said Dave's mum.

That's all? But suddenly, with all my might, I wanted to be in Mrs Brennan's warm tenement kitchen with the smell of the batch loaves that Dave told me she made every Monday morning.

'Now, Frances, this situation is unacceptable. You're to get this girl out of your life right now, do you hear? And you're to stop drinking. This is an order.'

I waited for her to chuckle or do *something* to indicate irony, but nothing came.

'Frances, David told me about these web romances you've signed up for. Please take your friends' advice and go on them. Stop filly-willying around, you hear?'

I nodded dumbly.

'FRANCES?'

'Sorry, Mrs Brennan. Yes. Right. No filly-willying around.'

'Grand,' she said. 'And stay away from that girl. You masochistic fool.'

In spite of everything, I smiled. 'OK, Mrs Brennan.'

'Good,' she replied, scraping back a stool. 'Well, I need to get on with my bread. Good day to you.'

''Bye, Mrs Brennan,' I said, slightly dazed. 'Give my love to Freya.'

But she'd already put the phone down. Dave's email followed a few minutes later.

> I can't put it any better than that. Behave yourself. Hope
> your mum's doing OK. Back tomorrow X

Strangely calm, I logged back into Facebook and, without pausing for a second, went into Account Settings and closed my account. Just like that. Gone. Poof. Then I emailed Dave.

> OK, David. I've just committed Facebook suicide. And I've
> taken Nellie's number out of my phone. I'll arrange
> another date by the end of tomorrow & I'll think about
> this drink thing.

I meant it. I'd try anything if it stopped me feeling like I had just been run over by a train.

I took a deep breath, started up an email to Hugh about the Pepys/blogger situation I'd pulled out of my backside and pondered the 'drink thing'.

Was there a drink thing? Guiltily I thought about the weekend. There had definitely been a drink thing this weekend. Leonie and I had agreed that a Bloody Mary seemed like a reasonable start to the day when we'd arrived at the Grand Union for a hearty burger yesterday. But while she'd gone home at four, ready to get on with some work-related thing, I'd stayed for another. And then another. I'd excused myself on the grounds that Leonie, who was a charity mugger, clearly didn't have any 'work things' to be doing on a Sunday and was thus going to meet Alex to Finally Have Sex. Bloody Mary was my antidote to this terrible possibility.

Later on yesterday, when I'd returned at seven o'clock to feed Duke Ellington and have some therapeutic banter with Freddy, Stefania had arrived in my kitchen looking very pretty with newly washed hair hanging over her shoulders. 'Vhat in ze name of Guru Nanak are you *doing*?' she had asked, as she stood in my doorway. It was a reasonable question: I had tried to open a bottle of wine by pushing the cork into the bottle with a pencil because I had lost the corkscrew, but unfortunately the pencil had splintered at the last minute so I was now sieving the wine into a bowl.

'I'm filtering for bits of pencil,' I explained.

Stefania shook her head. 'I have come to take you to my lodgings,' she said. 'It is time you consumed something healthy. Dave told me you ate a sack of doughnuts and now I find you eating pencils and vine on a Sunday night. Come,' she said pityingly.

'Dave told you I ate a bag of Krispy Kremes?' I said. 'Why are you lot talking about me behind my back? Bloody Gestapo! Stop it!'

'Ve are merely concerned for you. Come viz me.'

I brought the bowl of pencil-filtered wine with me,

accepting that Stefania was quite right to pity me. I was pathetic. Drinking pencil wine when my mother had just celebrated three whole days of sobriety after nearly twenty years of chronic dependency? I was disgusting.

'Er, morning, Fran.'

I snapped out of my ponder, paracetamol still half-way to my mouth. Alex was standing next to my desk looking very uncomfortable. In one hand he held a thimble of designer coffee and in the other a copy of the *Independent*. I stared at it with horror, half expecting a front-page announcement about Michael and Nellie's engagement. Then I stared up at him, mute. The agony of Michael's engagement had left me incapable of speech.

'Um, I need to talk to you about something,' Alex began awkwardly.

'NO!' I yelled, my vocal cords miraculously restored. 'There's no need to say *anything* about Michael. I just found out.'

Alex looked even more uncomfortable. 'Er, OK. Are you all right? I can't believe it, Fran. It's just terrible.'

I nodded glumly.

As he stared at me, cringing like a frightened dog, I marvelled at the bizarre turnaround that Leonie had effected by letting Alex into her life. Gone was the repellent confidence of News Producer Alex who would have revelled in my misery: here instead was

Gawky Teen Alex, who seemed genuinely anguished about my horrible situation.

'Sorry again for accusing you of selling Mum to the press, Alex,' I said eventually. 'And for the, erm, rude message.'

We both smiled awkwardly.

'Not at all. I'd have done the same. And I just want you to know the tape had nothing to do with me,' he said.

'OK. Fair enough. Let's just get on, yeah?'

Alex's pointy features broke into a genuine smile. 'I agree! Do you want to go for lunch, maybe?'

One thing at a time, Ratty. 'Er . . . Not sure. It feels weird, Alex. What with this Michael stuff going on.'

Alex looked wounded. 'It's terrible, Fran. I met up with him yesterday and he told me. I got really angry with him and said –'

I cut him off. 'Thanks. I hear you. I'll survive this somehow but I don't think I'm ready to have lunch with his best friend just yet.'

Alex sipped his coffee sheepishly. 'Yes. I understand.' He glanced awkwardly at the burgeoning election team. 'Well, better go. Lots to do.'

'I'm sure there is,' I said politely. I didn't want to hear about his busy job. It should have been mine.

'You could . . . um, well, if you don't hate me so much you could always come and get involved,' he said.

I raised an eyebrow, trying not to look too keen.

'I could clear it with Hugh. He didn't really want me to do the Nick Bennett interview on Friday, Fran, he wanted you to do it.'

'Thanks,' I said slowly. 'That would . . . That would be great. Let me know once you've got the go-ahead.'

As I watched his skinny legs scamper away it occurred to me that he'd probably be best man at Michael and Nellie's wedding.

Michael and Nellie's wedding. The idea sliced through me like a butcher's knife. Sharp, precise, deadly. *Michael and Nellie's wedding.*

'Coolest blogs in London,' I typed furiously into Google, determined to get through the day without giving in to the wedding-shaped dark cloud of despair that was lurking dangerously at the periphery of my mind.

But it was out of my hands. Two seconds later, as I opened the clublondon blog, my phone delivered a message from Michael. Fran, there's something I need to tell you. Can we please meet up as soon as possible.

I slammed my phone down on the table. And then picked it up, suddenly calm. I thought of what Mum had said last Wednesday. *It stops here.* If Mum was brave enough to take responsibility for her mental wellbeing, so was I.

I hit reply.

I know what's going on, Michael. Please leave me alone and don't contact me ever again. Fran.

Chapter Thirty-two

Fancy a game of pin the cock in the arsehole? Mickey xxxxx

'NO NEWS FROM CAMDEN,' Stefania yelled. I winced and held my mobile away from my face. Even through the music and beery chatter at Smiths of Smithfield I could hear her as clear as a bell. This was because, according to her usual custom, Stefania was conducting our phone conversation in an out-and-out roar.

My heart sank. Where was my little furry prince? Duke Ellington had failed to come in for his breakfast this morning, a completely out-of-character occurrence. Even in the event of a nuclear fall-out he would come in for his breakfast. It was his chance to reassert his reign of terror over our yard each day.

But nothing. I'd bashed away at his can and called him for more than ten minutes to no avail. Stefania, doing yoga on a mat in the yard in spite of the eight-degrees temperature, had seemed genuinely worried and had even scampered up the tree, like a mad little elf, to check that he wasn't stuck on either of our roofs.

He wasn't. I'd given her my keys and asked her to come and check later on in the day. Judging by the frequency with which she'd called me, she'd spent the whole day in my house waiting for him.

I couldn't help but feel horribly afraid. Duke Ellington was like my child. 'OK, well, let me know if you see him,' I said miserably. 'And thanks. You're a good friend.'

But she was off, chanting some sort of cat-finding prayer.

'Pint of Asahi,' I said, to the nice Brazilian barman. He smiled crisply and said, 'Be careful with beer. You have good physique. Do not ruin it.'

'Seconded,' said Dave, as he arrived next to me and pulled up a stool. 'Since when did you drink draught beer?'

I smiled wanly. 'Well, you kept bollocking me about drinking so I thought I'd transfer to something a bit softer.' I took a sip and promptly belched. 'Not sure it's for me, though. I forgot about my belching. Do you want this? I can get some wine.'

Dave looked down at his hands. He seemed to be struggling to say something. 'Dave?' I prompted. He was running them up and down his worn old jeans, exhaling slowly. After a few seconds he looked at me and smiled.

'OK, Franny Fannybaws. Here's the deal.'

I sighed and took off my duffel coat. 'Go on,' I said, resignedly. There was a ladder in my tights. Glam Fran was a bit sketchy today.

He coughed, then said, 'You're going to stop drinking and I'm going to do it with you. As of now. We're going to stop drinking together.'

This, I had not expected. I looked at Dave, who had obviously been subjected to a severe haircut by his mum over the weekend. He looked tired, but his face seemed a lot younger now that it wasn't so obscured by his mane. 'How old are you?' I asked suddenly.

'Thirty-eight. That's not the answer I was looking for, Fannybaws,' he added, with a smile. 'Back to this deal, please.'

I studied the pint of lager in front of me and realized that, in the last week, three of the people I cared about most had begged me to stop drinking.

And at that moment the thought fluttered gently into my head that they might actually be *right*. It flew around like a timid butterfly, refusing to settle, but it didn't leave.

Had my judgement been up to much of late? No. And if I really *didn't* have a problem with alcohol, what was the harm in trying a few weeks without it? Apart from anything else, I felt confident that it would do wonders for my skin and would get everyone off my back.

'OK,' I said slowly, biting my lip. 'But it'll be hard.

I like booze. How will I do Gin Thursdays without gin?'

Dave grinned and gave me a double thumbs-up. 'Because I'll be with you,' he replied. 'You'll be doing your mum a huge favour by not drinking. And your head'll be in far better shape for your Eight Date Deal.'

How I loved Dave. Quite why a big hairy scary man like him, with his legendary career and legendarily beautiful partner, gave a flying fuck about me and my pathetic gin-drinking, doughnut-munching habits was beyond me. I jumped off the stool and hugged him, knocking him into a group of suited money types who were buying cocktails behind him. He gave me a brief squeeze and pushed me away, picking up my coat, which had gone flying in the assault. 'How's about we leave this pint behind and go upstairs for some scran? You could do with a square meal.'

As I followed Dave up the stairs, I gazed happily down at the bar spread out below me. Framed neatly by industrial steel and exposed brick, the after-work crowd roared on, oblivious to whether or not I had a drink in my hand. *No one cares,* I mused. *The only person who gives a shit whether or not I'm drinking is me. And that's not enough.* Feeling overwhelmed but a lot happier, I surveyed the crowd one last time before turning the corner of the stairs.

And as I did so, my eye was caught by a burst of

beauty. A pair of people so attractive that the drinkers parted before them, like the Red Sea before Moses. I swear the music was even turned down.

It was, of course, Nellie Daniels.

Why not? And she was with a really exquisite man. She was flushed and happy and, dear God, she was clinging to his arm as if her life depended on it. A fairly sizeable rock sparkled visibly from her left hand, which was curled round his arm in a way that said, *We are going to have sex later.* What the blazes . . . ? I shuffled sideways to the turn in the stairs and peered round the corner as they headed towards the bar.

There, the man ostentatiously picked up a handful of Nellie's shiny hair and moved it reverently over her shoulder to her back. His hand remained on her neck and he whispered intimately in her ear before raising his hand to call over the barman.

'Fannybaws?' Dave said, coming back down the stairs next to me. 'What are you doing now, you mental?'

I pushed him back up the stairs. 'Don't move another *inch*, Dave Brennan!'

Dave put his hands in his pockets and watched me from a couple of stairs above. 'Will you explain this to me or am I to stand here for the rest of the night?'

'It's Nellie! She's here with some hot bloke and, Dave, I swear, they're having an affair! He's all over her! And she looks like she's having some sort of orgasm!'

'Fuck's sake, Fran, is that why you wanted to come here? Are we on a fucking stalking mission? Thanks a lot.'

'No! I had no idea they were coming.'

Dave got a packet of Golden Virginia out of his pocket. 'Whatever. I'm going outside to have a fag. By the time I get back I want you sitting down and minding your own fuckin' business, OK?'

I grabbed him. 'No! Nellie can't know I'm here . . . Dave this is big – look at them!' Nellie and the man were standing at the bar with their faces less than a foot apart. Nellie was grinning coyly into his face and he had her left hand in his. He was staring at her ring. Then he said something in her ear, which made her laugh uproariously. Were they laughing at Michael's taste in rings? Then he silenced her by kissing her.

I glanced sideways at Dave, who was really quite shocked. 'Fuck,' he said after a few seconds. 'Fuck, that's really bad. She can't seriously be after marrying Michael with this going on?'

I shrugged. Dave withdrew and sat on the stairs next to me. He looked pissed off.

'Why are you cross?' I asked him, confused.

'It's not looking good for Michael, is it?' he said eventually.

'What do you care about Michael?'

He shrugged. 'I guess I just don't like infidelity much. Never had time for it.' I watched his face, which was pitted with real irritation. It was quite touching. Freya's fear of Dave's foreign travels was obviously misplaced.

Then I had a thought that made my stomach slide out of my bowels. 'Oh, God, Dave. Maybe Michael proposed to her because she got pregnant. Maybe they were never that into each other but he's marrying her out of honour. That's *exactly* the sort of thing I'd expect him to do. That's why he sounds so sad in his messages! But how can I take him back if he has a child? With The DANIELS?' I clutched the banister for support as my mind raced.

Dave resumed rolling. 'Get a grip, Fannybaws. And stay out of it. Whatever's going on it's got nothing to do with you, you hear?'

I peered round the corner again but Nellie and the man had gone. I scanned the floor, looking for Nellie's wall of shining hair, and suddenly located it, about five metres from me, advancing up the stairs.

I considered my options: grab Dave and run to the first-floor wine rooms or brazen it out and talk to her. All I knew was that I didn't want to be trapped in any of these venues with Nellie and her bit on the side. So, after a lightning-quick consideration, I grabbed Dave's tobacco and rammed myself down on the step between his knees. I took a deep breath, closed my eyes and launched my face at him, kissing his mouth just as it opened in surprise to ask me what the hell I was playing at. Nellie's stilettos clacked past us and I heard her soft, husky giggle as she saw the tawdry little scene.

For a couple of seconds Dave didn't move, he just sat rigidly with his arms at his sides while I face-raped him. His face was all spiky and there was a definite aroma of fag smoke about him. Finally, he regained his composure, grabbed my shoulders forcefully and shoved me away. 'What the fuck?' he hissed angrily. 'Get *off* me!'

I checked that Nellie had cleared our line of vision, then removed myself rapidly from between his long legs. Dave, meanwhile, was dusting down his coat as if I had just aimed a slurry hose at him. I didn't want to be kissing him any more than he wanted to be kissing me but the force of his disgust was a little hurtful. 'Erm, sorry,' I mumbled, rearranging my hair and standing up. 'But there wasn't time to run off and hide.'

Dave just shook his head. 'Have some bloody respect,' he replied eventually.

I went red. Dave had just announced his views on infidelity to me and within seconds I had thrown myself at him. 'I'm sorry! If you want I can tell Freya and make sure she knows it was just a strategic move.'

'You can stay well away from Freya, Fran.' He was furious now.

'C'mon, Dave,' I said lamely. 'I didn't mean to snog you. It was just one of those things. Y'know, like when you go to Ikea for a picture frame and come back with a kitchen. I was just trying to hide from Nellie.'

Unable to help himself, Dave smiled. 'Shite analogy,

Fran. But you're OK. Let's forget about it, forget about Nellie and go and have dinner, OK?'

I nodded gratefully. 'OK. They're bound to be going to the third floor – that bloke looks minted. Let's go and eat on the second, right? And you have my word, no more face-raping. EVER.' He grimaced and offered me his arm.

As I scanned the menu my brain whirred furiously. What was going on? Was my pregnancy theory right? And, if so, did Michael know about Nellie's lover?

'Stop it,' Dave said, without even looking up.

'What?'

'This doesn't mean you can get back together with Michael. It just means the situation, whatever it is, is even more fucked than we thought.'

'But Michael's been cuckolded!'

I was half delighted, half appalled. I still loved Michael – right down at a cellular level – but with this amount of baggage his appeal was a little more complicated. It wasn't just baggage, it was like a full-on left-luggage convention at Heathrow.

Distractedly I ordered and then breathed a sigh of relief as Dave stood up to go to the loo. As he went he gave me a warning look.

I got straight on the phone to Leonie. '*Fuck,*' she breathed, awed. And then: '*SERIOUS fuck. Fran.*'

'I know,' I muttered furtively. 'What do you think's going on?'

Leonie thought about it, then said, rather to my dismay, 'I think . . . Oh dear, I'm sorry, Franny, but I think it's all completely rogered. Way too messy. I think you need to keep away from him. Sorry, my darling.'

I popped an olive into my mouth and chewed miserably. 'Yeah. You're probably right. But, Leonie, it's hard. I miss him. It still hurts every single day. How am I meant to deal with this? It's like the best worst thing that could happen!'

Leonie said nothing.

'Oh, God, Leonie, do you actually *know* what's going on? Did Alex tell you?'

'No,' she said immediately. 'I was just thinking. Fran, you *have* to trust me: I have not and will not talk to Alex about you and Michael. Do you believe me?'

'Yes.'

'I cannot for the life of me work this out but I strongly urge you to just keep the hell away. OK?'

'Understood. Thanks, Leonie. 'Bye.'

Dave would almost certainly go for a fag after he'd been to the loo. If I did it quickly, I'd be able to sneak up and get one last look at The Daniels. I scampered across the floor, signalling to the waitress that I was coming back.

Creeping up the stairs to the third floor, I realized there was something I could do here. Something that would settle once and for all what Michael was up to in texting me and whether he knew about Nellie's dodgy dealings.

I slid back the lens cover of the camera on my mobile and inched my head gingerly round the corner of the restaurant entrance. I was Fran the Charlie's Angel. I was Jack Bauer.

Perfect! Nellie and the man were sitting by the window with Smithfield meat market spread out majestically below them; the lights of the Thames glittered distantly in the background. They were both hunched over the table so that a gap of only a few inches separated them and their faces were flushed. As I began to take aim, I clocked a bucket of very expensive wine sitting next to them. They were in fact sitting at a table for four. Was Nellie *mad?* Going out in public with another man was insane enough; surely she wasn't so brazen as to invite others?

The man leaned over and kissed her. She arched her back, lifting her hand to touch his face.

I took aim and fired.

And, of course, my flash exploded across the serene white-tableclothed room like lightning. They both jumped and turned to me, frozen in the doorway, camera in hand. And then I heard a familiar, child-like voice to my right, saying, '*Fran?*'

It was Jenny. Jenny Slater. Jenny and Dmitri.

Time stood still. I looked at them, then back at Nellie and the man, who were both thoroughly startled. Somewhere in the periphery of my mind it occurred to me that Nellie was rogered now: not only had I just gathered pictorial evidence of her affair but

Jenny – *Michael's flesh and blood* – had seen the whole thing too. But I knew this wasn't correct. I knew that the picture of hell unfolding around me wasn't quite right. I knew it was me who was rogered.

In slow motion, I saw Nellie get up from her seat and start to walk over. She was wearing a simple slip dress and expensive tights with chunky velvet platforms. Beautiful silver bangles jangled at her wrists. 'Hi, babe,' she said carefully. 'Were you just taking a picture of us?'

I turned to Jenny, who was evidently perplexed. 'How *lovely* to see you, Fran! I . . . This is odd!' she exclaimed.

My heart thumped loudly in my chest. There was no escape.

And then something bizarre happened. Nellie kissed Jenny and Dmitri quickly, before turning back to me. She'd *known* they were coming?

'Babe . . . what's with the pictures?'

'Hi, Michael!' Jenny called. At this point I nearly fainted. Please, dear God, please let Michael not be walking up the stairs behind us.

And then I saw that Jenny was smiling and waving at Nellie's lover, the handsome, flashy man who was getting up out of his chair and coming over towards us. *Michael?* I heard Jenny's voice, as if through a cloud, tinkling, 'Congratulations, Michael! What wonderful news! And do you know Fran too? Well, this is all a bit funny, who'd have thought it?'

Nellie was engaged to a man called Michael. Who was not Michael Slater. Not my Michael. Not my boy. *She didn't have my boy.* Michael had never kissed her. I felt tears of relief and shock form in my eyes and, before I had time to do anything about it, they started falling. I sat down suddenly on the floor and leaned against the door frame. 'Oh, my God,' I whispered. 'It's OK. It's not Michael.'

I came to a few seconds later. Jenny was kneeling next to me, looking floppy and worried. Dmitri was striding over with a white-aproned waiter, who was holding a glass of water. Nellie's long, toned legs were rising up in front of me and this new Michael was on his haunches, staring at me. I pulled myself up a little bit so I was sitting properly rather than sprawling against the door frame. They all talked over each other and I drank some water, working out what the hell to do next.

The decision was taken out of my hands by a gravelly Glaswegian voice. 'Oh, bloody hell, Fran. What have you done? Get up off the floor!' Dave's hand was outstretched in front of me.

Jenny started telling him that I'd just sort of fainted and Nellie started to say hello to him, recognizing him from Meditation.

As the dizziness began to subside, I found myself in possibly the most embarrassing situation of my entire life. I took Dave's hand and got up slowly, dusting myself down. Five different pairs of eyes stared at me, waiting for an explanation. Jenny looked deeply and genuinely concerned, Nellie was a bit embarrassed, and the men wore the expression that men always wear when a woman has just done something inexplicably silly.

Dave's eyes were boring into me: he was daring me to make up yet another lie. As I cleared my throat he shook his head, a tiny, almost imperceptible movement, which only I saw. He was right. There was only one thing for it.

'Right. Hi, Jenny. Hi, Dmitri. It's nice to see you. Sorry I decked it. And, Nellie, erm, hi. And Michael, yes?' He nodded. 'Well, nice to meet you. In fact, Jesus, you have *no* idea how pleased I am to meet you.'

They were clearly bewildered. The waiter drifted off, already losing interest.

'Er . . . ahem. I . . .'

Dave reached for my hand and gave it a quick squeeze.

'Well, you see, the thing is, and you are totally allowed to have me sectioned or fired or something, if you want, but, um . . .' This was mortifying beyond my worst nightmares.

Dave squeezed my hand again. 'Come on. The sooner you do this, the sooner you can let it all go,' he murmured.

I glanced up at him for reassurance. He nodded and smiled.

And with that I began to smile too. 'Nellie, basically I thought you were going out with Jenny's brother Michael. He's my ex. He broke my heart.' Jenny flinched but I carried on: 'We broke up a couple of months ago and he said something about a Nellie. So I looked at his Facebook friends and found you and decided that he was going out with you. It's killed me. I've . . . well, I've been pretty much stalking you, trying to work out what's going on,' I said.

Nellie crinkled her brow, clearly disbelieving. 'But, babe, *how*? I mean, we met by chance at that meditation class.'

I looked at the floor. Nellie started laughing. 'Oh, my God, you're precious. You invited me, didn't you?' I nodded, scarlet. 'And the shoot with Isabelle? Oh, my *God*, babe, that's *soooo* funny! And the running club!' By now Nellie was really laughing, her smoky Sloane voice suddenly warm with affection and amusement. 'Oh, babe, and what terrible bad luck that Michael is called Michael! Of all the bloody names!'

Michael, standing next to her in an impeccably cut suit, was restlessly tapping his foot. He began to smile too. 'Women,' he said, raising his eyebrows despairingly at Dmitri. Dmitri jangled the change in the pocket of his equally impeccable suit and nodded.

Suddenly Jenny threw her arms round me. 'Oh, Fran,' she cried. 'Oh, my poor Fran, you must have been going out of your mind. God, this is all so wrong. You and Michael should be *together*! You're made for each other!'

I'd really missed Jenny. I realized now that in my

haste to stalk Nellie I'd kind of abandoned her as an ally. We pulled apart and she looked at me with eyes full of compassion. 'Poor old Fran,' she said again. 'Come and have dinner with us.'

I began to back away into Dave. 'No, no, I . . .'

She was firm. 'No, I insist. Nellie? Is this OK? My bloody brother has put this poor girl through hell. I promise you she's a good egg!'

Nellie smiled. 'Yuh, I know. We get on well. And I *love* that I had a little stalker! How cool! Yuh, Fran, you must join us. We're celebrating the engagement!'

I looked at Dave. He shrugged. 'Are you sure you're not freaked out?' I asked Nellie.

'No, babe! No, I love it! I'm a total full-on Facebook addict! I stalked my ex like a *fiend* when we split up! Oops, sorry, sweetie,' she added, patting Michael's sleeve.

'Yup. Come and join us. Waiter, two more, please,' said Michael, springing to life. He had a posh, assertive voice and looked like he'd exterminate you if you crossed him. The waiter all but ran to get the extra place settings.

An hour later, everyone was still laughing – albeit kindly – at my expense. The mood was relaxed and Dave was in excellent spirits, regaling everyone with tales of my insane tactics. 'I couldn't believe she went running with you,' he told Nellie. 'I mean, did you notice how fuckin' uncoordinated she is?'

'Shut it,' I told him. 'I'd like to see you running.'

Nellie giggled uncontrollably.

I'd avoided asking Jenny anything about Michael for the last hour or so. Since she'd said that he'd been miserable without me I'd been floating on a cloud of joy and relief; I knew I'd find out more in due course. All that mattered was that he missed me. Now she took my hand and started talking.

'I still don't understand why you thought my Michael was with Nellie, my love,' she said kindly. 'What was it he said about a Nellie that made you look for her in his Facebook friends?'

'Well, the day you went into labour you asked me to call Dmitri so I did and then I . . .' Jenny looked at me with such sympathy that I suddenly felt close to tears '. . . and, God, Jenny, I'm so sorry. I looked at your phone because I was so miserable and mad and I wanted to see if he'd texted you. And he had. He said he was with a Nellie. So I kind of called him and he thought it was you. He said he was with Nellie and she had some jumpers and he was walking her home and then coming to the hospital.'

'*Love* it, babe.' Nellie giggled.

Deep breath. 'And then I found her in his Facebook friends and Googled her and found she worked in PR. And I realized she must have been the fashion PR who'd been giving you free maternity clothes, and because she's so bloody beautiful, I just thought he must be shacked up with her –' Nellie smiled, obviously loving this '— and then when I called you in hospital a few days later he was there with Nellie. I heard both of them.'

I left out the bit when I'd 'borrowed' Nellie's Black-Berry and had seen a message from 'Michael'. There was a limit to how far I was prepared to shame myself. Jenny squeezed my hand. 'Oh, little Franny, you poor thing. How you must have tortured yourself!'

Nellie was all but squealing with excitement. 'Yuh, I was *totally* with Michael Slater the day you had Lily!' she crowed. 'But how funny, because you'd palmed him off on *me* for the day so you could see Fran!' Jenny nodded, smiling. Dave forgot himself and reached for the wine, remembering at the last minute and return-ing, slightly disgruntled, to his virgin cocktail.

'No offence, girls, but Michael isn't rully my thing. I mean, he's lovely but he's a bit, well . . . *sedate*,' Nellie said.

I started laughing. As if Nellie would ever be inter-ested in my boy. And once I'd started laughing, I couldn't stop. 'I'm a certifiable mentalist. I'll totally understand if you decide to press charges,' I said to her.

She cackled with delight. 'If you go down, I'll be going down with you, hon! I never knew anyone stalked as much as me!'

'See?' I said to Dave. 'See? It isn't just me. Every-one does this stuff!'

'Whatever, Fannybaws. You just tell yourself that.'

I looked at Jenny to see if she, too, was about to

throw her cap into the stalking ring but she seemed suddenly rather sad. 'Are you OK?' I mouthed at her.

'Yeah,' she said. 'But Michael's a mess. I'm so worried about him. He misses you so much — he's just not been himself since you split up.'

My stomach was churning again and I bit my lip. 'But, Jenny, he finished with me. It was all his idea. The separation, the ninety days without contact, everything. I just sat there and cried.'

Jenny nodded sadly. 'I know. He told me. He told me everything except WHY he did it. He . . .' Now she seemed on the edge of tears. 'He was going to propose to you that night, Fran. He had the most beautiful ring . . . It was our grandmother's, made for her in Egypt in the thirties. I just don't get it. It's so sad.' Her lip trembled a little and I felt tears gather in my own eyes.

'Oh, God,' I whispered. The table went silent. 'He had something in his pocket. I bloody knew it was a ring-box. I miss him, Jenny. So much.' A loud sniff to my left revealed that Nellie had decided to join in. I saw a single perfect pearl of a tear glide down her flawless cheek. Her empathy was the final straw and, without further ado, I started bawling. Not perfect pearly Daniels tears but messy, mascara-filled globules of sadness, full of the shock and horror of that night in Green Park.

The women cried while the men shuffled in their seats, embarrassed. 'Come on, girls,' barked Michael, half impatiently, half sympathetically. 'It's not the end of the world! They can get back together!'

Jenny nodded rapidly. 'Yes!' she cried. 'I so hope you do!'

I poked at my lamb cutlet. 'He's been texting me recently saying how much he misses me.'

Nellie mopped up her one tear and yelled, 'Traitor! Behind my back!' Her Michael shot her a warning look. I suspected his tolerance of this situation was beginning to fray.

'Yes . . .' Jenny paused. 'He heard you'd started seeing someone. Someone beginning with D? I can't remember. Is that true?'

'Oh, yes! Duke! What happened to him?' Nellie asked interestedly.

I blushed deeply but Dave laughed. 'Duke Ellington is Fran's cat,' he explained kindly. Nellie gasped, thrilled at my further deception. 'But she *is* dating,' he confirmed.

'I'm dating but it means nothing,' I said hastily. 'My friends made me promise to go on eight dates while I waited for the ninety days to be over. It's just a silly game.' Jenny's face showed relief. 'I thought I'd be more likely to get him back if I waited the ninety days like he suggested, and worked on being a bit less insane in the meantime. He's going to be my date number eight, I hope.'

'Good plan, Franny,' Jenny said. 'I think that's a great idea. Michael's a fool and this bloody ninety-days thing is a predicament of his own making. Let him sweat it out. Trust me, I know how much he's missing you.'

Dmitri had his head in his hands and was shaking with laughter.

'What?' I said to him.

'I just cannot believe, Fran, that you told Nellie you were dating your cat.'

I felt a little stab of fear, hoping that Duke Ellington was now back in my kitchen.

Half an hour later I was rooting around for my wallet. I needed to get home, first to find Duke Ellington, and second, to work out what to do about Michael.

'You're not off to see Michael already, are you?' asked Dave, suspiciously.

He was fully on my case. If I planned to see Michael before the eight dates were over, I'd have to do so in secret.

'Duke Ellington's disappeared. I need to go home and try to find him,' I replied.

'Seriously? That little fucker never strays far. Do you want a hand finding him?'

'No, no, don't be silly, it's miles out of your way.' I got out a couple of twenties and put them on the table. Michael waved them away dismissively. 'Really, please don't.' He shook his head and I noted that his expensive hairstyle didn't move.

Dave pushed his chair back. 'Thanks, matey,' he said to Michael. 'And may I apologize on behalf of my colleague here for her crazy behaviour?' he added, with a grin.

A chorus of 'Not at all' ensued.

I sighed, smiling. Fran the lovable clown was back in business. But she was a damn sight better than Fran the drunken stalker, even I could grasp that.

'I'm so happy to see you,' I said, as I hugged Jenny goodbye.

'You too, darling Fran. I've got my fingers crossed for March the twenty-third. Even Mum and Dad are hoping you two will get back together!' She giggled. We both knew that this was not true.

Nellie stood up and grabbed me in a warm embrace. 'So nice to meet another stalker, babe,' she enthused. 'We'll be cured some day, eh?' She looked affectionately at her gold-plated fiancé. 'Actually, I think I already am.'

'Did you look on the roof?' Dave asked, as we sped along St Pancras Way. He had a roll-up tucked behind his ear, and his eyes were dark and oddly foreboding as the shadows of London shifted across his face.

'Stefania did,' I replied.

'Hmm. Reckon I know where he might be.'

The taxi rumbled on. I hoped very much that he did.

'NOZZING!' Stefania hissed, as soon as we stepped through the gate. And then: 'Oh, good evening to you Dave.' She smiled warmly as Dave bent down and kissed her on the cheek. She was so pretty when she smiled. 'To vhat do ve owe zis pleasure?'

'Just thought I'd pop over and see if I can find that damned cat. Trust him to cause a bloody nuisance when Fran's a wreck.'

Stefania rolled her eyes in agreement.

Dave strode to the back of Stefania's shed purposefully. 'Oi, Duke Ellington, you little fucker, are you down there?' he said, as he disappeared out of range.

Stefania watched him go and smiled slowly. 'Aha! I zink he is looking in ze old pit where ze cars went.'

We heard a bang and a bit of a commotion.

'He's down here!' came a muffled shout from under the shed. 'And he's just fucking bitten my hand.'

'My baby! THANK YOU SO MUCH, DAVE!' I jumped up and down a bit. 'Do you need help?'

'No point all of us getting attacked, he's only – STOP IT, Duke Ellington, YOU BASTARD!' I giggled and started to fill Stefania in on tonight's events. Assorted bangs and curses from under the shed accompanied my recital.

Stefania was strangely silent. Eventually she said, 'Frances, I sink you need to vait ze ninety days before you see Michael. I sink zis very strongly. No, in fact I TELL you. Stefania is TELLING you, Fran.'

Startled by her ferocity, I began to explain that that was exactly what I'd decided to do but then an enraged miaow rent the evening air, followed by 'FUCKING BASTARD,' from Dave. I giggled. Duke Ellington had been excavated. A couple of seconds later, Dave's head emerged from under the shed, his large left arm clasping an angry, scrabbling cat. I clapped my hands, flooded with relief at the sight of my little grey weapon. Dave tried to hand Duke Ellington to me but my cat leaped out of his arms and galloped angrily up the stairs to my flat. The night was silent again.

Stefania had disappeared. I shrugged. This obsession she had with the Eight Date Deal really was quite ridiculous.

'Dave.' He carried on brushing himself down. 'Dave!'

'Aye, Fannybaws.'

'Thank you. For everything. You're a true friend. I am so grateful to you, for the drink thing, for Mum, looking after me tonight, finding my cat – everything. You're a bloody legend. Freya is a very lucky woman.' And with that I threw my arms around him.

Dave chuckled. 'No further assaults, remember?'

I removed my arms hastily.

'What did you do with Stefania?'

'Oh, she flew into a sulk about Michael. She's worried I won't complete your bloody date challenge. Honestly, the way you lot are carrying on about it!'

Dave hooked the roll-up from behind his ear. 'Just do it,' he said. 'Night.' He walked off, whistling.

'THANKS, DAVE!' I yelled after him.

Few people had friends like Dave.

Twenty minutes later, grateful to be going to bed sober for once, I was curled up with a rather cobwebby Duke Ellington and my phone cradled in my hand. A message to Michael sat on the screen, ready to be dispatched, the cursor blinking patiently. I'd read it approximately five thousand times now and I reckoned it was good to go.

I'm sorry about the other night. I thought you'd got engaged. Long story. 23 March is only three weeks away. Let's see each other then, OK? And you were right – no contact will make it all the better. X

I thought about it for a few more seconds, remembering all the pain and despair I'd felt over the last weeks. And then I thought of his grandmother's ring, and the sadness in Jenny's face when she'd talked about him, and knew it was OK. He loved me. He'd made a mistake. He'd panicked, for whatever reason, and now he was paying the price.

I was safe. I turned off the light and pressed send. Hugging myself, I smiled into the darkness. In three weeks I'd get my boy back.

Chapter Thirty-three

That was probably the most complicated compliment I've ever
received but thanks anyway. Much as I like your photos I am a
bit confused by your bi-polar wardrobe. Are you Power Woman
or Scruffy Bastard? You seem to be half and half.
Regardless, you're lovely. I wish I could meet you sooner. I'm
tired. Can't sleep. Fed up today. Hope you and your cat/mad
neighbour/weird friends are all well. Fx

'You look quite normal tonight. What went wrong?'
Dave asked me.

I peered at my jeans, Converses and an old H&M
stripy top. 'Well, just having a casual day . . .' I said.

Stefania started laughing. 'Stuff and nonsense! You
vore zose other clozes because you thought Michael
was making ze sex wiz Nellie! You thought you vould
pull him back viz ze tailoring! But you vere, of course,
very wrong.' I blushed. To soften her words, Stefania
laid a hand sympathetically on my arm. 'You are a
good girl, really,' she said.

'Can we stop blowing smoke up Fran's arse and get an
update on the Eight Date Deal?' Leonie said, slurping

her gin and tonic. She was wearing a really beautiful 1940s hourglass dress that on me would have been matronly but on Leonie was the sexiest garment ever made. She was wearing blue tights with yellow vintage boots and her hair was falling down her back in cascades of fiery red. No wonder Alex was wetting his pants over her.

'Yes, vot is the latest viz your dates, please?' Stefania chimed in, pulling out a little pocket book.

I burst out laughing. 'What the fuck is that? Are you taking *notes?*'

She nodded solemnly. 'Yes. Ve need to make sure sings are covered. You have less zan sree weeks to go.'

'I'm getting back together with Michael. What does it matter?' I said gently.

They all ignored me.

I sighed. 'OK. Well, in two days' time I have a date with Martin.'

Stefania started scribbling. 'And who is zis Martin?'

'Dunno. Don't really care. I just want this to be over. Let's see . . . I think it said he was six foot two, he's a banker and he lives in Parsons Green.'

'Good luck, Fannybaws. Sounds like a match made in heaven,' Dave said helpfully.

'Shut it. Yeah, he's about thirty-four, and he said he likes cheese. That doesn't sound too bad.'

Stefania continued to scribble. 'Income?' she asked.

'I don't know! I picked him because he was the best of a bad bunch!'

Stefania looked disappointed.

'I'm going on the date, OK? What more do you want?'

'I vant you to take zis more seriously, *zat*'s vhat I vant.'

'Er, guys, given that I've forced myself to go on four shit dates already, I do rather think you should be a bit more supportive.' Silence. 'Jesus, I went on them to keep you happy!'

'Stefania, it's OK,' Leonie said eventually. 'Personally I think we should have written into the rules that Fran had full sex with at least two men before she saw Michael again . . . but never mind.'

'*Rules?*'

'Of course,' Stefania muttered crossly, waving her notebook at me.

Leonie carried on: 'Anyway, three men to go before Michael. Maybe this Martin will be able to give you one on Saturday,' she said hopefully.

'Unlikely. We're meeting on Hampstead Heath for a picnic.'

'Perfect. Everyone has sex there,' she replied, apparently without irony.

'It's fuckin' March!' Dave said, horrified.

'Yes, but it's going to be nineteen degrees on Saturday. How awesome is that? And we can always decamp to Hampstead if it gets cold. For a cup of tea,' I added pointedly.

Dave raised an eyebrow. 'Do you fancy this chap then?'

'Nope,' I replied. 'Guys. Please get this into your heads. I love Michael. He's my One. And he wants me back. I agree that dating is a good idea but stop, I beg you, planning my freaking wedding to some geek off the Internet. Cos it ain't going to happen!'

'Vhatever,' Stefania said, looking bored. 'Anyone else?'

I smiled. 'Well, actually, there's this guy called Freddy. He's away at the moment but we're going to meet up when he gets back. Probably a week on Sunday.'

Leonie put down her drink with exaggerated precision. 'Excuse me, Frances O'Callaghan, is that a smile?' she asked incredulously.

I tried not to but somehow ended up with a broad grin. 'Stop it! No!'

'It damn well is,' Dave said, amused. 'Spill the beans.'

I told them all I knew. 'He makes me laugh,' I finished. 'But he feels sort of safe. You know. Not one of those ones you die trying to keep up with.'

Stefania nodded furiously. 'I know! I know! I know vhat you mean!'

I stared at her, surprised, and she blushed. 'Freddy,' she muttered, writing his name into her book.

'Do you like *him*, then?' Dave asked.

'Well, yes . . . I mean, he's good-looking, he doesn't mind me saying "cunt" and he likes Dire Straits. But it's all fantasy, meeting someone online. You can be anyone you want to be when you've got the protection of a computer,' I said.

Stefania wrote down, 'cunt/Dire Straits/fantasy'.

'I'm going to say this one more time, though, guys. I'm getting back together with Michael and that is that.' I downed my orange juice and went off to the loo, humming under my breath. The knowledge that Michael was out there, sad and jealous, torturing himself about my dating in the way that I had tortured myself over him and Nellie had completely turned things round for me. At work I'd suddenly been productive again and, although I said so myself, my afternoon helping Alex and the clever politics dudes yesterday had been nothing short of a gigantic triumph.

In the mirror I saw a scruffy girl staring back at me. But she had bright eyes and a whiff of hope and purpose about her. She wasn't crammed into some ludicrous Chelsea outfit and she was not sitting in a bush stalking anyone with a pair of binoculars. Instead she had three infuriating but well-meaning friends trying to help her, and an amazing sort-of-ex-boyfriend waiting for her to take him back.

When I emerged a few minutes later, Leonie was at the bar, holding court with the men from the table next door. They were insisting on buying her a drink and she was toying with them in a friendly but disinterested manner. This really was going to take some getting used to. But, then again, if Michael and I *were* going to get back together, and if things continued to improve between me and Alex, we would be the coolest foursome in the entire world! We would eat Sunday lunches in light and airy gastropubs and we would enjoy wintry trips to Brighton where we would take clever photographs with vintage cameras. We'd eat cupcakes in noisy cafés in the Lanes and discuss literature. It would be amazing. I would magically find myself to be as clever as Michael. I would finally be one of those Happy London People In Their Thirties!

As I turned towards our table I stopped. Dave and Stefania were talking intently about something and they were . . . well, *close*. They'd turned their chairs to face each other . . . and their knees were touching. Stefania's over-dramatic irritation of five minutes ago had been replaced by something a lot more – I choked slightly on the word – tender.

As I came into their peripheral vision they sprang apart, looking shifty. I wasn't sure I liked this. I picked up my glass and said, 'Top up,' before walking quickly back to the bar.

'S'cuse me,' I said to the men around Leonie. 'Do you mind if I borrow my friend back a minute?' One tried to give her his card.

'Actually, I have a boyfriend,' she said easily. They sidled off and I gawped.

'Shut up,' she said.

'Tell me, straight up. Are you going to fall in love with Alex?'

She gazed down at her vintage boots. 'Actually, I already have, Fran.'

It hung in the air between us, impossible to retract. And as her big brown eyes began to scan mine frantically for condemnation, I realized that I was truly, marvellously happy for her. Properly happy, in a way that even a week ago I couldn't have imagined being. I flung my arms round her. 'I frigging love you, Leonie,' I said.

She squeezed me, relieved. 'Mutual.'

'An orange juice and lemonade for my old drunk of a friend,' she said to the barman.

I thumped her leg. 'Hey, talking of which, Mum's been sober one whole week! Isn't that awesome? I'm off to Cheam soon for a celebration dinner.'

Leonie beamed. 'Yes, that is TRULY awesome. To Eve!' She raised my drink in a toast.

'Dave and Stefania are being really weird together,' I whispered.

Leonie glanced at them. They were sitting normally again, talking as old friends. 'How'd you mean "weird"?'

I thought about it. 'Um . . . Well, I know this sounds mad but I think they were actually *flirting*.'

'Don't be absurd! That's impossible!' She giggled and pulled her hair into a ponytail. The men stared at her with sad and furtive longing.

She was right. 'Yes, sorry. Moment of madness.

Dave's been with Freya since the dawn of time and Stefania is very clearly asexual.' Leonie smiled. I grabbed her hand. 'I really am happy for you, you know,' I said. 'God knows what Alex's problem was but he's been really nice the last few days. And he *is* good-looking, in a sort of East-Londonish way.'

'He's gorgeous. Empirically gorgeous. And you know what? He's not actually that skinny when you –'

'NO! NOT YET!'

Leonie raised her eyes to the ceiling. 'Hadn't you better get off to your mum's house, Fran?' she asked pointedly. I kissed her on the cheek and left, glancing at Dave and Stefania one last time.

Everything looked normal again. 'CIAO!' I shouted at them as I sailed out of the Three Kings.

Ninety minutes later, I walked into the house of my childhood. The lamps were on, Rachmaninov's Clarinet Concerto was tinkling merrily away from Mum's archaic music system and there were unfeasibly delicious cooking smells wafting through from the kitchen. Mum was showered and dressed – progress from earlier in the week – but she wasn't her usual self. There was no power suit, for starters, and her hair was pinned up roughly without so much as a whiff of hairspray. She was standing by the cooker, stirring something absently. When she saw me she looked simultaneously pleased and afraid.

'Mum! This smells amazing!'

She gave the curry another stir, then sat at the table, patting the seat next to her. 'One of the girls from the meetings came round and made it for us. She left about ten minutes ago. She did all this . . .' Mum gestured vaguely towards the lamps, music and unnaturally harmonious surroundings. 'I'm not up to much, Fran. I've been sleeping a lot. My head's a bit of a whirlwind without all the alcohol washing around.'

'Are you still craving a drink?' I asked. I'd half expected her to be having a face-off with a bottle of gin.

She thought for a minute. 'Right now, no. Earlier today? Yes. So badly I could hardly breathe. I'm a yo-yo at the moment. But I've got a sponsor and I call her whenever I feel bad. She's wonderful. I have no idea why she wants to help me.'

I stared at her. 'A what?'

'A sponsor. When I'm going mad, I talk to her rather than having a drink. It's hard to explain. Anyway, it's been a week since I drank, Fran. I feel insane one minute, elated the next. But I'm sober. Isn't that a miracle?'

'Yes,' I said, humbled. It was like talking to a fragile child. I'd never seen Mum so open or honest. She drifted off momentarily.

'So what do you all actually do? How does it work?' I asked, cursing myself for not having researched it first. I smiled encouragingly while Mum thought about her answer.

'God, Fran, I don't know how it works yet. I don't know anything. I just know that everything those people say makes sense to me. We're all so different and yet we seem to be the same person. They were talking about their families and it made me cry, Franny, thinking about you. I –' her voice started to wobble '– I just want to be sober, for you. I don't really care about me.'

'Mum, no. You're doing this for you. Not me. Not anyone else.'

Her eyes glazed. She was staring at the curry, which was beginning to bubble over. 'Yes. That's what my sponsor said earlier. I'm doing it for me. For sanity.'

I got up to stir the curry.

'I've got a big journey ahead of me,' Mum said steadily. 'And I'm really scared. It feels . . . a bit over-whelming, to be quite honest. But I don't think I have a choice.' She leaned towards me and I came over to hug her.

I felt choked with emotion. I dug my fingers into her woolly jumper and tried not to cry.

'I'm so proud of you, Mum,' I whispered, into the side of her head.

Much later on, unable to sleep and reading a dog-eared *Mizz* from the box under my bed, I pondered how miraculous it was that Mum was asleep next door without the aid of a bottle of gin.

Literally, a miracle.

I sat up in bed and pulled my laptop out of my bag. I might as well make use of this dead time and try to tie down my last remaining date. I had Martin on Saturday, Freddy a week on Sunday and, hopefully, Michael in nineteen days. 'Let's rack up one more freak,' I murmured as my dating site loaded.

Four messages had arrived in the past twenty-four hours. Four! I felt a little lift when I saw that one was from Freddy. It was a shame he was so cool, I thought fondly. Had things not done an about-turn with Michael I'd be really rather excited about meeting him.

Martin's latest message read: I shall bring a picnic. May I presume that when you say that you, too, like cheese, your palate extends beyond the average Camembert and Stilton platter?

Of course, I lied. My palate did *not* extend beyond the average Camembert and Stilton platter. In fact, if all the cheeses in the world were swept up in a terrible tornado and Camembert was the only survivor, I'd be absolutely ecstatic. But I was open to suggestion.

The next message was from an aspiring rocker called Jolyon. He invited me to go and see him in a gig tomorrow. Invitations like that were only one stop away from straightforward masturbation: invite a girl you've never met to stand alone in the audience while you play the drums? Sweet Jesus!

The next message was from someone called 'Benj'.

Hi, Fran. Liked your profile. It made me laugh out loud which is a rare thing on here. Was it written by some sort of Bratislavan convict? What do you do in telly then? I own a television; I hope that qualifies me sufficiently for a date with you. Oh, and I too am quite partial to a dough-nut. Hope to hear back. Benj.

I sat back and inspected his profile. He wasn't too bad, actually. Far too trendy for my liking – there weren't just fitted jeans in his pictures but full-on drainpipe situations, rolled up with orange socks and old leather brogues, and a selection of hats that meant he could only possibly live in Hackney. Like Alex, he seemed partial to low-cut V-neck T-shirts and he was also of the fashion facial-hair school. In more than one picture he was working on a Mac in a postmodern tea-house somewhere in East London. But I needed to slot someone in between Martin and Freddy.

I stared at his photo, weighing it up. Benj looked dangerously meeja and I didn't much like his Bratisla-van joke, but he did have an otherwise reasonable sense of humour and a nice enough face.

Please tell me about the sort of doughnuts you like, I replied, knowing that this would inevitably become date six. I felt a bit flat. This sort of date lead-up was always the same: witty banter, followed by excitement and then bitter disappointment when the real-life version turned out to have a massive bottom or cowboy boots.

Like saving the tastiest bit of steak for the end of the meal, I finally clicked on Freddy's message, ready for something delicious.

Chapter Thirty-four

Date five: Martin

I rolled up my jeans to expose two ankles so white that they were practically see-through. They seemed almost fluorescent on the plastic-backed tartan rug that Mum had left in my flat after a horrible drunk picnic a few summers ago.

The weather had delivered. It was a beautiful spring day, warm, green and brisk. Perky daffodils circled the trees and the first birds of the year twittered uncertainly in the unexpected heat. I took my sunglasses out of my bag and pondered the date ahead.

After Martin's last email – I look forward to our picnic with wild anticipation – I had realized I was in the hands of a man who possessed either a lot of irony or none at all. He would be either mad or magnificent. I prayed fervently for the former.

I glanced at Kenwood House rising up behind me, then turned back to appreciate the Arcadian bowl of grass, trees and lake that spread out calmly before me. It was a beautiful place to have a date. When I'd first moved to London I had often envisaged myself right here with a lover who would put a diamond on my finger as we gambolled like lambs in the dappled light of a beech tree. In my vision the man had worn white linen and he'd laid out a beautiful champagne picnic to celebrate our engagement. He was a delicate yet masculine man of classical good looks.

Clearly, Martin – who was now stomping towards me with a gigantic wicker hamper – had had a similar dream. Unfortunately, he was an enormous tank of a man with classical bad looks. Like a perversion of my pastoral romantic dream, he was wearing a vast linen suit, which even had a canary yellow handkerchief frothing over in the breast pocket, and a straw fedora, which sat awkwardly, rather than jauntily, on his head. Where the hell was his coat? This was not the outfit for a picnic in the windy spring sunshine!

In spite of his lack of coat he was sweating profusely. And I wasn't bloody surprised, given the size of the hamper: it was big enough to accommodate a string quartet.

Here we go again, I thought sadly, wondering what would happen if I got up and ran. I was reasonably sure he wouldn't catch me but I didn't want to be struck off the dating website for being nasty so I sat still and rolled my jeans back down. 'HI, MARTIN!' I shouted enthusiastically.

He arrived next to me, put down the basket and removed his hat. 'Frances, hello,' he boomed grandly. 'Martin Spencer-Hartley. A pleasure.'

'Nice to meet you. I can't believe you've brought a

hamper! That's wicked!' I said enthusiastically. Why was I talking like a teenager?

He paused and wiped a slick of forehead sweat on to his handkerchief. A large expanse of white hairy belly was visible through the gap caused by his straining shirt buttons. Martin wasn't fat, exactly, he was just . . . massive. All over. His hands were larger than my head. He bore more than a passing resemblance to Pavarotti, actually, but little resemblance to the picture I had seen online.

'I stopped at Fortnum and Mason *en route* from Fulham and bought refreshments,' he said eventually. I waited for an ironic twinkle in his eye but there was none. It was becoming increasingly clear that this man was taking himself seriously.

I glanced at the hamper, not without excitement. The date was already a write-off but there was at least some good cheese to be had!

He opened the hamper with a flourish. And what was inside made me want to cry. Not with joy, or even with laughter, but with pity. And vicarious embarrassment.

Martin had obviously ordered his hamper online. I knew this because on top there was a large receipt, saying 'Thanks for ordering with hamperkings.co.uk! Enclosed is your discounted Fortnum and Mason Christmas Hamper! We draw your attention to sell-by dates!'

Martin snatched away the receipt. Underneath, I'm

afraid to confirm, there were two Christmas pud-
dings, an assortment of pickles, a bottle of warm
champagne, and spice sachets for mulled wine. There
was a box of amaretti and a large panettone and –
particularly useful for a spring picnic – a tin of goose
fat. There was no checked cloth, no shining cutlery,
no sandwich selection, no smoked salmon. There
were probably some currants in the Christmas pudding but that was as close to strawberries and cream
as we were likely to get.

A horrible silence descended as we stared at
Martin's lie. I had to say something fast. This man –
who clearly wasn't any of the things he'd said he was
– had been carrying a massive, disastrous, out-of-
date, knocked-off Christmas hamper from God only
knew where. He must want to top himself.

'Oh, good, we can have an early Christmas,' I faltered, thinking that we could at least try to eat some
panettone and drink the champagne. But Martin was
utterly silent, staring in paralysed horror at the hamper's contents.

I felt desperately sorry for him. All that email bra-
vado, all that chivalrous masculinity, that big boomy
voice and . . . this. 'Tell you what, I need to nip to the
Ladies. How's about I pick us up a couple of ice
creams on the way back?' I said brightly.

Martin said nothing.

I went.

Sitting on the toilet, I tried to think up a way of

improving the situation but I couldn't. I started writing a message to Leonie to make myself laugh a bit but I knew there was nothing to say: it was just total mortification for poor old Martin.

And so, a few minutes later, when I walked back to the lawn, I was in no way surprised to find that there was a hamper but no Martin on my checked picnic rug.

I scanned around me. Just as he disappeared out of view I spotted him, a large white shape running at full tilt into the woods.

Chapter Thirty-five

Well then our date is confirmed. I am excited! Most girls off
   the Internet want to know if I have long-term plans to start
   a family; you want to know if I like 80s rap. I think I'm in
   love with you.
Actually, I'm not. You have a foul mouth and terrible taste in
   men by all accounts. What the fuck do you mean he
   brought an out-of-date Christmas hamper? I don't believe
   you. No one would do that.
Oh my God, maybe they would. Tell me more.

'VELCOME!' Stefania hissed, as I tried to slide
unobtrusively into the back of Meditation. 'I am
delighted you have returned to Meditation as you
come close to the conclusion of your dates!'

'Ssh,' I said, embarrassed. I was thirty seconds late
and the room had fallen silent in anticipation of Stefania's preamble. They goggled at me.

I threw my bag into the corner, straightened my
dress and sat on a chair near the back, closing my eyes

and stretching my neck from left to right. A finger jabbed me from the right. 'HI, BABE!'

I opened my eyes again. Nellie. For once it was genuinely nice to see her. The Daniels as a friend was a lot better than The Daniels as a foe. I smiled sideways at her. 'Hey. Thanks for not ignoring me.' She batted me away. 'Hon, I told you, I'm *soooo* happy to have found another stalker. I was stalking Michael's ex-girlfriend last night and I just couldn't stop giggling. We're two of a kind!' I looked wistfully at her impeccable white tailored shirt and super-smart high-waisted jeans, and knew we were nothing of the sort. I was wearing a shabby old dress that Leonie had rejected three years ago and there was a hole in my tights. But I enjoyed the warmth of her greeting. And, most importantly, she wasn't making the sex with my ex-boyfriend.

'OK, I vant you to close your eyes and try to relax,' Stefania crooned. 'Let us start viz a body scan. Start at ze top of your head. Are zere tense muscles zere? Let zem go . . .'

Afterwards I munched a vegan quiche and watched Nellie talking to some of the other media bitches. Back on show, she seemed as she always had – possessed, commanding and completely in control. And yet she was in reality a puppy, hysterically overexcited about her Posh Fiancé and prone to the same mad stalking outbursts as I was. *How funny life is*, I thought, trying to identify a strange rubbery ingredient within the quiche. People were so rarely who they appeared to be on the outside.

'I'm learning how much I compare other people's outsides to my insides,' Mum had said to me the other night after her AA meeting. 'I've spent my whole life thinking I know what's going on in other people's heads but of course I don't!' It was a pretty good point.

I picked up a little tablet of raw chocolate and popped it into my mouth. Urgh! Stefania was outstanding at raw chocolate but today's offering was like crunchy turd. As I tried to remove it from my mouth as inconspicuously as possible, she arrived in front of me with her arms crossed. 'Zis is not a good advert for my cooking, Frances,' she hissed. 'Vhat are you doing?'

I wiped my lips. 'I'm spitting out this chocolate. Have you tasted it? It's terrible! You're brilliant at this stuff, what went wrong?'

She reached over and put some in her mouth with a face of fury, then reached for the napkins and ejected it at high speed. 'Zeus! Zis is TERRIBLE!' She grabbed the plate and shoved it under the batique bedspread that was covering the table. 'I offer you a full apology! And a refund!'

'Don't be ridiculous. It's fine. You must just have had a bad day.' I pulled on my faded leather ankle boots and reached for my coat. Stefania didn't reply. She had gone red. 'Yes, I vas a bit preoccupied today,' she said, with a strange expression. It hovered somewhere between embarrassed, secretive and excited. A slight blush played at the edges of her porcelain cheeks.

I sat down again. 'Er, what's going on, Stefania?'

She pulled herself together, an imperceptible shift that closed me out. 'Nozzing. I was just distracted today sinking about your eight dates. Zat is all.'

'Bollocks.' I folded my arms. 'What's going on?'

'NOZZING, Frances. I shall see you tomorrow.'

'Aren't we going to travel back home together?'

She coloured again, this time more deeply. Blushing suited her. 'No, I have business to attend to.'

I was about to interrogate her further when Nellie bounded up, excitable and beaming, pawing my arm. 'BABE! We *so* need to talk! I've got something *rully* exciting for you!'

Stefania escaped delicately. I made a mental note to watch for her return later. She was *never* busy in the evenings. Ever.

'Sounds interesting,' I said to Nellie.

'Well, babe, here's the thing. My Michael also works in PR . . .' My eyebrows shot up. I would have put at least a grand on him working for a bank. '. . . and he has some clients who would be, let's say, *extremely* interesting to you. He called me earlier, asking what your exact role was at ITN because he's going to offer the project to your boss tomorrow.'

'Tell me more,' I said, trying to sound excited. The chances of any 'extremely interesting' project being given to me at the moment were slim.

But as soon as Nellie began to speak, I knew I wanted it. I didn't just want it, I really, *really* wanted it. I listened to her with growing excitement and despair, knowing that this could make or break me, but keenly aware that it would take an act of God for Hugh to entrust it to me.

Five minutes later, I stood up to leave. Nellie grabbed me and hugged me. 'I just *knew* this was up your street, babe! When Dave told me about the way you always weed out the normal people in your stories . . . well, I just knew it was perfect for you!'

I smiled, touched.

'Listen, babe, Michael's going to ITN with the offer tomorrow and unless they've lost their minds they'll say yes. So all we need to do then is convince them that you're the man for the job! Should I get Michael to put in a good word?'

I shook my head sadly. 'Nellie, I can't lie – it sounds like my dream project but there is just no way on earth Hugh would let me do it. I'm in the doghouse with him at the moment.' Nellie's face fell. She really was very sweet, in spite of her toned legs and power fragrances and wall of shiny hair. 'Trust me. He'll give this job to one of the old-timers. But thank you for thinking of me. It was really kind of you.'

'Oh, babe . . . I hope you're wrong. Well, I'd better scoot. I'm meant to be meeting Portia downstairs for a bottle of wine ten minutes ago.'

'Portia?'

'Yeah, you know – the blonde woman who was sitting closest to Stefania? She's the VP Worldwide Media Relations for Tower Media. I bloody want *them* on my books, babe.'

That was the difference between Nellie and me, I thought later, as I cobbled together a store-cupboard meal of canned sweetcorn and a half-defrosted beefburger. Duke Ellington was laying into his Tesco Finest rabbit terrine with gusto, casting occasional pitying looks at my student dinner. I believed in my career, and to a certain extent in myself, but I just didn't have Nellie's killer instinct. I was far happier sharing a dinner table with my evil cat than I was plying good contacts with expensive wines in exclusive West London clubs. Back in December when I'd asked Hugh about joining the politics team he'd just laughed in my face, yet Alex had come in and within three weeks had been given the frigging election special to produce.

'I'm a failure,' I told Duke Ellington, as I fired up my computer. He gave me an affirmative miaow. 'Shut up!' He started purring.

You have two new messages, my homepage told me. With a tiny but not insignificant buzz of excitement, I clicked through, delighted to see that one was from Freddy. Our emails over the last few days had been deliciously enjoyable. He really seemed to get me, this dude, and I felt good emailing him.

Hello again Fran.

I agree: I do look like an iconic film star in my photo. Yes.
But you've got the decade wrong, of course. It's more
1950s, non?

Anyway, I am on my way back to London in a couple of
days and looking forward to Sunday. Here is what we are
doing. 1. We are going to see my favourite mad transgen-
der folk singer at the Roundhouse. 2. Then I am going to
feed you tapas in a little place by Mornington Crescent. 3.
Then we will go home in opposite directions and I will
stare at my silent phone for weeks, wondering what
happened. Or we will go for a dirty hump on Primrose Hill.
Or maybe we will just have an awkward kiss/hug loaded
with the promise of more next time.

I sat back, grinning. 'This is quite exciting!' I whispered. Duke Ellington miaowed again. 'He likes the
sound of you, although God knows why.' Duke
Ellington marched over and allowed me to stroke
him, then spun round at lightning speed and scragged
my hand.

I typed with my left hand: Sounds ideal. ME LIKE TAPAS.
The cat just attacked me again. Cunt. Yours, injured, Fran X

'Little scrote,' I said, as I got up to wash my hand.
I was smiling. I liked Freddy. It felt easy with him. A
date with a truly nice chap just before I saw Michael
would give me just enough confidence to be able to
lay things out to him on my terms. My beautiful
Michael Slater with his slate grey eyes. Michael, who

slept curled up like a prawn. Michael, whom I admired more than any other man I'd ever met. Jesus, I honestly didn't know how I'd got through nearly three months of not seeing him. But he was going to have to give me answers. Good answers. And some things were going to have to change.

'This time round Michael and I are going to have more fun,' I told Duke Ellington.

There was a bunch of daffodils in one of Mum's jugs on the table. Spring was here. Michael and I would start again. The world was still turning. I was OK.

'Will you sodding well *stop* that?' I shouted at Leonie. She was snogging Alex, with tongues, about a metre from me. 'This is Gin Thursday! It's not a bloody sex show!'

Alex, looking thoroughly intoxicated, pulled away from her reluctantly and went a bit red. 'Sorry. I just can't keep my hands off her. You'd understand if you were male.' His long thin face was shiny and beaming, and his suspiciously clear-looking glasses were wonky. I smiled despairingly as Leonie giggled and grabbed his hand, straightening her cardigan. She rubbed a little bit of her scarlet lipstick off his chin but left the rest on, winking at me. Alex was so overwhelmed by the situation he resembled a small child.

It was funny to be feeling fond of Alex. But the transformation in his behaviour at work really had been radical. I'd been allocated to help his team three afternoons a week (albeit grudgingly) by Hugh and I knew that the things Alex was sending my way were producer's jobs, rather than the humble research and guest-booking I'd been quite happy to do. Only three hours before, he'd forwarded my Nick Clegg VT proposal directly to Hugh with a note, saying, 'This is from Fran. I think it's excellent. I wouldn't change a thing – do you agree?'

Hugh had replied simply, 'Yeah.' It would take a lot longer to win back his respect.

Nellie's Michael had arrived at three o'clock and left at five forty-five, but Hugh had said nothing to me. He'd merely called all of the politics producers into his office after Michael had left. There was *no* bloody chance of me getting my hands on that gig.

'What do you want to drink, Fannybaws?' Dave asked, as he came back in. He'd been outside on the phone for the last ten minutes and had come back in looking distinctly gooey. It was like being trapped in a restaurant on Valentine's night in this bloody place! I should have made my Freddy date tonight. 'Er, Coke, please. Was that Freya?' I asked.

'Nope. Stefania. She's not coming tonight.'

'Eh? What were you talking about all that time?' Since when did Dave and Stefania talk on the phone?

Dave didn't answer.

I watched him go to the bar, feeling a little unnerved. What was with the gooey face? Alex and

Leonie were clearly aware of my shift in concentration because they'd started snogging again. 'Pack it in!' I hissed at them.

Leonie raised a V-sign at me and continued, but Alex said, 'Sorry, Fran. You're right. Although you were just as bad when you met Michael,' he added slyly.

I smiled. 'Fair dos, Alex. After all, she is pretty awesome.'

Leonie nodded solemnly. 'Yes, I am.' We all burst out laughing.

Then Alex whispered, 'Tell her!' in a very loud, theatrical and unwhispery way.

Leonie slapped him. 'Alex! No!'

'Leonie has something to tell you,' Alex announced. He seemed liable to burst.

'Come on, Leonie. What's up?'

Dear God, they weren't . . . ?

'Ah. Well, I've been wanting to tell you this for ages but I got a bit shy.'

I laughed. '*Shy?* The girl who talks about bum sex with complete strangers is telling her best friend she felt a bit *shy?* Don't make me laugh!' Alex tittered, straightening out his blazer which was sitting rather lopsidedly over his expensive graffiti T-shirt. Leonie was actually blushing now. 'Leonie? What the hell's going on?' She blushed even harder. 'Well?'

Alex couldn't bear it any more. 'SHE'S WRITING

A BOOK!' he screamed, then clasped her even more tightly to him in the manner that a toddler throws his arms around his mother's leg. It was a truly hilarious spectacle.

Hang on. 'A *book*? Oh, my God! About what?'

'Um. Sex,' she said bashfully.

'Excuse me?'

'Sex. I'm writing a book about sex. In fact, that's a lie. I've *written* a book about sex. It's finished. It's done. But today I got an agent who wants to send it out to a load of publishers. This is the most exciting thing that's ever happened to me! And it's all thanks to you!'

I blinked. 'Um, I'm glad to be of service but how is this connected to me? Did you drug me and collect all of my sex secrets? Not that I really have any,' I added.

'When you got back from Kosovo in 2008 you told me I should write a book about sex. Like a manual or something. So I did! I've been writing it for the last two years!'

'Wow!' I said, genuinely thrilled. 'So that's why you shagged so many blokes in that time? Oh, no! Sorry! Actually, Alex, she didn't have sex with anyone! She was chaste.'

He seemed remarkably unfazed. 'It's OK,' he said. His normally reedy voice sounded full to bursting with happiness. 'I know she loves me.'

They had a private moment and I looked away,

embarrassed. The energy between them was intense. The last time I'd seen anything as tangible was when Michael had first arrived back from Kosovo. And now here was Leonie, having the same thing with his best friend. Love moved in funny ways.

'OK, break it up,' I said gently, after a few seconds. 'Leonie, my darling friend, I am so proud of you. This is absolutely amazing. What brought this on? Well, apart from me telling you that you should do it.'

She dropped her eyes modestly to her hands. 'I've always wanted to write a book,' she said simply.

It was true. It had saddened me that she'd abandoned her wonderful talents with wordsmithery and spent the last nine years charity mugging.

'But I started charity mugging as a tide-me-over and I met so many people who hated their jobs, I just thought, well, I didn't want to get on the treadmill. And then you joked about a sex book when you met Michael and you were so happy and glowing and really beginning to go somewhere with your life and I started to feel like a loser . . .' Alex put his arm round her and kissed the side of her head.

'You've *never* been a loser,' I said quietly. 'Ever.'

Dave arrived back at the table.

'Leonie's written a book about sex!' I cried.

Dave didn't turn a hair. 'Of course she has. I can't think of a better person to write one,' he said drily, smiling at Leonie and passing her a gin. 'Good work, kid – what sort of sex book is it?'

'It's a sort of contemporary housewife's manual,' she said. 'Lots of fifties-style diagrams and humorous anecdotes about baking cakes afterwards but with the kind of graphic detail you'd only get in a sex book now.'

I began to giggle. 'So, essentially it's filth wrapped up in a circular skirt and an apron?'

'Yep. That's the one.'

'Photos or pictures?'

'Oh, pictures, lots of them. All nineteen-fifties style.'

'It sounds amazing! Who illustrated it for you?'

'Um, I did.'

There was another stunned silence. 'This is amazing! I can't believe you didn't tell us!'

She blushed again. 'I know, I'm sorry. But I was scared. I didn't think it'd get anywhere. But this agent reckons it could sell. Can we not talk about it now? I'm embarrassed.'

Alex got up, nearly exploding out of his skin. 'This calls for champagne! Oh, are you two still off the booze?' he added, looking at Dave and me.

I turned to Dave. Were we? He nodded. 'Just for today,' he said.

Alex kissed Leonie again and trotted off to the bar.

'Stop it,' Leonie said, catching my smirk.

'Sorry. It's just so odd, though. It's like he's on drugs. You've completely changed him.'

'I honestly think he's always been like this. The

closed-book thing is just a front, Franny, he's quite a lost soul.'

'Well, I hope he's not too lost. You need a boy-friend, not a wreck.'

'I know. But, trust me, I have a boyfriend.'

The three of us burst out laughing at this completely improbable sentence.

'Now, how are you getting on with the Eight Date Deal?' she said, brisk once more.

Dave put his drink down and got a notebook out. 'Stefania gave me this,' he said, in response to my inquisitive look.

I sighed. I was not enjoying this 'Stefania and Dave = best friends for ever' thing. 'OK,' I began wearily. 'There's a Trendy Person on Saturday called Benj. I'm meeting him on Brick Lane. It's going to be a disappointment. He'll be wearing spray-on trousers and probably a moustache.' Dave sniggered. 'We've had a bit of banter but he's yet another clever-clever bloke full of witty quips and almost certainly no personality.' They nodded.

'And?' Leonie said impatiently.

I began to grin. 'Well, actually, the next one is on Sunday and I think he's a little bit ace. It's that guy Freddy I mentioned.'

Dave glanced up briefly. 'So you like this one, eh?' he asked.

'Yeah! I do! He looks like a film star! And he's quite rude to me. Keeps me in my box. Y'know.'

Dave smirked. 'Sounds like a wise man. And film-star looks too! Quite a catch, by all accounts, Fannybaws.'

'Seconded!' Leonie said. 'I like the sound of him. What are you going to do? Will you ask him to pop it in, do you think?'

'STOP IT! I AM GETTING BACK TO-GETHER WITH MICHAEL! But that doesn't stop me going on a date with Nice Freddy, though,' I added impishly. 'We're going to a gig at the Round-house. Some folky transsexual's singing. And then he's force-feeding me tapas and proposing a hard fuck on Primrose Hill.'

Dave sat back grinning. 'He sounds pretty different from Michael, Fannybaws.'

I nodded guardedly.

Alex was taking his change from the barman. 'Do you promise you're not discussing any of this with Alex?' I whispered at Leonie.

'Yes! Fran, I gave you my word.'

'Good. Thanks. Well, the ninety days is up in just under two weeks. You can talk about us all you like after that.' She squeezed my hand.

Later, when Leonie and Alex had resumed their mutual face-eating marathon, I sat at the bar with Dave, marvelling at how tiny and doll-like his bottle of Schweppes tomato juice looked in his hand. 'You've got absolutely massive hands, Dave,' I said absently.

'You've got an absolutely massive arse, Fran,' he replied.

'Have NOT!'

'Aye, true. Anyway. This business with Michael. Are you serious about taking him back?' He poured thick red juice from the toy bottle into his glass. It barely came to a third full and he was slightly dismayed. I poured mine into his glass.

'Yes. I've missed him horribly.' He took a sip. It left a big red semi-circle above his mouth, which I rubbed off with a tissue.

'That'd better not have your snot on it,' he said ominously.

'Nope. You're safe. Not a bogey in sight.'

'Why do you think Michael ended it in the first place, Fannybaws?'

I paused. I'd spent a lot of time trying to avoid this question. Because the truth of the matter was that I had *no idea*.

Jenny had emailed me a few days after the Smiths of Smithfield night, reiterating how much she hoped we'd get back together and how miserable Michael had been since we separated. I shook my head thoughtfully. 'Honestly? I don't know. I think something happened that day. Something really bad. You heard what Jenny said – he was going to propose. He had their grandmother's ring. It wasn't just a spur-of-the-moment thing, Dave, he'd obviously planned it. He'd decided he wanted to spend the rest of his life with me and then . . . *poof*. It's over. No contact for three months.'

Dave nodded.

'I need to find out what happened that day and do everything I can to make whatever it is better. I'm willing to go to any lengths. Whatever needs changing, I'm prepared to do it. I want the ring. I want Michael. I want us back.'

Dave stirred his tomato juice, his face inscrutable. 'Do you know *anything* about relationships?' he asked eventually.

I was taken aback. 'Er . . . *What?*'

'Seriously, Fran. "I'm willing to go to any lengths"? Where's your fucking self-respect?' His face was darkening. He downed his tomato juice angrily and stared off over my shoulder.

I waited for him to crack a smile but nothing happened. Confused, I cleared my throat. 'I see. Well, I'm sorry I'm such a disappointment to you, Dave. And I'm sorry that my relationship doesn't match up to the obviously perfect situation you have with Freya. But life isn't always like that. Most women aren't like her. Most of them are scared and unsure of themselves. I'm so sorry that I happen to be one of them.'

'You don't know *shit* about Freya, Fran,' he replied quietly.

I gazed at his angry face, appalled. '*What?* Dave, what's wrong?'

He toyed with his empty glass.

'Actually, you're right. I *don't* know anything about Freya any more because you haven't brought her out for as long as I can remember. Are you ashamed of us? Of me?'

Dave toyed with his glass a while longer, then put it down. 'I wasn't comparing you to Freya. I'm sorry.'

Dave had never been horrid to me in the entire history of our relationship. I didn't know what to say.

'Ah, fuck it. I'm going home.'

And he got up and walked out. I followed him out of the bar with my eyes, a big, angry man in a jumper with an old stripy shirt underneath. Trainers with holes in them. A face of thunder. Dave, a man I clearly didn't understand as well as I'd thought.

'I hate everyone,' I told Duke Ellington, an hour later. Leonie and Alex, oblivious to my bizarre altercation with Dave, had continued to snog as if a nuclear bomb was about to hit the Three Kings so, shortly after Dave had stormed off, I'd followed suit. Duke Ellington and I were munching a Hawaiian pizza I'd picked up on the way and I was firing up my laptop in the desperate hope of a nice communication from Freddy. The last message I'd sent him had been five hours ago and I needed a fix.

You have one new message, said my lurid pink homepage. I crossed my fingers.

Freddy!

Fran. You raving lunatic. I give up. Whatever. But I'm not giving up on Sunday. I'll meet you outside the Morrisons petrol station, OK? If you're really lucky I'll buy you a microwavable pasty.

I'll be the one wearing a Phil Collins T-shirt and carrying an enormous bunch of flowers.

Seriously, I can't wait. You are properly awesome. Promise not to grope you during the gig.

Freddy X

I liked Freddy. A lot.

'If it doesn't work out with Michael, I'm jumping this bloke,' I told Duke Ellington. He was wrestling with a piece of pepperoni and took no notice of me. I threw a dough ball at him and went back to my message.

Chapter Thirty-six

Date six: Benj

Spring was definitely here. I knew that not because of the weather but because I had commenced applying fake tan every other day. It was for this reason that I was staring at my stripy orange palms as I waited for Benj-the-music-composer/producer/probably-a-bit-of-a-cock at a table outside the Vibe Bar in Brick Lane.

It was heaving with fashionable types wearing battered leather jackets, weird hats and slightly optimistic sunglasses in a variety of silly colours. While I waited for Benj I shared a table with two blokes who were discussing how much they hated their girlfriends. Moments like this reminded me of how much I loved men. So loyal, so honourable, so kind. 'She just doesn't understand why I need to go to a spoon-making workshop,' one lamented, as if his girlfriend had chopped off one of his testicles.

His companion nodded sympathetically. 'Tough, dude. Tough. But she'll get there. She's only nineteen.' I balked. These guys were at least thirty-five.

As always, I was early. I liked being early for dates. I took a swig of my soda water, which I'd asked the barman to disguise as gin and tonic, and looked around. Still no sign of Benj. The afternoon sun was hard and pale but still warm; it illuminated thousands of little bubbles cruising round and round in my glass and bathed the fashionable people around me with a lovely antique sort of glow, like a sepia picture, suspended in 2010, young, happy, beautiful.

Ten days until 23 March.

Bored, I pretended to read a leaflet about something called 'Dances with Cupcakes' in Dalston. *Dances with Cupcakes?* For crying out loud!

I got my phone out to call Leonie, knowing this would make her day. But as I did so, Benj plonked himself down opposite me, dumping a breezy kiss on my cheekbone on the way. He didn't bother to take his Wayfarers off and I knew immediately that I would not find love with him. He had a fashion moustache.

'Hi there, Frances,' he whined, pulling limply on the sleeves of his jumper. 'Sorry I'm late. I was, y'know, tied up with some really difficult shit, man. God, life can be so fucked up at times, but I'm just playing it cool and letting everyone else run around screaming. Oooh, bit of an accident with fake tan on your hand there.'

I downed my 'G and T' and wished it was the real thing. I'd not missed alcohol all that much but the prospect of two or three hours in the company of this whingey moustache person suddenly made a glass of wine seem like the greatest thing on earth. 'Oh dear,' I said brightly. 'What's happened?'

'Well, I'm running this creative event with my ex-girlfriend and she's being really difficult about it – Oh, shit, man, you've got one of our flyers there. Well, you'll know all about "Dances with Cupcakes", then. She's cooking the spare cakes, right, and she wants me to go halves with her on the ingredients and even the bloody *electricity bill* for her flat. And I'm just like, "Flora, this is about *creativity,* not electricity bills," and then her flatmate gets all arsey with me and, well, you know what it's like. Now they're stressing and sending me pissy texts and, fuck it, I'm so not in that sort of a space right now.'

I wondered if it would enrage him further if I asked for a sneak preview of his most recent cupcake dance when his phone went.

'Flora. Dude. Can we not fight? I'm on a date.'

Way to go, Benj.

Flora, even if she'd only been calling to make peace, let rip completely. I blotted them out and thought about Dave. He'd sent me a very sincere email of apology this morning, which had been full of remorse and humour. 'I've had a bit of a rough time of late,' he'd said. I wondered what that meant. Dave generally didn't have rough times; his life was universally regarded as peachy. Beautiful girlfriend, top-ranking news cameraman in London, and owner of stunning old house in Wimbledon Village. Had he and Freya fallen out? Or was something going on with his family in Glasgow?

I glanced back at Benj. His face and voice had taken on a thundery tone and he clutched his iPhone with the kind of ferocity that Duke Ellington employed when holding on to my feet during an ambush. Keen to escape I raised my hand and eyebrows in a pint gesture and he nodded.

Relieved, I went inside where they were playing rather unexpected piano music. Next to a clump of teenage trendies, a single old lady sat at the bar wearing a pinafore dress over a ribbed turtle-neck jumper with long socks and sandals. The incongruity of London never failed to delight me. 'Pint of Kronenberg and another fake G and T,' I said to the barman, and fished around in my wallet.

The woman tapped me on the shoulder as I handed over a grubby tenner. 'Young lady.'

She had a lovely face, knowing if not a little wild, and bobbed grey hair pulled back under a neat tortoiseshell clip. 'Hello,' I said. She seemed like the most normal person here.

'I saw you outside just now. You looked like you were contemplating suicide,' she said, without any trace of irony.

I sniggered. 'Not far off. I'm on a bad date.'

She nodded, as if she already knew. Was I talking to some sort of witch?

'Yes, I saw that. Dear, I felt that your heart was elsewhere. Not with this man. Am I right?'

I suddenly had a vision of the first time I'd met

Michael, so clear and sharp that it almost winded me. There he was, standing in the doorway of the UN office in Mitrovica, winter sun splicing over his shoulder, looking sleepy and kind. In the third person I watched myself, young, silly, dressed like a 1980s Easter egg, buffooning my way through our first five minutes in each other's lives.

The woman was watching me in a kindly manner. She cocked her head to one side.

'Yes,' I said slowly. 'My heart is *definitely* somewhere else.' She beamed. 'And, in fact, you've just done me a favour. Thank you. I don't need to be here,' I said. I took the drinks and the change from the barman and stood before her, smiling. 'I'm going to go home.'

She smiled.

This was all a bit bizarre. 'Er, thanks . . .' I added lamely.

'No problem. A contribution to my beer fund wouldn't go amiss,' she said.

Amused and appalled in equal measure, I handed over a fiver from my change and left. This was not the place for me today.

I snaked my way back through the tables to where Benj was sitting, still yelling into his iPhone. I felt very calm and clear. Unless I was going to fall wildly in love with Benj, which I was most definitely not, I would far rather be cracking open an elderflower cordial on the steps with Stefania and Duke Ellington, and preparing myself for my reunion with Michael. It wasn't honest for me to sit here and talk to this waz-zock about his cupcakes.

I put his pint in front of him, picked up my coat and caught his eye. He saw what was going on and waved me off dismissively.

I was free. I bought a pot of Ethiopian stew from a smiley man at a stall and got on the bus home, feeling unnaturally serene. When a teenager sat next to me and started playing speed garage through his mobile phone, I jiggled along with him to the flavas.

I arrived back in my yard forty minutes later to find Stefania exploding from her shed looking flustered. I began to say hello but was cut short – very short, in fact – by the sight of Dave shuffling out behind her, blinking like a mole.

I was stunned. 'Dave! Er, what's going on? You're not having an affair with Stefania, are you?'

He reached for his fags. 'All right, Fran. Er, no. I was having a massage.'

'A *what*?'

He raised his eyebrows and lit up.

Stefania and I said, 'Stop smoking,' at the same time.

'A massage. My back's all fucked up from shooting all the time. How was your date?'

I sighed. 'Oh, useless. I walked out on him, actually. I couldn't take it.'

Dave whistled. 'You walked *out* on him? Jesus, that's a wee bit rude, isn't it?'

'No. He was a complete bell end. How he'd managed

to take time out of his busy schedule masturbating lovingly in front of a mirror I have no idea. Anyway, what on earth are you doing having massages at six p.m. on a Saturday? Are you *sure* you aren't knocking off my neighbour?'

Stefania went back inside abruptly.

Had I hit on something? *Surely not* . . . I felt a bit ill.

Dave's smile had disappeared. 'Your manners, Franny, are fuckin' bad,' he said softly. 'Stefania is wonderful. Stop embarrassing her.'

I felt a little bit uneasy. *Why* was Stefania massaging him in her shed? She came back out with a broom and started sweeping the yard.

I was mortified. 'Dave, you know I adore her,' I whispered, as Stefania stalked across towards the tree. 'Why are you being so weird?'

But he was off.

Astonished, I watched him walk out of my yard. 'Hey, Dave,' I called.

'Aye.' He didn't even bother to turn round.

'Dave, I was just messing. Come back.'

Now he turned and smiled wanly. 'You're OK, Fran. No worries.' And with that he was gone in a cloud of messy hair and fag smoke.

Stefania was still sweeping. 'Stefania, what on earth was that about? Since when did you start giving people massages?'

She carried on sweeping. 'Since always. I just do not invite you for ze massage because you are a pain in ze fanny and you vill always be vanting ze massage,' she said, smiling evilly.

'Come up to mine for some of that elderflower stuff. I want to celebrate getting to the end of this Eight Date Deal.' Her eyes narrowed suspiciously.

'*Nearly* to the end,' I added.

She smiled and came with me.

I managed not to interrogate her about Dave but it was hard. A busy roll-call of possible explanations was tapping away in my head but none of them really felt right. Why the hell was she giving him massages on a Saturday evening? Something about this situation was wrong. I felt uncomfortable about it. And I felt uncomfortable about feeling uncomfortable.

After twenty minutes I was dragged out of my reverie by my first ever text message from Freddy, which restored my smile pretty quickly. Fran. Freddy. I hope your date today is shit. Our date tomorrow is going to be amazing. I giggled. Freddy was awesome! It was really quite a shame I'd met him at a time like this.

'Who is zat message from?' Stefania asked suspiciously. She was curled up on the sofa with a large cup of horrible green tea.

'Freddy, my date for tomorrow,' I said, as I closed my phone.

She beamed. 'And he sends a good message?' she asked.

'Yeah, he does, actually. A really good message.'

Stefania beamed even harder. 'I sink maybe he

could be Ze One!' she announced excitedly, karate-chopping the air. 'Seriously, Fran! Zis could be it!'

'Stefania, do you not want it to work out with me and Michael?' I asked. 'Do you not care how I feel about him?'

She eyed me beadily. Stefania really did have quite amazing eyes. Dark, feline and secretive, shaded by long eyelashes that had no need of mascara. 'I do care,' she said abruptly. Duke Ellington, who was sitting quietly on her knee, as if he was the sort of cat who always sat quietly on knees, looked up benevolently at her. 'But I sink you are forgetting zat he ended ze relationship, Francees. I vant you to be viz someone who really, really loves you. A wild love! A crazy love! I want yours to be ze greatest love story of all time!' She threw her arms wide and grinned ecstatically.

'And you think I'm going to find this with Freddy off the Internet?' I asked eventually.

She shrugged. 'Vhy not?'

I decided that Stefania was functionally insane. 'Have *you* ever felt love like that, Stefania?' I asked suddenly. She looked down at her tea and I knew straight away I'd made an error. Time after time we'd been here – me asking about her personal life and her turning into a brick wall. So when she broke into a seemingly uncontrollable smile I was more than a little surprised.

'Yes,' she said simply. 'Yes, I know vhat it is like to

love someone like zat.' She smiled down at Duke Ellington. 'And, Fran, it's vonderful.' Then she giggled and hugged herself.

Later on as I twirled some home-made coleslaw round my plate, I pondered this bizarre exchange. Stefania did not make faces like that. Stefania did not giggle like a schoolgirl and hug herself. Stefania liked to scream and karate-chop things! *What was happening?*

I batted away the image of Dave coming out of her shed earlier on. It was impossible. And wrong. And . . . something else, which I couldn't put my finger on.

As I changed into my pyjamas a few minutes later, my phone buzzed. I smiled: Freddy!

But it wasn't Freddy. It was Michael. And his message was the best thing I'd ever read. Furthermore, it proved that this was *exactly* the kind of fireworks-and-explosions love Stefania had described: Franny. My beautiful girl. Sorry for breaking the rules but I can't take any more! I'm in Paris working & I want you to come out here this weekend. I know it's 2 days too early but I've taken the liberty of booking you Eurostar tickets & have all my fingers crossed you'll say yes. Have emailed details. Love you so much. M xxxxx

I shrieked, delighted. Paris! Me, Michael and a tearful reunion! Not to mention steaming cups of *chocolat chaud* and berets and moustachioed chaps playing accordions! And sunsets over the Seine and lovemaking in a grand and splendid bedchamber, and maybe a cheeky wedding proposal in the shadow of the Eiffel Tower! This was perfect!

It was official: THIS WAS THE GREATEST LOVE STORY OF ALL TIME.

Chapter Thirty-seven

Date seven: Freddy

Bonnie Tyler drawled sexily about being in love, lost somewhere in France, while I poured some Whiskas cat milk into Duke Ellington's bowl and danced around my kitchen. Sunlight was streaming in through the window, which I'd opened wide even though it was only March. I didn't care. I was the happiest girl on the planet! I sat down at my table with my phone and some marmalady toast and wrote a grovelling cancellation text message to Freddy.

It was a shame to miss out on meeting him, really. He'd made for a very lovely distraction from the cesspool of Internet dating but it would have been mean to meet up with him now. It was all about Michael Slater for me, the man of my dreams who did posh journalistic assignments in Paris for the *Independent*. MICHAEL AND FRAN: the greatest love story of all time! I could barely contain myself!

I pressed send and mouthed an apology: *Sorry, Freddy. In another life, maybe.*

I took a large bite of toast and wriggled my legs excitedly. This time next week I might have a beautiful old Egyptian ring on my finger! I might know what it was like to wake up with Michael again! *I might not be on my own.* In my state of wild overexcitement I forgot that it was only nine twenty-three a.m. and I called Leonie.

'Mmpfff?'

It was Alex. 'Oh, God. Sorry. I'll call another time. 'Bye!'

Gross.

'Holding Out For A Hero' came on and I started jumping and dancing. I had to share this with someone.

Stefania! Surely the Parisian development would be enough to convince her that Michael and I were serious. I scampered off to my room to put some jeans on and looked out of the window to check that her red-and-white curtains had been opened for the day. I stopped in my tracks. Stefania was just walking into her shed. Not in a Sunday-morning-just-popped-out-for-some-rye-bread kind of outfit but in a Saturday-night *date* outfit. I stared as she unlocked the shed door and then wandered in, distinctly floaty and happy and sort of . . . *post-coital.* I shut my curtains quickly again. This was insane. *Stefania didn't have sex!*

And if she did, who was she having it with? A small tendril of unease wrapped itself delicately around my stomach. Something wasn't quite right here. Surely she wasn't . . . Surely it wasn't possible that . . .

No. Today was not the day for these thoughts.

Today was the day for celebration and whooping. My boy was waiting for me in Paris! Life was good!

I tried Mum.

'Hello, darling! Are you OK?'

'Yes! I'm amazing! How are you?'

'Putting one foot in front of the other, Franny. It gets a little less awful every day. I just booked myself a little trip to Devon, actually, for next weekend. Lots of walking, hearty meals, time for me to do some of my AA stuff. I was going to call you and ask if you wanted to come. I'm a bit scared about it but I can't lock myself in the house for ever.'

I bit my lip, feeling horribly guilty. 'Oh, Mum, I'm sorry. I'd have loved to. Count me in next time. But I can't, I'm going to be in Paris.' My mind raced. Should I cancel? Go to Devon with Mum? Or was this something she needed to do on her own?

'Don't worry. I'm not sure I'd be great company anyway, darling. I'll probably be really ratty and horrible, worrying about whether or not I'll crumble and drink. So, Paris! How exciting! Are you going with Leonie?'

'No. I'm meeting Michael. The ninety days are up, Mum, and he sent me a message saying how much he loves me and that he's bought me tickets to go over there for the weekend!'

Mum paused. 'Well, that sounds lovely, Franny. And you think he wants to get back together?'

'Er, yes! You should have seen his email, Mum, he's

booked us into this amazing hotel and we've got tickets for the opera and stuff. I'm beside myself!'

Mum laughed hesitantly. 'I can hear that,' she said.
'But, Fran, just be sure to think it over properly first.
And make sure you find out exactly why he ended it,
OK?'

'Oh, Mum, not you too. Can't anyone be happy for
me?' I asked sadly.

'I hear you, Fran. Just be sure that you're happy
with his explanation.'

'Fine, fine. I will. Look, would you like me to cancel and come with you to Devon?'

'No. I've got my challenge, you've got yours. Just
make sure you do the right thing, OK?'

Deflated, I sank on to my bed. Bonnie Tyler was
still pumping away in the kitchen but I wasn't in the
mood for her now. *It would be nice if someone could be
excited for me,* I thought darkly. My phone buzzed with
a message from Freddy. Gutted. But thanks for being so
honest. I hope your ex really does redeem himself because
you sound ace.

I considered going back to bed for a while but the
sun was streaming quite insistently through the window
on to my face. This wasn't a day for bed. I'd go for a
walk. I'd go to Hampstead Heath, stride up Parliament
Hill, get some colour in my cheeks and munch a scone.

Children watched in wonder as their kites tore through
the breezy March sky above Parliament Hill. Dogs gal-

loped foolishly after frisbees that they would never catch, and sturdy, good-looking dads carried their sturdy, good-looking children on their shoulders. My hands were shoved deep in my pockets as I sat on a bench overlooking the city, with a pair of slightly hopeful sunglasses sliding off my nose. My thoughts jumped in a very scrambled manner between Mum's words of warning, Stefania's possible love affair, Freddy, Leonie, Alex and, of course, Michael. I wondered what he was doing right now. My guess was sleeping. I smiled to myself, imagining him unconscious and prawn-like in a gigantic Louis XIV bed somewhere.

What happened that day, Michael? Why did my thirtieth birthday begin with you running me a bath and end with you breaking my heart?

I threw a ball for an unfeasibly silly Labrador and settled back into the bench to go over the events of that night one last time.

When I'd burst into Reception at ITN, higher than a teenager on White Lightning about my new job on the election team, Michael had been oddly unenthusiastic. 'It's OK,' I'd reassured him, tucking his scratchy scarf inside his coat. 'It's just until May. I'll only be working insane hours for a couple of months.'

He'd looked at me for a few seconds, and then his face had cracked into a wide, warm smile. 'Happy birthday, Frances O'Callaghan. You're ravishing!' he said, throwing his arms round me. 'And congratulations,' he whispered. He hugged me for a long time. Hard.

I grinned into his face, like a toothy lunatic. 'We can talk politics in bed now!' I leaned forward and kissed his nose. 'Any news on your promotion?'

'No,' he said briefly. 'As in, no, I didn't get it. But it honestly doesn't matter. Let's go and celebrate.'

'Oh, Michael, I'm sorr—'

'Honestly, it's fine. This is your night. There will be plenty more opportunities, Franny.' He really did seem fine. Normal. Michaelish.

As we went to leave, an exhausted-looking Stella and Dave arrived, Stella gulping down a large coffee and Dave, like a big hairy giant in an old sheepskin coat, carrying his camera. He saw us and came over, shook Michael's hand and ruffled my hair. 'Where are you two lovebirds off to tonight, then?' he asked. He put his camera down and started assembling a roll-up, smiling as I tutted my disapproval.

Michael put his arm round my shoulders. 'It's a secret,' he said, winking at Dave. Dave laughed and shoved his fag behind his ear, picking his camera up. 'Well, I hope it's somewhere special. Nothing less than the best for Princess Fran on her thirtieth birthday.' He kissed me on the cheek and walked off, whistling 'Happy Birthday'.

Grays Inn Road was bustling and utterly freezing. But I couldn't feel the cold. I was thirty years old, I was a specialist news producer who was about to crack politics, I had the best boyfriend in the world (who might, or might not, be about to propose to me) and life felt good. Scrap that, life felt bloody *amazing*.

'Where are we going?' I asked Michael eagerly, sounding like I was en route to my tenth birthday treat in the Wimpy Bar.

He looked sideways at me and smiled. There was something strange about his voice when he said, 'You'll have to wait, young lady.' He put his arm round me and pulled me into his side. And that was when I felt it. Something hard, small and square in the inside pocket of his coat.

My stomach flipped. A ring-box.

A million comets whizzed around my chest and my head swam with excitement.

Michael retreated into silence once we had hailed a cab and I wondered if he was practising his speech. I silently tried out my tearful acceptance as blinking Christmas lights slid over his face. We passed through Holborn and then along Shaftesbury Avenue towards Piccadilly Circus, tourists swarming round our taxi. London was pulsing with life and here I was at the centre of it with the loveliest man on the planet about to get down on one knee. In taxi. Think you might be right about M proposing. So nervous, I wrote to Leonie.

Eventually, and somewhat to my surprise, Michael asked the taxi driver to pull up outside the Ritz. Leonie texted back: FUCK! TOUCHING CLOTH!

I grinned uncontrollably. Michael knew I loved

nothing more than a bit of gilt and gold plating. How sweet of him to bring me here!

He paid the driver and helped me out of the taxi. His hand was shaking violently. I smiled encouragingly at him, thinking about my wedding dress. It would be raw silk and knee-length. I'd be carrying three lilies and my hair would be pulled back into an elegant knot at the nape of my neck. I'd get Dad over from Spain to walk me down a rustic aisle and hope that Mum didn't get too drunk and punch Gloria, Dad's wife.

'Let's go for a walk first,' Michael said. He sounded terrified. 'I knew you'd be late so I booked a table for nine. We could go and sit on our bench.' And with that he drifted off down the ramp into Green Park with me following reluctantly. Much as I liked going back to the bench where we'd drunk weird Slavic meths on our first proper day as a couple, I was keener on glamour and diamonds tonight.

Michael sat down on the bench and stared out at the park. My heart started thumping again.

'Franny. I need to talk to you about something,' he began.

Oh, Jesus! On a bench? I couldn't believe it. My eyes filled immediately, stinging in the freezing air, and I smiled so hard that my cheeks hurt. I raised my eyebrows to let him carry on.

He looked tortured, the poor thing.

'Fran. I don't know how to say this. I can't believe

I'm sitting here saying this to you on your birthday. But we have to break up for a while. I'm so sorry. I need a few months on my own.'

A police car was roaring up Piccadilly from Hyde Park Corner, sirens blaring; its flashing lights flickered across Green Park. As its urgent beacons lit up his features I knew, however impossible it was, that he meant it.

Less than an hour later, Leonie had half carried, half dragged me into my flat, which felt like it had been abandoned months ago. Michael's tea mug was on the table, but beyond that, there was no trace of him. He had spent most of the day moving his stuff out. He'd told me this in comforting tones as if I would somehow be grateful for his foresight.

I wailed.

Leonie had thrown open the door of the sixties faux-teak drinks cabinet she'd bought me for my twenty-first birthday. 'Fran, what the hell is going on in here?' she murmured, sorting through bottles of Co-op Irish Cream and weird foreign liqueurs that had been festering in there for years. Eventually she hauled out a bottle of Grey Goose that Michael had forgotten to take.

Duke Ellington had arrived through the cat flap, something alarming in his jaws. He eyeballed me for a while, then proudly deposited a half-mouse on the kitchen floor.

I wouldn't mind being that half-mouse, I thought. Head

eaten off, not a care in the world now. 'Hello, Duke Ellington,' I mumbled. He gazed at his half-mouse and miaowed.

'Duke Ellington, if you aren't nice to Fran tonight I'll skin you alive,' said Leonie, as she'd rummaged in my freezer for ice. He'd flicked his tail haughtily and minced off to sharpen his claws on the leg of the dining table. Through waves of misery I smiled. If nothing else, I still had my horrible cat.

'Right.' Leonie had handed me a vodka. 'So, can I get this absolutely clear, please? Michael says it's not working for him and he's suggested you both take three months out of the relationship.'

I nodded, tears sliding down my face into my vodka.

'And he wouldn't explain why?'

I shook my head.

'*Nothing?*'

I shook my head again. 'No. It was like . . . it was like he didn't even know himself.' Michael had just kept rocking backwards and forwards, crying and muttering, 'I just can't do this right now, Fran, I can't do it. I can't be with you.'

'And no contact between now and . . . what? Late *March*?' Leonie had been visibly appalled.

'He said a clean break would be better. Said he can't work anything out if we're still in touch.' A big, suffocating hollow was beginning to open in my chest. 'He said he'd call me at the end of it.'

Leonie had downed her drink and thought for a few minutes. 'Right. Well, for starters I'm confiscating your phone. Next I think we should probably get wasted and wake up in a pile of our own vomit. Then at some point tomorrow I'll make you a bacon sandwich. Deal?'

Now a sturdy dad ran past me with a child hanging off his back. 'RARRRR!' he yelled. I smiled. What on earth went wrong in people's brains when they had kids? Would Michael be like that if we became parents?

Thinking about that night had left me feeling pretty strange about meeting him next week, And, as usual, I had drawn a blank. There had been nothing, *nothing*, in what he'd said that could explain his motives. I'd literally begged him to explain but he'd just got up and walked away, leaving me howling like a werewolf on a lone bench in Green Park. Even the man who looked like he was there to flash people had given me a wide berth.

Mum and Stefania were right: I was going to need a very, very good explanation. The immutable fact was that Michael had left me howling in a park on my thirtieth birthday and he was damn well going to have to tell me why. *Should I demand an explanation before I go?* I wondered uneasily. *Before I pack my heart into a suitcase and get on a train heading for the Gare du Nord?*

My phone buzzed. Freddy again. Still gutted. Let me know if you change your mind. I bet your ex is a cock. I deleted it irritably, but another arrived only a few seconds later.

And then I smiled. This one was from Michael. Just woke up and realized that you'll be here this time next week. So excited. Can't wait to start again. I'm so sorry about my fuck-up, I was just a bit mad for a while. But I'm sane again. And I LOVE YOU!xxx

It was OK. It was fine. Everyone was allowed to have one breakdown, surely. I was safe! I smiled at the *rarrrr*ing dad and strode off down the hill in search of scones and other bread products. Date seven had been aborted but in its place something far better was brewing.

Chapter Thirty-eight

DRAFTS
....

To	Subject	Saved	Time
michael@michaelslater.com	Why?	19/03/2010	00:33:51

Michael . . .. I sort of wanted to ask, before I get on the train, why this happened. Why did we have to break up? Was it because I

ARRRGHHHH NO FRAN JUST GO TO BED YOU COCK YOU WILL SEE HIM TOMORROW

It was Clever Politics Thursday. Currently I was helping Alex and his team on Tuesday, Wednesday and Thursday afternoons, but unofficially I'd been beavering away at home, on the bus, in my breaks and during any downtime I had on my own news desk. There had even been one occasion on which I had taken work into the toilet with me in the aftermath of a prawn vindaloo. My schedule did not permit diarrhoea breaks.

Alex's pathetic gratitude for even the tiniest of tasks was beginning to grate, though, and I was currently practising my please-calm-down speech in the bathroom mirror. 'There is no need for this sort of behaviour, Alex,' I told my reflection sternly. 'Leonie likes you *regardless* of how you treat me. You can't send flowers to thank me for working till ten – I've been doing it for nearly five years!'

'I wouldn't bother, Fran,' Stella Sanderson said, emerging from a toilet cubicle. 'Alex is a man possessed at the moment. I can only imagine what your friend must be doing to him in bed.'

'Stella! Sorry, I didn't know you were there.'

'Going over my script for tomorrow's feature. I do my finest work in this toilet.'

I giggled. 'Me too! I had a vindaloo on Sunday, right, so I was a bit you-know-what on Monday and I came in here and spent a good half an hour –'

Stella cut in: 'No. I meant that I came in here for the peace. I put the lid down, Fran. I don't work and defecate simultaneously. Although it surprises me in no way that you do.' And out she strode.

I looked at myself in the mirror again. 'Fuck's sake,' I muttered.

'All right, Fannybaws?' Dave said, as I walked out of the loo.

I brightened. 'Dave! Hey. Where've you been all week?'

He shrugged. 'Out. Working.'

I waited for him to expand, but he didn't. I bit my lip. 'You OK?'

'Yep. You?'

'Er, yes, fine. I just made a twat of myself with Stella, I admitted to coming in here and doing some work when I had the shits and . . .' I trailed off. Dave wasn't smiling.

'Hugh was looking for you,' he said, after a pause. His mobile went and he fished it out of his pocket, smiling briefly. 'Gotta go.'

'Oh, OK. See you later for Gin Thursday?'

'Nope. Can't. Have plans. Sorry.'

'Oh. Right. Well, see you in a bit.'

I thought hard as I walked to Hugh's office. What was going on with Dave? He'd eaten my head off last Thursday, then apologized, and he'd stormed off on Saturday when I'd found him in my yard. Now he was being weird again. What was his problem? *And why was he in Stefania's shed?* a little voice asked. I brushed it off nervously and knocked on Hugh's door.

'COME IN,' he screamed, in his usual welcoming manner. I scanned back quickly for any stupidity or laziness on my part over the last week or two but nothing came to mind.

'I thought I told you I hated those bloody romper things, Fran,' Hugh said, glaring at my perky little Topshop ensemble.

'Well, I missed them. The corporate look didn't work for me either.'

Hugh snorted derisively. 'True. Now. First, shut the fuck up. Second, shut the fuck up. And third, I'd like you to make the film Michael Denby brought in.'

I opened my mouth in preparation for a loud scream. 'SHUT THE FUCK UP!' Hugh shouted, but he was smiling. 'You weren't my first choice – in fact, given recent behaviour, you were probably my last – but with the election I'm short on people who can do this sort of thing. I think you can do it but I want Dave Brennan to film it. Keep an eye on you.' I nodded enthusiastically. 'It's all yours. Please do your research, come up with a script and get back to me in three weeks ready to go. Your filming period begins during the week before the election and at that point you will lose your position helping Alex's team. I can't guarantee that you'll get it back come election night. Is this satisfactory?'

I did a brief mental calculation. Glamorous, exciting live election show versus ten-minute film about an ordinary person. For me it was a no-brainer. I nodded enthusiastically.

'Excellent. I wasn't giving you a fucking choice anyway.' He smiled. 'Stella will send you a full brief. She was going to do it but I needed her on the live election show.'

I bounded out of Hugh's office, beaming. This was unbelievable! Never in a million years had I thought I'd get a gig like this! I ran over to my computer and wrote an IM to Nellie: You won't believe it – my boss has given me the doc that your Michael brought in!! She pinged back: WONDERFUL, BABE! I bloody loved Nellie! I wrote: Would you like to join Gin Thursday tonight? It's the final debrief before I meet

Michael in Paris this weekend! Dave can't come but you know Stefania from Meditation and you'll love my friend Leonie.

Thanks, babe, but can't. Stefania invited me at Meditation last night but then she called me earlier to cancel.

I sat back, surprised. Really? Stefania's a regular at Gin Thursday. You sure?

Yeah, babe, she had something on.

Stefania had *what* on? Stefania never had anything on except a pot of hippie stew.

A few seconds later I was grinning again. This was it! My big break! A project that combined all of the things I loved – politics, characters, real life – which might be watched by literally millions! *And* I'd be in Paris with Michael in three days. Things were looking up.

Where was Dave? I needed to tell him! I scanned the news floor and eventually located a mop of messy hair retreating into the staffroom. Bounding up from my desk, I saw Hugh watching me from the door of his office with a face of amused despair. I blew him a kiss and he grimaced, retreating back to his cave.

'DAVE! GUESS WHAT!' He was sitting eating a Müller Fruit Corner. I smiled. How nineties and how typically Dave.

He looked up briefly from his yoghurt. 'DAVE! HUGH'S ASKED ME TO DIRECT THE

DOCUMENTARY THAT NELLIE'S BOY-FRIEND BROUGHT IN!' I jumped up and down on the spot.

Dave sat back in his chair and put another spoonful of yoghurt into his mouth. His face was strangely inscrutable. 'That's great, Fannybaws,' he said carefully. And then something – who knew what? – changed inside him and his face cracked into a broad smile. 'Actually, no, that's *really* fuckin' great. Well done, you little trouper!' He jumped up and hugged me. I smiled into his jumper, enjoying his smell. I'd always loved Dave's smell. Probably a bit too much fag smoke but there was a lovely whiff of soap and spice and cloves and cologne about him. Sort of like a smoky Christmas stocking. 'Well fuckin' done,' he said, into the top of my head.

I pulled away. 'Guess what else? You're filming it!' I threw myself back into a hug, butting his chest as I went. He jumped. 'Oof, sorry,' I said, from his armpit.

He smiled down at me. ''S OK, you mad fiend. So when do you start planning it?'

'Today! I'm so excited! Dave, I want it to be *beautiful*. I've already got all of these ideas and I'm so glad you're doing it because you're amazing!'

His eyes flashed with pleasure. 'Clever girl. And about time Hugh gave you a break too. I'm really proud of you, Franny.'

I beamed back at him. 'Are you sure you aren't free

for a quick celebratory apple juice tonight?' I said, as I switched on the kettle.

'Yep, quite sure. I'm busy. Sorry, love.'

I got a cup out of the dishwasher. Before I had time to think about it or stop myself I swung round. 'Are you meeting Stefania tonight?'

Dave looked surprised. 'Eh?'

I started to blush. 'Are you seeing Stefania tonight? She cancelled Gin Thursday too and I . . . I want to know.'

He was flustered now, and not completely innocent either. 'I'm not sure it's any of your business,' he said gently. 'Enjoy your cuppa. And well done on the doc. We'll do a great job of it.' And with that he got up and walked out of the staffroom leaving his nineties yoghurt only half eaten on the table.

A heavy feeling of unease settled in my stomach. I didn't want Dave to be meeting Stefania behind my back. I got up and trotted off after him. 'Um, Dave.'

He stopped and sighed. 'Fannybaws.'

'I didn't mean to pry. And I know it's none of my business. I just thought you and her, recently you've been as thick as thieves.'

Dave raised an eyebrow, nonplussed.

'But of course you've got Freya, and it's nothing to do with me, so I'm sorry. Er, yep. That's it. None of my business.'

He was peering across the news floor with a very

397

complicated expression on his face. After a few seconds he looked back at me and said something that nearly sent me into cardiac arrest. 'Freya left me actually. We're not together.'

I blanched. 'Oh, my *God* . . . Dave, I'm so sorry! I . . . *Why?*'

He shook his head and walked off. This time I didn't follow him.

'Could Dave and Stefania be having an affair?' I asked Duke Ellington. He looked keenly at me and miaowed. 'That's no help. One miaow for yes, two for no.'

My cat hopped into my suitcase.

'Out. OUT!' He ignored me. 'Bloody animal.' I tried my best to arrange my new Paris outfits around him and considered the evidence.

1. Dave was single. (This I could hardly believe. Dave and Freya had been together since *for ever*. How in the name of Jehovah had it gone wrong?)
2. Dave and Stefania had been caught looking strangely close at Gin Thursday.
3. Stefania had been entertaining Dave in her shed which did *not* contain a massage table.
4. I'd spotted Stefania doing the Walk of Shame twice.
5. She was generally behaving weirdly. Talking gushingly about love and also wearing

makeup. Neither of these things were in any way normal.

6. Dave was behaving weirdly too. He was blowing hot and cold quicker than my shower.

7. If he wasn't meeting Stefania tonight then why didn't he deny it? Instead he'd told me to mind my own business. Which was guilty-person's speak for yes.

I called Leonie. 'Do you think it's weird that Dave and Stefania both cancelled at the last minute?'

'No' she replied immediately, laughing.

'Excuse me?'

'Er . . . I just said no, I don't think it's weird. They're both obviously just busy.'

'But you said "no" really quickly. Why?'

'Fran, you're being mental! Dave and Stefania? Please! Look, have an amazing, amazing time in Paris this weekend, OK? You *have* to keep me posted. Regular texts. Only take him back if he begs for mercy.'

I smiled. 'OK. Promise.'

'Where are you meeting him?'

A delicious warm fuzzy feeling spread across my stomach. 'I don't know! It's a surprise. He just told me I have to be at St Pancras at eight thirty on Saturday morning. I'm to pick up the tickets and await further instructions!'

Leonie chuckled drily. 'Jolly good. Well, I'll leave

you to your packing. Good luck, my darling! Love you!'

As I upended my suitcase to eject Duke Ellington, I opened a Dave and Stefania file in my head. I wasn't done with it yet. 'I'm going to get to the bottom of this,' I told my angry cat.

Chapter Thirty-nine

Date eight: Michael

A man with twinkling dark eyes helped me off the train with a gloved hand. '*Merci!*' I breathed excitedly, surveying the scene around me. The Gare du Nord was packed. It was everything I'd imagined: massive, chaotic and exciting. There were glamorous women with neckerchiefs and sunglasses, men in suits scuttling along with briefcases, the smell of coffee and pastry and chocolate, and luscious sexy Frenchyspeak spilling down from elegant platform speakers. Thousands of voices filled the cavernous arches and sun spilled through the old leaded windows. *Mon dieu!* I was here at last!

I beamed at the nice gloved man who'd been serving me in First all the way from St Pancras. He smiled indulgently. '*Bonne chance, Mademoiselle.*' (Every time he'd arrived with more coffee I'd given him a nervous earful about Michael.) He handed me my suitcase – which looked rather shabby among the Louis Vuitton luggage that was descending from the train – but *nothing* was going to trouble me today. I was in the world's most romantic city, fresh as a daisy after an unexpected trip in First Class, only a matter of hours from seeing Michael Slater. I'd chosen my outfit carefully – tight jeans, smart boots and a seventies floral blouse that showed just the right amount of collar bone – casual but well groomed. My hair had begun to grow out of its bob and I'd pinned my fringe to one side in the way that I imagined *une Parisienne* would do. My heels clicked steadily along the platform with my suitcase trundling obediently behind me. I felt fabulous.

I stopped at a Presse newsstand on the main concourse for an impulse purchase of *Le Monde*. I wanted as many souvenirs of this weekend as I could find and I rather liked the idea of Fran *avec* French newspaper.

A few seconds later I handed it back to the man at the stand, red-faced. I had forgotten to bring any euros. 'Erm, *pardonnez-moi*,' I muttered, and scurried off.

After a quick tussle with a cash machine I was free, standing in the sun on the rue de Dunkerque under the awesome edifice of the Gare du Nord. I texted Michael: I'm here! Standing outside Gare du Nord. What next?

While I waited for his response I walked off to find a French Snack, filling my brain with Paris. Even here, smack bang in the middle of Tourist Central, it felt magnificent. I ran into a little bakery crammed between a bookshop and a rip-off tourist store and bought a coffee and a brioche, just because I felt that this was what one should do. I paid nine euros. I left, a little outraged, but amused. Only the French could pull off a stunt that audacious.

Munching the buttery pastry I felt quite overwhelmed and it took everything I had not to start dancing on the spot. In fact, had my phone not been ringing, I probably would have. It was Leonie. 'OH, MY GOD!' I screamed, by way of answer. No reply came, just a lot of hissing. 'Leonie, I can't hear you,' I shouted. 'I'll call you later when I've got an update!'

As I cancelled the call, the next message came through: Turn right out of the station and walk along Dunquerque. Look for a silver Beamer parked by a flower stall. Get in it!

I started jigging up and down with pure, childish excitement and ran towards the car, which was only metres from me. 'Françoise?' the driver said, with a lovely French smile.

'*Oui!*' I breathed, hopping in. We pulled off smoothly and I hugged myself. I couldn't believe he'd done this for me!

I knew now that I would do pretty much anything to get him back. Whatever he wanted, I'd give it to him.

Michael's next message said, You're coming to meet me for lunch in my fave brasserie. Exploring this afternoon. And then something very special tonight . . . X

As we passed through the streets filled with people I drank in the city. Bikes with baskets containing small dogs, chestnut trees laden with fat fluorescent green buds, smiling people drinking coffee on pavements and then – I drew in my breath – the pyramid of the Louvre. I saluted to the *Mona Lisa* as we chugged on towards the river. 'Wow,' I whispered as Notre Dame cruised into view.

The taxi driver cocked his head in the opposite direction. '*Regardez*,' he said. I regarded.

'Triple wow!' I breathed. It was only the bloody Eiffel Tower! '*J'adore Paris!*' The misery of the last few months evaporated out through the window across the Seine.

Leonie tried me a couple more times but there was no sound and eventually I turned my phone to silent. I wanted to be able to concentrate fully on my boy.

And there, twenty minutes later – as I stood in the doorway of a cavernous art-deco brasserie called La Coupole – he was.

My stomach somersaulted. My precious Michael Slater with the slate grey eyes. Sitting alone at a table by the window, fiddling with his stiff white napkin. Under the high ceiling, surrounded by gaily chattering diners, he seemed small and lonely but rather romantic. He was thinner than last time I'd seen him; he was wearing my favourite of his jumpers and his shoulder bones seemed sharply visible underneath. Even across a crowded restaurant I could see the fear in his face. It made my heart burst as I manoeuvred my way through the tables behind the maître d. *I'm coming, Michael. I can make whatever it is go away. I can fix this!*

I stood in front of him and he looked up. For a second, he didn't do anything, he just looked at me, almost shocked. And then the smile started. The smile I'd fallen in love with the moment I'd met him. The slow, lazy smile that made his eyes sparkle and his cheeks dimple. I felt the same stirring in my womb I'd felt on the day I'd walked into his life with Barry Manilow hair.

'Franny?' he said eventually, getting up.

'Actually, yes. Do I look like someone else?'

'No, I– What?'

I started giggling. 'Sorry, it's just you put a question mark after my name. As if I was someone else. I'm definitely Fran.'

'Thank Christ for that.' And then he did what I'd been desperate – *desperate* – for him to do every moment of the last three months: he pulled me into his arms and kissed me properly on the mouth. Then he hugged me so hard that I feared for my ribcage. 'Michael! I can't breathe down here.' Nothing. 'Michael! You're killing me!' A deep rumbly laugh travelled out through his rather spare ribs and jumper and into my ear. Eventually he let go. 'Christ, I've missed you. So badly.'

He traced a finger along my collarbone in exactly the way he had in my mind when I'd bought this blouse. I didn't trust myself to speak. There was so much to say and so much pain to try to file away.

Instead of saying anything I began the meal in the

405

way that only I knew how, which was to smash a glass off the table with my handbag as I sat down. A large, beautiful wine glass, which splintered into a million rainbow-tinted pieces as it hit the floor. Unsurprised but mortified, I sprang to my feet to pick it up while Michael laughed. 'For God's sake, Franny! You haven't changed.' He bent down to help me.

'I'm so sorry!' I whispered, puce. I didn't dare look up at the people around us and kept my eyes on the shards of glass all over the place. Something wet fell on them. A tear. Me? A quick mental check confirmed that I wasn't crying. Michael? Yes, Michael. He was picking up glass and *actually* crying.

'What the blazes is going on?' I whispered to him. 'Why are you crying?'

He made a weird snuffly noise like the one he made when he was sleeping. 'Because I've missed you. Even your bull-in-a-china-shop ways. I need you in my life. I can't function without you,' he said simply.

That seemed a very decent explanation. I tried to put my hand over his briefly but stabbed him with a glass shard. 'Oh, fuck, sorry!'

'Ssh!' he hissed. 'You can't say "fuck" here!'

People were by now ignoring us as we scrabbled around on the floor. 'We're in France, Michael. These people speak French. Of course I can say "fuck"!' The waiter arrived and swept the glass briskly into an elegant silver dustpan, which he whisked away. We sat down and looked at each other.

Michael's eyes were watering but he'd stopped crying. 'Sorry to start blubbing,' he said ruefully. 'Didn't plan to do that straight away. But it's true. I can't live without you. You don't know what the last three months have been like.'

I took a deep breath and straightened my top with shaking hands. 'So why did you end it?' I said. I wasn't far off crying myself now. All the pain, the shame of stalking, the nights where I'd cried myself to sleep, the stupid dates, the SOS calls to my friends. Why had we both gone through this? The waiter came back. He scanned the floor quickly to check I hadn't broken anything else and then got a bottle of wine out of a bucket behind Michael. Bloody hell, it was Puligny Montrachet.

'Yes, great,' Michael said distractedly, after sipping the sample the waiter gave him.

'Très bien,' the waiter muttered waspishly. He poured wine into our glasses, deposited vast leather-bound menus on the table and turned on his smart clicky heel.

'Um, I can't drink at the moment,' I said.

Michael looked surprised. 'Eh? You're a born drinker!' I flinched. 'What's going on?'

'Er, antibiotics. Anyway. You were about to tell me why the hell we've spent the last three months in Purgatory, I believe.'

Michael had coloured slightly and my heart melted. He looked so precious and vulnerable. And thin. I resisted the urge to get up, hurl myself into his lap and curl up there with my arms around him.

'Because . . .' he said eventually '. . . because you abandoned me, Franny. You had left the relationship. You were living on your terms and finding time for me as and when you could fit me in. I just couldn't take any more.' He stopped, anguished. 'By the time we got to your thirtieth I felt like you weren't giving me anything at all. I felt like this hanger-on and I just cracked up, Franny, I couldn't take any more.'

'Um . . . Go on,' I said slowly. My brain was exploding with confusion, frantically re-scrambling my picture of our last few months together and cross-checking it against what he was saying.

'Fran, I know you worked on the six thirty news so you were never going to put in really normal hours, but it just felt you were throwing your whole life into it. When you weren't working, you were out with Leonie *drinking*,' – he spat the word out as if I'd been shooting up skag – 'or hanging with bloody *Dave* or, worst of all, you were looking after your *mother*.'

I put my hands up. 'Whoa, Michael, Mum was sick! I saw her once a fortnight. What are you *on* about?' But he was crying again. Silent sobs that convulsed him in agonizing spasms. 'Franny, I was so lonely I didn't know what to do with myself,' he said. 'I just felt like I was spending my life waiting for you to come home from your big important job or from nights out with your big important friends. You completely abandoned me. I couldn't take any more.' Silently I passed him a slightly snotty tissue from my handbag. He winced as he appraised it before blotting his tears.

I was rendered completely mute by now so he carried on: 'I always loved you, Fran. From the moment we met. I wanted to be with you for ever. I still want to be with you for ever. I was going to ask you to marry me that night on your thirtieth and then you kept me waiting for an hour at ITN while you were calling Nick Bennett and trying to get into the election team, and when you finally came out all you could talk about was that you'd got the job even though I'd *said* I didn't want you doing it. It was like you didn't even care. And I realized I had to get away from it all and sort my head out. I wanted to spend some time apart so I could figure out whether or not you wanted to be with me and whether I was prepared to accept you on your terms.'

I stared at him.

'I heard from Alex that you were dating and it nearly killed me.'

'That was why you started texting me,' I whispered.

He nodded. 'But then eventually you replied and Jenny said she'd seen you and that you'd been miserable too and you'd been stalking Nellie Daniels thinking we were together and . . . well, I suppose I realized you were in as much of a state as I was.'

I was flabbergasted. 'You mean the three months was a *test*? To see how hard I'd try to get you back?'

He looked sheepish. 'Not so much a test, I just needed to know if you cared.'

'JESUS, Michael, you told me not to contact you for three months! It was the only bloody thing you *were* clear about! If I'd known you were testing me I'd have been on the phone twenty-four hours a day! I nearly had a breakdown. Seriously.' I felt hollow and exhausted. 'I nearly had a breakdown,' I repeated softly.

He studied my face closely and put his hand over mine. 'I know. Jenny told me. I realize now it was a stupid thing to do. I should have been straight with you –'

'You're not bloody wrong there. I can't believe you did this to me.' I regained my composure. 'You do know that my friends made me go on those dates, don't you?' He nodded. 'And that nothing came of them?' He nodded again. I made a mental note to ensure the story of my sleeping with Charlie Swift was deeply buried.

'Michael, the last three months have been the worst in my life. And if it's been that bad for you, too, then quite frankly I think you're insane.' His face clouded. 'I just think it was a ridiculous thing to do and it didn't pay off. I thought you were sleeping with Nellie and you thought I was dating everything that moved. And we were both miserable. If this is going to work, you're going to need to be honest with me. One hundred per cent honest.'

The waiter came over and hovered slightly malevolently, pointedly ignoring the fact that we were engrossed in a deeply personal conversation. I looked up at him with watery eyes. 'Er . . . pâté?' I said, taking a stab at what might be on the menu. *'Et, um, moules frites?'* The waiter nodded and I smiled wryly, grateful for my GCSE French. Michael muttered, *'Moi aussi,'* and the waiter swept off.

Michael smiled and put his hand on the side of my face. 'I agree, honesty is the only way. So here's me being super-honest, Fran. I love you. I've missed you terribly and I want us to be together. I just need to know that you're serious about us. I can't go on feeling alone in our relationship.'

Scared of losing him again I gabbled, 'Of *course* I'm serious about us. I'm so sorry you felt abandoned, darling Michael. I never intended to make you feel that way. I promise I'll spend less time drinking – in fact, actually I lied about antibiotics. I'm not drinking at all these days' – Michael was stunned – 'and, anyway, Leonie is in complete La-la Land with Alex and Dave's being weird, but none of that matters. Even if they want to see me every night I promise I'll make more time for you. In fact, I'll give up Gin Thursday, OK? That's it. Gin Thursday's gone. Done. Finished.'

Michael nodded hopefully.

'And Mum's in AA! She's sober! It's a miracle, but she doesn't need much looking after now; she's got all these people from AA she hangs out with and she's talking about working again and she's seeing her old friends . . .' Michael smiled. It didn't feel quite right, batting away Mum as a drain on my time, but I couldn't lose him again. 'And as for work, well, I . . .' My new project was going to take up a lot of my time.

I looked at Michael's face and knew what I had to do. 'As for work, I was just asked to make a prime-time documentary for the ITV news. It'll take up hours of my time, there's no point denying it.' Michael lowered his eyes to his napkin. 'But there will be other opportunities.' He looked up again. 'If Hugh trusts me with this I'm sure he'll trust me with a similar thing when you and me are solid again. Maybe for now I could quit the six thirty news and apply for a transfer to the lunchtime bulletin so I'd be home earlier.'

He fiddled with his fork, evidently still concerned. My heart pounded. I could not go back to where I was three months ago. *Nothing* was worth that sort of pain. 'Michael, I'll do whatever it takes, OK? I'll put you first. Just please believe me when I tell you I'm sorry because I love you and I am willing to make *whatever changes* I have to for this to work.'

The waiter returned, wearing a rather horrid smirk, and we stopped talking as he replaced our starter cutlery with pâté knives. Michael was thinking hard. *I had to get him back.* The waiter swept off again.

'OK.' Michael smiled. 'Let's do it. Let's be us again. I trust you. I love you. I want to be with you.' He leaned forward and kissed me softly on the lips.

I felt a Mexican wave of relief go off inside me. I grabbed his hand and smiled, weak with relief. 'Thank you,' I whispered. 'Thank you for giving me one more chance.' We kissed again.

The meal was delicious. Rich gamey pâté with squares of light brown bread and glorious salted butter, followed by mussels in a sauce so exquisite I had to fight hard not to lift the bowl up and slurp at the end. We talked and laughed as if none of the last painful ninety days had happened, me filling him in on Duke Ellington's evil machinations and him groaning about Alex's descent into complete Leonie-based insanity. Apparently he had been obsessed with her from the moment he met her. 'Does he talk about it all the time?' I asked.

Michael shrugged. 'Don't bloody know. Since he got involved with her I've not even heard from him. He is *totally* under the thumb.'

I let him in on my suspicions regarding Dave and Stefania, which he seemed to enjoy immensely. 'Surely not! *Stefania?* After someone as beautiful as Freya?' he breathed, scandalized.

'Er, hang on a minute . . . Stefania is wonderful, Michael, and she's really very pretty if you ignore the outfits. But I know what you mean about it being sudden. *Maybe* I'm barking up the wrong tree . . . I suppose we'll have to see.' The conversation turned to Michael's work: he was out here writing a feature on the Sarkozy family and, as ever, I was dumbstruck by his success. And, well, his *cleverness*. I listened for ages to the tales of his journalistic exploits tracking down Sarkozy-haters in secret cafés in Montmartre and pulling up old newspapers in dusty records offices, feeling the usual overwhelming sensation of pride. He was so awesome, this man of mine! Quite why he wanted a thicko like me was beyond me.

While we waited for dessert, Michael took my hands in his again and looked me in the eye. 'Thank you,' he said quietly. 'Thank you for agreeing to give more to us. I know it can't have been easy for you.' I smiled at him and he kissed me. He didn't lean back again but stayed very close to my face, gazing searchingly into my eyes.

Suddenly he seemed scared again. He cleared his throat and started speaking hesitantly. 'Um, I was going to ask you tonight . . . I have this perfect romantic location lined up but right here, right now, feels perfect.'

He put his hand into his pocket and I started seeing things in slow motion. Out it came. A ring-box. And it opened. And inside it was a beautiful, delicate, sparkling ring made of a smooth silvery metal. Three diamonds sat in a perfect rectangular art-deco clasp. My ears started tingling, so when Michael said, 'Franny, will you marry me?' I could barely hear him.

I nodded slowly, wondering if I was possibly fainting. He took my left hand and put the ring on my finger. And then he got up, came round to my chair

414

and kissed me and hugged me, muttering, 'Thank you, thank you, thank you,' into my ear. We stayed there for a good five minutes by which time the waiter had served our dessert and wandered off in disgust with the cream jug.

'I've just got engaged!' I whisper-shrieked, at the stylish old couple who arrived at the table next to ours when Michael went to the loo half an hour later. They looked at me blankly. Ah, yes, they were French. I waved my left hand at them instead, adding squeaks to clarify the situation.

'Ah! *Félicitations!*' said Madame, kindly. The man pretty much ignored me but she laughed softly. '*Appelez votre mère!*' she whispered.

Dear Christ! Mum! Madame was quite right. I pulled my phone out of my bag and waited for the ring tone. Nothing. Dammit. Of course, I'd not been able to hear Leonie this morning. Perhaps I could text Mum.

There were three texts from Leonie. The most recent said CALL ME IMMEDIATELY. The one before said: DID YOU GET MY MESSAGE? THIS IS SERIOUS FRAN. Now nervous, I opened the first message.

URGENT: DON'T SEE MICHAEL. CALL ME. DON'T EVEN GO NEAR HIM. I'M NOT FUCKING AROUND.

Oh, God, I thought. This didn't sound like anything to do with the Eight Date Deal. This didn't sound like a kindly caution. This was bad. As I stared at my phone, another message came through. FOR

FUCK'S SAKE, ARE YOU GETTING THESE? FRAN YOU MUST NOT MEET MICHAEL.

'*Pardonnez moi*,' I said, grabbing the waiter by his apron. He looked disdainfully at my hand. I removed it. 'Erm, *j'ai besoin d'utiliser votre téléphone*.'

'I see. It is over by the maître d's desk,' he replied in English. I was off and running. Michael was coming back from the toilet on the other side of the room. I smiled and waved my telephone at him; he nodded and carried on back to the table.

'Fran? Is that you?'

'Yes. What the fuck?'

'Darling, I don't know how to tell you this.'

'What?'

'Franny. It was Michael who sold your mum – and, indeed, you – to the press.'

Silence.

'Franny?'

'What are you talking about? Charlie did! He knew everything!'

'*Yes yes yes*, that's how it looked, I admit. But it seems Charlie kept his mouth shut. Perhaps he really did like you. Doesn't matter. Franny, it was Michael.'

I gulped, goldfish-like, unable to take this in. 'What the hell are you talking about? How? Why are you telling me this now?'

She took a deep breath. 'I told Alex this morning that you'd gone to Paris to meet Michael. I figured that if you two were getting back together, we could talk about you at last. But when I said where you were going he went mad. Got really angry. Called Michael a cunt and all sorts. Honestly his language was filthier than when he —'

'LEONIE.'

'Sorry. Christ. Look, Alex hasn't talked to Michael in weeks. They'd been drifting apart for a couple of years because once Michael found you he didn't really need Alex any more. But then they went out a few weeks back, when Alex told him you were dating, and Michael basically got drunk and told Alex he'd sold the story. They had a massive fight and haven't spoken since.'

I was speechless. 'But why? Why would he do that? He works at the fucking *Independent*, Leonie! Why the hell would he bother selling the story to the *Mirror* when he could break it in his own broadsheet?'

'He doesn't work at the *Independent*. He was a total failure there. The day he dumped you, he lost his job. They made him redundant because he was shit. Remember how you never saw his name in the paper? And he told you it was because he was in a more editorial role? That was bollocks. He just couldn't write. He was unemployed for two months after you two split up and then eventually sold your mum to the *Mirror* so that he'd get some freelancing there.'

'But he was great at his job. I *know* he was. I saw him in action!'

Leonie interrupted: 'He was OK-ish as an on-camera correspondent but only because he had a good team

417

around him. He didn't get early dispensation to leave Kosovo, Fran, they let him go. They got rid of him.'

My mouth had stopped working. I made a strangled honking noise.

'Oh, Fran, I'm so sorry. But if you don't believe me, ask Hugh. It was him who let Michael go. He said the quality of stuff Michael was sending in from over there was so bad he'd have better luck employing a turkey with learning difficulties.'

That certainly sounded like Hugh.

'But . . . but he's in Paris writing a piece for the *Independent*.'

'Of course he's not.' Leonie took another deep breath. 'And, Fran, if you don't believe me, I need you to think seriously about your relationship. Look, I always wondered about this a bit, in fact we all did, but Alex confirmed it a hundred per cent for me this morning. Michael needed you not because of who you are but because of what you did for him. You put him on a pedestal right from day one, Franny, and told him he was amazing all the time. You fed his ego day after day, you listened to all of his self-important bullshit and made him feel like he was the greatest journalist alive. Apparently he's always had some downtrodden sidekick doing this for him since he was a schoolboy. Alex was his punchbag for years when they were younger. But then your career started to really take shape and he couldn't cope with it. The more established you became, the less you did what he *wanted* you to do. He couldn't take it. He used to be really scathing about your work behind your back.'

Another blow to the stomach. 'He *what*?'

'I'm afraid so, darling. And he *was* going to propose to you on your thirtieth but only in the hope that you'd agree to become some sort of housewife. But that very day he lost his job at the *Independent* and you got your promotion on to the election team and he lost it.'

I reeled. 'Leonie, you don't know any of this. As if Michael would tell any of this to Alex! It was *Alex* who was always being rude about my work! Michael told me what he used to say. How do I know he's not just making it all up?'

'FRAN! Wake up! Think about your relationship!'

I went silent, but nothing much happened in my head. This was too much. Just too much.

'Franny?'

'Yes, still here.'

'Franny, what has he said to you about why he ended it?'

I felt an unbearable lump of sadness form in my throat. 'He said I'd abandoned him,' I whispered. 'He said I hadn't given him enough time or put enough effort into the relationship.'

'The FUCKER!' Leonie roared. 'And do you think that's true, Fran?'

'No.'

'Damn right it's not. You were always running off home to him to make sure he was OK. When we

419

were at Popstarz the other week I was thinking, God, it's been months and months and months since me and Fran did this – we used to do it all the time.'

'Yes, I thought the same,' I said sadly. It felt as if my world was ending. Again.

'What did you say to him when he accused you of abandoning him?' she asked.

'I said I was sorry. I said . . .' I started to cry '. . . I said I'd stop Gin Thursdays and spend less time looking after Mum because she was in AA now, and I said I'd –' A loud sob escaped and the maître d' handed me a white napkin without looking round. 'I said I'd resign from the documentary.'

Leonie was silent. 'Poor Fran,' she said eventually. 'You know that was the wrong thing to do, don't you?' I nodded, even though she couldn't see me, blowing my nose. 'And you know that you were a wonderful, committed girlfriend to him, don't you?' she asked gently.

I nodded again. 'Mmmppff.'

'So what are you going to do? Do you need re-inforcements? I can see if there's any seats on the Eurostar today, my love?' Leonie's kindness was almost as heartbreaking as the situation.

'I'm going to –' I cried even harder. 'I don't know what I'm going to do. We just got engaged.'

'Oh, Franny,' Leonie whispered. 'Darling, I'm so sorry.'

*

420

After the call ended I looked at him, sitting in the restaurant window, completely relaxed and blissful. *How dare he?* I thought numbly. *How dare he propose marriage to me when he picked up a phone and told the press that my mother is an alcoholic? That she blackmailed Nick into staying with her?* How had he envisaged our wedding day? What would he have said in his speech, for fuck's sake? 'And a special thank you to Eve, whose family I'm truly honoured to be joining'?

'Can I assist wiz, er, *le situation*?' the maître d' said quietly at my shoulder. He glanced at Michael and raised his eyebrow. 'I am presooming that your engagement is no good.'

I started mopping away the now-drying smudges of black mascara with the napkin. I continued to watch Michael, who wore an expression of pure childlike happiness on his face. 'No,' I whispered. 'No good.'

'He cheated wiz you?' he guessed, looking excited.

'No. Worse.' He whistled.

I'd wanted to be with Michael from the *moment* I'd met him. I'd dreamed of it; I'd dreamed of *him*. I'd watched him sleep and imagined us in the same bed in forty years' time. I'd watched love and hope and disappointment flash across his eyes. I'd made dinner as he'd talked to my cat. I'd cleaned skidmarks out of the toilet without swearing. All because I loved him.

In response he'd used me as a prop. As an ego-inflater. Confidence-booster. He'd laughed at my career behind my back and he'd sold me and Mum to the fucking *Mirror* just because his career wasn't working out the way he wanted it to. `

I balled my fist. Anger had arrived and it was riding a big furious don't-fuck-with-me horse. The maître d' peered down at the fist and nodded enthusiastically. '*Oui*. Fight him.' He removed his jacket. 'But no fighting in the restaurant. I will get him out for you. And then you may fight to your heart's end.'

'Heart's content,' I said automatically, as if the man were Stefania. But then I stopped. 'No, you're right. Heart's end is spot on. This is *over*.'

'*Yes!*' he hissed. 'Over! We have too many engagements in this city! It is time for break heart at La Coupole!'

Together, we marched over to the table where Michael sat gazing dreamily into the middle distance. A happy smile lit up his face as I approached him.

And my anger left as rapidly as it had arrived. 'It's OK, actually,' I said to the maître d' quietly. 'I can handle this.'

He was bitterly disappointed. 'The engagement is still on?'

'No. It's still off. But there won't be any fighting.'

He smiled sadly and shuffled off.

'Hello,' I said, as I arrived back at the table.

'Hello!' he said warmly, taking my hand.

'So, the engagement is off,' I said, as I sat down.

He smiled. 'Yeah, I second that. We're a shit couple!'

I said nothing, just looked straight at him. I didn't move.

Eventually, a small chink of doubt wormed its way into his face. I continued to say nothing as it flourished gradually into a shadow of pure fear. He looked at the maître d', who was replacing the telephone under his desk. And then he looked at me again.

He knew.

I watched excuses flicker across his face like a silent movie – lies he could tell me to buy himself more time, insults he could throw to make himself feel better, insistences that Leonie, or Alex, or whoever had blown his cover, was mad.

I shook my head gently and eventually he nodded, understanding. Slowly, I took off the ring.

It was beautiful. A finger of afternoon Parisian sun bounced gaily off the main diamond and flashed into his eye briefly.

'I'm sorry,' he said quietly.

'I know. But I can't be with you now, Michael.'

He exhaled slowly.

I thought of Mum, of that day when the press were camped outside her house and she'd begged me like a child to go and buy her gin. About the shame I'd suffered at ITN. And I thought about our relationship and the overwhelming amount of love I'd poured into someone who needed me only because I bolstered his ego. Someone who cared so little about me he'd sell me and my family so that the nation could laugh at us.

And then I got up and left. I cut through the clink of cutlery and glasses and the low hum of conversation and walked out at four o'clock, on 20 March 2010, to the rue du Montparnasse. I took a deep breath, pulled my bag over my shoulder, and started walking.

Chapter Forty

I think you were right. It wouldn't have worked. Your mother
would have destroyed our relationship eventually.
Sender: Michael Mob 07009 704462
Message centre: +447999100100
Sent: 20 Mar 2010 19:00:05

'*Un café très, très grand,*' I said to the bored teenager
trundling through economy coach D with a drinks
trolley.

My phone started ringing and I looked at it warily.
I didn't want to hear any more of Michael's bullshit.
He'd sent me five messages already, each containing
more denial than the one before. But instead it was
Alex. I answered.

'Hi, Alex.'

'Fran?'

'Yes. I'm on the train home.'

A silence.

'I . . . I know,' he said uncomfortably. 'I . . . Fran, I
owe you an enormous apology.'

'I don't think so,' I said. The train started to move.
'Michael is who he is. It's not your fault I didn't realize
that.' I was exhausted. I didn't want to talk to Alex or,

indeed, anyone else. I pulled my new, pointless négli-
gée out of my bag and put it between my head and
the window.

Alex wasn't having any of it. 'No, Fran, it was awful
of me not to tell you about Michael and your mum.
I've been torturing myself over it. I thought you knew.'

'Why on earth would I have gone to Paris if I'd
known?'

Alex sighed. 'That Monday morning when I came
to your desk and said I needed to talk to you about
something. I was going to tell you then. I had the
speech planned. But you stopped me – you said you
already knew. What were you talking about? What did
you "know" if it wasn't about Michael selling your
mum to the *Mirror*?'

I tucked my phone between shoulder and ear and
smiled sadly at my newly manicured hands. 'I thought
he'd got engaged,' I said. 'I thought he was shacked
up with a girl called Nellie Daniels. Didn't Leonie *tell*
you all of this?'

'No,' Alex said. 'We agreed at the start we wouldn't
talk about Michael and you. Leonie was insistent.
And I . . .'

I laughed briefly. 'You do everything she says.'

He went silent.

'Alex, I'm only joking. So . . . that Monday morning
you were trying to tell me what Michael had done and
I stopped you. Oh, God, I remember . . . you said
you'd seen him the day before. While Leonie and I

were eating burgers. Fuck . . . So I could have avoided all of this if I'd just listened? Great. Another triumph. Amazing work, Fran.'

'Don't be so hard on yourself,' Alex said. There was kindness in his voice. It was in great danger of choking me. 'You were just trying to protect yourself. After the amount of shit you'd been through I'm not surprised.'

I didn't trust myself to talk. Alex sounded genuinely stricken. And kind. And warm. I didn't understand it. Where had the weasel gone?

He cleared his throat. 'And, Fran, I'm afraid there's something else I need to talk to you about.' The train was passing through ugly, neglected railwayside buildings and darkness was falling. I could begin to see my reflection in the window; tired, sad, small. 'Go on,' I said hesitantly. This didn't sound good.

'I've been wanting to say this for a long time,' Alex began, and then stopped.

'Go on,' I repeated, now nervous.

'Fran . . . you've been led to believe that I've had all sorts of opinions about you that just aren't true. Apparently you were told that I was very disparaging about you and your work on the ents and culture news desk. And that I thought you were a bit silly and frilly. I cannot emphasize strongly enough how completely untrue that is. What you've done on that news desk is amazing! I'd bloody *love* to know the stuff you know about popular culture and arts and stuff!' He

427

added, 'And I only had good things to say about you. From the very start.'

I sat back, surprised. This in no way tallied with what Michael had told me.

Which meant, I realized slowly, that . . .

'Michael made it all up,' Alex said firmly. 'All of it. Sorry, Fran, I don't want to point fingers but I can't have you thinking those things about me. It's not for me to put words in someone else's mouth, but I do rather wonder if he used me as a way of expressing his *own* prejudices.'

I felt disbelieving. Then angry. Then sad. Defeated. It had to be true. 'Wow,' I said, after a pause. 'What a . . . what a bastard. How could I have been so stupid, Alex?'

'You're not,' he said. 'We all make mistakes in who we fall for.'

'So you really didn't try to get me sacked,' I said slowly.

'No,' he said, very firmly. 'In fact, I found out the other day that the reason your tape was in the bin was that Dave put it there. He was worried someone would find it and you'd get sacked. Obviously it went a bit tits up! But . . .'

'Right,' I said. 'So really I owe *you* an apology.' This was not a situation I'd ever imagined being in. I felt extremely embarrassed. God only knew how rude I'd been to Alex over the last two years, presuming he loathed me.

'No, it's the other way round. I shouldn't have let you shut me up when I tried to tell you about Michael. I should have insisted that we talked about it.'

'Don't be silly. I told you I knew about it – what were you going to do? Hold a biro to my throat to clarify what exactly I "knew"? It was a misunderstanding, Alex. I . . . Look, I'm glad you called me. Things are making a lot more sense now.'

'Are you OK?' he asked.

A painful lump lodged in my throat. 'Not really. But I *will* be OK. He's wasted two years of my life. He's not getting any more.'

'Good girl. You're brilliant, Fran. You have a lot of fans. You'll be just fine.'

'Thanks. Um, I'd better go. We're probably about to lose signal. Thanks again, Alex.'

'Let's have lunch!' he cried excitedly. 'Monday!'

I smiled. 'OK. Monday. And thanks again.'

The train gathered speed.

As we headed into the now-dark countryside and I settled down to sleep, my phone delivered a message from Dave. The sight of his name in my inbox made my spirits lift a little. I heard. I'm so sorry Franny. But I know you'll be OK. Michael was wrong for you. He couldn't have made you happy.

No, I thought. *No, he really couldn't.* It came to me, as I stared at Dave's message – Dave, around whom I'd always felt so safe and normal – that I had been . . . *scared* of Michael. Scared of his brain. Scared of what he thought. Scared of not being good enough. And as we cut silently through France, I saw that that was exactly where he'd wanted me.

You're right. Thank you, DB, I replied.

Come back to London Fannybaws. We're all waiting for you.

I smiled, knowing I was going to be OK.

The train shot on into the night.

Chapter Forty-one

'Oh, my God! Dave! It's *brilliant*!' I breathed.

He smiled lopsidedly and got two bottles of alcohol-free beer out of the mini-fridge in the corner. 'That's down to you, not me,' he replied.

'Rubbish! Dave, it's brilliant because of how beautifully you've filmed it. You great big talented Glaswegian!' Dave grinned as he cracked open a Bitburger and handed it to me. He'd had his hair cut – in preparation for this long hot summer we were being promised   and he really looked quite normal. Nice, in fact. A lot less homeless.

It was 14 May, and Dave and I had shot the final scenes of my documentary three days before. We'd been waiting for these all-important final scenes so we could finish editing and now – at last! – it was done. Polished, complete and ready for Hugh. I glugged the Bitburger and high-fived Dave, dizzy with tiredness, relief and achievement. 'We're wrapped, David Brennan!' I said. 'Team Documentary disbanded and awaiting debrief!'

He nodded. 'Yep. And you've done bloody brilliantly, Fran. I'm proud of you.'

'Shut it, Dad,' I muttered, as scarlet invaded my face.

I was truly spent. On my return from the ill-fated Paris trip in March I'd started my documentary and simultaneously been drafted in to help Alex's election team pretty much full-time. 'Help them whenever you aren't tied up with your film, Fran. I don't want to see you so much as going for a shit. YOU HAVE NO SPARE TIME, UNDERSTOOD?' Hugh had barked.

I had understood. In the weeks that had followed I'd completely lost track of time. London at three a.m. had whizzed past my taxi window night after night; Gin Thursday had ground to a halt (or was flourishing without me, I didn't even know) and my relationship with the outside world was reduced to a mumbled conversation with Mum once a week from the ITN toilet, a one-way stream of smutty text messages from Leonie and a regular supply of healthy stews deposited through my cat flap by Stefania. Duke Ellington had long since taken to ignoring me completely and had instead cultivated a close relationship with the automatic feeder. He ate when the timer popped open and then departed silently for Stefania's shed.

Stefania. I'd not had time to snoop around after her but something extremely scandalous was definitely going on still. Apart from the fact that she had taken to wearing makeup, I'd arrived back from work at two thirty a.m. a couple of weeks ago and heard the deep bass notes of a man's voice murmuring in her shed. And this morning when I'd left at six to get to our breakfast briefing she had been arriving home on the walk of shame with a smile of not-particularly-secret joy on her face.

'FRANCES!' she had shouted, although I was only three feet away from her. She grabbed and hugged me. 'Ve are missing you, me and Duke Ellington!'

I extricated myself from her bony grip and grinned, clutching my flask of coffee for support. 'It's mutual,' I replied. 'And you are so unbelievably lovely for leaving me those dinners. I've been taking them to work in Tupperware boxes every day. Everyone thinks I've lost it, rocking up with bloody okra curries, but I swear that stuff is what's keeping me on it!' My taxi beeped outside the gate. 'I have to go. But don't think you're off the hook. At the end of today it's all over and you, madam, are due a very severe grilling.'

She smirked and mimed zipping up her mouth. 'Stefania vill discuss not matters viz you before she is ready,' she said craftily.

'Just like Fran had to go on eight dates LONG before she was ready? No chance. Expect an interrogation!' I shouted, jumping into the calm haven of my taxi. As we passed through an already busy London, I pondered for the millionth time who her lover was. I still had a horrible suspicion it was Dave. He'd mentioned her often of late, and more times than I cared to remember during the filming of my documentary, I'd caught him gazing into the distance. I was rather glad that I'd been too busy to give the matter much thought. Because I simply didn't like it. Dave wasn't meant to be with Stefania. Stefania wasn't meant to be with Dave. I couldn't really make more sense of it than that.

I put down my bottle of Bitburger and pulled an embarrassingly warm bottle of champagne out of my handbag, which I gave to Danny, the editor. 'Thanks so much,' I said. 'Between you and Dave you made it really special.'

He guffawed. 'Cheers. But you guys gave me some wicked material to work with! You make a well good team!' My blush returned and I looked sideways at Dave.

He smiled briefly, then answered the internal phone. 'It's Stella,' he said, peering at the caller display.

Under normal circumstances, Hugh would have signed off the documentary before we left the edit but he was so flat out on the general election that he'd deputized to Stella. We were waiting for her now.

'She's late. Half an hour. Let's take a break,' he said, as he replaced the receiver. Danny grinned and went off to smoke.

'It's lovely outside,' Dave said to me. 'Wanna go up to the roof for a wee stroll? There's been a shoot up there, the door's open.'

'Yes! Ace!'

We went.

Dave chinked my bottle as the lift slid quietly upwards. I grinned at him. 'I know we've been filming

434

together but I feel like we haven't talked in weeks,' I said.

Dave swigged his Bitburger. 'Aye, it's been a funny old time. But don't you worry about me. I've been fine,' he said, with a wink.

I punched his arm. 'What have you been up to? What was that wink for?'

'Ah, nothing much. I've been working a lot too. They've had me down in Westminster every second that I've not been filming the doc with you.'

'And what else have you been doing?'

'Moochin' around,' he said vaguely.

We got out of the lift and walked into the sun. London sprawled away in all directions, its customary honking and revving muted by the roar of air-conditioning vents. A tiny but significant early-summer heat haze shimmered over the sea of satellite dishes.

Dave leaned on the south-facing wall, and beckoned me over when I didn't join him. 'C'mon, Fannybaws! Bloody well relax for half an hour!'

I trotted over obediently, only to be enveloped in an enormous hug on arrival. 'Well done, kid,' he said, into the top of my head. 'You did so well. You're going to blow Hugh's arse away when he sees it.' I lost myself in his stripy T-shirt for a few seconds.

'Thanks. I needed a hug,' I said, as I emerged. 'Fuck knows how I haven't lost my mind.'

'Well, you didn't,' Dave said, ruffling my hair. 'And

that's even more to your credit. Live election shows and quirky documentaries are two pretty difficult things to juggle, Fannybaws. Particularly when you have shit to deal with elsewhere. There aren't many people in this place who could've pulled that off. For a mentalist of your calibre it was an outstanding performance.'

'Nonsense. I'm just a baby in comparison to most of the people here.'

Dave reached for my hand. 'Not true. Look at me, Fran.'

I obeyed. He was smiling. 'You really aced this, love. You should be so proud of yourself. And even if you're not, I am!'

I grinned up at him. The afternoon sun was hitting him square on his right-hand side, picking out little auburn bits in his stubble. 'Dave! No way! You've got a ginger beard!' I got my mirror out of my bag.

He squinted at his reflection and shrugged. 'Whatever.' He walked over to the west-facing wall. 'How's your mum getting on?' he asked, looking out at the city.

'Good. Well, up and down, but good. She seems to be realizing how bad she's been. It's amazing, seeing her revisit the last twenty years with different eyes.'

It was true. Last weekend Mum had come round to cook a roast while I was rewriting the voiceover for my documentary. After chiding me for trying to eat Yorkshire pudding while watching footage and tapping frantically at my laptop she had suddenly put down her knife and fork and told me how sorry she was for absconding from her role as my mother. 'I lost my grip on reality,' she'd said.

'I did always know that, Mum.'

'But to think of how lost and lonely you must have felt . . . Michael leaving you, and the business with that other girl . . . Oh, Fran, it must have been terrible. I want to make up for it. I want to be your mother again.'

Of course we'd both cried.

'I'm so glad,' Dave said. There was real pleasure in his eyes. I loved Dave.

Then an almost imperceptible change flashed across his face. 'How are you feeling about Michael?' he asked tentatively. We'd spoken about it, of course, but only in the few snatched moments that we'd slumped in the back of taxis loaded with camera kit, or in the fluorescent glare of the news floor at three a.m. And the truth was, now that Dave had asked, I didn't actually know.

'I feel . . . I dunno. Numb. No, sad. Disappointed. But after I'd had it out with Alex and discovered how much shit Michael had stirred, I suppose it just got rid of any doubts.'

Dave was watching me closely. 'And has he contacted you?'

'Nope. Nothing. *Nada*. He's probably found someone else to massage his ego,' I said sadly. 'I really thought I was going to marry him. When he got that ring out, I thought that was it. Us. For ever. And now, seven weeks later, I'm thirty and single and I don't even know what country he's in.' I lined up my bottle on the wall next to Dave's so the shadows spilled on to the concrete under our feet. 'But ... I'm liking myself more now he's gone.'

Dave nodded. 'Fannybaws. I'm only going to say this once, cos God knows, I've thought about it enough. But here's the truth. Watching you spending all your time trying to impress Michael – trying to be *good enough* for him – it broke my heart. Leonie told me you even agreed to leave your fuckin' *job* for him in Paris. She said you told him you'd spend less time with your mum, with us – fuckin' hell, Fran, you even told him you'd ditch Gin Thursdays!'

I bit my lip. 'Yeah. Sorry. Really shabby behaviour.'

He took my hand for a second and squeezed it. 'No, I'm not making a row with you.' I looked away, embarrassed. In the quiet moments as my taxi had slid through early-morning London I'd spent a lot of time trying to work out why I had been so willing, over the last few months, to change everything about myself. How I looked, what I did, who I hung out with, how much time I spent with my own *mother,* for crying out loud. I'd been happy to throw away every detail of myself to become someone that Michael would want to be with.

Michael, who had left me on my thirtieth birthday because I wasn't giving him enough.

Dave ran a hand through his hair. He looked lovely today. 'Fran, I'm just saying, or I'm trying to say . . . whoever you end up with, Fannybaws, you shouldn't be changing a thing for them. Nothing. Don't be with anyone if you can't be you. Because you're bang on just as you are. OK?' He started fiddling very studiously with a loose thread on the hem of his T-shirt.

'Erm, thanks. Appreciate it. You sentimental old gay.' I gave his hand a quick squeeze to let him know how much it meant to me. Because it did.

'Right, well, better get back for the viewing,' he said, suddenly brisk.

I groaned inwardly. I was so tired of Dave's yo-yo behaviour. One minute he was a lovely great big huggy bear, the next he was as abrupt as a full stop. It had been like this since before I went to Paris. 'It's only been ten minutes!' I protested. 'Stella won't be there for at least another fifteen!'

Dave was off, though, his shoulder blades moving powerfully through the old faded stripes of his T-shirt. He had a nice big bear-like back, I thought, as it retreated from me. The kind of back that was good for throwing one's arms around. Was this the back that was making Stefania so damn happy? I hoped not.

'Oi, Dave!' I yelled.

He stopped and turned. 'Oi, Fran,' he shouted back.

'Dave, are you seeing Stefania?' He looked round, as if I was asking someone else. 'Yes, you. Are you seeing

Stefania?' I walked towards him, draining the dregs of my now-warm fake lager. Dave smiled privately.

'Bloody hell, you are, aren't you?' A brief clutch of something unidentifiable, but not particularly lovely, grabbed my stomach.

He raised an eyebrow and shoved his hands into his jeans pockets. 'How would you feel if I was, Fannybaws?' he asked.

I noticed that his twinkly eyes were a lot more visible now that he'd shorn off a load of mad hair.

I didn't say anything.

His phone started ringing and he answered it, smiling. 'Hey, hey!' He disappeared through the exit.

'Fine,' I said, after he'd left. 'Yeah, I'd feel great about it. There would not be a problem at all. Not even a tiny one. I'd be really happy for you both.'

When I got back to the edit, Danny was sipping his warm champagne on his own. Stella had not arrived and Dave was nowhere to be seen. 'Oh, that guy, the one who works on the live show, was looking for you, Fran.'

'Which one?'

'The skinny fucker. Posh bloke. Glasses. Bit of a twat.'

'Alex. Actually, he's all right. What did he want?'

'Dunno. He had a butcher's at this film, though – looked well impressed. Went off to meet his bird.'

I wandered out to Reception on the off-chance and struck gold. 'Franny!' Leonie screamed. She was jumping up and down, holding Alex's hand, a manic grin stretched across her face.

'I've missed you so much!' I gasped, as we hugged. 'Bloody work! We have some SERIOUS catching up to do. What's going on?'

Leonie could barely speak she was so excited. 'PENGUIN!' she yelled. Alex was laughing. Bless Alex. He was so happy, these days. He waited for her to explain. I was baffled, and a stream of nonsense came out again. 'PENGUIN!' was the only word that made any sense.

'You've bought one?' I ventured. 'Adopted one?'

'THEY'RE PUBLISHING MY FUCKING BOOK!' she yelled, grabbing my hair in two clumps and jumping up and down.

'Ow!' I had to jump up and down with her so that my hair wouldn't be ripped out. And then I grasped what she was saying. 'Oh, my God!' She nodded madly – still jumping – and emitted a series of hoots.

The security guard was watching us with a raised eyebrow, and Alex clapped his hands like a young girl. I grabbed Leonie and hugged her. We jumped up and down some more until a bony assault from our left announced that Alex had joined us and we were now a three-way bouncy ball. Squeaks and roars and whoops abounded.

'THIS IS THE BEST NEWS EVER!' I shouted, extricating myself eventually.

'Isn't it?' Alex cried. His glasses had slid round to offer enhanced vision to his left ear and in his excitement he seemed not to have noticed. Leonie moved them back on to his nose, which she kissed briefly.

'Oh, you guys,' I said, suddenly emotional. 'This is totally awesome. I'm so happy. When are we celebrating?'

'Er, right now?' Leonie said. 'How long till you finish? Surely if Alex's mad hours are over you're in the clear too.'

'Nearly. I'm just waiting for sign-off from Stella. But you two go. I'll join you in a bit!' I hugged Leonie again. 'I'm so fucking proud of you, my clever sexpert friend!' I stood back and surveyed her, all five foot nine of my wonderful, beautiful, talented childhood chum, clad in a beautiful full-skirted dress from the 1950s: she had finally got the career and aristocratic boyfriend I'd always imagined her to have. I felt like a proud mother at the nativity play. I loved her with every part of my body.

'I have to go to the loo before we leave,' Alex cried, and skipped off.

We smiled indulgently. 'He really loves you, doesn't he?' I chuckled.

'He doesn't fail to amaze me, Fran. I always thought he was such a penis and he's just . . . he's just wonderful! He's so humble. And so open. He always wants to know about me and my day – I have to practically wrestle him to make him talk about his.'

'It was kind of the opposite with Michael and me,' I said.

Leonie looked sharply at me. 'Well done, Fran.'

I glanced back at her, confused.

'Well done for saying that sort of thing out loud. It's true, of course, but it's important you acknowledge it. I'm proud of you.'

'Well, there's no pretending otherwise, is there?' She shook her head. 'Did you always think that about him?' I asked.

'No, actually, I didn't. I knew from the start that you saw him as some sort of god but I didn't realize that was because he *made* you feel like that. I thought you were just a bit mad and carried away.'

'Well, I was that, too.'

'Perhaps. But it was him, Franny. He was toxic. God, the stuff Alex has told me . . . Michael needs to sort himself out and stop using other people to do the job for him. Poor Alex took a right beating over the years. No wonder he comes across as such a wazzock the first time you meet him!'

I giggled. 'He's definitely one of the good guys, Leonie. I'm so pleased for you! I've really loved working with him these last few months. Who'd have thought it, eh?' I paused, looking out of the huge glass swing doors at the busy pavement outside. 'How funny that it should have worked out like this. You and Alex all loved up, me and Michael totally incommunicado. Not what I saw when I imagined the future.'

Leonie nodded sympathetically.

'I'm seeing more and more how much Michael fucked with my head. He was really . . . really subversive, y'know? I dunno how he did it – he just somehow got under my skin and made me feel like he was the best thing that could possibly have happened to me.'

'Well, he's history. You're free to meet the man of your dreams now, Franny.'

'Yeah.' I thought for a few moments and started giggling. 'And you know what, Leonie? Here's a little something for your book. Michael used to yell, "FIN-GER IN BOTTOM!" just before he came.'

As Alex bounded over, puppy-like, from the Gents, Leonie and I clutched our stomachs and howled like werewolves.

Chapter Forty-two

'Let's get this fucking thing started,' Hugh barked.

I shot a look of pure fear in Stella's direction but she smiled. 'He'll love it,' she whispered, as Hugh settled himself on the viewing sofa. Dave nodded his agreement and gave me a cheesy thumbs-up. He sprawled next to Hugh.

Finally, it was time for Hugh to watch the film. It was signed off and awaiting transmission, but the only thing that really mattered to me was whether or not he liked it. I was quaking in my boots and had spent some time in the toilet this morning quite without the need for a prawn vindaloo the night before.

The music started – I'd chosen a delicately humorous Handel Piano Concerto for the opening sequence – and I steeled myself for condemnation and scorn.

Michael Denby, Nellie's rich and, it turned out, highly influential fiancé, had come to us with a simple idea for something that no one else could possibly have gained access to. Michael was the PR for an old, distinguished and largely unheard-of company who supplied key staff to Downing Street and other Whitehall buildings. To become a member of their team it appeared you had to belong to a different era in which people spoke with efficient 1940s accents and had strong command of skills such as silver-polishing and chutney-bottling.

One of their longest-serving clients, a lovely, soft-spoken woman called Esther Bonningham, was the chief housekeeper at 10 Downing Street. She had been due to retire and leave at the same time as Gordon Brown, if he lost the general election. And, of course, he had. Michael had, somehow, gained access for a tiny crew of director and cameraman to follow Esther in her last few weeks at Number Ten. The idea was two-pronged: on the one hand it was a glimpse behind the scenes during the biggest election in decades, and on the other it was a simple character portrait of an unassuming woman who ran the most important house in Britain.

I'd been with Esther during the chaos of the week leading up to the election, then right through the purgatorial weekend when the country had stood still, waiting for a government to be formed. I'd been with her in the still of the morning when she'd stood at the window with her clipboard, thinking back over her forty-five years of service in the house, and then later on when it was all systems go and she was presiding over the boiling of *perfect* eggs for the Browns down in the Great Kitchen. The beauty of it was that the Browns had passed through the back of shot a few times but they had merely been off-stage characters. This was Esther's story.

How I'd managed to get through it without making some massive blunder – without breaking anything or swearing or getting arrested – was a source of great wonder to both Dave and myself.

Hugh stared at the screen, silent, as the final scene played. While Gordon and Sarah Brown had left 10 Downing Street holding their children's hands on 11 May, a far more moving scene was taking place at the staff entrance. Esther was handing her uniform, carefully folded, to a security guard and removing the ID lanyard from her neck for the last time. She took one final glance around the silent, abandoned hallway, then smoothed her skirt, picked up her bag and left.

As the cameras flashed at the front of the house, a small, erect figure slipped quietly away at the back.

Dave had shot it beautifully. It looked like a feature film. Every tiny twitch of her lip as she left the house she'd run for forty-five years, every nervous flick of her fingers through her hair, he'd got it. I gazed at him as he sat on the sofa next to Hugh, engrossed. He was sporting an old white T-shirt and the same jeans he'd seemed to be wearing every single day since I'd met him. Watching the film so absorbedly he looked young, almost boyish. I smiled, thinking that he was probably the most quietly talented man I'd ever known.

The film finished and no one said anything. Stella sipped her coffee and I yawned nervously, crossing my arms over my jumpy stomach. *Please go easy on me*, I thought.

Hugh scribbled a few things on his notepad, then signalled to me that I was to pass him the phone. What the fuck? I stared, anguished, at him. Even Dave seemed a bit frightened.

'Kate. Hi. Hugh from ITN here. Kate, I'm suggesting you make space for an independent ten-minute film straight after the six thirty bulletin one night next week . . . I know, I know. Your schedule's fucked as it is. But, trust me, I have something extremely fucking special for you.'

I began to smile.

'No, Kate, I can't fucking put it into the main news. It'll get lost there. This thing needs time of its own. We got access to Gordon Brown's housekeeper and filmed her last two weeks. We were there right through the election. This is must-see viewing. In fact, it's a fucking masterpiece.'

I hugged myself, and caught Dave's eye. He was beaming at me.

'Well, speak to whichever fucking commissioner you need to. Tell them I'll come and show it to them today. Trust me, they'll want it. Wasted on the news.'

I couldn't believe what I was hearing.

'Good, thanks, Kate. And I suggest it's on a big news day. Cameron's first shit as prime minister or something. You'll want a lot of people with their TVs switched on when this thing goes out. OK. 'Bye.'

He handed me back the phone, still refusing to make eye contact, then stood up. 'Good job, Brennan,' he said. Dave nodded briefly. 'And can someone tell Danny I'm very pleased with his editing too?'

He was nearly out of the door when he turned to me, gave me a proper smile and said, 'You, young lady, have just made a fucking outstanding little documentary. I am extremely fucking impressed, Fran. Dave was right. You deserved that gig. You two are an excellent team. It's only a shame that you won't be able to work together again.'

And with that he was gone.

I turned round to find Dave standing behind me, getting some Rizlas out and smiling at me. 'The man's right. It was a masterpiece. And you deserved it,' he said. 'Fancy a tomato juice?' He sounded strangely detached, given the circumstances.

I grinned. 'No, I fancy a fucking magnum of champagne! Am I allowed to drink yet?'

He shrugged. 'It's up to you. I'll drink tomato juice if you want to stay dry.'

I giggled. 'You're plain weird, David Brennan. Since when was there a dry Glaswegian?'

He tucked the new cigarette behind his ear and put the tobacco back in his pocket. 'Aye. We're few and far between. But, actually, it's not so bad, is it? This not drinking thing?'

I thought about it. I was being pummelled by waves of happiness still. 'Actually, no. I don't mind it. You're right, let's go for a tomato juice. Oh, my God! He loved it!' And leaving Dave with no choice in the matter I threw myself at him and smiled as his arms closed round my back. 'He's right. We're a fucking great team!' I shouted into his chest. He hugged me harder.

We sat at a rickety table outside the Apple Tree where sunlight drizzled through the acacia tree and on to Dave's forearms.

'It was because of you that I got this documentary, wasn't it?'

'Nope,' he said. And then: 'Cheers, Fannybaws!' He knocked his tomato juice against mine.

'Don't wriggle out of it. You convinced Hugh to give me the job. Dave, he all but told me so just now!'

Dave smiled. 'Well, you deserved the break. It had your name written all over it. And you didn't just meet expectations, you exceeded them. You may be a mental but you're a damn talented one, love.'

'God, Dave. I owe you so much. You are amazing. What would I do without you? I dunno what Hugh was on about when he said it's a shame we can't work together again! As far as I'm concerned, I ain't doing another one unless I can work with you. I have leverage now, you know, Brennan!'

I busied myself with the Worcester sauce and Tabasco; I'd asked for a Virgin Mary but instead had been given a tray of condiments and a crappy little tomato juice. Dave lit his fag and laughed. 'That's going to taste fucking dreadful, Fannybaws,' he said.

'Shut it,' I replied automatically. Then I looked up at him. He was watching me with what could only be described as intense sadness. I put down my celery stick. 'Dave?'

He took another drag. 'Hugh said it's a shame we won't be working together in the future because I'm leaving for Afghanistan in a few days.'

I felt the colour drain from my face. 'You're *what*?'

He was watching me keenly now. 'Aye. Afghanistan. I've missed those war zones. I only came back because Freya made me and, well, she's not part of the picture any more. I've been working through the transfer for the last few weeks.'

No.

This was all wrong. I didn't want Dave to go. He was my Dave. My Scottish sidekick who ate Fruit Corners and wore jumpers with gnomes on them and listened to soft rock. He was Dave who made me feel like I could do my job and that my clumsiness and ability to put my foot in it were fine. He was Dave who gave me big, warm hugs and said I was bang on just as I was.

'Are you serious?' I said. My voice had come out a bit wobbly so I sat up straight and tried to look commanding.

He nodded.

'But, Dave, you might get killed. Or injured. Or taken hostage. Anything could happen, you –' I broke off. I had no idea what to say.

'I know, Fannybaws. It's a risk, of course, but I've done it before. I know the drill and I'm well trained. They do their best to keep us safe.'

I looked at the place on his left hand where his little finger should have been. How did he know that the next accident wouldn't be more serious? 'But what about Stefania? I *know* you've been seeing her, Dave. You can't just go off and leave her!'

He laughed a little and fiddled with his tomato juice. He hadn't drunk any. 'Frances O'Callaghan. You're remarkably good at deciding who everyone's sleeping with but you're always bloody well wrong. Of course I'm not seeing Stefania! Jesus! I'm way too scared to mess with the likes of her!'

I stared at him.

He continued to chuckle. 'Can you imagine if you were late for a date? Christ, that wee girl'd bake you into one of her fuckin' stews! She'd string you from the ceiling! No, I adore Stefania but I haven't been seeing her. Another classic case of Fran the crap detective.'

I realized I was about to cry.

'Hey, what's with the long face?'

I fought hard with tears and for a few seconds they remained in my eyes.

'Fannybaws, no . . .' A big fat one rolled down my cheek and plopped into my tomato juice.

Dave reached forward and gently removed the next one from underneath my other eye with his finger. 'Don't cry, Franny, I didn't mean it. I'm sure you'll make a cracking detective one of these days.'

I shook my head, trying to regain control.

'Oh, come on, I'll be OK! I'm tough shit. You should see the bullet-proof vest they gave me last time – it was the size of *you*.'

Two more tears popped out. A big, sad, Dave-shaped gulf was expanding across my chest. I'd be completely lost without my big, funny, talented friend. 'I don't want you to go,' I whispered.

He passed me a napkin from my tray of condiments. 'Sorry, Fannybaws. But I'm a war-zone cameraman at heart. I need to get back to it.'

'When are you going?'

'Thursday.'

'For how long?'

He shrugged. 'Indefinitely.'

*

I know. Devastation : (said a text from Leonie. I pushed open the gate to my yard and put my phone back in my pocket. For some reason I'd kind of been hoping that Leonie would tell me it was all just a massive porkie and that Dave was really only going on a week-long caravanning holiday in Bognor Regis.

Duke Ellington sat lazily in the sun as I closed the gate behind me. When he saw me he rolled over on his back in the dust, inviting me to come over and scratch his tummy so he could destroy my hand. Instead I sat next to him. 'Dave's leaving,' I told him glumly.

He waved a paw in the air, still on his back. 'Look at my nice, soft, inviting furry tummy,' his eyes said. 'Wouldn't you just love to stroke it?'

'I've just lost my Dave. I'm not losing my hand. Leave me alone.' Duke Ellington rolled back over and sat up. After a few seconds' consideration, he offered me a short sharp miaow. 'I know. It's shit, isn't it? I'm going to really miss him. I mean, I'm glad he's off to do what he loves doing but, Duke Ellington, I feel so sad.'

Duke Ellington watched a large fat bumblebee, which was flying dangerously close to his face.

'Don't. Stay away from it, you mentalist.' And then I started crying again, thinking that that was just the sort of thing Dave would say to me. Duke Ellington miaowed crossly by way of comfort.

I took a very deep breath and tried to pull myself

together. It was a beautiful day, not the sort of day that should be wasted in crying. It was the sort of day when one should be wearing a floaty summer dress and frolicking in the sun with a crowd of vital-looking people drinking sparkling grape juice and eating Brie. I stood up and gazed down at my cat. 'I don't know what to do with myself,' I told him.

Just at that moment, I heard a gust of sharp, Slavic laughter and the rattle of keys. Stefania. And then, rather shockingly, the unmistakable rumble of a man's laugh. I stared at Duke Ellington. 'Fuck!' I whispered at him, and we both shot up the tree. It was probably the world's easiest tree to climb but I still only made it up by the time they walked through the gate. I peered through the canopy of leaves, trying to find out who the man was.

'Vhat are you doing in ze tree, Frances?' Stefania said curiously.

'Oh, hi! I was just up here chatting to Duke Ellington,' I explained, clambering down.

Stefania was laughing again as I dropped on to the ground.

And there he was. A man. The Man, whoever he was. He looked really rather nice, like a nutty professor but of the younger generation – the kind of intellectual genius who knows about astral physics and is able to tweet humorously about it on Twitter. He had cropped sandy hair and nice cheekbones.

'Oh, hello! I'm Fran!' I said, offering him my hand.

He pumped it enthusiastically. 'Hi. Roland. I've heard a lot about you.'

I shot a look at Stefania. How could she have hidden him from us for so long? She just grinned back impishly and put a sly hand into Roland's. 'Roland is the apple of my online search,' she said shiftily.

Roland and I both started giggling and spoke at the same time. 'No, you,' I said to him. 'I'm more than happy to resign as unscrambler of Stefania's idioms!'

'Fruit of my search or apple of my eye,' he said kindly to her. He pinched her nose quickly and gave her a grin. 'But apple of my search works just as well.' She smiled up at him, her sharp little face quite transformed.

Bloody hell! Not Stefania too! At this rate Duke Ellington was going to fall in love! 'So?' I said to them both.

Stefania giggled again: quite an unusual sound. 'Vell,' she said, 'I vas vaiting for the right moment, Frances. The love of Stefania and Roland is sanks to you and your technologies! Ve have been brought together by your lapside computer!'

Duke Ellington wove round her legs and I waited for further clarification of what on earth she was on about. She offered none but just bent down and started talking to Duke Ellington in some language I didn't understand.

'I'll put on some nettle tea, right?' Roland said.

Stefania nodded vigorously. 'Make it viz love,' she said.

Roland went into the shed, saying, 'Tea for three coming right up!' He was quite the most enthusiastic, smiley man I'd met in a long time.

'Great!' I said, even though the thought of nettle tea made me want to run. 'Right, over here, *now*!' I said to her, pointing to my steps. 'What the hell is going on? What have my "technologies" got to do with this man? How long's it been going on? And why the hell am I only finding out about him now?'

Stefania smiled evilly. 'I thought, if I told you, you would arrive in my shed to take notes on him,' she said. 'It is a liability having you as a neighbour, after all!'

'STEFANIA! That's a horrible thing to say! I'd NEVER spy on you! I've known there was something going on for weeks and I haven't said a word to anyone!'

'No no no, I am not being serious.' Suddenly her eyes were veiled. 'Frances, I have a confession. I used your computer. I liked vhat I saw on ze Internet dating website and I made a profile for myself. I met Roland on my first date. I did not vant to tell you because then I vould have to admit to using your computer vizout ze permission.'

She hung her head guiltily and I roared with laughter. 'Stefania, you have been coming in and out of my flat as you please since I moved in. Why on earth would I mind? I'm bloody *delighted* you've met someone! It's wonderful!'

She patted my arm. 'Sank you.'

457

'Oh, my God! So that was why the bloody website was always at the top of my browsing history. You minx!'

She looked confused. 'Mink?'

'No, minx. It means … Oh, it doesn't matter. Stefania, I'm truly happy for you. I'd begun to think you just weren't interested in men! You've been alone in that shed for years, taking pots of food to the homeless and to other charitable causes such as me … I'm delighted!'

She fiddled with her orange leggings. Mixed with a traditional French gingham cotton blouse they represented a real pinnacle in her sartorial efforts.

'So what changed? Why did you start looking for someone now?'

'Vell, I am a princess, as you know. And princesses must marry eventually. I needed to find a partner.'

'Stefania, please tell me what really happened. Come on, I've met Roland now. No need to be shy!'

She returned to her leggings. 'Ze love of Stefania and Roland is a result of years of searching in ze soul. But ze searching had to stop. I am a princess. And your interdating website was vhat I needed to start my hunt.'

'Can you please stop being a weirdo and tell me what actually happened before Roland comes back with the tea?' I said gently.

'I am telling you zis twice now. I am a princess. I had to get married.'

Stefania had been telling me she was a Balkan princess/Russian noble/close relative of the Polish royalty for a long time now. I shook my head irritably, demanding some straight talk.

'No, Frances, I do not sink you understand. I *am* a princess. My name is Princess Stefania Mirova Karađorđević. I am a direct descendant of the House of Karađorđević. We were kicked out in 1945 when ze Communists took Yugoslavia. My family is still recognized by many as a royal family. Zey have zis barmy belief zat zey can be restored viz ze srone, one day.'

There was a pause. I snorted. 'Um, Stefania. I'm sorry, *what?*'

'It is true, Frances,' she said wearily. 'Zis is vhy I do not talk about myself. People laugh as if I am telling ze lies.'

'You're serious, aren't you?'

'Perfectly,' she snapped.

'Shit! You're a real princess?'

She smiled shyly. 'Yes.'

'Then what the flaming JESUS are you doing living in my shed?'

Roland came over with a knobbly wooden tray bearing three clay mugs. He was smiling in the vague way that nutty professors always smile. A sort of distracted one-part-of-my-brain-is-dealing-with-you-and-the-other-part-is-fixing-the-hadron-collider smile. 'Er, Stefania has just outed herself as a princess,' I said uncertainly. If a joke was being made at my expense he'd blow her cover.

Instead, Roland grinned in a more focused way and pushed his glasses to the top of his head. 'Oh, goody,' he said enthusiastically. He had just the edges of a Yorkshire accent. 'I do love this story, although it's so sad!' He took her hand and sat down next to her.

I sipped nettle tea and listened in amazement.

Stefania had been engaged, aged nineteen, to some bloke she'd been to school with and had been going out with since she was barely legal. By the sound of things it had been a pretty intense affair, and even though her family wasn't delighted by her choice, the wedding plans were in full swing on 17 July 1999 when he was killed in a motorbike accident on the outskirts of Belgrade. Stefania had been utterly heartbroken. She had dropped out of university a couple of years later and wandered off into Eastern Europe. She'd hitched her way across Europe over the course of three years and stayed with travelling communities until eventually she'd arrived in London in 2005, only a few months before I moved in. 'You were ze first person who talked to me,' she said. 'You let me live here. I am for ever grateful to you.'

Feeling as if I was watching some sort of historical thriller I just goggled. 'Carry on!'

'Vell, zat is it, really. I left my life behind in Serbia because I could not bend it –'

'Bear it,' Roland and I said simultaneously. Then we both said, 'Sorry.'

Stefania waved us away. 'Does not matter. I could not bear it. So I have spent ze time here listening to ze mad drama of your life, Frances, and hanging around with your cat, and trying to help some people even more sad zan me. But vhen you had ze heartbreak I realized zat I could not carry on being me in my shed. I needed to start my life again. And so I stole your lapside computer every day vhen you vere at vork and found Roland! Ze love of Stefania and Roland has awoken me! I am alive once more!'

Roland sipped his horrid nettle tea enthusiastically. 'My little roaming gypsy!' he said, with gusto.

I liked Roland immensely. 'So does this mean you're rich?' I asked incredulously.

'Vell, since I have been living here I have not been in contact with my family so I had only ze remains of ze money I brought viz me. But vhen ze love of Stefania and Roland began I wrote to zem and all is well. Zey sent me money. I do not know if I am rich, but I sink zere is enough to do somesing good.'

'WHAT?' I breathed, enthralled.

'Vell, I am sinking of moving to India and starting a retreat,' she said casually, as if this were a pretty common-or-garden thing to be doing. 'You know, meditation, cleanses, body purification – vhat is the name of zat process vhere you have ze tube in your bottom?'

I burst out laughing. 'Colonic irrigation?'

She nodded. 'Yes, zat one. I believe it is a powerful tool for cleaning out ze –'

'OK, OK, enough. Stefania, that is the best story I've ever heard . . . but how utterly tragic the circumstances,' I added. 'I can't believe you've looked after me so much when you've been grieving. I feel awful!'

She smiled fiercely. 'NO! Do not feel bad! It is only by caring for ze community zat ve are able to escape our own heads!'

I chuckled. 'Yes, that sounds apt. Care in the community. I like it.'

A tendril of her hair had escaped from her customary mad topknot and I smiled as Roland tucked it back in with a face of reverence: it was as if he was restoring a missing jewel to a priceless crown. And then, for the second time that day, I found myself feeling unbearably sad. 'Everyone's leaving me, Stefania. You can't go too!'

'Who else?'

'Dave. He's leaving for bloody Afghanistan on Thursday. Indefinitely.'

Stefania went white. 'No. Zis cannot be! Dave cannot go!'

I nodded sadly. ''Fraid so. He's off. It's all sorted. I tried to make him stay but he wasn't having any of it.'

Stefania looked as if she was going to have a heart attack. 'We'll just have to hope he meets some hot journalist out there who drags him back to the UK with her.'

Stefania's eyes narrowed. 'I hope for nozzing of ze sort,' she said.

Chapter Forty-three

DRAFTS
....

To	Subject	Saved	Time
David.Brennan@ITNNews.com	Don't go!	19/05/2010	01:39:40

It was Gin Thursday. Probably the most special Gin Thursday in the history of Gin Thursdays. I realized that there wasn't a person there I didn't care about. Even Hugh. He was swearing away at the bar with gay abandon, the epitome of news editor with beige cords and glasses hanging round his neck. It was a late-May scorcher and everyone was wearing summer clothes: London was awash with a sea of white arms and legs. I surveyed the blotched fake tan on my right ankle and shrugged.

Stefania and Roland were talking, rather improbably, with Stella Sanderson who, to my surprise, was roaring with laughter and clutching Stefania's arm, and even the Fit Blokes from the C4 news had somehow got invited and were standing in a group looking Fit while Chatting Manfully. Nellie was honking with posh laughter with Mona Carrington underneath the large TV screen, and Michael Denby, even posher and richer than I'd remembered, stood next to her, like an advert for Thomas Pink in crisp chinos and a light pink shirt with not so much as one wrinkle on it. His gold cufflinks kept being picked up by the rather inexplicable disco ball, which was revolving above us, in spite of the fact that it was seven fifteen on a Thursday evening in a disco-less London pub.

Mum was sitting at a table near the door with an orange juice and a wide smile. She was talking animatedly with Leonie and Alex, Leonie relaxed and confident as ever and Alex all but hopping up and down in his desperation to please the mother-of-his-girlfriend's-best-friend. A tiny little bead of perspiration kept forming between his brows, which Leonie would mop off every now and then with her long vintage Hermès scarf.

I felt very fond of Alex, these days. What a turnaround to feel so indifferent to Michael and so maternal and affectionate towards Alex! And, I thought, as my eyes travelled across the table, what an incredible turnaround to see my mother – my *mother* – sitting in a pub looking relaxed, happy and, well, normal. No power shoulders. No bouffant. No pearlescent lipstick or pearls or smudged wine glass. Just Mum in a flowery dress I hadn't seen since I was about ten. Her arms were freckled and slender. The change in her was incredible. She'd transformed from Drink Voice Woman to the Mum I remembered from my childhood. I loved her. My mum. I watched as her face lit up at the sight of someone arriving, someone I couldn't quite see – largely because he was obscured by Mum's enthusiastic hug. She kissed him on the cheek.

Blimey! Mum wasn't *dating*, was she? Then, to my astonishment, Leonie got up and hugged him too. What the . . . ?

Slightly incredulous, I picked up my drink and began to pick my way through the crowd to investigate. Leonie said something to him and they both turned to me.

'DAD! OH, MY GOD!' I took out Eddie from Entertainment as I pummelled my way to their table. I threw my arms around him. It had been more than a year since I'd seen Dad. His Costa del Sol pot-belly had become a bit of a beery paunch and his skin was a bit Torremolinos for my liking but those were minor details – it was my DAD!

'Hey, little Franny!' He kissed and hugged me. 'Couldn't miss this! Eve called me on Tuesday, I'm bloody proud of you, my girl!'

It was too much. 'RARRR!' I yelled like a Hampstead Heath dad, completely beside myself. Everyone laughed. 'This is the BEST!' *Well, nearly the best*, I thought, as I checked the door again quickly.

My heart sank a tiny bit. No Dave.

I knew he wasn't coming. It was completely impossible. But if he'd walked in it would have officially become the best night in my life, so much the best, in fact, that I would have submitted an announcement to that effect to *The Times*. I realized Leonie was watching me and turned my attention back to the group. 'Let me go and get some drinks,' I said. 'Dad?'

'Tia Maria, please, darling.'

I giggled. 'Dad, what's happening to you?'

He winked. 'Gloria got me on the Tia Maria,' he said easily. Nothing embarrassed him. 'The drink of kings!'

I rolled my eyes. 'Whatever. Mum?'

'Just a soda water, thanks, Franny.'

Dad looked at her and winked. I felt a warm swell in my stomach. Dad and Mum were over and had been for a very long time, but to see them talking as friends again – well, it felt good. Something I'd been hoping for since I was an angry teenager with a rolled-up school skirt and a biro-crunching habit. I took every one else's orders and picked my way to the bar, with Leonie bringing up the rear. 'I'll get these,' she said.

'No! Everyone's come to watch my film. It's the least I can do to thank them.'

'Shut it,' she replied briefly, and assumed position at the bar.

I let her. For Leonie to be able to buy a round after all these years of poverty must have been quite something. And, of course, within seconds a slavering young man stood waiting eagerly for her order. Catching me looking wistfully at the door, Leonie touched my arm. 'I know. It's shit. Is there no chance of him coming?'

'No. His flight's at ten thirty. He'll be checking in any minute now.'

'You're going to miss him, aren't you?' she said.

I nodded glumly. 'Yeah. A shit load. How many men do you meet who you can discuss things like nose-picking with? ITN's going to be rubbish without him. Gin Thursday's going to be rubbish without him. In fact, life is going to be rubbish without him.'

Frustration glimmered on Leonie's face but disappeared as soon as it had arrived.

'Anyway, sorry, I'm sure I'll get over it. We need to have some serious fun tonight, Leonie. This is your night too! Long live *Baking and Blowjobs*!' She handed me a glass of champagne, then snatched it away. 'Oh, bollocks, sorry, Fran. What do you want instead?'

'Well, if I can't drink champagne tonight, when can I?' She looked suspicious and I smiled. 'Seriously, I haven't missed it. I was just going through a mentalist phase. I feel as indifferent towards a glass of champagne as I do your chapter seven on bum sex.'

She smiled and handed me the champagne. 'Cheers,' she said, and chinked hers against mine. 'I'm so proud of you.'

I reached round and pinched her bottom. 'And I'm so proud of you. This is a good night!' I took a sip. It tasted nice. Nothing more.

'Stay here,' she said. 'I'm just going to give these to your parents and Alex. I'll be back. I need to talk to you, Frances O'Callaghan.'

I nodded obediently and leaned against the bar, surveying the scene. How very lucky I was! My Tourette's
boss, all of my friends, all of my family, all of my colleagues: all here to watch my humble little documentary!
All of my friends, that was, except Dave. There was no
denying it. I wanted desperately for Dave to be there. I
wanted the warmth of his crinkly eyes smiling as I said
the wrong thing to someone or fell over a bar stool. I
wanted the safety of his rangy frame standing near me.
I'd even have tolerated him smoking.

Dave not being here was all wrong.

'You OK?' Leonie said, as she arrived back.

I nodded. 'Yep. So, what's up?'

'Oh, not much. I just wondered if you were thinking of starting Internet dating again.'

'Oh, Leonie, fuck OFF! I went on eight dates!
They were terrible! I am *never* doing that shit again!'

She looked sulky.

'Stop it! No way! I'd rather have sexual relations
with a stuffed animal.'

She sipped her champagne and thought about it.
'As it happens, Fran, you only went on seven dates in
the end.'

'Well, yes, but I cancelled the seventh because I
thought I was about to get back into a long-term relationship with the eighth. It would hardly have been
fair.'

She stuck her lip out a bit. 'I think it's a shame.
That Freddy guy seemed like he was really wicked.'

'How do you even remember his *name*?'

'Because he seemed really wicked. And, correct me if I'm wrong, Stefania alleges you told her that it was like this guy could see into your soul. How often do you get that kind of feeling for some guy you've never even *met*?'

'I was just carried away. I'm sure he was a nice guy. But the matter is closed.'

Then Leonie did something extraordinary. She took my glass out of my hand and thumped me. Properly. On the side of my head. 'FUCKING HELL, FRAN!' she exploded.

I was stunned. 'Um, excuse me? What was that?'

Leonie was clutching her skirt as if she was about to erupt. 'YOU ARE THE MOST FRUSTRAT-ING FUCKING PERSON ON THE PLANET. WHY CAN'T YOU SEE IT? WHY CAN'T YOU SEE WHAT'S UNDER YOUR OWN BLOODY *NOSE*?'

I stared at her face and then at her champagne. 'Leonie, has someone Rohypnoled you or something?'

'ARRRGH! FRAN! Wake up! Wake up, you fuck-wit! Don't you have any curiosity about Freddy at *all*?'

Leonie looked like she was about to give birth to a pumpkin. That had spikes. And was on fire.

'Er, Leonie, do you need medical assistance? Why are you getting so angry about some bloke off the Internet?'

'Ladies and gentlemen! Quiet, please! We have one

minute until transmission!' Hugh roared across the pub. I glanced at him and then back at Leonie, who had turned into a charging bull. She let go of her skirt and handed me my champagne. 'As I said, right under your nose.'

She pushed through the crowd, back to her table, and I watched her, astonished.

'Ladies and gentlemen, could you –' Hugh was losing a battle against the pub noise. 'OH, JUST SHUT THE FUCK UP' he roared a few seconds later. The pub shut the fuck up.

Right under your nose. What was she on about?

'We can have speeches afterwards but for now, I present Fran's début documentary for ITN news!' A roar went up, and the sound of lots of thighs being thumped by people too lazy to put their drinks down and clap properly. I worked my way over to the table where Mum and Dad were sitting and checked the door one last time.

No Dave.

As the music started and Esther's face came into view, sliced across with cold morning light filtering through the kitchen blinds at No. 10 Downing Street, I felt a wave of deep, almost unbearable sadness. 'Thank you, Dave,' I whispered. 'Thank you for making this possible for me.'

And then my heart went into a mild form of cardiac arrest.

Oh, my God. *Right under my nose.* A spasm of panic

471

crashed through me and I bombed under the table, grabbing my bag from somewhere alarmingly close to Alex's crotch. Cursing, I scrabbled with the zip on my laptop sleeve and tore it out. *Please, God, let there be Wi-Fi here.* I looked up briefly for a Wi-Fi sign. There was one right next to me. I caught Leonie's eye. She was watching me, smiling slightly.

Fucking come on! I screamed silently, as my wireless roved leisurely through the available networks. It took no notice. Just as I began to wonder if I should call a pre-emptive ambulance for myself, lest I die of an aneurysm, it connected. I typed in the URL of my dating website and started praying that my login was still valid.

It was. *Eureka.* 'You have 34 new messages!' *FUCK OFF, ALL OF YOU*, I thought frenziedly, scouring down to the oldest message. There it was. Freddy: 14 March 2010. I opened it.

Dear Fran.

I had a feeling you'd cancel our date. I can't pretend I'm not gutted.

Fran, I think I'm I love with you. In fact I know I am. I have been for years. My girlfriend left me two years ago because she realized I was in love with you. I'm sorry I never told you that we'd split up. I just didn't know how to explain it.

I can't take another moment of being in London knowing that you don't feel the same way. I've tried to do it for five years now and it's not working. I'm putting the wheels in motion for a foreign transfer so I can try to sort my head out and get over you abroad.

I should have told you how I felt a long time ago, but I thought it would be hopeless. So I'm telling you now, knowing you'll probably never even read this. I love you, Frances O'Callaghan. I love everything about you. You're the most ludicrous excuse for a woman I've ever known – seriously, how could you not have spotted that I used a photo of James fucking Dean in my profile? – but there isn't a centimetre of you that I don't think is perfect.

I will miss you so much but I have to go. I have to get over you.

Take care of yourself. Please.

Love,
Freddy

Tears were beginning to pour down my face as I clicked on Freddy's name to open his profile, so by the time it loaded I could barely see. But I could see enough. I could see his new photo.

A mop of mad hair. A pair of blue crinkly, sparkly eyes. A careful, almost bashful smile.

Dave.

A thunderous round of applause and some frenzied whooping from Mum and Dad announced that the film had finished. I did my best to pull my hair over my face and raised my champagne glass over my head in acknowledgement. 'Whoop!' I yelled vaguely.

Oh, God. Dave was in love with me? My stomach was engaged in complex gymnastics. Dave being in love with me felt like the best news in the history of the whole universe.

'Dave is in love with me?' I said to Leonie, who had appeared at my side with Stefania. Hugh was fighting his way noisily to a spot underneath the TV screen.

'Vhat do you sink?' Stefania shouted.

'I don't . . . I don't believe it. Dave isn't in love with me – is he?'

Leonie's gasket blew again. 'HE FUCKING WELL STOPPED DRINKING FOR YOU!' she roared. 'HE'S A SCOTSMAN! HE DRANK FUCKING TOMATO JUICE FOR YOU!' I blanched. *Dave had drunk tomato juice for me.* Lovely manly Dave had spent weeks drinking Diet Coke and tomato juice and silly frilly virgin cocktails just for me. Further tears exploded from my eyes.

'What's going on?' I heard Dad asking Mum.

'Oh, I think Fran's realized her best friend's in love with her. We've all been wanting them to get together for years,' Mum said matter-of-factly.

'Oh, fuck,' I said.

Stefania nodded gravely. 'Oh, fuck,' she echoed.

'WELL! I think you'll all agree that this film was fucking eggzellent,' Hugh yelled.

Alex giggled. 'He's pissed,' he whispered to Leonie, and then must have seen me. 'Oh. She's worked it out then,' I heard him say. My hair was still curtained across my face.

'AND I WOULD LIKE TO THANK FRAN, DAVE AND DANNY FOR THEIR EXCELLENT WORK!' Further cheers. 'Whoop!' I shouted again.

'Am I in love with Dave?' I whispered to my friends. They nodded frenziedly.

'And I can't think of a bedder moment to announce that I am making Fran producer of special features across all news desks. As I'm sure you'll agree, she's got an excellent eye for this sort of thing and we don't want to lose her to some fucking dogumennary company. So, ladies and gentlemen, please be upstanding for our new special features producer FRAN!'

This time complete pandemonium broke out. Dad, fresh off a plane from Málaga and completely overwhelmed by the situation, forgot that I was now a fully grown adult and picked me up off my stool, whooping. Mum burst into tears and even Nellie let out a few husky huzzahs. I found myself being propelled to the front of the crowd and started frenziedly scrubbing my face with my sleeve.

And there I was, standing in front of everyone, mascara hieroglyphed across my cheeks and a little river of snot running calmly out of my left nostril. There was a sharp group intake of breath. 'Er, sorry,' I stammered. 'Bit emotional. Y'know. Carried away.' A gale of relieved laughter. *Phew! She hasn't lost it!* 'So, er, yes, it was a massive honour to be asked to do this, and an even greater one to hear about this new job – thanks, Hugh, I'll accept – but I need to thank a few people . . .'

A loud primal noise escaped from my lungs. I pretended it hadn't happened. Nellie and Michael were watching me with faces of absolute horror.

'Bleugh . . . First I need to thank Michael Denby for bringing Esther to us. She was an absolute gift. Anyone could have made a great documentary about her.'

Nellie whooped again and shouted, 'Michael Denby!' Michael gave a curt nod.

'And then, of course, there was the wonderful Danny who cut this thing in a matter of days.'

Further whooping. Danny flexed his biceps.

'But most of all, I owe the success of this film . . .' another loud noise, sort of like a baby bear cub trying to roar because its mother has left, escaped me '. . . to, er, Dave Brennan. Who is about to board a plane to Afghanistan.'

Silence.

'And who . . .' another mad sound 'who . . . oh, God, I have to go.'

'Are you going to Heathrow?' Hugh yelled, as I tore across the pub floor.

'YES!'

The loudest cheers of all. I left the pub at a flat-out sprint to roars, stamping feet, clanging glasses and cries of 'Go get him!' and 'At long fucking last!'

'TAXI!' Stefania screamed. The cab driver approaching us saw her maroon riding breeches and Roland Rat T-shirt and swerved, visibly afraid.

'Fuck,' I said. My head was full of Dave. I felt his hand ruffling my hair and heard him laughing kindly at me. 'Oh, no! I need to be there NOW. RIGHT NOW.'

Another taxi was approaching. Leonie kissed Alex briefly, said, 'Sorry,' and walked out into the middle of the road, lifting up her dress. She stood with her baps poking gaily out into the darkening evening until the taxi stopped. A milk float on the other side of the road kerbed it and stalled.

'Heathrow. Now.'

'Which terminal?' asked the driver, dazedly, as Stefania threw me into the back. After a moment's hesitation, she threw Leonie in too and climbed in herself. She slammed the door. 'ALEX! FIND OUT ZIS INFORMATION!' she barked. 'And you. Just drive! Ve vill tell you vhen ve know!'

'Roger that. I'm on it!' Alex shouted, whipping out his iPhone.

The taxi driver pulled away and, two seconds later, ground to a halt at traffic-lights.

'No no no,' Stefania said. 'Zis is not ze kind of driving ve are looking for. Zis is a matter of life and death. My friend vill show her breasts to any police-men who stop us. Just drive, fast, and break ze law as much as you need to.'

477

The taxi driver floored it.

Leonie put her arm round me and kissed me on the side of my head. 'Sorry to punch you, old thing,' she said conversationally, 'but you really are a numb-nuts.'

Stefania nodded sagely. 'Is true.' She offered me a striped hanky that smelt of Parma violets.

I blew my nose and Leonie rubbed off the remainder of my mascara. 'Crack a smile, Fran!' she said, and squeezed my boob.

'Not until I know we're going to get there on time. Why hasn't Alex called you with the terminal yet?'

'Because we left him only two minutes ago, Franny. Don't stress. He'll be phoning in flight numbers, check-in desks, grid references and vegetarian meal options within the next fifteen minutes. Of that you can be sure.'

I smiled in spite of myself. 'How did you know Dave was posing as Freddy? And why didn't you tell me?'

Leonie raised an eyebrow at Stefania and they both started laughing. 'Ze Eight Date Deal, you STU-PEEED CABBAGE, was designed to get you and ze Dave togezzer before Michael had a chance to drag you back into his life,' Stefania told me. 'But zen you interfered and ruined it!'

I looked at them incredulously. '*Seriously?* You organized the whole Freddy thing?'

'Yes. I have been vorking on this plan for a long

time, Frances. You remember ze night zat you were drunk and Dave brought you home and let you sleep it off on ze steps to stop you throwing up all over Michael?' I nodded, colouring slightly. 'Vell, I saw him before he saw me. He vas holding you like a child. Ze look on his face . . .' Stefania paused. Dear God, her lip was trembling! Her eyes were filling! Although, come to think of it, mine were too. The idea of Dave watching me sleep was causing an out-and-out riot in my stomach.

'Ze look on his face vas beautiful,' she said simply. 'He vas vatching you, all drunk and disgusting on his lap, as if you vere his first-born child. Michael had only just arrived in London and I knew zen zat you vere viz ze wrong man.'

I was bewildered. 'But you kept this from me – why?'

'Because you vould not have listened!' she hissed. 'You vere in love viz ze Michael!'

I nodded. 'Yep, fair enough. But he said something about Freya leaving him *two years ago*. That bit's surely got to be bollocks? He would have said!'

'No,' Leonie cut through. 'He didn't tell any of us until you and Michael split up. We had a Gin Thursday while you were holed up in your room and got quite drunk and Stefania just came out with all this stuff about how she thought he liked you' – Stefania nodded proudly – 'and after a few hours of interrogation he broke. He literally put his hands up and said, "Aye, fair enough, I'm in love with Fran, what of it?" I nearly *shat* myself, Franny!' I imagined my great big lovely Dave putting his hands up and admitting he loved me. It made my heart stop.

'But why? Why didn't he say anything about Freya?' I winced as we hurtled past a number 14 bus on the inside lane of Piccadilly.

Leonie shrugged. 'It was as he said in his email. He didn't know how to explain it without telling us the truth about why she left. Remember that Gin Thursday when she found out he'd recommended you for promotion? That was the death warrant. She'd been on to him and you for years.'

I stared at her. 'Freya left him because of me. Fuck.'

Leonie nodded. 'He'd do anything for you, Franny. Remember that tape that turned up in Hugh's office? The one from the shoot you faked to stalk Nellie?'

'I'm not likely to forget that in a hurry.'

'It was Dave who talked Hugh into keeping you on. He told Hugh and Alex that you were an outstanding producer and Hugh would be insane to let you go.' Leonie paused, looking quite emotional herself.

I sat back. 'Fuck.'

Hyde Park Corner screamed past us. This taxi driver was full-on Scalextric. He was mega. *Please, my lovely Dave, please still be there.*

'I – I guess I'm really surprised that Dave would have got involved with the Internet dating, though,' I said eventually. 'I mean, it's hardly his thing.'

They laughed. 'Oh, ze battles I had viz him!' Stefania crowed.

'Stefania basically didn't give him a choice in the end.' Leonie chuckled. 'And how could he say no anyway? He was madly in love with you, that great big bloody Glaswegian heart of his bleeding all over the place, and there was Stefania in his ear twenty-four seven telling him that this was a foolproof plan. Of course he caved in!'

Stefania shot me a look of malevolence. 'It *vas* foolproof until you started messing with it,' she muttered darkly. 'I could have cut your face off, Frances. If Leonie hadn't stopped me I vould have decked you out.'

I giggled. 'Sorry. But if I hadn't put the whole Michael thing to rest, we wouldn't be here now, would we?'

They looked at each other and then at me. 'No,' Leonie said doubtfully, 'I suppose not. But you'd better bloody well hope we catch him, Fran.'

I bit my lip, suddenly afraid again. We were only at Harrods, its lights twinkling gaily as if nothing was happening. 'Yep,' I said. 'Please God let me not have messed *this* up.' They smiled sympathetically at me.

'We're not imagining it, are we, Franny?' Leonie asked gently. 'You *do* love Dave, don't you?'

My stomach tightened again. I thought about Dave's eyes sparkling the first time we talked in the Apple Tree. I remembered his affectionate laughter and reassuring hand on my arm as I bungled a red-carpet interview in 2007. I remembered his solid warmth in Kosovo; the apple pie he'd brought round to my house when I'd had flu last year. I thought about the way the afternoon light had shone on the side of his face last week on the roof of ITN when he'd told me I was bang on just as I was and my heart ached.

I nodded. 'Yes. I do love Dave. I really love Dave.'

Leonie glanced anxiously at her watch. Stefania, for once, said nothing.

Then Alex's call came through and it was all hands on deck again.

Twenty minutes later we were heading down the M4 at 85 m.p.h. and Alex was phoning through departure status updates every other minute. The taxi driver was hunched over his wheel, Stefania was scribbling in her notebook and Leonie was studying floor plans of Heathrow that Alex had sent through on her iPhone.

It was a military operation. I counted streetlights as they whizzed by and knew that Leonie was right. It *had* been under my nose. For a very long time. I imagined touching his face and my stomach exploded. *Please, God, create some terrible delays at Heathrow. Make Dave get stuck in a toilet or something. Please, please, please, don't let him leave the country without me. I love him, God. I love Dave.*

Chapter Forty-four

FREDDY, YOU HAVE A NEW MESSAGE FROM **FRAN!**
HERE'S WHAT SHE HAD TO SAY!

DAVE. Freddy. Whatever your name is. I made a mistake. Please
still be at Heathrow when I get there. Please. Fran

xxxxxxxxxxxxxxxxxxxxxxxxxxxxxxx

'No! This way! Stefania, fucking come back!' Leonie
yelled as we sprinted into Terminal 5.

Stefania ran back with a luggage trolley. 'What the
hell is that for?' I shouted frantically.

'I DON'T KNOW,' she yelled, abandoning it and
running off.

We stopped abruptly under the departures screen.
Terminal 5 was far too busy for my liking. I scanned
wildly down for the 22.30 departure to Kabul. My
heart stopped.

'BOARDING! FINAL BOARDING CALL!'
Leonie shouted hoarsely.

I slumped to the floor. 'Oh, God, no!'

But Leonie grabbed me by the strap of my vest
and pulled me back up. 'Get a life,' she muttered.
'Come on, let's just be sure.' We started running again,
this time towards Security.

'Where's Stefania?' I shouted.

'Dunno. Probably riding a luggage trolley. Forget it, we haven't got time.'

We split up and trawled the long snaking queues into Security. People shuffled along with their bags, chatting and staring into space. None of them was Dave. I looked at Leonie, who had finally given in. She shook her head sadly and I felt my heart begin to break.

'I'm sorry, my love,' she said, as we began to walk back to the entrance. 'But you can call him as soon as he gets there. Maybe you could go out and see him.'

'Great. I could visit him in a trench in Helmand Province,' I said, fighting tears. This was all wrong. I'd let him go. I'd let him walk out of my life. Precious, lovely Dave.

Suddenly a loud, honking yell of 'FRANCES!' hit us. Stefania was proceeding in our direction at a gallop. 'Right, take zis and go,' she yelled, thrusting a flight ticket and my passport into my hand.

I gawped. 'What?'

'I took ze liberty of breaking into your house and stealing your passport,' she said.

'But the ticket? How?' I asked, with wonder.

'I have ze money from my family. I vant to repay you for use of ze shed. GO!' she yelled, propelling me forward. I smiled gratefully at them both and ran.

'GO, FRAN!' Leonie yelled.

I sprinted round the corner towards Security and bulldozed straight into a little old lady who was crying into a handkerchief. She staggered backwards but, much to my relief, she stayed upright. 'Oh, no, I'm so sorry!' I cried.

'Fool! Hooligan!' she yelled, in a shrill Scottish accent. 'No fuckin' manners, the youth of today!' She pulled her bag back on her shoulder fiercely and stared me angrily in the eye.

My jaw dropped. 'Are you Mrs Brennan?' I asked.

Her eyes narrowed. 'Aye, who are – Oh, sweet Jesus.' She whistled. 'You're Fran, aren't ye?'

I nodded, suddenly terrified. Mrs Brennan was tiny, but she was not someone you'd want to mess with. I was reminded of how she had warned Freya practically at knife-point that she had to feed Dave broccoli three times a day.

'You silly little girl,' she said witheringly. 'You're too late.'

I put my face in my hands. Too late. Dave had gone. I'd lost my chance. Something horrible and dead settled in my stomach.

Then she cracked a smile. 'Well, there's no harm trying.' And with that she stood on her toes and gave me a kiss on the cheek. Her lips felt dry. I wanted to hug her. 'Go and get my boy back,' she whispered less firmly. Her eyes were wet and her hand, which she briefly pressed on to my cheek, was none too steady.

He was sitting with his back to the queue, staring out of the window at the vast plane that was hulking outside. Bent double after a flat-out sprint, I stood and stared at him as the queue filed into the plane. Dave. Dave Brennan. Dave Brennan, who probably understood me better than anyone else in the world. Who was in love with me. The thought of which was making my stomach do things that no stomach had any business doing.

I looked at the side of his face, defeated, sad and silent, and I knew, finally, just how much I loved this man. And that I had probably felt like this for a very long time.

Right under your nose.

I went and sat quietly beside him, shaking from head to foot. I could smell his familiar spicy Christmas-stockingy smell and grinned.

Dave continued to sit slumped forward, his chin resting on his hands. Afraid and awkward, I did nothing.

Come on, Fran, you massive wazzock, I thought. I cleared my throat and readied myself to say something hauntingly beautiful.

'Erreugh.'

It hadn't worked out quite as I'd planned. But it was enough. Dave glanced at me and did a double-take, dumbfounded.

'Er, evening,' I tried.

He looked incredulous.

'Um, so, er, yes. Hi, Dave.'

He just stared.

Jesus. This was hard. Nothing like the scene in *Love Actually* where the kid storms Passport Control and gets to kiss his love interest amid fondly smiling parents and bungling security guards. This was real life. It was a real airport. The man sitting next to me, staring at me as if I was a ghost, was quite probably the real love of my life, and now I had verbal constipation.

I cleared my throat and resumed my efforts.

'Yes, so. Er, I've been a fool. A total knobhead. Like, the worst knobhead in the history of the universe. I'm so sorry, Dave. I messed up, but I'm here now. I don't want you to go without me.'

Dave leaned away from me in total disbelief. '*Excuse* me?'

'I said, I've been a knobhead and I fucked up and I don't want you to go without me.'

Dave gazed at me warily. 'I don't believe you, Fannybaws,' he said quietly.

I held up my ticket. 'I want to come with you. I want to be with you wherever you are, whether it's in a dodgy bed-sit in Kandahar or a five-star hotel in Barbados. Not that you get much call for that as a news cameraman. But never mind. Look, Dave, I'm serious. Let me come. I'll cook you broccoli three times a day and just – just be near you.'

Dave remained mute.

'Dave, please,' I said, struggling with tears. 'Please let me come. I don't have anything, not even a clean pair of knickers, I just want to be with you. I want to come to Afghanistan. I've been chasing the wrong man. It's you I want. It always has been. I just didn't realize it.'

Still nothing.

I was crying now. 'I want to share your life, Dave. I want to sit in a trench with you and make sure you're safe. I want to worry about you. I want to work with you. I want to sit and talk to you over a can of beer. Alcoholic or not, I don't care. I want to know if you snore or not.'

He began to smile. His eyes crinkled up in the way I had loved for years. There was a hole in his jumper by his elbow that I wanted to stick my finger in.

'You see, the problem is, Franny,' he said eventually – and then stopped, looking keenly at me. I didn't want to hear about the problem. 'The problem is, I've seen you in action in war zones. You're a liability. You start punching the air when people riot in the streets. I'm not sure I'd want you with me in the middle of an exchange of gunfire.'

I ventured a smile.

'I need to know you're serious,' Dave whispered. His forearms were tense.

I decided I was even in love with Dave's forearms. 'I'm serious, Dave,' I said. 'You're the only man I've ever been myself with. When shit goes wrong I want to call you. When shit goes right I want to call you. I love watching you at work. I love watching you doing nothing. I even love watching you smoking.'

Dave raised an eyebrow.

'Seriously! But the one thing I didn't love was thinking you were seeing Stefania. That bit I hated.'

Dave smiled a little bit more. I smiled back at him. The flight attendant was looking at us uncertainly, trying to decide when to bundle us on to the plane.

'How do you think I felt when you got together with Michael?' he said.

There was a wary silence.

Then I said, very clearly, 'Dave, I've probably blown it by now but, regardless, I want you to know that I'm in love with you. Chronically so. In fact, I love you so much that I probably won't ever love anyone else. So I think you should let me come with you.'

He looked at the floor and then at me again. I tried not to evacuate my bowels. I prayed. I begged God for mercy and apologized for all the times I'd said 'cunt'.

'How about,' he said slowly, 'we see how we get on in London before we start planning holidays to war zones?'

'Do you mean it?'

He nodded. I felt faint with relief.

We looked at each other shyly. Then we smiled into each other's eyes and my insides started doing crazy things again.

'I love you, Dave,' I said.

'I love you, too,' he whispered. 'I love every part of you.'

Slowly, I slid my hands into his. They slotted in perfectly. Dave seemed dangerously close to tears.

'You make the first move,' I said shyly.

'No, you.'

I blanched. 'But I'm scared.'

'Me too,' he murmured.

We stared at each other a little while longer and then, after what felt like a lifetime, he leaned towards me and rested his forehead on mine. From point-blank range his eyes were enormous. They were full of love. For me. Dave loved me. I touched his cheek and felt a wave of happiness break over me.

I was home. Finally, we kissed. And it was perfect.

Epilogue

Dear Fran

I'm watching you sleep. You are sucking your thumb. (We're going to need to talk about this.)

I can't pretend you look like a delicately slumbering princess, because you don't. Apart from the thumb business you are twitching around like a ferret and about ten minutes ago you pulled the entire duvet over yourself and left me with nothing. But I've never loved you more than I do right now.

I love you so much. I hope we can have a life together. There's so much I want to say to you. Please wake up soon.

Freddy X

PS Duke Ellington says he doesn't mind you that much either.

Acknowledgements

Thank you, first and foremost, to the wise and wonderful Carla Bevan, then editor of marieclaire.co.uk. Without her I would never have a blog, let alone a book. And on a similar note, I'd like to thank my blog readers; an extremely awesome bunch of women whose messages of scandalized support and hilarious identification got me through all sorts of dating horrors.

Thanks to Kieran, then Sarah, then Viv – housemates extraordinaire in London and Buenos Aires, who allowed me to take over the kitchen table and tolerated my self-indulgent writerly outbursts. Thank you, also, to people who kept me sane – you know who you are – especially Karen and Aisling.

Thanks to Lola for reading my early drafts, to Kate Fisher for her help with all things journalistic, to Lexie Minter for midwifery advice and to Laura for her help with Fran's mum's story. If I've got things wrong it's my own fault.

Thank you so much to my completely brilliant agent Lizzy Kremer for the huge amount of time and effort she's poured into this book. I am in awe of her and her talents and look forward to many more amusing conversations in her book-lined office. Thanks also to Laura West and the other fine folk at David Higham Associates.

Above all I am hugely grateful to Mari Evans at Michael Joseph for publishing me and being so enthusiastic about my book. I still can't believe there's a Penguin logo on the front of my first novel! Thanks also to Alice, Liz, Francesca, Claire, Nick and all the other people who've worked so hard.

Finally, a big thank you to my lovely George for ruining my dating blog and for being so amazing and tolerant and kind. And to my family, who are wonderful and bear no resemblance whatsoever to Fran's. Your support and excitement have meant the world to me.

Good grief! An acknowledgements page! A book! It really is a miracle.